For Steven, my imagination buddy for life.
For my family, who didn't think me too insane.
For my friends, who were just as crazy.
And for that starry void in our heads that we call wonder.

Copyright © 2015 by I. A. Ashcroft.
ISBN-13: 978-1-944674-00-7
ISBN-10: 1-944674-00-4

Printed in the United States of America.
Cover by Dane Low.
Visit I. A. Ashcroft on the web at ia-ashcroft.com.

RAVEN SONG

BOOK ONE OF INOKI'S GAME

I. A. ASHCROFT

PROLOGUE

A boy lay on the broken sidewalk, eyes closed. He was pale and thin, looking not a day over ten years old. His half-clothed body shuddered against the chilly night air. His bony frame scraped against the grime of the street as he curled into himself, trying to keep back the cold. Overhead, the stars hung bright and lonely.

In the alley, almost invisible against the midnight darkness, a man stood tall over the boy. His well-pressed suit was as black as the shadows, as his skin, and as the raven on his shoulder. The way he hovered over the child, he seemed a strange guardian. But his eyes were turned upwards to the sky, away from the boy's plight, as if it was no real matter. In those black eyes the stars were mirrored, impossible and brilliant. Those eyes stared back into the past, when the celestial lights were loved and revered, when each constellation had a story.

Once upon a time… this was when the world had sung to him, the dream-walker, the song-weaver, the star-stringer.

Once, before humans had forgotten his name.

Now, the starry sky was almost hidden by the glowing blue haze of the Barrier, a shield cast over what was left of the city: proud New York, ruined, rebuilt, defiant.

The stranger kept staring upwards into oblivion, even as the boy let out an unhappy whimper, chills wracking his weak frame. The raven flew from the stranger's shoulder then, alighting onto the sidewalk, picking past the weeds and rubble. It rejoined its fellows who had settled amicably around the child, oblivious to the fact that ravens were all supposed to be dead. One hundred years ago, poison had leeched into the earth, into the grass, into the grazers, and into the corpses left behind. The blight spared little, its kind no exception. Regardless, this impossible creature affectionately brushed at the boy's dark hair with its beak.

At the touch, the boy awoke with a start. His wide, uncomprehending eyes took in the world as he struggled to sit up, his head swinging around wildly, past awnings and high rises he had never seen, past scrawled words and graffiti he could not understand. He teetered to his feet, then fell back down again as his knees gave out, sending the birds around him into flight.

He saw no starry eyes in the darkness, no stranger standing nearby. He was half-naked, shivering, hungry, and alone, his head aching down to his teeth. The nameless boy shook off the dreams he couldn't remember and wondered where he was.

If there had been any passersby on that cold autumn night, they would have sworn that this boy hadn't been there a minute ago, and no stranger or ravens had been there at all.

CHAPTER ONE
A Dreamer

Eighteen Years Later

Jackson's shriek pierced the air. He lunged up out of bed in a cold sweat, a dream ringing in his ears, his breathing harsh.

Then he blinked at the darkness of his bedroom and sighed in relief, running his hands through his hair. His head drooped, his exhausted eyes closing. Nightmares.

Always nightmares.

There had been a teeming crowd in his head this time, screaming, bloodthirsty. Jackson could still smell the rank sweat, feel the oppressive crush of bodies dragging him in like the tide. There were makeshift weapons flashing in the light as two men danced around each other on center stage, feet smearing the blood-spattered concrete. A sharply dressed man in red towered above them all, narrating, his voice slicing through the air as if it was a velvet knife.

And, perched at the edge of a bleacher, watching the fight, was a hunched man with dark eyes, eyes filled with stars. He had turned to Jackson, and he had laughed.

Jackson shook his head. *It was just a dream*, he told himself, easing into the comfort of his wake-up ritual, running through his checklist. His night terrors weren't real. The arena was a place that had never existed. He'd never heard the sound of breaking bones or death whimpers.

I am safe.

He still saw the arena's host turning towards him, smiling a chilling grin. "You're up next," he had hissed, a cold promise.

Jackson shuddered. *I am safe.* Feeling his heartbeat ease, he cast a glance out of his bedroom window. His skin prickled. A raven was perched on the sill. It gave him a long look, then flew off into the night.

Jackson watched as it left, then scowled. He could still see the darkened sky through the blue haze of the Barrier. His clock told him it was 12:30 in the morning on July 21st, 2147. Also, it was predicted to be sunny and unseasonably hot, once the sun could be bothered to rise in six hours or so. Another darktime of insomnia.

It seemed that his companion from last night had left, probably when he'd started thrashing in his sleep. Oh well. He didn't remember much about her, anyway.

Jackson grimaced as he padded to the bathroom, hands shaking. He rested his forehead against the cool glass of the mirror for a long minute, trying to quell the pounding in his head and the roiling in his stomach. *I am safe.* It seemed to get harder to remind himself of this, every time. As the years went on, it had gotten harder to feel as if there wasn't something horribly broken in his head.

The therapist had told him it might have something to do with his missing years before he had been brought into the orphanage, half-feral, frostbitten, and almost starved to death. The doctor gave him routines, things to calm him, things to help. It worked—sometimes.

Some dreams, like this one, clung worse than others.

He had seen how the announcer had bared his teeth in a lunatic smile as one of the fighters had been slaughtered.

How the crowd had roared.

No more whiskey before bed, he promised himself again. Just dream tea. That's what he needed. Dream tea. It would make him feel much better. Then, he could get to work, a head start on the day. Slowly, he raised his gaze to the mirror. His dark-rimmed eyes stared back. When he spoke, his reflection quoted his adopted father: "Business waits for no man."

It was almost twenty minutes before he was present enough to stagger out of the bathroom and down the stairs. He didn't bother getting a flashlight as he began foraging for ingredients in the kitchen, his eyes well used to seeing in the dark.

That raven was at the window. Again. He tried not to linger on it. But, gods *damn* the things. Jackson's insistence on their existence had very nearly gotten him committed as a boy. They were extinct, everyone said. Therapists didn't like hearing stories about dead animals following children around. They didn't like stories about shadows slithering up the walls either, or monsters in the dark. The nightmares had been enough for them to handle.

These days, Jackson tried to ignore the little black-feathered bastards clustered on the sill or roof. He refused to talk about them anymore. *Stop thinking about it. You'll make it worse.*

His hands shook as he finished grinding his tea herbs with a pestle, filling his cup to the brim with steaming water. There was a soothing wash over his nose of lavender, coriander, and something else, something he'd never been able to identify. It was something the magic-dealer selling the mixture to him had refused to reveal.

He sighed, breathing in the scent of tea. His... *crazy tea.* It was well overdue. Time to get all better, as Dad used to say. No more bad dreams or bird talk. No more books flying off of the shelves or visions of shadows. All better.

His adopted father had always hated it when Jackson called it *crazy tea.* Jackson felt this did not make it any less true.

He took a sip. The knot between his shoulders loosened and his headache retreated. The dream seemed less important now, the blood and fear a faraway note. There it was: a good feeling. He was not going to let a dream ruin his day. He had things to do, people to see, a business to run. This was the Jackson most people saw. He was young, but if pressed, any of his colleagues would have said he was an articulate, professional boss. Jackson was very good at keeping his secrets, his therapy, and his dark-rimmed eyes behind closed doors.

He leaned back on his couch, thinking nothing of his hallucinations anymore, only his tea and the reality before him. In fact, he wished the residential electricity grid was on at this hour so he could turn on a fan and circulate the humid air. Not even his nice neighborhood granted him an exception from darktime, though. Oh well. He didn't feel like bribing a militiaman to turn a blind eye to frivolous generator use.

The day's worries began to hum. Jackson began flipping through his briefcase, retrieving his datapad. He felt his headache start to return as his eyes flickered over what he had been reading the previous night: the proposal to cut staff by almost a quarter. Ah. There. The reason he had gone out seeking drink and company in the first place. Quite a few hours were ahead of him before he was expected to turn up for the meeting to discuss the proposal, rebut it, somehow.

His father would have known how to do it, how to make the finances wiggle about and get back those lost contracts. His father would have gone into fits of rage at the mere suggestion of layoffs.

But, though Jackson knew he had done well by the delivery service, he was not his father. At this rate, they were only fighting against time.

The nightmare danced at the edge of his thoughts, the victor of the death match pacing, smiling. The fighter had been painted like a tiger, his gaze looking for weakness, a place to sink his teeth.

No. Don't think about that. He took another sip of his tea, trying to veer back to thoughts of meetings and proposals. It was difficult.

The nightmares were getting worse, weren't they? It was now almost every night he was waking up like this. He'd missed only one dose of tea that week, and the repercussions had never been so sudden and vivid. Jackson yawned wide, his jaw cracking, feeling queasy from exhaustion.

This could not continue. His thoughts were jumbled, unfocused, and his work was suffering. His work was all he had.

Damn it.

It was time to do something he did not want to do if he was going to get himself under control.

He was going to have to consult Theodore Huxley.

Gods DAMN it.

Still, Huxley would talk to him. Huxley wouldn't write off his nightmares and visions as crazy. He and Huxley had history, and it wasn't *all* bad. Still, Jackson hated skirting around The Order of which Huxley was a part, hated the deal in life they'd handed him.

The messenger on his datapad was sluggish to respond, as if it too wanted nothing to do with the letter Jackson was about to write. He worried his bottom lip with his teeth, deliberating, letting his fingers consider the words. *Huxley,* he began.

This opening troubled him for a full minute, but he realized that no matter how many years it had been, he had never grown into using his former mentor's first name.

He continued. *I need to speak with you in person. My dreams are worsening. The tea doesn't seem to be helping anymore. Perhaps my stock is old. I'm also seeing the ravens, more than before. I would respectfully request your advice.*

There. That should do it. Jackson was well aware how stiff and formal the words sounded, but he wasn't feeling friendly enough to change it.

For a few moments, his fingers hovered over Send, uncertain. There had also been that man in his dreams, the one with the stars glittering in his eyes. He'd been in his dreams before. Sometimes, he was watching from behind a tree, or sometimes from a crowd. He was always dressed in different clothes, yet always grinning the same, as if an amusing secret was just behind those sparkling teeth. Huxley had once thought patterns in Jackson's dreams would give insight into his *talents*, back when he was being evaluated for the Order.

No. What did it matter? He was never going to be in the Order. Huxley had made that *quite* clear.

Jackson sent the letter and sipped his tea again, feeling a little more focused. He hoped the old mage would deign to respond soon.

Suddenly, his datapad began vibrating on the coffee table. This was far too soon to be a reply from Huxley. It was probably work. *Oh come on. It's not even 1 AM.* But, the datapad kept inching across the wood until it *tinked* up against an empty shot glass. Jackson sighed, knowing it was business, and checked the caller ID. Frank. Of course it was Frank.

"Hello?" Jackson knew he looked like hell. He gave a bright smile anyway.

The stern face staring back at him crinkled into powerful disapproval. "Boss? Geez." Jackson winced. Balding, beady-eyed Frank technically worked for him, but he behaved more like a gruff uncle, the kind who kept a sawed-off shotgun in his trunk and knives in his boots. This was fine when Frank was being an overseer of Dovetail Parcel's less-than-legal deals. It was not so much when he felt Jackson needed a talking-to. And so, Jackson was glad when Frank skipped ahead to the business at hand instead of a lecture.

"Look, boss, I need you to come to the warehouse. We've got a problem."

Jackson went on the alert, fuzziness evaporating. "What? Why?"

Frank smacked his lips, giving Jackson a look that said, *If I could tell you on the phone, I would have already, you idiot.* "Just get down here. Now. Do it quiet. And get your ass sober."

Then, the screen flickered out, and Frank was gone.

Jackson cast the rest of the scalding tea down his throat and took off back up the stairs. Frank's few, grim words were always placed with care. When the man said *now*, he meant yesterday, if Jackson could help it. Something was wrong, something big, on top of everything else. Perhaps Jackson should be grateful for the dream waking him so early.

He was dressed and slamming the door behind him minutes later, keys almost slipping from his sweaty hands. His heart thudded as he settled a white courier hat over his hair, hiding his eyes under the brim. In the ill-fitted uniform, he looked little like his daytime self, the businessman with briefcase in hand. Now, he was a worker at the docks.

Frank wanted this to be quiet. Taking his car was out. The train it was.

A raven posted on the walkway railing fluttered, disturbed by the door slam. It looked up at Jackson as if offended. He ignored it and set off into the night.

CHAPTER TWO
A Government Miracle

Brooklyn at night was a treacherous beast. Jackson's street shoes clicked on the broken pavement in a way he always thought was too loud. Few had good reason to be outside after dark in this industrial sector, wandering past empty, grafittied buildings and crumbling concrete, breathing in the oppressive, finely-churned stench of the Gowanus Canal. Breather masks were customary, if no longer necessary. Jackson wore one now.

An old man with skin like leather and a scraggly, overgrown beard looked his way as he passed, sprawled back on the sidewalk, hand starting to stretch outwards as if he was about to ask for something. Jackson saw cancerous sores running up his arm. Probably a scrounger, picking up the odds and ends of the past beyond the dome for a little money.

His eyes were unseeing. The cancer had taken them. Retired scrounger, then.

Jackson carried nothing beyond subway fare. He averted his eyes and moved on.

Twice, Jackson was certain someone was following him. Twice, he ducked down side streets, adrenaline surging, clinging to the shadows, trying not to be seen. Each time, the follower simply passed him by.

In reality, it was only a matter of fifteen minutes to go from his home in Queens to the station. It was as much time to get to Dovetail Parcel's primary shipping center once he stepped out into the early Brooklyn morning. But, to Jackson's nerves, it was *hours*.

The warehouse seemed desolate, still. He let himself in. In the gloom, Jackson could see endless stacks of crates, boxes, and bins, categorized, labeled, ready for loading into the fleet of trucks and boats waiting outside. The clack of his shoes was the sole echo in the vast space, except for the occasional quiet skitter of a rat or two. In less than four hours, this facility would fill with people in white caps and jackets, clutching their dear coffees. Lifeblood, his father had called the company's couriers and sorters.

Three generations ago, as his father was fond of saying, the Dovetails had made their name, had been there to re-establish communications between domes when the military could not. They been there to deliver medicines, supplies, and more when great New York was forgotten by cities that had more survivors and their own problems. They had made their city flourish, had helped the survivors of The Bombings make a life again.

Jackson shuddered to consider that the dream and name of three generations of Dovetails might end with him, the adopted boy. Perhaps it already had.

Yellow light suddenly flooded the shipping floor. Jackson instinctively flinched behind a bin, although he suspected he knew who had entered. Sure enough, a shuffling step made its way over the catwalk above, one he knew well. He jogged up the stairs to find a thickly-built, broad-shouldered man dressed in a matching courier uniform, squinting in the new light, scowling. Frank's eyes flickered to him.

"Did ya know, boss, that it's frickin' creepy to stand around in the dark?"

"I don't know how you can't see without the light. It was fine."

"Was dark as up in the devil's ass. That's creepy. I stand by that." Frank licked his lips, as if considering his words. "Anyway. There's business. Special client. New one."

Jackson made a rolling gesture with his hand, indicating, *Go on?* Frank was the kind of man who laid his thoughts bare whether or not anyone wanted them. This reticence was uncharacteristic.

"He's… Coalition."

Jackson stared, then snorted with laughter. But, Frank was not doing the same. "Wait. What? You're serious?"

"…Yeah."

Jackson let the implication settle on his shoulders, and his voice dropped to a whisper, even though no one was there to hear. "The *Coalition* wants to *smuggle. With us.*"

"They're not here for our generous bulk discounts on three-day shipping, boss."

"*Why?* They're the government. They can do whatever the hell they want."

Frank rolled his big shoulders like they pained him. Not for the first time, Jackson wondered if arthritis was setting into Frank's bones. "Apparently, there are some banned items they want to get to their base inside the dome. They don't want the local authority raising a stink about it. So… here they are."

Jackson did not like this. *Very* few objects met Frank's description, at least that the Coalition could want. Most of those things were high-powered weapons, and that was far outside their smuggling operation's scope. "You're telling me they can't tell the Mayor to turn a blind eye? The Coalition *owns* the trade routes."

"There's more to it," Frank continued, his voice just as quiet as Jackson's. His hand brushed the gun on his hip as he crossed his arms, like he half expected he'd need to grab it at some point. "Political crap."

Jackson didn't see how this mattered. There was *always* political crap, politicians shouting and local militaries grandstanding. It was nothing New York had a stake in right now. Hell, New York usually wasn't invited to the summits to get a *chance* to shout. "And?"

"Moscow's pissy."

"They always are."

"Some uproar about the Coalition illegally confiscating their shipments, this time. Everyone on that goddamn ship is real sensitive about local versus federal authority right now. They get caught doing something against the Charter behind New York's back? That's why this agent contact says they want *us.*"

Jackson *harrumph*ed. He found he didn't mind the Coalition getting itself into well-deserved trouble. It wasn't as if they made his life any easier. He could, however, care if they got him caught alongside them. "How the hell did some Coalition agent even find out about what we do?"

Frank made a face, one of deep distaste and *I told you so.* "Huxley."

Jackson blinked, coming to a full stop. What? Huxley was recommending Coalition agents to him? No forewarning? Another secret? *Was Huxley getting senile?* Gods *damn* the old mage. "Wonderful."

"Yeah." Frank grimaced. Jackson knew Frank's opinion of Huxley had never been high. He'd never liked the "hoodoo" that followed a visit to the Huxley house, thought it unnatural at best. Not many knew of the magical dealings in New York, but Frank did, and he would rather be returned to ignorance. In Huxley's presence, Frank would shift like his skin was crawling off his body, and he would look as if he was barely refraining from spitting on the ground in the old man's wake.

Mercifully, Frank did not choose to give Jackson another round of opinions on magic. "You can fix that leak later if you want. But, this agent claims he's got papers for us in case this run goes south. Says it makes it all legal beagle."

"*Sure* it does."

"Boss… I know. I knew it looked like a sting from a million miles away. But, I had some connections vet it. Wouldn't have bothered talking to you about it if I hadn't."

Jackson shook his head and cast a sidelong eye on the ocean of parcels under his feet, feeling as if he was sinking. Frank knew how desperate the company was, or he wouldn't have bothered vetting the offer at all. He was man who had spent the better portion of his career *evading* the Coalition. The fact that he was in his fifties and wasn't sitting in prison was a testament to how good he was at his job.

Jackson also knew that Frank hadn't been paid in a month, and that could affect even the judgment of his most trusted advisor.

"Boss, it is for a *hell* of a lot of money."

"Oh?" Jackson swallowed. "How much?"

"Ten million credits."

Jackson stared at him for a few seconds. "Did you say *ten million?*"

"Yes."

"Ten. Million."

Frank gave a sly old tomcat grin. "*For today.* It's ten million per run, and there are five runs."

"So... so... damn. Are you sure?"

"Yeah. We decide to meet the agent in the next two hours for the first trip, or we decline the whole thing. Said it's just that urgent, and that's why they're willing to pay so much. We go on paper as being their primary shipping service in every dome we reach. They mark it as us delivering their office supplies or whatever. We keep the real nature of the job quiet. Like we do."

Jackson found he had to lean against the catwalk railing, slightly dizzy. Yeah. That *was* a hell of a lot of money, and that was substantial legal protection—to become New York's only sanctioned smuggling operation? It was as preposterous as it was tempting. Who would even audit the Coalition's papers, anyway? Themselves? The government was opaque and corrupt, and everyone knew it.

He found himself nodding. Perhaps Frank wasn't just being desperate.

Frank clapped him on the back. "Don't worry. Your meeting is in forty minutes at the spot at Red Hook. Guy calls himself Agent Walker."

With that, Frank strode out the door, leaving Jackson alone with his thoughts under the glare of the catwalk lights.

Though it was yet before four in the morning, the docks were coming alive, the businesses that catered to its workers standing with doors open and generators buzzing, their lights shining in the gloom. Despite the morning rush, Jackson needn't have worried about how to find the government man at "the spot", a coffee shop frequented by his couriers. Agent Walker was the only man in one-way Coalition sunglasses.

The agent was alone at a tiny round table, a black suit in a sea of white uniforms. The moment Jackson entered the door, the agent stood. This "Walker" was holding a coffee in one hand as he ran the other over his short military hair. As Jackson approached, he extended the offer of a handshake. Jackson accepted, noting that the agent's grip was strong, his stance balanced. Athletic type, then, perhaps a field agent.

"Thank you for taking time to meet with me. I understand you must keep a busy schedule as president of the company." Walker's voice was soft, polite, and his smile was as generic as his shined Coalition shoes—the kind with no marks or tread pattern, every pair the same. Jackson smiled in return, tensing, and took his seat at the small table.

In the close quarters of their negotiation space, the air carried the sour scent of the radiation inhibitor Quarantine. Jackson swallowed a gag.

"I assume you're filled in," Walker continued, expression blank. "We don't have a lot of time." He slid a datapad across the table, the places to sign already highlighted and glowing. Jackson's practiced eye skimmed the contract. He, of course, saw the words "smuggling" and "contraband" exchanged for phrases such as "classified delivery" and "undeclared materials". But, nothing else jumped out. It was as Frank claimed. Direct. Short. Legally defensible. This troubled him more than anything else. The government was being... forthright. Above board.

He didn't like Walker, not his suit nor his sunglasses, and certainly not his proximity. Of course, he knew any parcel delivery company in New York's borders would feel their teeth on edge with the government watching them.

He read the contract again.

Fifty million. Gods.

Did he have a choice? Could he afford to turn away such an opportunity?

He found his finger signing the glowing line.

The agent slid the datapad back and smiled in his generic way again. And, Jackson found he was tenser than he'd been before, when he was poorer by millions. "Thank you, Mr. Dovetail. We look forward to working with you.

Regarding today's delivery, the pickup site is at these coordinates." A few taps, and a map appeared on the datapad screen. A dot hovered fifty miles north of the city, near badlands territory, but the route was accessible by the main roads for the most part.

"This is going to require my papers to make an unscheduled pass at the checkpoint today." Jackson narrowed his eyes as he voiced this, wondering if that would be a problem. It was a riskier gambit, bringing himself on the same truck that would soon carry illegal cargo, but the guards at the gates would only be so forgiving. The truck would need an alibi. He had gotten through several times by proclaiming that he had business dealings in the settlements, his journey necessitating a shift in the delivery schedule. If the local militia ever got the resources to verify his story, well, he had a connection that would vouch he'd spent three hours that afternoon sealing bargains in New Pleasantville.

Walker only cleared his throat. "I will be accompanying you as well." Jackson raised an eyebrow. "You're going to need my clearance for the handoff. Besides, as I said, time is short, and necessary explanations will have to occur en route." He brushed a credit chit in Jackson's direction, across the table. "The first half of payment, of course."

Jackson palmed the chit without looking at it. The two nodded at each other, businessman and client, faces straight, questions unasked, as they would be in any operation worth its salt. Walker stood. The discussion was done.

In only minutes, Frank wheeled a solar-charged truck from the shipping center, and with the agent in tow, they took off into that promising morning, the Sapphire City's blue dome sparkling overhead against the dawning sky. At the checkpoint, a bored guard logged Jackson's papers and reasons for travel. As expected, given his status as an upstanding citizen and moneymaker for the city (dearly paid for with the right people), they waved him through, not even logging Frank's or Walker's papers. Jackson noted the agent's papers were false anyway, reading "Richard Nakamoto". *The Coalition would rather its passing not be marked, it seems.* He wondered if this was why Walker, before they left, had insisted on changing into a courier uniform as well.

At least Walker seemed impressed with how smoothly the last-minute arrangement was running. When Jackson glanced over his shoulder to the back seat, he was met with a bland smile.

Just five runs. Then he could be rid of the agent.

"Director," Walker spoke to the air, one eye on the shacks and crumbling border homes passing them by. "We're on our way."

It was a private commlink, and Jackson could not hear the response. Walker nodded to no one, and reached into his jacket. Frank edged his hand closer to his gun, his eyes trained into the rearview mirror.

The corner of Walker's mouth might have sparked into a small smile. "No need to be tense. I'm not the trouble you should be worried about." It was true. A fat delivery truck like theirs? Raiders might be out there watching. Jackson shook his head at Frank, who eased a millimeter.

Walker retrieved what he had been fishing for in his pocket. There were three needles of telltale purple serum. They were pre-measured, as if someone had calculated everyone's height and weight well before their encounter.

"That shit's not necessary," Frank snapped.

The agent, for the first time that day, removed his sunglasses, stashing them where the needles had been. This revealed an unimpressed expression. "Yes," he said, "it is."

Jackson found Frank's unhappiness contagious. "You stated nothing about Quarantine in the contract."

"I wouldn't think I'd have to. Going out this far in the wastes, I would have thought it would be a standard precaution to protect the lives of your workers."

"Our routes go *around* established hot zones," Jackson said. "Unless the coordinates you gave me were false."

"Oh, no, not at all. This is for a *new* hot zone." Walker rolled up a sleeve and injected himself with a dose, a clean, surgical hand at work. "I understand your trucks are shielded on the inside to protect from environmental radiation. Smart. What we are bringing back to New York may be somewhat radioactive itself. The truck's lining should suffice. But, you all need a dose of Quarantine.

Just a safeguard, really. As much as you boys don't like the government—and I can tell—we're not out to see you get sick and die." He gave his flavorless smile again, although Jackson could swear there was a glimmer of genuine mirth in his voice. "Besides, the Coalition will need your services in the future. Sort of stupid to poison you all now."

The argument was quite logical.

No one volunteered their arm.

"Mr. Dovetail," Walker sighed. "My superior is not going to allow me to let you step out of this vehicle into potentially lethal doses of radiation. You can accept the Quarantine, or we can turn around and I can find someone else. Pegasus Deliveries seems well-funded enough—"

"Pegasus *hardly* has the flexibility we offer," Jackson reassured, scowling only in his mind. They had lost three contracts to Pegasus that month. "I only mean to say, we have suits on-hand."

"The suits may not be sufficient. We insist on protecting our investments. You understand."

Jackson frowned. What Walker was speaking of shouldn't have been a problem. It wasn't as if raiders had nukes, no matter how sadistic they got—and intense, new radiation spots didn't just *appear*. But, Jackson swallowed back the question. Interrogating his clients was not the nature of his agreements. He had signed on for this. He was going to have to live with it.

The dashboard began to click and chirp, Geiger counter taking external readings. They had left the main road a couple miles back, and were nearing their destination, somewhere a few miles south of the ghost town of Elmsford.

"Radiation shouldn't be this high this soon," Frank intoned.

"Mr. Dovetail."

Jackson sighed, rolled up his sleeve, and thrust his arm in the agent's direction, unable to watch. The injector bit into his skin, and a cold feeling crept through his veins, lingering in his shoulder. He shuddered as the agent withdrew the needle. "You next, big guy," Walker said. And, Frank, stubborn as he was, did not argue, thrusting his arm back while he drove onward with one hand. The boss had done it, and so would he. It didn't stop him from glaring at the road ahead as if he wanted to punch it in the windpipe.

Ugh. A sour taste started blooming in the back of Jackson's mouth. No one enjoyed Quarantine, no matter how life-saving it could be. The truck cab probably smelled like it was inhabited by a scrounger team now. Jackson snagged his flask from his breast pocket, taking a swig. A comforting ball of whiskey heat slid down his throat, washing away the taste and his nerves.

"We're here," Frank grumbled, and the truck rumbled to a stop, parking off-road in a bare patch of dust and weeds.

Jackson heard the creak of the seat as Walker leaned forward. "Team, the transport has arrived."

The sun was unusually harsh to Jackson's eyes, raw yellow light beaming through the windshield, unfiltered by the Barrier. The Geiger counter was clicking steadily now. Nothing was around except a few buildings demolished by time and one forlorn tree, bent like an old man, long stripped of life.

"Team, this is Agent Walker. Respond."

Jackson saw Frank tense. Something was wrong.

A buzzing sensation began at the base of Jackson's skull. It was washing over the cool rush of Quarantine, tingling through his fingers and down his neck and spine. His mouth went dry. That feeling. He knew that feeling. It wasn't a side effect to the radiation drug. The bark on the tree seemed to pulse. The air tingled. *Oh gods. Not now.*

A shadow washed across the dust, small, quick. A large black bird, one he knew well, flared its wings, coming to rest in the tree at the apex of the branches. It regarded him and opened its beak, sending out a cry Jackson could swear he heard even through the shielded glass.

More shadows of birds flickered along the ground. Jackson turned his eyes upward. Ravens wheeled lazily in front of the sun, an entire flock. He hadn't seen so many at once since he was a teenager.

It's a hallucination. The buzzing feeling set his adrenaline rising, his heartbeat quickening. *Stay calm. Don't let it show.*

Walker cleared his throat, a noise altered by an air filter. While Jackson had been staring outside, eyes glazing, the agent had wrestled on a protective suit.

"Please, remain in the truck. Communications seem to be down. I am going to go investigate." With that, he opened the door, slipped out past Jackson's seat, and shut it ever so quietly behind him. Jackson watched, stunned, as Walker went down into a full crouch behind the truck, then began creeping forward on his hands and knees towards a spot on the horizon, moving between bits of rubble and concrete for cover. A weighty handgun was ready in his hands, the safety turned off.

"You've got to be kidding me," Jackson said, turning to his bodyguard. "Is this turning into a firefight?"

Frank shrugged. "Which is why we don't usually let you come along. We can leave that G-man out here, right?"

"You know we can't now."

"Yeah. I know." Frank gave a resigned sigh. Then, he drew his own handgun. It may have even been the same make as the one the agent wielded, though the numbers had long since been filed off. "Stay here, boss," he muttered.

"What?"

"That idiot's going without backup. I'm not going to wait and see what happens," Frank smoothly checked his clip and clicked off the safety.

Jackson's skin was tingling with unpleasant shocks, pinpricks of sweat breaking out on his neck and forehead. He was struck with the dead certainty that he needed to leave the truck. If he left, his craving spoke, the feeling would stop. "Does this glass look bulletproof or something? I'll come with you."

"Does the *air* out there look bulletproof of something? Yeesh. Just crouch in the back seat. It's safer. You've already done your part."

Jackson was aware the most risky part of his job was usually smoothing the concerns of armed and puffed-up clients. No shots had been fired at him, *yet*, even if a few guns had been waved, and he preferred to keep it that way. But, he could not swallow back the insistent pulling in his stomach, the buzzing in his skull of a hundred bees. "I can't stay here. I have to go outside. I think there's something I need to see."

Frank gave him what could only be described as *a look*. "Are you dumb?

Like what?"

"I can't explain. I just have to." The call in his bones denied words. The dream tea dosage that morning hadn't been enough, not against whatever was going wrong in his head. The buzzing was roaring in his ears now, his hands shaking. Above, the ravens were still circling, chittering, watching. "Look. This truck will be a target, if raiders are about. I have to go with you. I have to go see the... the thing."

"*No.*" Then, a pause. "Wait... Christ, boss. This isn't that spooky weird New Age shit again, is it?" At Jackson's guilty silence, Frank grumbled under his breath for almost half a minute, pressing his hands to his temples. "I know that look. I swear to God, every time you get that look, the paint starts peeling and crap starts flying off the walls."

Jackson had nothing to say to that, preoccupied with his rising nausea.

"Christ. I'm getting too old for this. *Fucking hoodoo.*" Frank set his gun to the side, and grabbed one of the protective teal suits from its compartment, beginning the difficult task of putting it on while sitting. "I'm not gonna tell you again. It'd be best if you hunker in that back seat rather than doing this freaky-deaky shaman crap. That makes this whole business *a lot* harder."

Jackson grabbed another suit from the compartment and began pulling it on as well. There was more grumpy grumbling, but he recognized Frank's resigned tone. Frank would obey and protect him, even if it was a risk he did not understand.

Frank was a little afraid of him, he knew.

The two crept out of the truck, Jackson's bodyguard moving like a panther, despite both his age and the undignified squeaking of the suits. "Clear here," Frank intoned from his side of the truck.

"Clear here," Jackson replied. Frank quickly converged with his path, ushering them both forward, eyes always on the horizon.

A hundred yards ahead, Jackson spied that Agent Walker was rising from his position on his belly, his pistol lowering to his side. It seemed there was no immediate danger in that direction. Jackson could now see that, where Walker stood, the flatness of the land gave way to a valley. A strange smell wafted their way on the breeze, making it even through the air filter. It was coppery, rank, and seemed to stick on Jackson's tongue. His nose wrinkled in disgust.

Jackson came up behind the agent and peeked over the valley edge.

A score of ravens dotted the dirt, just like the ones wheeling up high. They scampered and jockeyed with each other on the reddened earth, snapping at choice bits of food, cawing throatily. One bird turned and stared at Jackson, then turned away, pecking at a malformed lump. Jackson only realized what he was truly seeing as the raven took flight, tearing away an eye in its beak.

The government team was dead.

CHAPTER THREE
A Curious Box

Agent Walker finally turned. His gaze was a little vacant behind the mask. Frank gave no hint of being surprised nor disturbed by the sight below. Blood spatters. Limbs, flesh, *liquidated*. Bones, pink, slimy. Jackson's stomach turned, and he looked away. The ravens croaked and cawed in his ears.

"What the fuck…" he breathed.

"This is a couple hours old," Frank intoned. Jackson shuddered. Of course Frank would know something like that. The smell on the wind, now identified, was making his eyes tear up, like it was a noxious gas. Frank continued, "Tire treads, recent ones, heading outta here. Probably the same assholes that did this."

Agent Walker nodded, his voice soft and robotic. "Yes, I saw that. Whoever was here left." He looked up as if seeing them there for the first time. "Why the hell aren't you all in the truck like I asked?"

"The guys who did this could be back," Frank snorted, ignoring the question. "We can't stick around. We move out."

"…We can't leave yet." Walker stiffened and clutched his gun until his knuckles turned white. "We need to see if they took the package."

"Are you kiddin' me? Even for this money, this ain't worth—"

"Search, then." Jackson closed his eyes, breathing only through his mouth so he couldn't smell. "Be quick. Very quick." His stomach was doing small flip-flops. He suddenly realized he had not seen a dead body since his father's funeral, and this was different. The mess below used to be human life, and his brain struggled to accept it, couldn't process that alongside the mad buzzing ricocheting between his ears and the need to throw up inside of his helmet. Blood stains leapt out at his eyes from every patch of darkness on the earth. He lolled his gaze up to the hazy, sick yellow clouds above, wondering desperately why any of this had happened.

About two hundred yards in the distance, he spotted a shimmer in the sun, a patch of brightness amidst the dread. A box. It was strangely rectangular and narrow, like a coffin, atop of which was perched a single black-feathered bird.

He started to walk towards it, away from the stench of carnage, his stomach, for an instant, forgetting to heave. Seizing on that respite, he began to stride in earnest, eyes leveled on the strutting raven.

"Where the hell are you going?" Frank demanded.

"I need to walk."

"Yeah, good. 'Cause we're gonna *walk* back to the truck right now."

"You say the area is clear, yes? Let me walk. Two minutes. Then I will go to the truck. I won't leave it. I will live in that gods-damned truck for the rest of my life." Jackson inhaled again to center himself, but forgot to breathe only through his mouth, and a recoil shuddered in his throat. The stench of death. He hoped the agent was expedient. Whatever the hell had done *that* to the government team, he did not want to meet it.

A hundred paces later, the worst of it was behind him. He found his words again. "That wasn't raiders, was it?" Frank's movements may have been silent, but he knew his advisor and bodyguard was not far behind. Always reliable, Frank.

"I dunno," Frank replied. "That... that was bad. Shouldn't have gotten involved in this."

"Noted. Also noted: your idea." Frank made a grunt, then grumbled something under his breath that was probably very insulting. Jackson didn't care. If he could keep down his bile, remain professional, and drag Walker out after the search was done, successful or not, perhaps they would get through unscathed. Was this worth it? It would have to be. They couldn't back out now.

Not for the first time, Jackson questioned the wisdom in keeping up the smuggling operation his father had left him. Keeping the company afloat would bring him no joy if he was dead.

What they hell were they shipping, anyway? He had wondered during the trip, settling on perhaps a cache of plutonium, given Walker's interest in the truck shielding, but this incident... *revised* his expectations. This sort of massacre had never happened to his people or anyone he'd ever known, even over military-grade arms. Raiders, bold as they were, knew better than to piss off the Coalition so badly, *to slaughter their very agents.* The Coalition was going to rain hellfire from the sky if they found out who had done this.

As he gnawed on his thoughts, he realized he and Frank were almost upon his mental checkpoint, the gleaming steel box in the sunlight. The raven stopped pacing, and leveled its sidelong gaze at them as they approached. It cawed in greeting. *Hello,* Jackson thought, dipping his head in acknowledgement, then feeling foolish for doing so. "Do you see that bird on the box there?"

"What fucking bird? The hell are you on about?"

No, then. He was on the right track. The tingling feeling in his spine was growing stronger with his nausea, as if it might overflow through his fingers and toes any moment, electrifying the earth.

Then, the overpowering sensation simply stopped, just as their feet did.

The raven gave Jackson one last inscrutable look with its beady black eyes and took off in a flurry of dark feathers. Jackson watched it go with the same curiosity and longing that he usually felt, wishing it could tell him something, anything. He sighed, disappointed, and looked over the crate.

There, where the raven had perched, was a tiny shred of paper taped to the lid. Jackson examined it, finding letters scrawled at a manic slant in purple crayon. Agents did not write in crayon. What sort of childish...?

Reading the words set off an apprehensive fluttering in his chest.

JACK, the paper said. *They told me to leave this for you.* Jackson squinted, mouth dry, then peeled the note off, but found nothing more. "No one should know we were coming out here, right?"

Frank plucked the note out of his hands, skimming it, a confused look on his face. "No?" Jackson shook his head, tamping down dread. No need to feed into his growing panic. *Jack* was a common enough name; why should he scare himself by assuming it was written for him? Besides, everyone called him *Jackson*, not Jack, never Jack. A bizarre coincidence.

The crate, however, bore examination. It wasn't a coffin like his imagination had first thought, but was about the same size. It was also sealed with electronic locks, and emitted a faint hum. It had a built-in generator, perhaps? He hunched over the puzzle box, noting that the top was covered in a glossy one-way glass. That had been what gleamed to him from so far away. "I want to know what they left for Jack."

"Who's Jack?"

"The one on the note."

"What—"

"Shhh, I need to figure this out. I want to know why this hell went down and why I'm here."

"Why? We don't ask questions, boss. I think that goes for now more than ever."

"You question me *all* the time, Frank."

"I don't question government spooks that could jail me for treason without trial."

"Well, I can't do *that*. But, I could fire you."

"You won't. Look, just leave it be. Let the government boy over there mess with it. I don't like it."

Jackson fiddled with a few of the buttons. Once before, he had seen a box like this in the possession of a gunrunner—Frank needed firearms in his line of work, after all. The smuggler had used translucency sliders on the glass to allow window shopping while keeping the weapons locked up. Was this the same? "I think we can look inside without opening it."

"That's not the point."

Ah! There it was. A switch. Jackson's fingers brushed it to the right. The opaque black began to fade.

And there, behind the glass, was no gun stash, no bombs, no drugs, no illicit data chips.

It was a woman, a young woman, eyes closed as if asleep.

Jackson blinked.

"Well, shit," Frank said for both of them.

Who the hell was this? The pale girl looked to be in her mid-twenties, with gnarled, matted blond hair draped over her frame. Her arms were folded over her chest. She was also... very naked.

Something like a chime sounded in the back of Jackson's mind, a familiar note, a feeling he'd seen this woman before. He brushed the glass with his fingers, as if asking a gentle question. Then, he yanked his hand back and shook his head to clear it, almost repulsed by his own reaction. What was he thinking? She was a complete stranger, and likely hurt, or worse. "Um. Frank? What do we...?"

His bodyguard did not answer right away. Then: "Fucking bandits." After another pause: "We get her out of there. And we be quick about it."

Jackson leaned down and scanned the controls. Was she cargo in a human trafficking ring? Had she been left behind by the raiders? His eyes narrowed. Was the woman even alive? He peered forward for a closer look, to see if he could notice breathing.

Suddenly, the woman's eyes opened, and Jackson started back. Her blue gaze was unfocused at first. It drifted across the sky above in wonder. But then she saw him, and her eyes widened in shock, her hands thudding and sliding against the glass. Her mouth opened, and she began to scream. And scream. *And scream.*

Jackson's eyes staggered over the unfamiliar controls as he began to panic, her horrified wails reverberating dully through the case. "How do we—"

A fist shot straight up through the glass, shattering it. Jackson reeled back as Frank yanked him away and behind him, leveling the gun. "She's just a—" Jackson started, but his words died. Whatever it was that she was, she was kicking and cracking through her metal cage like it was made of paper maché. Her form erupted outwards from the case, glass tinkling, her terrified screams reaching a fever pitch. Then, she went silent. She stood before them, eyes wild, whipping her head around to take in the scene, panting heavily. Her hands and arms were cut and bleeding, but before Jackson's eyes, the wounds closed up and vanished.

Oh gods. She has... she has magic.

The strange, familiar chime whispered in his ears again.

It was then Jackson realized that the woman was no longer standing. In fact, she was floating, some two inches off of the ground. "Do you see...?" he asked Frank.

Frank didn't respond, mouth only gaping, gun wavering. His gun had never wavered before.

They stared at each other for a long moment, the woman's eyes darting between them, her breathing ragged. Then, in a voice thick and rough from misuse, she made a sort of questioning grunt.

"It's alright," Jackson managed, holding up his hands. "We aren't going to hurt you. I... er... I'm Jackson. Who are you? Are you okay?"

The floating woman shook her head for a moment as if to clear it. Jackson noted tears had begun to streak down her face, though she was neither sobbing nor appeared to be hurt anymore. Her throat made several guttural noises as it cleared. Slowly, she began to sink in the air, her feet finally touching the earth. There she stood, staring at them, trying to speak.

"What's your name?" he tried again.

"*Anna,*" she struggled with a croak. Then, she collapsed, and Jackson could only lunge forward to catch her.

CHAPTER FOUR
The Impossible Woman

Anna's vision was full of spots, her head veering with vertigo. She put her hand over her eyes to block out the bright light, feeling like sandpaper was lodged between her bones, grinding. Someone was holding her up, thick, plastic sleeves on her skin. She struggled to right herself, but the world was unstable, tipping, sliding, taking her with it.

A thought struck her then, an echo in her head, as if she'd heard it on a dying radio station. *"Message received."*

Anna didn't know what it meant. Her breathing was shallow and frightened as she leaned into whoever was stabilizing her, trying to clear her head. She'd woken up in a coffin, screaming and pounding to get out. Tears streaked down her face as she sucked in air, the old nightmare of claustrophobia strangling her.

Where am I? What happened to me?

It was data that her frantic mind grasped for. Last night, she had been in her room. She had fed her cat. The affectionate feline had gotten underfoot, made her trip and hit her head on the way out the door. Maybe she had a concussion? Maybe she was dreaming?

She had gone to work, to the test site. Yes, the sun had been so bright on her way there. She remembered fishing for sunglasses in the glove compartment, finding nothing.

Then… there was nothing where her memories should be. She had woken up in a box. A claustrophobic, horrible box.

Why was her throat hurting so much? Why was it so dry? The spots cleared, and now she saw that the person propping her on her feet was head to toe dressed in teal, an environmental suit, though not one from her facility. Surprised, unfamiliar eyes were watching her through a visor on the helmet. "It's going to be okay, Anna." His tone was that of someone trying to soothe a wounded animal. A burlier teal-suited person was behind him, gloved hand clutching a gun. "It's okay. No one's going to hurt you."

Anna could only nod, staring at the gun, her throat a swollen ache. Even saying her name had taken everything she had. *Did I crash my car? Why are they wearing radiation suits if I crashed my car?* She had so many questions trying to surge up and out that she barely noticed a third stranger arriving until he spoke. "Who is this?" the new man asked. "What the *hell* is going on?" The edge in his tone made her wince, and she pulled her arms around herself.

She noticed then, in a distant way, that her palms felt only bare skin. Anna looked down, blinking, recognizing suddenly the warm brush of wind on her thighs, the hot scrape of earth on the soles of her feet. Her clothes were completely gone. She made a raspy, shrieking noise, sinking to the ground in a ball, covering herself as best as she could with her arms, the world tipping and rocking again.

"She needs medical attention." The first man's voice. "Frank, get her a spare uniform from the back. We need to go. Agent, tell me you're ready. The counter's going crazy."

"The package *isn't here*."

There was then some angry whispering between the two. She couldn't make it out, just snippets, words like "hospital" and "customs". And, in truth, Anna could barely focus on what they were saying anyway, nausea and distress making her fingers grip her kneecaps until they were white. *What happened to me? Why am I naked? Should I ask them to call work for me? Oh God, I'm going to get fired!* Anna felt her stomach drop, remembering she was supposed to meet with her mentor first thing that morning. They had to discuss the simulation numbers before their input was presented to the Pentagon, and she was in the middle of nowhere, naked, scared, and couldn't remember—

"Anna?" It was the first man, and his voice was gentle. Anna swallowed, winced, and turned. "There's water in the truck. You should come back with us. It's not safe out here, and you need a doctor." She nodded, weak, wondering if she could even stand. Her muscles shook as she tried. *Breathe. Breathe. Dr. Appleby will be able to read my notes, do the presentation, even if I'm not there.* She felt hot tears slide down her face, though, betraying her nerves.

It was at this moment that the big burly fellow—Frank, had he been called?—returned, a bundle of white fabric in his arms. He approached her with a cautious step, sliding his eyes away as he proffered the clothes. Anna took them, grateful, and more grateful still as they all turned around to let her dress, giving her a little space.

The white uniform was crisp against her skin, as if it had just been dry cleaned. As soon as everything was in place, she felt the panic start to sink back beneath the surface, but only just.

Bold letters on the cap made her pause. "Dovetail Parcel: Since 2042". That date wasn't for another 20 years. *Maybe some movie reference?* She wearily tugged the cap down over her hair, not caring enough to ask.

Her eyes were grateful for the relief from the bright sun. For the first time, she gave a hard look at the landscape around her. *Where am I?* This wasn't along her route. There was no crashed car, no Joshua trees, nothing to betray how she'd gotten there. The world before her was dust, concrete, and scraggly weeds, marred with sad used-to-be-buildings. Some kind of ghost town? *Did I get dragged out into the Mojave?* The cool air carried an awful, putrid smell. God, her head *hurt*.

Was I kidnapped? Was I drugged? She felt so sick and slow in the head. "I'm okay," she muttered weakly, though she knew she wasn't really okay, nothing about this was *okay*. A doctor. Yes, a doctor might be able to tell her what had happened.

The man with the gentle voice offered her a shoulder as a brace, the other one coming up on her left side and doing the same. She nodded, thankful, and licked her cracking lips, knowing it was going to be a long stagger to the truck. As she heaved one leg in front of the other, on top of it all, she realized she was hallucinating. Her feet looked like they were floating off of the ground, as if she were *hovering* forward. She glared at them. In a slow, dreamlike way, they began to meet earth again. *Drugged. I'm drugged.*

Her vision started to swim again, so Anna shut her eyes as she walked. *If I was kidnapped... what did they do to me?* She tried sensing herself, trying to feel out how badly she'd been hurt. But, she felt no twists or scrapes, no pain except the dryness of her throat.

She was still grateful to be seated in the back seat next to the man with the kind voice, who offered her a bottle of water, wonderful water, which splashed down her chin as she guzzled. Not even her aching throat could stop her from draining it to the last drop.

Finally, *finally*, her head cleared a little.

"Thank you for finding me," she whispered. She knew the Mojave was no place to get lost in. She might have died.

"Where are you from?" It was the frustrated stranger that had been so tense before (Walker?), who was riding in the front seat. He was giving her a hard, unblinking look through his visor. None of the men were removing their suits. She wondered if there had been a drill at the facility, or, if, heaven forbid, there'd been a contamination leak.

"Las Vegas. I work for Falcon."

Walker cocked his head at her, squinting. Anna realized she didn't have energy to say anything more. She rested her head back on the seat, feeling sleepy. She heard him ask something else, but she was already drifting.

...

...

Anna snapped awake. The truck was still rumbling down the road, a very ill-maintained road, which bumped and jarred them as they went. It looked like someone had built a highway and forgot to fix it for decades. Nothing but dirt, weeds, and dilapidated houses were outside the window still, the sky an overcast white.

The air seemed thick, too damp for the desert. Anna wondered if she'd been out for long. Her travel companions were silent.

Anna had never had the benefit of a groggy mind when she woke up. Her troubles immediately returned. She felt a pang in her chest. Home. She wanted home. She wanted to walk in the door and collapse face first onto her bed, maybe treat herself and order a pizza. She could almost smell her sheets and the little vase of lilacs she'd bought for herself on her dresser.

I hope I'm not fired. Being kidnapped, sure, it was a pretty good excuse for ditching the most important meeting of her fledgling career. But, that didn't make her failure to turn up easy to let go. She had worked *so hard* to land her job after college, get Falcon to take a chance on her unproven mind. At the test site, she was a minority on the scientific team, a young woman in a swath of men. Anna knew she had to meet a higher standard. Now on today, of all days, the day of her subcritical test presentation, the day that would see her first big contribution to their work...!

Panic began to simmer again.

There was a clicking noise, growing more rapid. The big guy in the front seat checked something on the dashboard, muttering, "Whose counter's sounding off? Outside measurements are clear."

Walker drew a boxy contraption from his side, and it made telltale whistling clicks that Anna knew well, though the gadget itself was smaller and sleeker than the ones she was used to. *A Geiger counter?* "It's mine. I don't understand... I'm getting almost 400 CPM here. You sure the dashboard is reliable?"

Anna's eyes narrowed. 400 CPM was a *lot* more than just background radiation, even if it wouldn't make a person sick right away.

"The truck's systems were accurate on the road down," the man next to her said. "Do we need to take a different route? There aren't that many roads from here back to New York."

Wait. What? "New York?!"

The clicking noise hit a frantic pace.

"Shit. My backup's saying 800 now," the driver growled.

"Something's very wrong," Walker muttered. "This would indicate the source of the radiation isn't outside. It's in here." His eyes widened. Slowly, he moved the boxy device near Anna. The clicking became more rapid. He pulled it away. It slowed. The truck ground to a screeching halt as they braked, and then, the three men simply stared at her. Anna pushed herself back into her seat.

"She's contaminated," Walker announced.

"That's ridiculous," the mutter came from her left. "The counters would have gone off ages ago if it were her."

Anna agreed. It *was* ridiculous. *Everything* was ridiculous. She couldn't take much more of today. Her eyes started to well up again. "I just want to go home." She wasn't sure when she had done it, but her legs were curled up in front of her defensively. She buried her face in her knees. "Please."

There was a hand on her shoulder. It was the man with the gentle voice. "Relax. It'll be alright; we just need to get you to a doctor. Frank, keep driving. We don't really have proper decontamination equipment here. And, well, these aren't alarming levels yet for us anyway."

"Boss...?" Frank asked.

"He's right; step on it. She needs help, and this is the quickest way back," Walker agreed.

"Drive, Frank."

The truck resumed its rumble down the road, and the man next to her turned, watching her.

Anna tried to think, and not to panic. Decontamination shouldn't have even been a problem. She hadn't been near anything radioactive in well over a week, and there had been no incidents at the facility that would have exposed her. It wasn't as if she made a habit of rolling around in uranium ore dust. Anna tried until tears squeezed out of her eyes, but she couldn't remember what had happened to get her there, what had been done to her during her blackout. *Naked and on the other side of the country.* "I don't understand..." The words were rasps still, and every one of them hurt.

"It's okay. You'll be alright." It was the gentle-voiced man. Anna looked up.

Wasn't he the one that had found her in the box? He must have gotten her out. He had gotten her clothes, and then water. She was alive because of all of that, and she didn't even know his name.

"Thank you…. who are you?" she managed.

"My name's Jackson. Don't worry about it. Just try to breathe and relax. Take one thing at a time."

Anna closed her eyes. He was right. One thing at a time. "Is there any more water…?" Her training finally kicked in. If she could wash, she might be able to remove some of the radioactive particles on her skin.

"That was the last." He made an apologetic nod at her bottle. "Sorry, this was an… unplanned trip. We are short-supplied."

Anna nodded, squeezing the plastic. No panicking. A doctor would help. And, if she was near New York for some unfathomable reason, she probably had enough savings to get home.

I'm okay. I'm okay.

The clicking continued in the front seat, unsettling and confusing.

I'm not okay.

"If it helps," Jackson continued. "I can tell you a story to get your mind off things."

It struck Anna that this was an odd solution, like something one might offer to a six year old afraid of needles and about to get a vaccine. But, she found herself nodding anyway. If he was talking, she didn't have to listen to the anxious voice flailing in her head, one far too close to boiling over.

Jackson leaned in, his voice taking on a quiet, conspiratorial air. It had a strange effect, as if cordoning off the space around the two of them. Then, in an authoritative tone, he began relating a fairy tale. It was something about a sailor's wife who went out to sea to find her husband, taken by mermaids.

Even though she was only half paying attention to it, the strangeness of it all did distract her, even if she felt a little childish. Her breathing evened. The fear slowly started to go back beneath the surface. The tears stopped.

"Huh…" Walker reported. "Readings are slowing."

Maybe it was a fluke? Anna's hopeful inner voice relaxed her a little more.

Jackson concluded the fable, the eyes behind the visor still looking a little concerned, but she nodded in thanks. If she had been asked, she wasn't sure if she could recount most of what he said, but the way he had said it had helped. She closed her eyes, weary.

I'm so tired.

And, she slipped into sleep again for a little while.

When she awoke, the atmosphere in the truck was hushed, the sun sinking past its noon zenith, the shadows shifting. "We're still going to New York?" she rasped.

"Yes," Jackson replied.

"How far away…?"

"We're here."

Anna glanced, confused, out of the front window again. Skyscrapers had burst into view on the horizon, a city skyline she had always wanted to see. She breathed a sigh of relief at civilization. Help was on the way.

Yet… something was strange about the buildings. She squinted. Something shimmered in the air, a strange glow, an unnatural, gem-like blue against the sky. Her eyes struggled to make sense of what she was seeing.

A giant glowing dome was settled over New York.

Anna almost vaulted into the front seat. "What the heck is *that?!*"

Three pairs of eyes turned to stare again. "What is what?" Walker asked.

"THAT!" She pointed at the city. They continued to stare in puzzlement. Her brain spun for a second, desperately trying to make sense of it, and then arrived at the most logical conclusion. *It's not real. I'm still hallucinating.* "I… um… I'm sorry. I'm seeing things. I think I was drugged."

Jackson cocked his head. "What are you seeing?"

"Some kind of bubble over New York. Sorry. It's stupid, right?"

He blinked owlishly. "You mean The Barrier?"

"…The what?"

Walker interrupted. "You've probably never seen one like this…? That's the reason for the name 'The Sapphire City', of course."

Anna's stomach twisted as she wrung her hands. "You can see it too."

"Yes...?" Walker replied.

"It's *real.*"

"Yes?" Jackson agreed. His tone seemed to ask why she thought it was so abnormal, a question that made the anxious voice inside scream louder.

"I'm drugged worse than I thought." Anna rubbed her eyes, leaning back. What if... what if none of these people were real? Could that be true? Maybe she wasn't even kidnapped or contaminated. Maybe she was in bed, dreaming.

"Las Vegas has one too," Walker intoned from the front seat. "Though I don't know the color."

"No, it doesn't. I live there." She coughed, trying to quash the fear, her throat too worn to continue.

It's okay. It is *a dream. That's why I don't remember how I got here.* A pearl of relief settled into her chest. *None of it is real. Oh, thank God. I just have to ride this out.* If one thing was certain about dreaming, it was that she would wake up eventually. The adrenaline had destroyed her body's need to go back to sleep, though, so she supposed she would just wait, watch, and see. The panic and the tears dried up. She clasped her legs tighter against her chest, marveling at how her brain was able to make her feel the bump of every pothole in the derelict highway, how she hadn't even questioned if it was real before now. *Dreams are always like that, I guess.*

At the blue bubble's edge, the truck stopped at a checkpoint. The man named Jackson passed forward some papers, began arguing with the woman who took them. It was about their extra, contaminated passenger. Anna, detached, peered out the windows, wondering at her imagination's workings. Right up until the glowing blue line of the dome, people milled. There were stores, apartments, and restaurants selling food from countries she'd never heard of. It was all things her brain had probably picked up from seeing New York on TV, a little grimy, a little under construction, but lively, energetic, the streets all grids and angles that ushered along a river of humans. The truck started moving again. The flow of the crowd was as if everyone needed to get to where they were going right that minute, pushing, jostling, one or two even running in front of their wheels. The driver kept a serene posture as he blared the horn, though she heard a soft diatribe behind the air filter in his suit.

The minutes passed, and the truck rumbled up a bridge now. Dark water flickered beneath them in the sunlight, and Anna caught glimpses of a handful of little white ships below, jostling with the gentle current, maybe fishing boats, or ferries. *I think I saw this in a travel article once.*

It was almost a disappointment when they left the bridge behind. Now, all the buildings were an unmarked, sandy brown. The truck ambled into the heart of what seemed to be a complex of some kind as the driver followed Walker's instructions, and Anna sunk in her seat as she saw a perimeter fence pass them by, four times her height, barbed wire glinting. A flickering of dread rose again.

The truck stopped.

"We're here," Walker announced, turning and looking at her expectantly.

I'd like to wake up now, Anna requested of her mind. But, it didn't happen. Jackson was holding out a hand, an offer to help her out of the truck, and she took it, unsure of what else to do. She thanked him as her shoes touched the cement, realizing her body was still shaking. Anna willed it to stop, but it would not. Shouldn't she be able to do whatever she wanted, now that she realized it wasn't real? Lucid dreaming; wasn't that what it was called?

As she was willing her wobbly knees to stay straight, a man was coming up to them in a uniform of charcoal gray, a sky-blue insignia of two shaking hands over his heart. Anna had never seen a uniform like it, though she encountered the military at the test site all the time.

He nodded at her, his face stoic, his eyes hidden behind dark sunglasses. Anna nodded back.

And then, a stinging pain bloomed in her neck. Her hand whipped up, the instinct rising to swat at some biting insect. A little yellow nodule came away in her palm. A… dart…?

Anna closed her eyes, an airy feeling building in her head. She felt like a balloon about to float away. "Whuzzat?" she failed to articulate.

She didn't even feel it when she hit the ground.

CHAPTER FIVE
Negotiation

The interrogation room was dark, cold, and smelled of bleach and artificial lemon. They'd called it a "debriefing room", but Jackson knew better.

He gingerly touched the bruising area on his shoulder that his escort had left and winced, trying not to think about why they would need to sanitize this room on a regular basis. He had almost come to blows with the agent that had sedated the Anna woman—what the hell were they thinking?—only to be grabbed himself, shown to this room, and locked up. He supposed he ought to be *grateful* they hadn't deigned to tranquilize him, too.

Where had Frank been taken? Jackson had heard a lot of angry yelling behind him when the agents had seized him and marched him off. Gods, he couldn't imagine Frank responding to government coercion in any way other than *badly*. He hoped no one got shot.

The helm from his protective suit sat askew on the table in front of him now, the rest of it discarded by his chair. His nervous breathing through the filter had begun making his head dizzy, the safety lining making him sweat. How much time had passed? An hour, maybe two? They'd taken his datapad. He had no way of knowing.

During their journey back, Agent Walker had been whispering into his communicator, and Jackson didn't like this at all. Something that Walker had said to his superiors had triggered this reaction to Anna's arrival at the base;

he was certain. Likely, the man had told his Coalition cronies that she was radioactive as hell. Jackson saw no reason why Walker wouldn't disclose the fact that *she'd been floating,* either.

He found he was shaking in his seat, his back and face still sweating hot pinpricks, even without the suit. He weaved his fingers together in front of himself to still the trembling and pretended to examine his fingernails, as if bored rather than terrified. He didn't know who might be watching him behind the opaque window near the door.

There were stories he remembered from when he was a child, science fiction bits about the government stealing away *different* people, those mutated in the radiation. Those people would disappear, or become experiments. To most children, they had been stories. To him... especially after his father's and Huxley's warnings...

Of course, this wasn't just about him right now. There was Anna, as well. Jackson was not a man given to fretting about the well-being of strangers, but... she was like him, wasn't she? She had *magic.* She wasn't contaminated at all. When she stewed and grew frightened, the radiation had flared out, just like the shadows did for him, before the tea had put him back in control.

Well, mostly in control, at this point.

He suspected that she was experiencing what Huxley had told him was a *flare,* an uncontrolled burst of channeled magic. Because of this, he wasn't surprised, though he was glad, when soothing her had calmed down the radiation levels as well. At least she hadn't started flying again.

If the Coalition let either of them walk out of this compound alive, perhaps they would share a cup of crazy tea and figure out what was wrong with them both.

If the Coalition let them leave.

The door suddenly slammed open, flooding his eyes with searing light. A figure entered, and the bulb overhead blazed. Jackson felt exposed as the darkness fell away, and he squinted at the new arrival. Agent Walker. Of course it was.

"Mr. Dovetail," Walker greeted. He strode to the table and sat across from

Jackson, stretching out his legs and setting down his datapad.

Jackson seethed, but he knew the value of diplomacy in the face of scrutiny. Besides, he'd only been paid in half so far. For the company and his own health, Jackson forced a smile. "How can I help you? I can't say I'm certain why I've been brought here."

Walker removed his sunglasses. The dark-eyed gaze underneath was that of a man about to wager something. Jackson did not trust this lack of hostility, and watched, wary, as Walker opened one side of his Coalition-issued jacket, extracted a thumb-sized recording device, and set it on the table, making a show of switching it to *Off*. "Everything you and I say in this room is off the record. No one else is listening."

Jackson raised an eyebrow. "Okay?" *Right. Sure they aren't.*

"Now, what I wanted to talk about was *magic*."

What? …Shit.

Jackson swallowed, threading his hands together in front of them, fidgeting with his fingers. He smiled again, this time apologetic. "I'm sorry, I'm not certain if I heard you correctly."

"Magic, Dovetail. Magic. What happened out there in the wastes is forcing me to tell you things a lot sooner than I'd like." Jackson remained still, face and posture neutral. "Full honesty? I didn't come to you because I needed a smuggler. There are other smugglers, some of them doing better than you, and some of them already in the Coalition's employ. I came to you because I've been watching you for a while. I know you were Huxley's student, not for the piano lesson nonsense he advertises. I know you did get a very basic magical training at least, even if the Order vote was against you."

Shit. Shit. It was everything in Jackson not to react. He just kept smiling, but now the way one would at a child insisting they'd seen a fairy. He leaned forward, staring directly into the agent's dark eyes, and summoned his talisman against the government agents who might still be listening, regardless of Walker's assurances. "Magic doesn't exist, Agent. What is this really about?"

Walker sighed, and leaned back, massaging his temples. "You're making this difficult. I come from a magical family myself. My mother… she was from the Morimoto line." He paused, as if he was seeking recognition, but this meant nothing to Jackson, whose mind kept racing, trying to nail down the agent's angle. "They were well-established in Texas, using their abilities to keep the water and food supply uncontaminated. They even ran a small Order there, until the plague, anyway. Came up here. She was all that was left, and me."

Jackson remembered hearing once about the tragic rash of disease in some of the Texan settlements, and frowned. So, the agent was claiming to be a mage? He had never met a mage other than Huxley, had always been denied the chance. But, Jackson also knew what Huxley said, what his father said: *Keep this quiet. No one must ever know.* And to spill to the government? Jackson licked his lips, choosing his words with wariness, coloring them with disbelief. "So you're saying you practice *magic.*"

"No. I didn't get The Gift. It went with my mother."

"Oh." Jackson was uncertain if he was disappointed or even more wary. "And why are you telling *me* this?"

"I need you to know I'm *in* on this business," Walker said, "And, that in mind, I need you to tell me what this is about." He reached into his pocket and pulled out a small scrap of paper, one that made Jackson's stomach sink like a stone.

JACK, the note read, *I left this here for you.*

Walker must have gotten it off of Frank, he realized. *Damn it.* "It was taped to the box Anna was trapped in when we arrived on site." Jackson shrugged. "I doubt it's addressed to me. No one knew of our journey. I didn't even have coordinates until I was in the truck with you."

"Tell me, Jackson, did anything unusual happen regarding either this note or Anna? And, I think you know what I mean by *unusual.*"

The agent had switched to using his first name. It was likely a ploy to create artificial trustworthiness, a common business tactic. "No, *Agent Walker,*" Jackson said, thinking back to the buzzing in his ears and ravens in the skies. "Nothing at all."

"I don't think that can be true," Walker replied. "I really don't…" He turned the note back to himself, squinting at it. "...Jack."

"I've never gone by *Jack*."

"Oh? Not ever? Well, I don't suppose any of *this* is familiar to you?" Walker tapped his datapad, propping it up so Jackson could better see. An image flickered onto the screen, a photograph of the destruction and death they had seen earlier. Jackson's stomach made a queasy shift. Walker swiped the picture away, and in its place was another dead body, battered, old blood running down his face. "This is Mr. Chao Wu. He wasn't at the scene today. He died about a week ago. Wu's brothers were arrested for buying arms at a raider black market, and for kidnapping New York citizens to use as *coin*."

Jackson's shoulders groaned with tension. To be implicated in the vile slave trade—something he'd made sure to stay far away from—was as good as a death sentence. "I'm afraid I still don't understand, Agent. I don't know a Chao Wu." This was the truth.

"Like I said, Wu's brothers were arrested, but we couldn't find the man himself. That is, until he turned up like this. We found him at a raider camp, beaten to death and his brains liquidated. That's what's on his face, there." Jackson swallowed back bile. "The raiders didn't do that to him, you know. We don't know what the hell did. But, his body was delivered to the camp before we got there, and the raiders were so spooked, they abandoned shop, making a friend of mine very unhappy when his sting operation fell through."

"That's... unfortunate..."

"Mr. Wu had this stapled to his vest." Walker swiped the image away. There, in its place, was a photograph of a brown-stained, crumpled piece of stationary. And, in familiar, frantically tilted purple crayon letters, were the words, *Stay out of my city*.

Jackson squeezed his fingers together, the hairs on the back of his neck rising, his fingertips tingling with adrenaline. "I don't have anything to do with this."

"I know." Walker closed the datapad, and Jackson's shoulders eased, just a little. "And I'm certainly not looking to avenge Wu's death. He deserved what he got. But, I have tens of other pictures, other stories, dead criminals and bystanders alike. A lot of my coworkers following up on these cases think they're unrelated, or the local militia will just handle it, but I found the pattern: the notes. You see, these letters have a little bit of magic on them. The eyes tend to slide past the writing unless they're meant for you... or you know what to look for. So, you see, I saw them, could read them, and my coworkers simply can't."

Walker's fingers tapped an even rhythm on the table. "And," he continued, "since you can see the notes just fine too, either it *is* addressed to you, or your denial about being ignorant of magic doesn't wash."

Jackson realized his breathing had gotten shallow. He tried to will it to even out, to force his body to at least stop sweating. *JACK, I left this here for you.* What did that even mean? That Anna was left behind *for him?* Was Walker lying, trying to trap him? Frank had been able to read the note, hadn't he? Thinking back, had Frank done anything more than give a confused grunt when he'd been handed the paper?

"Originally," Walker continued, "I was just going to work with you on smuggling runs, monitoring you to see if I could eventually approach you as a magical source. I don't really trust the Order here, and I could use your expertise, based on your history."

Jackson's mental wheels were humming, questions bubbling. *Why don't you trust the Order?* "My... expertise."

"Yes, but, well, now twenty agents are dead—butchered—and this person has his eye on you. The Coalition is about to get very involved in this business. You can see the need for a change of plans." Walker drew his hands together, leaning forward, and Jackson was glad he knew this posture. It wasn't one of aggression. No, Walker was about to deliver *an offer.*

"I need to find out who is behind this, but I need magical resources, and none of my coworkers can help me. Right now, I'm alone in a sea of well-intentioned agents who don't know what magic is, and if they were informed, would make some very bad decisions." His expression grew pained, but he did not comment further on it. "Jackson, it seems you have a powerful Gift. If you can help me track this person down, I can help you in turn."

Jackson gave him a sidelong stare. *Powerful Gift...? His research mustn't be that good, then.* He kept his voice flat and neutral, though, exploring the offer. "How do you mean?"

"I've seen your medical records. I know you have certain issues with your memory. I can get you answers about your past, your lineage, everything about what you are. I can get you spellbooks, artifacts, and more that the Order controls here, without them knowing. My family had a lot of connections, and knew almost every other major magical family on the East and West Coasts."

Well. There it was. Jackson licked his lips, trying not to scowl about Walker digging into his medical history. He could team up with this agent and delve into the crimes of a magical madman, and in return, he would receive information, forbidden, rare.

Jackson considered it for only two seconds.

"No."

"No?" Walker actually seemed startled. "Auras like yours don't just pop into any family tree. You were related to *powerful* mages. Don't you *want* to know who you are? Who your family was?"

Jackson drew his lips into a thin line. "That would be unnecessary. Peter Dovetail was my father. That's it."

He of course knew he didn't have a choice but to help Walker either way. If he didn't, the government contracts were probably as good as gone, and he didn't like the idea of turning up murdered with a purple crayon note stuck to his jacket.

Let it not be said, however, that Jackson could not barter.

"I find it hard to believe that you're not curious at all. Do you really want to have a made up birth certificate forever? Not know anything about your lineage, or what happened to them?"

"Oh? You really think I should care about that?" Jackson crossed his arms, irritated—he knew why Walker was taking this tack, dangling the hopes of many an orphaned boy. "Let me tell you about when I was adopted, when it came time to file my citizenship papers, and transfer me from being a ward of the state into Peter Dovetail's care." The agent cocked his head. "No one knew my birth date, of course. And, Peter Dovetail, this man who was taking me in, he turns and asks if I should like to put down October 24th as a birthday. I didn't get it then, of course. It just sounded as good as any other day."

Walker drummed his fingers, clearly not certain what Jackson was getting at.

"I later learned that a few years before he adopted me, he had a wife. I'm sure you turned that up in your... *research*."

Walker frowned. "Yes. She died in a car accident, from what I understand. It was a tragedy."

"Yes. Yes, she did. She and their unborn son, Jackson, who she was scheduled to deliver on October 24th."

Walker straightened, mouth opening and closing. "I... see..."

"So, Peter Dovetail came to the orphanage and decided I was to be his son, and he my father, and that's that. You don't need to dangle my biological relatives in front of me like a carrot for a poor orphaned rabbit. I am a Dovetail."

Walker leaned back and regarded Jackson with an inscrutable stare. The seconds passed. Then, "Very well. I can still help you with information regarding your Gift. I know the Order makes it difficult to get resources if you don't keep to their ranks."

Jackson shook his head. "I have little use for your books." He did not say he could not even read them, that the Language of Magic was nothing more than crude squiggles to him. It still stung, in some ways, and he refused to discuss his being *defective* with a stranger. Perhaps if Walker had offered this ten years ago, he would have leapt at the chance. But what did he have now? Just some nightmares that, if all went well, Huxley would help him get under control.

"Very well." The agent's jaw tightened in frustration. There was, for just a moment, a tic of tension under his left eye. "So I can't give you spellbooks, genealogy, or a place in the Order. Whatever. How about money?"

Ah, there it was. Something useful. Jackson smiled, pleased Walker had arrived at the proper bartering tool on his own. "How much?"

The agent shook his head. Then, he frowned even deeper, like he'd just figured out the game they were playing. "I don't know why I didn't offer you that in the first place. I guess I assumed you were a man of interests beyond *smuggling* and *money*."

Jackson snorted. The less Walker knew of his interests, the better. "How much, Agent Walker?"

"I can afford twenty thousand per month. That is it. No more."

Jackson blinked. Twenty thousand? The agent must have decided to get this agreement off the books. It was a far lower amount of coin than his other contracts. Still... it wasn't for the company, just for him. And, it would more than make up for Frank's backlogged paycheck. "Under the table?" he clarified.

"*Yes*," Walker growled. "But for that, I want another favor."

"What?"

"Anna. I'm sure you've pieced together there's magic around her, a lot of it. I'm not even Gifted and I can see the signs."

"I thought she was simply contaminated. Nothing a quick wash and check up won't solve."

Walker stared. "...Stop that. I know a flare when I see it. Once she's mentally stabilized, she's going to need someone to explain her magical outbursts to her. I'm not the best fit, without the training. And, it's not like the Order will break in here, trying to keep a low profile as they are. Wouldn't trust her to them anyway. It was *you* that calmed her down in the truck."

Jackson wondered again what dirt the agent had on the oh-so-mighty Order.

"So, you have a rapport with her. I can make that excuse enough to get you visitation rights. You might be able to help her, *quietly*, and if I'm going to get her transferred out of here, she cannot flare again. It must look like a fluke contamination. And... well... I can't really hide it if she starts *flying* again, so this needs to happen soon."

Now Jackson uncrossed his arms. Walker claimed to want to help her? He couldn't see the angle. "You're the one that insisted we bring her here."

"Yes, and I stand by that. I have orders. She's dangerous, and there isn't a single civilian hospital equipped to deal with her if her outburst gets worse. It's going to be a fine line between whether she's going to get this under control and leave, or if she..." He trailed off. "You know what, I am not certain why you would care."

Jackson was certain he did. Were the stories of secret government programs true? "What *would* happen to her, Walker?"

The agent clenched his jaw again. "Classified, Jackson. Classified. But I'd rather it not be. Can you help her?"

"I..." Jackson hesitated. He had thought he had Walker's measure, but... could he really help? ...Maybe. Should he get involved, though?

Jackson slid his eyes down to his white-knuckled fists, a strain of memory turning his stomach, a sick feeling of fear from long ago. He had been thirteen, slamming the bathroom door, hands slippery on the lock. The ravens had croaked at his window all night, but that had been far from the worst of it. There were shadows, endless shadows, unnaturally pooling near him. Without warning, they were coming for him, slithering off the walls, becoming solid against all reason, knocking things off tables and shelves. They reached to him, grasping, yanking, dragging. At 3AM, he had fled to the bathroom while brandishing a kitchen knife, not sure anymore if he was awake or dreaming. A horrible, discordant buzzing was in his head.

His first flare, or at least, the first he remembered.

His father had broken down the door, had seen him waving a blade at the walls, and had shuddered in horror. But he had stayed, and he had embraced his adopted son, and he had promised he was going to find a way to make everything alright.

"Okay," Jackson finally said. He lifted his eyes from the weight of lingering memories. "I accept these terms."

Walker hadn't seemed to notice the weary shift in his demeanor. "Finally." He put the recorder back in his pocket. "That mountain of a bodyguard of yours is sitting outside, stewing. Tell him not to draw his gun on any more agents in the compound, okay? You're free to go. You'll get a call when you're needed." He chucked a small electronic card Jackson's way, who barely caught it. "And here's the rest of the pay for today."

Walker rose and went to the door, banging on it three times. Two agents entered, one of which collected Jackson's radiation suit. The second of them grabbed back onto the tender spot in Jackson's shoulder, pushing him up and along, down the intricate maze of gray hallways, and finally, out into the sun. It had already sunk beneath the skyline, casting the area in a false twilight. They left him there amongst the vehicles, slamming the door to the compound behind them.

Frank stood by the truck, face contorted as if he was currently eating a rotten egg. Jackson hoisted himself up into the passenger seat, and Frank took his place behind the wheel, rolling down the window, then spitting on the ground for good measure before driving out of the gate. "Fucking government," Frank grumbled.

"Yes," Jackson agreed.

CHAPTER SIX
Out of Time

Anna dreamed.

She dreamed about many things: her home, her friends, occasionally even her mother and father, as distant as their relationship had been. In her dream, her family was having a Thanksgiving dinner, no snide remarks about her lack of husband, or her looks, or her life. Her mother hugged her. It was like when she was three, and her aunt and uncle had still been alive, and everyone just got together and ate and ate...

She dreamed of work, too. She would sit at her desk, calmly entering the day's radiation measurements, making sure they were in normal parameters. It was serene, familiar. There was some project Dr. Appleby was asking her to join; it was in a folder on her desk, and she was so curious to look at it. If nothing else, it felt like it might be a break from the monotony.

Then, something in the air *shifted*, a sour taste filling in her mouth. Anna looked up from the folder, dread worming into her mind.

There was a scream, and she was then in the hallway beyond her desk. She didn't know why, but she began to run, gasping with every stride, terrified beyond reason. Something was chasing her. It was a horrible thing, just outside of her field of vision. Thunderous cracks and screams echoed in its wake, but she didn't know what it was. Her breathing had gone harsh and her mind was spinning—the thing was coming for her, was going to end her life. She shrieked for help. Gunshots blared, and she was drowned out by all the other screams in her ears.

Anna would wake up, heaving with frantic breaths and crying, every time this dream came to her. And, it seemed to come often. Anna would sleep, and then, she would run, and she would wake, and she would cry, never knowing what it meant, pulling her knees to her chest and trying to comfort herself. *Just nightmares. It's just nightmares.*

The lights flickered on, and Anna looked up again to the whitewashed quarantine room, eyes burning from her frightened tears. She swallowed the last of her sobs and uncurled herself, steadying her breathing.

Her eyes meandered to her window, her only glimpse at the rest of the facility. Two people in environmental suits were taking notes beyond the glass, probably discussing her, though not using the intercom to let her in on it. She could have well been a bit of furniture.

Anna rolled out of bed, stretching, trying to keep the back of her hospital gown from showing itself to the window. She was convinced that she should have woken up days ago to her apartment, to her life, but she hadn't. Here, deep in some facility, there were no clocks, no conversations, no explanations. Her only way of keeping time was to eat, sleep, dream, and count how often she did these things.

She still remembered nothing about why she was here.

One, two, three.

Anna stretched and touched her toes, trying to work out the cramps from laying down for so long.

One, two, three.

Her muscles ached in strange places. Her calves and thighs had started getting nervous tics when she rested. Since she had awoken here—she thought it might have been about a week ago—she'd begun getting shaky spells, spasms, and a weak feeling in her fingers. This sudden downturn in her health haunted her. It was the memories of radiation suits and Geiger counters. *What's wrong with me? Radiation poisoning?* She was well aware how bad it could go for her if it was. She was young and healthy, but radiation didn't care, and lingering pain and death would be waiting for her at the end of that road.

So, Anna did stretches, trying not to think about the sickness that might be eating her from the inside out, or the delirium that had preceded this room. She tried not to be scared at the thought of dying across the country, if she was, in fact, in New York, in some quarantined hole. The technicians never said a word, and none of the men that had brought her here in that truck had returned. She was alone in her silence.

Anna wondered if anyone was searching for her. How many days could she miss at work? When would her roommate call the police?

The first day, Anna had cried a little, yelled at the window and the door, pounded on the glass. Then, she organized, thinking through her weakening body. She composed a checklist of questions, and confronted anyone who would listen with them. "Where am I? Why am I being held here? Are you affiliated with the U.S. government? Is there anything medically wrong with me? When will I be allowed to leave? May I have a phone call?" And so on. The questions, however, turned out to be little more than a meditational chant, because no one answered any of them, no matter how long or how frequently she asked.

Once, a man with icy brown eyes and a black suit had come to her window, memorable only because he wore no protective gear. She'd shouted her questions at him until her throat went hoarse, but he only shook his head at her and left.

Anna sat back on the bed, done with stretches, feeling dizzy again. She wrapped her arms around herself, clammy skin under her palms. Her grasp was weak. Her muscles were turning to gelatin.

Her stomach gurgled. And, the room suddenly felt like it was tipping. *What is...?*

Then, the world *jumped*.

One second, she was staring at the window, considering calling for help as her vision swayed and blurred. The next, she was lying back in the bed, a bright light shining into one eye.

"You're awake," a male voice said through a filter. She bolted upright, before the dizziness returned, then sank back onto her pillow. "Easy now. You passed out. You're going to be fine, Anna."

"Who are you?" she whispered, her throat sore. "Where am I? Why am I being held here? Are you affiliated with—"

"Relax. I'm here to answer your questions. I'm sorry it took so long. I'm Special Agent Walker, Coalition. You can call me Jaden if you like." His face was hidden behind a teal helmet again, but now, she placed his voice and the name. The man from the front seat in the truck. She must have made a face, because he sighed. "I know I brought you here, and it's been very confusing and frustrating. This is the first visit I was allowed to arrange. It's been two days, and you haven't been well, so visitation was restricted while your ailments were analyzed."

This shook something inside of her. She could have sworn it had been a full week! She'd slept so often, gotten so tired... it had only been two days? "What's *wrong* with me?"

"I'm sorry. We still don't really know, though I can tell you it's no infection or virus."

"There has to be..." Anna struggled to sit up. "...more tests you can do, something, right? You have to have some idea, if I'm in quarantine."

Instead of answering, Walker asked, "Do you remember anything that happened before you came here, before we found you?"

Anna paused and thought back. "Sort of? I was at work. I work at a research compound a few miles outside of town—Vegas, I mean—in the Mojave. You know, the Nevada National Security Site? Then... I don't know. I think something happened? But it's a blur. I'm sorry. I just don't know. I woke up in that box. Everything hurt."

Walker nodded, his suit making the sound of plastic squeaking against itself. "The company you work with—is it Falcon, by any chance?"

"Yes! Yes, that's it. You can call Dr. Appleby. He's my mentor. Well, my boss, really. He can verify for me." Anna bit her lip, then. She wasn't sure why, but thinking about Dr. Appleby made her feel sort of empty inside. "Is it radiation poisoning?" she finally asked. "I know the signs. I had to learn them backwards and forwards."

"Strangely, we don't think it is."

She stared at Walker for a long moment. "Wasn't there a Geiger counter…?" The truck ride was a blur in her mind, mixing parts that might have been real with parts that definitely weren't. She wished none of it had been real at all. Still, a small bit of hope sprung up in her chest. Perhaps she hadn't been handed a death sentence.

"Yes, we found you in an irradiated area, and by all accounts, you ought to be badly poisoned. But we've done some tests, and you show no signs of anemia, damage to your tissues… nothing. You're a miracle." The way he said *miracle* sounded tired and sad, however, and didn't make her feel better. "There's something wrong, but it's not that."

"Then what *is* it?"

Walker was silent. This response rang in her ears. Anna swallowed.

"So… I'm in New York."

"Yes."

"Has anyone figured out how I got here?"

"I'm sorry." Walker motioned to scratch his head, seeming to forget the helmet was in the way. He let his hand fall with an awkward, embarrassed flop. "Your memories might come back later. And if they do… please let me know. It could be very important so I can help you."

Anna nodded. "What… what day is it?" *How long have I been out of work?*

"It's July 24th, about oh nine hundred hours."

"But…" She gaped. "A *month?*" Her voice was coming out in a tiny squeak; she didn't even know she could make such a mousy noise. "I've been out for a *month?*" Her newfound dizziness didn't have anything to do with the sickness; Anna leaned her head back and let the sterile white expanse of the ceiling fill her eyes.

"Anna." Walker spoke. Anna didn't find the wince in his voice comforting. It was as if his words had sharp edges that needed to be tucked away before they were handed to her. "Do you know what year it is?"

"2022." Her voice sounded flat and robotic, even to her own ears. And then, something in her gut prickled. "…Why?"

"Anna…" Walker shifted again, whispering. "I need you to understand that whatever is wrong with you, it flares up when you grow frustrated or upset. It's very important that you keep your emotions as much in control as you possibly can."

Considering what was happening, Anna felt she'd been *very* calm. She said as much.

"Yes, well, there's some news, and it's going to sound pretty… unbelievable. There are cameras in here. If we keep our voices *very* low, they aren't going to pick up what we're saying." Anna turned to him with curiosity and trepidation. Why did it matter? Why the secrecy? "I'm trying to get you better and get you out of quarantine, but if you make any loud exclamations, it's going to make them keep you here longer. You do *not* want to call attention to yourself. Do you understand?"

Anna nodded, not sure why, just wanting him to tell her what he was trying to say.

"Alright. Now, I need you to take a couple deep breaths, okay?"

"Okay…?" Anna nodded. Then, she demonstrated. "Alright, I'm breathing! Why am I breathing?"

"It's very important that you remain calm."

"Yes, I get it." Anna narrowed her eyes.

"It is 2147."

Anna stared. "…What is 2147?"

Walker hesitated. "The year. The *year* is 2147."

Anna cocked her head. Then, she laughed, feeling a bit lighter for the first time since she'd woken up. "Ha! Alright, alright, you've made me laugh. I feel calmer now." She snorted, shaking her head, grinning. "What is the *real* serious thing you wanted to tell me?"

"I… just did. It's 2147."

Anna felt her smile fade. She stared at him for a long time, unable to see his face, unable to read anything about him. Her mind went still again, blank. "Why would you say that?"

"I'm telling the truth."

Anna shook her head. "I maintain warheads. I'm not a time traveler. I'm pretty grounded in reality, Mr. Walker. *Agent* Walker."

He sighed. "I don't know what to tell you, how to make this easier in some way… Anna, you don't even have to believe me. It's just *very* important you don't reference the world as if it's 2022. A psychiatric evaluation, on top of all of this, well…"

"Why would you even tell me this? Why?" Anna didn't mind reading sci-fi; heck, she had her own little library at home. But this nonsense, after everything that was happening to her?

"Your story. I found a *very* old record of who you say you are." He spoke so low that she almost had to lean forward to catch it. "Dr. Anna Matthews, with Falcon. Your face matches hers exactly." He shook his head. "That in itself was hard to come to terms with but… I'm sorry. Let me ask you. What's your assignment?"

Anna gave him an frustrated stare. "I run safety simulations on the stockpile, but…"

Walker gave a resigned nod that stopped her protest. "That's… that's what the record said. That's not public data. Christ…" He was silent for a long minute. "Anna, if I'm even going to consider what you're saying is true, you ought to be either very old or very dead after going through a hundred and twenty five years, then taking a nap in six grays of radiation outside of New York." He shook his head, slowly, as if in disbelief. "I don't know what this means. Maybe you're not insane. I've seen impossible things before, and you were found in the middle of something almost worse than this."

Anna continued staring at him, without words. *You thought I'm insane? Are you serious?*

Her mind whispered to her of the hallucinations she'd seen during her drive to New York.

A ghost town, a wasteland.

A giant blue bubble over a city skyline.

A uniform: *Dovetail Parcel: Since 2042.*

No no no. Time travel wasn't something that happened to people like her. It wasn't something that happened to people *at all*. It was stupid! It was *crazy!*

"Please," she said quietly, with such certainty that it was if she was trying to force the universe to comply. "I don't want to talk about this. I don't care about your game. I want to go home."

Walker bowed his head. "I'm sorry. I don't know where home *is* for you anymore. This complicates things. But, I promise you, I am working on it."

Anna felt her eyes burning, but no tears were coming, not yet.

Walker stood. "I have to go. They didn't give me much time." He shifted from foot to foot, as if he was seeking words that would somehow make her believe him, and finding few. "I know it's a lot. You're going to have questions. I promise I'm here to help. You remember Jackson? I'm going to send him in tomorrow to help you, too." His voice hushed again. "There's some people here that want to keep you. I'm doing everything I can to make sure they don't turn the Director's ear. You just have to keep the year you think it is to yourself— and the radiation. Just be calm as you can, and friendly, and listen to Jackson's advice. Can you do that?"

That was it? Just, nod and agree to think about what he said, all the impossible things he said?

Anna continued looking at her hands. Walker seemed to take her silence as an affirmation, and left. The door made a huff of compressing air as it closed behind him.

Her head ached; her stomach churned.

Anna simply sat, and thought, and then, finally, cried herself to sleep, not knowing what else to do.

When she awoke, the next day was much the same as the first: an austere, white room, a silence, and a sickness in her body. There was now a simple gray uniform waiting for her on the table. Anna changed clothes, glad to rid herself of the gown, and went about her hours thinking, even getting up the courage to do her stretches again. This time, she did not get dizzy or collapse, though her muscles shook a little harder, and she sat before she exerted herself much.

She didn't know how many hours passed before the door swooshed open again, and despite everything, it was a welcome change to the *nothingness* of the room.

"Hello, Anna!" a chipper male voice greeted her. This newcomer was also in a suit, face hidden. But, though they'd only met once, Anna thought she knew the brown eyes behind the visor, the friendly tone.

"…Jackson?"

There was a silence, and she had the strange certainty that he was smiling at her. "How are you doing?" he asked.

Anna said nothing. Some part of herself wanted to automatically respond, *Fine, how are you?*, but it felt like too big of a lie for her to handle right now. In fact, his friendliness was almost unsettling after so much isolation.

He seemed to take her extended silence as an answer. "May I sit?" He nodded at the chair where Walker had been the day prior. Anna nodded, not really knowing what else to say. When Jackson approached the chair, he gave it an exaggerated spin so it faced her, and sat.

"So…" She let her question trail off, her expression more than finishing her words. *What are you doing here, talking to me, the girl in quarantine who's either gone crazy or is going to?*

Jackson hesitated. "They asked me to meet with you."

"…Oh."

"I *wanted* to talk to you too," he added quickly. "See how you were doing. I want to help. I'd like to get you out of here, and I'm sure you'd like that too."

Anna regarded him with a wary eye. "Alright. Well… do you work here, too?"

"*Gods*, no," he snorted, waving a dismissive hand at the door. "Independent contractor. I do deliveries. That was my mail truck we brought you back in when you were hurt."

Anna found she believed him, his energetic movements and light tone wholly apart from Walker's. Something about talking to "agents" of any kind unsettled her. Back at Falcon, she did that regularly. She always had the feeling they were analyzing her, waiting for her to do something they didn't like, not unlike the ice-eyed man that had been at the window earlier. "I never got the chance to thank you. You rescued me. Even if I did wind up here."

Jackson nodded his head, the suit squeaking. "Of course. We couldn't just leave you out there for the raiders!"

"...Raiders?"

Jackson made a wavy motion with his wrist, as if summoning an image to mind. "You know, raiders, bandits. Outside the city walls."

Anna blinked. "Um." This was a strange assumption that he seemed to think she should be making about the world.

"Oh... right. Walker told me about the... er... *year* problem."

Anna's eyes narrowed, expecting a challenge, but it didn't come. She didn't argue, remembering Walker's warning, then wondered why she was taking such a warning seriously. *Wanting me to pretend I'm a time traveler... why on earth...*

"You don't remember anything?" Jackson asked. Anna shook her head. When she tried to tease her memories out, a cold, sick feeling would form in her stomach, like she was trying to touch a hot oven, knowing it would hurt. And so help her, she didn't want to talk about it, and if Jackson wanted to pry, or repeat that ridiculous 'What year is it?' game— "Well, don't worry about all of that right now. Right now, you look like you feel queasy. You're confused, and probably a little frightened. Right? I can help you feel better."

"...And how's that?" It wasn't in Anna's nature to be suspicious or defensive, but right then, she didn't know how else to feel. "I... I do want help. But I just don't understand what's going on."

Jackson's voice dropped to a whisper. "Walker told me you're radioactive."

Her own voice was less quiet. "Yes, I know he thinks that." She recalled the revelation in the truck. "And, not unlike other things Walker said, it's *scientifically impossible*. Someone cannot be radioactive to the degree that everyone needs to wear *suits* around them. Not without being a lot more sick than I am."

"Anna, he's right." Jackson's tone fell into a soothing cadence. She remembered how he spoke with her when she was first found. "We can't talk a lot about the why's or how's here. It's not safe. And, I'm told you're not allowed a Geiger counter of your own yet to see for yourself. But, it doesn't matter. I'm going to help you get this radioactivity nonsense under control, so you can leave." His palms were up, in an almost supplicating gesture.

Anna, regardless of anything else, found that his tone seemed sincere. She swallowed. "I want to go home. Can you get me that?"

"I don't know. But getting out of here is a great start."

Anna nodded. "Alright." Perhaps he was right. It didn't matter if she could see it for herself. Maybe it didn't matter if she believed these assertions. Other people seemed to, and they were keeping her here. "What do you want me to do?"

"Well, for one, you need to breathe." Anna wrinkled her nose. "I'm serious. You need to be as relaxed as humanly possible."

"I, er, don't know if I can *relax* here."

"Then sit with me." Anna hesitated, but dragged the chair a few inches, and sat. Jackson's eyes were still smiling at her through his visor. It put her off balance. She was so used to be scared and angry now that this friendly attitude was almost… she wasn't sure. She didn't know if she liked it. "Tell me about yourself."

Anna blinked. "Uh."

"Do you read much?"

Anna wasn't sure how much further he could catch her off guard. Why ask this? "I… yes. I like to read."

"What kinds of things?"

She bit her lip. "Anything, I guess. But, I do like nonfiction best."

"Wonderful. Who's one of your favorite writers?"

Anna thought for a moment, still confused. "Well… have you ever heard of John Livingston?"

"I have not."

"He's a chemist. That's not really my field… but, I love how he explains things, boils them down, tells you how the world works. It's beautiful." She paused. "Anyway, I know most people find that boring, but…"

"Nonsense. It sounds like an interesting thing to read about. I love to read too. Fiction." He reclined back, his posture suggesting that, if he were not in an environmental suit, they might be two acquaintances sharing coffee.

She hesitated, then asked, "Tolkien, maybe?"

"I adore Tolkien, though more Hobbit, less Lord of the Rings."

Anna didn't understand why, but Jackson moved from books to music to films, and the strange line of conversation about nothing at all carried on for another half hour. All the same, after the stress of her ordeal, these safe subjects put her at ease in a way small talk usually never did. He was speaking as if there were no threats or pressure, as if they had all the time in the world to shoot the breeze. His hands would move around a great deal, punctuating the air while he summarized a story or two, and in spite of her uncertainty, Anna began feeling a smile or two pull on her lips. She forgot her problems, if only for a moment or two.

The door swished open again. "Jackson? Anna?" It was Walker's voice. "Visit time is up."

Anna found herself disappointed. This had been the first real human interaction she'd had in days, not counting Walker's conversation, and... "Hey," she mumbled. "I guess I am a little more relaxed."

Jackson's eyes smiled again. "I can come back tomorrow, if you like."

She shrugged. But, she realized she *would* like it, even if it wasn't of any objective help in getting her free. It sounded like a welcome relief when she thought about the sterile white walls and the silence. "Okay. Yeah. Sure."

He stood, spinning the chair back into its original spot. "If you start feeling anxious," he said, "Just think about reading Livingston. Breathe."

Walker came close before escorting Jackson out. "I took a reading. The radiation levels are dropping," he whispered. "Not as much as needs to happen. But, they're dropping. Keep it up."

"Keep... keep what up?"

Walker shrugged. "Whatever Jackson said." She saw then, for a moment, his eyes flicker to her window. There stood the ice-eyed man again, mouth downturned into a deep frown. She shivered as he stared at her. "And don't talk to Reeds, there," Walker whispered, eyes filled with warning. "Don't give him *anything.*"

The word of caution was so quick and quiet that it took Anna a moment to parse it, and by then, Walker was turning away. She hugged her arms closer to herself as the door cut her off again from both him and Jackson, giving her back her hated solitude. Then, she glanced up at Reeds, nervous, wondering if he would try to use the intercom, wondering if he was a threat. His eyes bore down on her like he was dissecting her with his mind.

Then, he *smiled* at her.

She shuddered, and he left.

CHAPTER SEVEN
Bitter Magic

Frank picked Jackson up from the Coalition facility, though he had refused to park too close, forcing Jackson to walk a good three blocks before he could get in the truck. "So." Frank sneered at no one as Jackson took his place in the passenger seat. "How'd it go?"

Jackson, in response, tossed a credit chit into his lap. "Well."

Frank raised an eyebrow, pocketing his pay. "How is she?"

"Anna... she's scared." Jackson let his chin rest on his hand, thinking back to her guarded stance. "I mean, you know, she's doing things she can't control and the government is staring her down." He left out Anna's claimed displacement from time. Walker had filled him in, and he suspected the agent, for some reason, was actually on the fence about believing her. As for himself? Ha. The strange and impossible, sure, he'd seen it, but time travel? It almost seemed a step too far.

"Is the Coalition gonna be a problem?" Frank, since the run outside of the dome, had begun indicating he thought Jackson's proximity to this matter might make him explode in a firework display of *hoodoo*, bringing the entire government down on their heads.

"It's fine. I'm fine. Don't worry about it."

"You know your dad told you to stay away from that magic shit when you could. Nothing but trouble."

"He did *not* say that." Well, Peter Dovetail might have *meant* it, in so many words and warning looks. But Jackson wasn't going to concede that to Frank.

"I still think this is a dumb idea."

"She needs help, Frank. She really does. I can't give them a reason to make her some kind of experiment." He shuddered. "It sounds like some of them got wind of the existence of magic users. And Walker doesn't sound like he trusts any of the ones that have. I don't like the idea of her being in there much longer. I don't know if she has a chance if they decide to keep her."

Frank gritted his teeth and said nothing.

Jackson sighed. "She doesn't deserve this. She seems... nice." *Even if the whole time travel thing might call her sanity into question.* He wondered, if they had met under different circumstances, if they might have been friends. Perhaps... he might have even asked her out for a drink. He'd had several first dates that had gone far worse than his first conversation with her.

Frank gave a grumble, and looked unhappier than he did before, though he drove the truck without further comment. Jackson had a business meeting to get to, a legitimate one this time.

Jackson's next two visits were much the same, since it seemed Walker had no new information on the mysterious writer of crayoned notes, nor what had happened out in the wastes. He taught Anna breathing exercises and talked about everything and nothing with her, and so far, radiation levels had continued to fall.

Walker implied he thought Jackson was doing some secretive ritual during his visits that had helped, but there was no such thing. Dealing with a flare was no high-level mage secret. Chitchat was something he'd learned as an invaluable skill when any of his clients were nervous and there were no real reassurances to give. If he was charismatic enough and got them talking about themselves, almost invariably, they would relax. It helped, he imagined, that he himself was not one of the people holding her hostage.

She'd begun opening up about her job as a scientist. And, she'd been given some houseplants to brighten up the room, though she was a terrible gardener, and killed them in two days. Or, the radiation had. But, Anna preferred to think she was just bad with plants. Jackson found her optimism refreshing.

Frank never smiled at any of his stories, but Jackson had started looking forward to the visits at the end of his day at the office. Perhaps it was the fact that she was magic too, but Jackson felt a strange hum around her, one not unlike the one he felt during his visions—though it was almost peaceful, not frantic. It was something that left him feeling more in control of his own problems after he left. He couldn't help but like her, even if they could never speak of truly personal things.

Jackson's dreams persisted, though, and Huxley was disturbingly silent. And, that night, Jackson found his sense of control was only a fragile illusion.

It began when he realized he was standing in a dark warehouse with no idea how he'd gotten there. He smelled brine and sweat, and in an instant, he was terrified, though he didn't know why. Around him stood a hushed audience, the tension poised, the air itself waiting to *snap*.

What the hell—

Then, lights flickered on, illuminating an arena stage, and the crowd cheered, the rumbling of their roar vibrating the warehouse's steel pylons. "THE *TIGER*! THE *TIGER*!"

A painted beast-like man on the stage roared in return, the gladiator from Jackson's nightmares. A young man was pinned under his foot.

The announcer, all in red, impossibly drifted through the air like a marionette, though there were no strings. He laughed into the microphone, a high, joyous sound slicing Jackson's ears. "Show them!"

The beast man turned, his lifelike tail thrashing. He unholstered a crude spear from his back, slamming it down as if he was pinning a fish to the earth. This was no fight. It was a demonstration. His victim eventually stopped struggling, and the crowd went wild. Jackson turned, bile in his throat, desperate to flee the press of bloodthirsty savages, but there were no doors, no windows, no escape.

The crowd had turned on him, knew he was trying to run. Fingers grasped and tugged and tore, fingers holding papers marked with scribbles of crayon, trying to drag him down, pin their notes to his chest.

Jackson woke up screaming. He thrashed out of bed, realizing his legs and arms were pinioned, and hit the carpet with a grunt, cutting his lip on a tooth.

He breathed, and ran through the checklist. It was a dream. He was dreaming again, just a recurring nightmare. Floating announcers and tiger men, they didn't exist. Nothing was going to hurt him. He was safe.

Slowly he felt his muscles unwind. Yet, he still felt unable to move, pinned like the man in his dream. Jackson's heart thudded as he licked the coppery taste from his bottom lip. Cold tendrils squeezed his legs and arms, and his limbs throbbed painfully, like the circulation was getting cut off. *Oh no. Not this. Please, not this.* He knew what the tendrils were, could never forget what they were, even if it was impossible to see them in the dark. Gods, the shadows. They were *back*. He had gotten so bad, *the shadows were back.* They'd covered him, bound him up, and he couldn't run now; he could barely breathe.

The tea wasn't working—he'd had a dose last night. No one was there to help him this time. He was alone, and he was trapped.

Jackson struggled to suck in air, to slow his heart. Panicking would make it worse. Already, the shadows squeezed tighter.

His datapad made a pinging noise, like a message had arrived. Jackson turned to look, and the shadows surged, the device flinging from the nightstand, sailing ten feet, hitting the doorframe with a crack.

He squeezed his eyes shut and tried slowing his breathing again. *Oh gods. Oh gods. Oh gods. No. No. Calm down. You are in control of this.* He wasn't really sure if he was, but it didn't hurt to think he might be. *It was just a dream, and you are going to calm down, and you are going to make this go away. Then, you are going to go check your gods-damned email.*

Jackson fell deep into his head, into a breathing exercise from his teenage years. He was glad he'd rehearsed it with Anna the previous day—though it occurred to him he should have done it in earnest, not just for recollection's sake. It took half an hour of steady breathing and meditation, his limbs nearly going numb. But, finally, his body uncurled, his bonds evaporating. The tendrils sank back into the normal shadows in the room, unmoving, lifeless. The coldness left. Jackson finally stood. He shook for a minute before making a wobbly step to where he'd thrown his jacket down the night previous, reached in the pocket, and retrieved his flask. Then, he downed all the whiskey that remained.

There was an argument to be made for liquor being better than dream tea. The burn boiled his anxiety away.

Jackson's eyes flickered around the room anyway as he held his breath. No shadows moved. He resumed breathing.

His datapad had a huge crack running down the screen. Getting a replacement meant being put on the city's month-long waiting list, unless he wanted to pay out the nose at the black market. Thankfully, it still looked like it worked. It was just uglier now. And, one thing was there that eased his unhappy mood, something that he never thought would have that effect: a message from Huxley. *Jackson*, it said. *I am concerned. Please come see me today. Take two cups immediately. You may experience some side effects, but fight through them.*

Finally, *finally*, he might get some relief. Jackson rubbed his burning insomniac's eyes, internally bidding goodbye to the nightmares and shadows for good. He slammed down the recommended two cups of tea without any hesitation. *Time to get all better.*

After the sun rose, when Jackson arrived at Huxley's mansion at the dome's western edge in Harlem, he wondered if he was gatecrashing. He transferred a few extra credits to the driver as he peered out the window, asking the man to wait for a while. The cabbie nodded and shrugged, saying something in a language Jackson didn't fully understand, but took to mean "Okay."

Two ostentatious stone gargoyles stood guard at the high gate, and were watching over a group of people strolling down the pathway. There were perhaps fifteen of them, and they seemed dressed for a breakfast party or some event, though it was only 6AM. Jackson had never seen anyone visit the old man other than himself. He began to walk to meet them, intrigued.

Then, only for a moment, he saw the sleeve draw back on a young woman's arm, saw the *mark*. Slender black stalks wove about a stylized eye on her wrist, a pattern Jackson had seen in Egyptian history books and upon Huxley's own forearm.

This, this was the Order!

As if sensing his eyes, the woman dragged her sleeve back over the tattoo, glancing his way with a piercing stare. Her bright red lips dragged down into a frown.

Jackson kept walking as if the silent exchange hadn't occurred, head held high, thoughts buzzing. He'd pleaded with Huxley once, as if his very life depended on meeting these people, learning from them. And now, here he was, spiraling out of control, and here they were—having a magical potluck or gods knew what. It was only a moment before all of them were staring back at him now, and some tugged at their sleeves, subconsciously ensuring their marks remained hidden.

He could hear their whispers cease as the crowd parted to let him through, feel the hair on the back of his neck rise.

One of them glared outright, as if daring Jackson to speak. He was a lithe man in fine clothes, and into his black, tapered beard, he had shaved simple runes. It was a conspicuous bit of flair for someone so concerned with remaining secret. *The hell did I do to you?* Jackson wondered at the evil eye. *Exist?*

It wasn't his fault he wasn't good enough for them.

And so, Jackson decided to smile at the glaring man (*Good day, asshole!*) and kept walking. No one tried to stop him as he passed the gargoyles, not even the rune-bearded man, though Jackson felt the stare in his back long past the gate.

That one knew who I was. Why was he angry I was here? Jackson sighed. Like anything else relating to The Order, he knew he stood little chance of getting answers to his questions. Besides, it was no time to pick a fight. *Priorities.*

The manor stood beyond a smattering of oak trees. It was a freestanding expanse of sturdy wood and stone that had risen up only after much of Harlem had burned, back in the days when it stood beyond the dome's protective reach. It had weathered the riots, the anarchy, and no less than two coups on the local government. It then weathered the peace that had followed, affecting an air that it would be there for another few centuries to come. Of course, it didn't hurt that the Huxleys had once been bountiful in numbers, able to carve out their sanctuary in the chaos—and defend it—thanks to their *unique talents*.

The house now stood quiet, all of the windows dark, rooms empty of life.

An elderly gentleman with an overgrown mustache was slouching in a chair on the front porch, arms drawn over a substantial curve of belly. He popped upright as he saw Jackson approach, face splitting into a beatific smile, a hand running through what was left of his curly white hair. "Jackson, my boy! Welcome!"

"Huxley," Jackson greeted, voice stiff with tension. His abdomen gave a strange pang. "I'm here regarding your message. The situation has worsened, I'm afraid."

The old man's prominent eyebrows huddled in concern, his fingers fiddling with his many rings. Opal and obsidian shimmered in the sun. "Of course, of course, come inside."

Jackson followed him over the threshold, the scent of incense and furniture polish carrying him back to when he'd first entered while hiding behind his father. He was desperate then for answers, just as he was now. No one went to Huxley to merely shoot the breeze.

The elderly mage ferried Jackson along to the study, a pocket watch wagging at his side. This study was a spacious room, well-lit by a tall east-facing window, letting the morning sun dance across a small fortune's worth of dusty manuscripts, scrolls, and oddments. Huxley wouldn't hear of just using a datapad to store his library—never had figured out how to enchant a data file, he said. Jackson supposed he couldn't judge; he kept a few paper-printed books as well. Still, these were books in piles, stacks, and sprawling shelves, no order to them other than one the mage understood.

The man himself settled in cozily at his desk, pluck in the center of his book hoard. On the desk, a golden-eyed tabby cat shifted her bulk, allowing him access to her belly. Jackson nodded at the cat, Tabitha, he recalled. She blinked slowly in greeting, feline smile showing one fang.

"So, what brings you here, Jackson?" Huxley was smiling in his polite, grandfatherly way as he rubbed the cat, his brown eyes shining with curiosity. "Sorry I didn't answer your messages earlier. Much business to attend to. I was hosting an event."

Jackson shifted uncomfortably as his stomach creaked and groaned. Something was going on down there, and he didn't like it. "Was it an Order event?"

"Oh, nothing like that."

"I saw the tattoos." The bitter part of Jackson was unable to resist prodding a little further. "Don't know exactly what I did to that one with the rune beard. Stared at me like I might set him on fire. Do you know if he knows me?"

Huxley did not make eye contact. "I do not." Jackson expected no other answer, whether or not it was true. "I think it might do you well to have another cup of tea." Huxley added. "You seem upset."

"I—" Jackson thought for a moment, then bit his tongue. He was picking at an old argument, years past the point of meaning. *Priorities!* he reminded himself again. "Sorry. It's been a stressful few days."

"Not to worry," Huxley was nodding at the corner of the study, and Jackson saw an aged butler in black creeping away, likely to get the tea. Jackson recalled Ducat. The butler had a way about him that made him seem like one of the dusty, ill-maintained armchairs. Jackson's insides burbled in displeasure, though he hid his discomfort, and Huxley smiled again. "Do tell me about your emergency."

Down to business. The sooner he could leave, Jackson felt, the better. "Several emergencies. First, I'm seeing the ravens again. A lot of them."

Jackson saw Huxley's hands clench ever so slightly. "How many?"

"There's been one or two on the gate or at the window for about a month now. A few days ago, on a delivery, I saw an entire flock. I got that buzzing feeling in my head... it was unbearably *loud*." Jackson winced thinking back, stomach lurching in time.

Huxley was silent a long moment. "And you've been taking your tea every day?"

Jackson fidgeted. "Yes."

Huxley's perceptive, piercing stare had not fogged in old age. "...Have you now?"

"I missed one dosage the night before I saw the flock. But that's *it*." Jackson continued to stare back at Huxley until the old man looked away, accepting the lie. To be fair, it had been years since he'd bothered taking the tea daily. It had just never been a problem before, had never made him fall apart so quickly. "I took a double dose today before I came, like you said. I had a dose last night. But, this morning, I woke up from a nightmare, balled up in *shadows*."

"The shadows are *back?*"

"I can't... I don't want that to happen again. I need a stronger tea, a better solution, *something*." Jackson heard the desperate edge seep into his voice. He hated to show this much weakness, but he had no other path anymore. Huxley was the only man in the world that could have answers.

The old man thought, and as he thought, he smacked his lips, something Jackson knew he did when he was displeased. "The content of your nightmare?"

Jackson sighed, not sure why it mattered. "Last night, I saw an arena in a warehouse. There were two men fighting to the death, and this man in red—he was grinning like a demon, and wearing this mask—he was narrating or something." Huxley's eyes turned hard, and Jackson trailed to a stop, wondering if he'd said something wrong or important. "Does that mean anything to you?"

Huxley smacked his lips again, eyes casting upwards. "Yes."

"What?"

"That you need to be better about taking your tea."

Jackson huffed. "I suppose."

At this point, Ducat returned, ferrying a silver tray. It gleamed under Jackson's nose, and he lifted one of the delicate teacups, allowing the grim butler to pour some liquid into it. Huxley fished in his desk for a moment, withdrawing a packet of herbs, then made a beckoning gesture at Jackson, who handed over his cup. The mage doused the entire packet under the liquid, and instantly, Jackson caught the spicy aroma of the drink he knew very well.

"Extra dose," Huxley urged.

"I had two before coming, like you said."

"I highly recommend another, with what you're telling me. Drink up."

Jackson nodded, but bile rose up in his throat as he took the cup back, his stomach almost heaving then and there. *Side effects*, he remembered from Huxley's note.

He placed the cup on an aged yellow doily, choking back his unhappy stomach.

"What's wrong?"

"Just wanted to let it steep. It's very hot," Jackson lied. He couldn't show any more weakness. Huxley pitied him enough as it was. He just… needed a moment for his system to settle. "Anyway, my problems aren't limited to me. I met this woman."

Huxley's eyebrows went up. "Not a lot I can advise you on *there*, boy, if you haven't figured it out by now."

Jackson snorted. "It's not like that. The ravens I saw during the delivery led me to her. She was trapped in a box. I thought it was part of a human trafficking ring. And for just a moment, I saw that she had… er… *abilities*. She was floating."

Huxley's eyes were hard again, his voice sharp. "Where was this?"

"On the road up to Yonkers. Badlands territory." The old man was casting aside papers now, as if looking for something. Jackson continued, "We brought her back for medical attention. She seems very confused, like she doesn't know when or where she is. She was also kicking off radiation. I think it's a *flare?* Like what was happening to me? I needed to know… well… everything I can tell her, to make sure she doesn't get hurt. I've helped her curb her anxiety, but that's all I know how to do."

Huxley was now blowing dust off of an old reddish-brown clay bowl, crumbling tiny flakes of pungent herbs between his fingers, mumbling, eyelids fluttering. A tiny fire sparked in the bowl's depths. Jackson was somewhat taken aback. The elder mage rarely used magic in front of him. Jackson hadn't been sure if it was out of respect or some sort of Order code, but now, Huxley was in his own world, and had driven it in to him that casting could be dangerous without deep focus. So, Jackson remained quiet.

The rolling chant came to a stop a few moments later, and Huxley blinked as if clearing his head. "So strange," he whispered to himself. "There weren't any new flares... but now she's clear as day..."

"...Huxley?"

"Oh?" His eyes snapped into focus. "Just let us take care of it. We'll send someone out to evaluate her, see how strong The Gift is, and if she needs additional training. Thank you for bringing her to our attention."

"Huxley, she's locked up in the Coalition facility out on Staten Island."

"She's *what?*"

"They may have noticed the *radiation* part I mentioned."

"Oh. That's no good. That's no good at all." Lip smacking went into high gear. "Secrecy must be maintained. The Coalition should not pry into this."

"Your concern for her safety is touching." Jackson scowled. "Look, I've been encouraged to visit her. Just tell me what I need to know, and I can help her get things under control until she can talk to you."

"No, no, no. That won't do." Huxley's fingers were tapping now, a quick, nervous rhythm. "Given your *condition*," he continued, and Jackson dug his nails into his palms, "being around someone magically flaring for the first time could agitate things further. You're already having *lapses*."

"I don't really have a choice. When I said the government encouraged me to visit, I meant I was told to do it. Besides, you know that while she's left in the dark, something dangerous could happen." He didn't know why he had to explain this. Huxley had given him countless lectures on the dangers of untamed magic, namely, his own.

The old man wiped sweat from his forehead. Jackson realized he was suddenly a little flushed too, feverish, even though it wasn't hot at all in the drafty study. His stomach continued to cramp. "You must get out of seeing her somehow," Huxley said. "For your health."

"But in case I can't—"

"You *must*."

"But what about—"

"*The Archmage won't have it.*" Huxley's light demeanor fell to a dark look, his voice gaining a thrumming resonance and power. "Take your tea. *Triple* the dosage. Do your meditation exercises twice a day. Forget this girl, and let us handle it." For a moment, a flicker of sympathy crossed his commanding expression. "Live your life, Jackson. You have a good one. There is no point pining over what you can't have."

Jackson was taken aback, nausea rising. "Of course," he replied, his voice tight with bewilderment... and a little resentment. Just drink more tea? That was *it?* Oh, and stay away from a woman he'd already decided to help, or else the Archmage, who he'd never even spoken with, might get his panties in a twist? "Do you have any *other* advice?"

"Come back in two weeks if you still have nightmares or you see *them*. We will try a magic binding. It's an unpleasant alternative, but far better to be safe than for something... dangerous to happen." Huxley prodded the still-steeping tea towards Jackson.

Jackson nodded and fought down his gag reflex, using the time it took to chug down his medicine to grasp for a response. He didn't like the threatening implications in the mage's words, and he hated the renewed sour feeling the tea left behind in his throat. Tabitha the cat gave her feline smirk, as if satisfied with Jackson being put in his place, and leapt from the desk with a *thump*.

Where she had been, Jackson stared. On Huxley's desk was a letter.

FOR JACK was declared with a flourish on the envelope, not in Huxley's handwriting, but in two-inch-high purple crayon.

He snapped his eyes back as if he saw nothing, softly setting down his teacup. His stomach was roiling now like it contained a stormy sea.

"Is something wrong?"

"No, I... I'm just not feeling well." Jackson considered Huxley's stern stare... always the stare the mage used when telling him to not question too far. *You lying sack of...!* Huxley was hiding something from him—*though should I be surprised?*—and part of it was this letter, left for him, unmentioned, undelivered. The murderer was trying to contact him again, through the Order this time. Had it been Huxley's age that had let him leave it out in the open? Absentmindedness? Was it luck? Fate?

Jackson began sweating in earnest, feverish sensation rising with his nausea again. He didn't trust himself to keep his composure and he rose. "I should go home. I think with some rest, I'll be fine." He swayed. "Would you mind showing me out? I haven't been here for some time, and my head's a little blurry right now…"

"Of course!" Huxley stood, and the cold look in his eyes was gone, the grandfatherly twinkle back. "I hope you feel better soon. No good coming down with something, a busy man like you."

Jackson let Huxley take the lead. And, without hesitation, as soon as the mage's back was turned, he scooped the letter from the desk, curled it and slipped it up his sleeve, and fell behind Huxley without missing a step. Tabitha gave a growl from below, but Huxley didn't turn back.

How angry would the old mage be? Well, Jackson knew he should be long gone by the time his theft was found out.

They reached the door. Huxley twiddled his mustache between his thumb and forefinger. "Well then, goodbye. And don't be such a stranger. I promised your father I'd help you out, you know, keep you safe."

Jackson nodded, on autopilot. "He'd appreciate it."

Just as he stepped across the threshold, Huxley spoke. "Wait a moment."

Jackson stopped and kept his face carefully neutral, his arms crossed so the letter didn't fall back out of his sleeve. "What is it?"

The old man smiled and handed him a fresh bag of dream tea herbs. From where he'd gotten it, Jackson didn't know, but he nodded, politely smiling, and accepted it. "On the house, for that last shipment coming early. Keep well, Jackson."

The door shut at last.

Jackson walked behind one of Huxley's hedges as if attending a sober business meeting. He checked the time on his datapad, rolled up his sleeves, and flexed his fingers. Then, he threw up everything he'd had in the last twelve hours. Black liquid pooled, his head turning dizzy and weak.

Tea… side effects. Three cups. Too much.

Just… just going to go home and rest. Lying bastard mages.

Yet, Jackson knew that if he slept, the shadows could come back again, especially if he'd just rejected all the tea in his system. He couldn't sleep until he'd had more. But when would he be able to stomach another cup?

Oh gods, not another cup—just thinking it made his stomach heave out a second time. Jackson wiped his mouth, praying the rest of the Order outside was long gone, and considered his other problem.

Did I really just steal from a mage? He had, in the past, seen Huxley light fire in his hands. *I'm losing my mind.*

And yet, he felt no remorse or fear, only sickness and anger, and the vindication in taking something back that was his. A binding spell? The way Huxley had said it, his hackles rose and his heart beat faster, his bile rising again, barely staying inside this time. He tried to remember anything he'd heard over a decade ago about bindings. It had been something about out-of-control spirits, trapping them, draining them until they just… disappeared. Was that it? Would they bind the wayward energy in him until it was gone?

Magic was part of the soul, Huxley had always said. Was that what a binding would mean? Strangulating a part of his soul until it was extinguished? Was that what it would take to make him normal?

He shuddered, clutching the letter up his sleeve so hard it crumpled, and began to eke a dizzy stagger to the waiting cab. When he finally arrived home and stared up at his raven-free gate, he realized he'd blacked out for half the journey, not even remembering leaving the vehicle or paying for the trip.

With his last bit of strength, he opened the door. And then, he collapsed.

CHAPTER EIGHT
The End of the World's Not So Bad

Anna dreamed.

She was running again, tearing down the hallway of the research lab, breathing in gasps, screams in her ears. Her heart pounded until it felt like her entire chest would seize. She tried to shout for help, but as it always was in this dream, her voice died, drowned out by others' screams of pain and fear, and the thunderous bangs from the monster that chased her.

Then, she saw it, a thing that a part of herself knew shouldn't have been there, the part of herself that ran these corridors every time she slept and knew this for a recurring nightmare. What she saw was a door.

Desperate, she yanked it open. Utter darkness lay beyond. Anna didn't care; she flung herself inside to hide, slamming the door shut behind her.

Then, everything *stopped*. Her breathing evened. The air felt lighter, warmer, inviting. The thing pursuing her wasn't following her anymore, and she didn't question how she knew this. It was just... gone.

Anna gazed into the pit of darkness, confused, and a flicker of fire appeared, far away. She no longer felt afraid. Stumbling through the dark, she groped for the lab's familiar drywall, but her hands found nothing. So, she staggered forward towards the fire, towards the light that drove back the horror.

There at the fireside sat a man. She later couldn't remember very much about him, other than that he was tall, his clothes were black, and he had a pearly, mischievous smile. There was something about his eyes that was strange, Anna would recall, but she couldn't put her finger on what. She couldn't look at him for long. When she did, her head would fill with twinkling lights, stars in the darkness.

He said something to her, but his voice was like the vibrations of music underwater, indistinct, just out of comprehension. He let her sit by the fire, however, and for a time, she was warm, safe, and happy.

The lights flickered on in the facility, and Anna opened her eyes, once again seeing the austere quarantine room, white filling her vision.

She rolled over, heaving a sigh, the dreams slipping away. Rubbing her eyes, she tried to remember what had happened. It had been something different, something important.

No. It was gone.

She sat up, and immediately felt a tremendous change in her body. Nothing shook. Her stomach didn't turn. Her vision didn't blur. Anna touched her hands together, finding them a little warm, but no longer clammy and feverish. She stood, and for the first time in days, felt almost normal.

Anna swung her legs out of bed, touching her bare feet to the cold tile, feeling like she might dance. The clock she requested told her it was a bright and early 6 AM, and Anna fell into her morning stretches with gusto, marveling at how *good* she felt. It was like the sickness had just evaporated.

One, two, three! she called out in her mind as she stretched.

Compared to yesterday, she felt *alive*, no longer pinioned under malaise and bad luck. Yesterday... well, first, there had been a shift in the food. The rations they gave her were never exactly delicious, but breakfast, lunch, and dinner were only a heated gruel. It had an indefinable gluey feel to it that made her just want to leave it in the bowl. Then, there was Walker. She'd been very invested in the visit he was supposed to make that day, for some kind of update. Anna couldn't argue that the numbers on Walker's counter were sinking every time she saw him and Jackson, even if she didn't understand why they were there at all (and they refused to give her the tools to run her own tests). But, Walker hadn't shown up, and no explanation had been given. Thirdly, the agent named Reeds had sat at the glass, watching her for almost a full hour. It had been skin-crawling. He'd turned up more and more throughout the week, staring, smiling when she glared at him.

The final blow to her mood had been that Jackson had been supposed to visit too, his fourth time since their small-talk chatter when they spoke of Tolkien and Livingston. She'd come to look forward to their conversations, the only friendly ones she got down here. He could waffle on for as long as she'd let him on nearly any subject, pulling stories and anecdotes out of the air with ease, waving his hands around all the while. They would sometimes be allowed a small deck of cards, too, and they'd play a few hands of poker, something she wasn't very good at, but still found a lot more fun than staring at the walls.

But, he hadn't shown either.

Yet, it all seemed far away. Anna felt good, better than good, really. She felt energetic. She felt like she could show them all how healthy she was, and that there was no reason to keep her here any longer, no matter what strange psychological game all of this 'What year is it?' nonsense was about.

Anna finished stretching and settled down in a chair, closing her eyes, breathing. She'd never been into meditation before, but Jackson had talked her through a few exercises, and she'd found it really did help cope with her anxiety, the repetitiveness of her days, and the anger at her questions forever going unanswered by anyone in charge. It had helped her regain hope, however little, that she might see her way out of this mess. Perhaps it had been that visit, his third one, that had made her decide he might be a friend.

He'd swung into the room, chirping his bright hello, spinning his chair to face her before sitting in his fanciful way. She'd awkwardly said hello back and he'd launched into chatter, asking her about her day and sharing his own, a day filled with, apparently, smooth-talking a disgruntled client. She almost wasn't surprised he was a businessman. That might have been where his ease of conversation came from. Anna found herself opening up a little, talking a bit about her job, or, at least, the parts she was allowed to talk about (the funny thing about maintaining warheads was that her employer preferred no one know the details.)

She wasn't sure what she'd said that had triggered the reaction. But, when she spoke of talking to U.S. soldiers on occasion, Jackson had grown quiet, and had remained so for a long time. She'd seen a sort of sadness in his eyes behind the visor, and she'd talked over it, though she heard her voice grow a little more edged and frantic.

Walker's words kept following her, and Jackson dancing around them every visit… she hated it, but it was starting to shake her.

"2022." His eventual whispered statement was simple, accepting—no sarcasm she could hear, no assertion that she was delusional or damaged.

"And… and you'd tell me it's not 2022. I know. I get it. I don't want to talk about it, because that's crazy."

"I've seen a lot of strange things in my life." He shrugged. "You believe you're from over a hundred years ago?" He flourished a hand again, as if brushing away everything else. "Unless your memories change on the matter, then that's that."

Anna stared.

"And anyway," he continued, "It sounds nice, being able to commute out of the city without being armed. The raiders crawled out of the woodwork while the cities were still rebuilding, scavenging everything they could. Not all of them stopped robbing and murdering everything when the cities turned stable. They're a good reason not to leave the Barrier without protection, of course."

Anna clenched her jaw and wrung her hands. She'd been comfortable with their conversation, and now, she was sitting on needles. Walker had tried telling her about a "bombing", a different world. He'd said he was just trying to prepare her for what waited outside. Anna just wanted to wake up, to be let go and to go call her mother.

"So," Jackson said suddenly. "We should talk about your radiation problem some more."

Anna was a little startled by the sudden shift, but looked up again, glad to be talking about something only slightly less insane. "You, uh, told me to keep relaxing and breathing. Walker comes in with his Geiger counter every so often and tells me the readouts. They... they are dropping..." She bit her lip. "I still don't understand what's happening. But, they're dropping."

She'd always put a lot of faith in accurate instruments, solid readings, and logic. And, she'd tried many things over the last few days, in fact, trying to influence those numbers, the one outcome she thought she could try to control. Walker had brought her a little 'datapad', a crappy tablet that seemed to be locked down, only letting her have access to a note-taking app. She recorded every aspect of her stay, trying not to go mad.

Jackson's eyes widened as he looked over her extensive notes on everything she'd done trying to influence the Geiger counter's CPM. Then, he chuckled. "You... stood on your head?"

"I have a lot of time in here, you know." She paused, feeling a twinge of emptiness. "*A lot* of time."

"Did you try any meditation exercises?"

Anna sighed. "Yes, I did, here, on page twenty-two..." She swiped across the datapad, the page loads stuttering on struggling hardware. "Breathing exercises, five minutes, cleared mind, etc. Continued for ten minutes. No change."

"Ten minutes? 'Cleared mind'? Well, that's your problem right there."

She cocked an eyebrow in challenge. He seemed rather self-assured on this point. "Oh?"

"Here, let me help. I know a thing or two about things like this."

"You know a thing or two about radioactive girls unable to stop shooting gamma rays out of their skin?"

"Well, no." His hands waggled excitably again. "Not *exactly* like this, but *kind of* like this! Trust me."

Anna gave a reluctant huff. But... well... what did she have to lose?

He didn't wait for her to verbally agree, instead bringing his feet up, shifting to perch on the edge of his chair like some sort of bird. He steepled his fingers to where his chin would be under the helmet. "Okay. Get comfortable."

Anna scrunched herself up into the yoga posture she had learned, legs twisted into a minor pretzel.

"Is that really comfortable?"

"...No...? But this is how it's done, isn't it?"

"Sure, for those people. But if you're not comfortable, it won't work, so sit... normal-like." Anna, confused, untwisted herself, resting her feet on the floor. *Jackson's perch doesn't look normal or comfortable either.* But, he seemed quite at ease. "Alright, close your eyes, and breathe deep." Still feeling awkward, Anna did so. "Now here's the key. Keep breathing deep, but you're going to reach back for some memory, alright? Something that made you feel at peace. Some place. Someone. Doesn't matter what it is, and you don't have to tell me about it."

Anna thought. When she graduated? No. No, she was nervous as heck then. Just remembering giving that speech made butterflies return to her stomach. She heard the counter on Jackson's belt click faster.

"Try something else," Jackson suggested dryly.

Anna sifted through her thoughts, unsure of what to do, a thin veneer of nerves layered over almost all of them. College had been wonderful, but stressful. Her peaceful memories with boyfriends or her parents were tainted by other memories, sad ones, angry ones, hurtful ones, thoughts of what came later. Thinking of her sanctuary, her apartment, her cat, just made her heart ache, missing it.

The counter ticked a bit more rapidly.

Anna bit her lip. "I'm not very good at this," she said.

"Keep trying. You must have something. Just clear everything out of your head and remember being happy. The rest will come with it."

So, Anna did. She tried remembering what it was like to smile without stress. Something in the back of her mind responded, something warm and safe.

And then, something else came. Sand. There was sand between her toes, gritty and cool. A cold wash of saltwater rushed over her ankles. Sun was kissing her skin like she was made to stand under it. She breathed out slowly, trying to remember. Pink. She'd been wearing a pink swimsuit, little polka dots. Yes… the beach. The memory was dusty, faded around the edges—she had to have been what, five? But she remembered other children, and she remembered her parents letting her run up and down the beach all day, not once calling her back, not even paying attention to her, really. She'd met the sort of friends children meet and ten minutes later swear eternal friendship with, though they'd never see each other again. There was laughter, and she'd found a starfish, thrown it back into the waves after talking her new friend's ear off about it.

She wasn't sure how long she sat there, remembering. Jackson only once broke in, telling her to just work over every detail, lose herself in the memory. And, she did.

Finally, she breathed out, unable to retain it anymore. She opened her eyes. A much slower, steady click greeted her, and she glanced to the side. "How did…? How?" The Geiger counter remained low, the lowest it had been in a week. The levels in the room weren't completely safe, no, but they were getting there. Anna let out a happy whoop of joy.

Jackson crossed his arms and was quiet, and Anna still couldn't see his face, but she could almost feel the self-satisfaction oozing off of him in waves. She would have rolled her eyes had she not been so grateful for it.

"Thank you! How did you know that would work?"

"Oh… I learned that exercise to deal with my own problematic stress as a teenager. I had a hunch it would do the same for you."

A… hunch? Seriously? Anna cocked an eyebrow, certain there was more to the story, but let it go for now. It worked. That was the important thing.

From that point onwards, Anna looked forward to Jackson's visits. She'd even started peppering him with questions about this supposed 'future' she wound up in, just curious about what he would say. His tales were less grim than talks of bombings. People went about their lives as they always had, trains running mostly on time, the mail getting delivered. Gradually, she found herself participating in the conversation like she almost expected to live in the impossible future he spoke of, like she might build a life in it, though at the end she always reminded herself that it was a distraction, that she didn't really believe it. It seemed radiation techs were in high demand, even if her degree might not mean much. It was absurd, Anna thought, to really consider that she truly traveled through time, but what else was there to talk about?

If this future was real, it meant whatever had happened to her had destroyed her life as she knew it, and the horrible, gaping hole of memory in her mind became even more something she didn't want to consider. It would mean everyone she knew was dead.

It was a very good thing, Anna knew, that it wasn't real.

And, now, as she finally felt her health improve, she felt this much closer to stepping out of this quarantined hole, and that thought made her smile, even though no one was around. The fact that Jackson and Walker hadn't shown up when they were supposed to probably didn't mean anything. She shouldn't listen to the little stone of worry that was settling in her stomach.

Then, the door swooshed open, and Anna looked up, for just a moment, hopeful.

There stood a medical team of five, something she could only glean from the medical kit in the lead one's hand. They were all in the standard teal blue environmental outfit. Anna remembered to be polite and cooperative, and gave the lead one a bright smile, waving.

They did not acknowledge the greeting. The lead came up to her, and, for the first time in a week, she heard a voice that didn't belong to Walker or Jackson. "Hold out your arm." Anna did. The doctor withdrew a needle, and Anna bit her lip, flinching as she sunk it into a vein and began extracting blood. Time passed in silence, and they drew three vials worth, packing them up without further instruction.

"Hey..." Anna finally said. "I've noticed the radiation levels in this room have dropped a lot, to almost safe levels, actually, in the past couple of days. Today, I feel really good, like I was never sick at all. I think I'll be ready to be released soon. Or have visitors, right? What do you think?"

One of the technicians paused, placing the last vial in a case. "Our charts show you here for the next year," he said.

She blinked. "What?"

"Cranston!" The head doctor barked, and the technician who spoke froze. "Get those vials to the lab. Now."

"Wait," Anna turned to the doctor. "The next year?"

The doctor sighed, shifting in her boots. Anna saw a conflict in her eyes, as if she was grappling with the idea of having a conversation Anna suspected she was ordered not to have. "Yes, Miss Matthews."

"Can... can I talk to Walker?" Anna's eyes narrowed, her stomach starting to turn.

"He's no longer on your team."

"*What?* Who do I talk to, then?"

"Director's prerogative. Sorry, Miss, I can't say much more."

"Don't I get a say in this? I'm safe, aren't I? You can see my readings—"

"Miss..." The head doctor gained a note of sympathy in her voice. "You've been designated to be moved from radiation quarantine to Project Esper. No outside visitors until the Director says otherwise."

Anna stood then, calm long gone. "What? You're just going to keep me down here indefinitely? What's wrong with you people? I'm getting better!"

"Please calm down, Miss Matthews."

"No! You people just keep bouncing me around like a ping pong ball, never telling me where I'm going or what I'm doing here! You've locked me up without access to anything! Now, what, I'm barred from seeing anybody? You're taking my blood and telling me all this crazy stuff about bombings and raiders and the future—"

"Miss Matthews, calm yourself."

"NO! Do you know how many human rights violations you people are probably committing? I want to talk to someone, *now!*"

In retrospect, she imagined it was jabbing her finger at the doctor's chest that did it, the action that changed everything, toppled it all over. It was a very pointed jab, even, for Anna, a forceful one, full every frustration and indignity she had suffered in that quarantine but let pass unremarked, full of *I'm sick of this, and I don't want to take it anymore!*

All four technicians were suddenly on her, twisting her arms, pinning them behind her back, dragging her down.

"NO! NO! NO!" she heard herself yelling. The counter began wildly clicking.

Somehow, she yanked herself free, panicking, flailing and kicking. Three of the technicians stumbled backwards and landed hard, even though they were much bigger than she was. She backed up, feeling nothing but a wall behind her, tears of desperation starting now. "Please, I just—!"

A tech dove into her, tackling her down, and though she fought, she felt a cold needle jab into her neck.

Her breathing slowed. Her vision grew fuzzy, and her tongue felt thick and heavy.

For a while, everything went black.

And when she awoke next, she was tied down to her bed with thick leather straps, unable to move at all.

CHAPTER NINE
Witchbane

Jackson faded in and out of the waking world. His stomach roiled and seized. More than once, he awoke to roll over and dry heave, but nothing more would come out. Jackson curled up in a ball on the carpet, wondering if he was about to die.

You're not dying. It's side effects from the tea. You're just going to ride this out until it goes away.

His stomach disagreed. It pulsed with pain in time to his heartbeat now, the pain spreading into his kidneys and radiating out through his fingers and toes. Where was his datapad? Should he call a doctor? No, what would he tell the doctor if they asked what he had taken, and why he'd done it? It wasn't as if they could help him. Not with *this*.

I'm so thirsty.

Jackson stumbled to his feet, not sure how much time had passed since his last blackout. The room had gone dark, the lights dead, no power anymore. *Darktime. Did I miss my visit with Anna?* A twinge of disappointment at himself resonated in his chest.

But, he had more to worry about. The hallway seemed skewed to one side. Jackson braced himself against the wall and took small, shaking steps toward the kitchen. He saw small pools of black on the carpet where his head had been lying.

Finally, after one shuddering step in front of the next, he leaned over the sink, panting. It felt as if his head was about to slide off his shoulders, down, down into the drain. He almost wished it would, if the nausea would go with it.

There was a buzzing in his pocket. With fumbling fingers, he mashed at his datapad's screen, not looking at it. "Hello?" he slurred.

"Jackson," a prim, exacting voice came over the link. His stomach took another painful turn. This voice belonged to the headmistress of his old orphanage.

"Rosita?" Jackson scrunched up his face, trying to regain his bearings. When business was good, he made sure a bit of money always went her way, but she had no reason to call now. So why...? Gods, he didn't have the energy or time to deal with this.

"Jackson, you have to tell me something now." It was a tone she used so often when he was a boy, when she *knew* he'd done something she disliked. It made him, irrationally, stare down at his feet and straighten his appearance. He wiped his mouth, and more black came away with his hand, making him shudder.

"What?"

"You need to tell me what happened in that classroom."

Jackson blinked. "What...?"

Rosita was silent in response.

There was a cold finger of dread in his spine he didn't understand. "Um." *What classroom?* "I don't understand."

"You need to tell me, Jackson."

"Rosita," he said, voice rasping, wondering if she was beginning to show signs of dementia. "I have no idea what you're asking about."

His stomach turned again as he listened to silence. Frowning, he examined the datapad closer. It seemed the call had gone dead. Grumbling, he resumed staring down at the sink drain.

Turning on the water, his joints grinding, he filled his palms and drank. The tiniest bit of relief hit his throat. Then, a hot lance of pain pierced his abdomen, and he cried out, staggering back. Barely with enough presence of mind to turn the water off, he staggered into a chair by the kitchen table and slumped over to rest his head in his arms.

His chest hurt. Everything hurt.

But, gods, his chest!

A buzzing had settled over it on the left side, radiating in time to his stomach pain. Jackson clutched his hand over his heart, alarmed, and felt his fingers meet the stiff crinkle of paper. *What?* Unsure, he reached in his pocket, pulling out the envelope he'd stolen. *FOR JACK.*

The pain lessened, and the tingling moved from his chest to his hand. The sensation was reminiscent of the buzzing he felt during his visions and episodes, but the frequency was foreign, queasy, and erratic. Jackson dropped the letter, and the buzzing dissipated.

Jack. He didn't like this letter. He didn't like that *name*; he never had. Perhaps it was Rosita's odd call that unsettled the memory, but no one had called him *Jack* since he'd been in her care. He'd been found with no memory or name of his own, and the invention *Jack* had been jotted into the ledgers instead, an unwanted second skin. Something about it just didn't sit on his shoulders like it should have.

It was Peter Dovetail, on a donation visit, that had first (mistakenly) addressed him as *Jackson*. Oddly, *Jackson* had felt *full*, had felt *right*. Perhaps this was why he'd followed in Peter Dovetail's footsteps like a shadow after that, and refused to go by anything else.

The fond memory of his father was driven back by his stomach pain. *FOR JACK.*

Jackson wanted nothing to do with this letter, even if he'd gone to the trouble of stealing it. Every time his hand drew nearer, it was as if ants began crawling up his arm, his head getting lighter.

I'm too sick for this. I... I need to sleep. Jackson shoved the letter away and let his head droop, the pain in his abdomen lessening a little as he curled in on himself. *Maybe the shadows will come. And the nightmares. Maybe they won't. But I'm so tired.* Jackson just wanted to stop feeling like he was about to die, wanted to stop throwing up black ooze.

His datapad buzzed again, and Jackson groaned, slamming it on the table, answering it through muscle memory. "What?"

"Jackson, you need to tell me what happened in that classroom."

"*I don't know!* Look, it's a really bad time."

No response. Scowling, Jackson glared down at the screen. It looked like the call had gone dead again. *What the hell, Rosita?*

Jackson gritted his teeth as his head pulsed in pain again and closed his eyes, unable to concern himself with the matter any longer. The room seemed to wobble on its side as he shoved the datapad back into his pocket. The wood of the table was cool on his cheek, and as he wrapped his arms around his head, alone and confused in the dark, it occurred to him... maybe... he really... ought to... call... that doctor...

Jackson faded out of the waking world. And, for a time, he didn't think of anything at all. He drifted through darkness, and in time, he began to hear laughter, soft, but insistent. His thoughts were rumbles of ghosts, nonsense and dreamstuff, nothing he paid attention to for long. An undercurrent of music and pain was in the distance of his mind. The laughter tittered louder.

He opened his eyes, exhausted, wanting the giggling to stop.

A whitewashed wall greeted him, familiar only his memory. It was a wall he'd stared at as a boy, and a part of Jackson realized he was dreaming, that he'd dreamed of this place many times. This was his punishment for mulling on the past. The lights were off, sunlight beaming through a window. The desks were pushed askew, the aisles cluttered with the detritus children brought as they were ushered through life. In a haze, he wondered if he could put his head down on the desk, go back to sleep. This was what he got for letting Rosita bother him, for letting that letter disquiet him: memories of a classroom, one in the orphanage. And, Jackson had no desire to examine the dream, the memory, further.

Then, Jackson realized he wasn't alone. Laughter sounded again, and Jackson looked to his left. There was another boy, his dark, messy bangs almost down to his wide eyes.

"Jack," the boy said, his words whistling, "I caught a really big bug. Wanna see?" His grin showed off a prominent gap in his teeth. Jackson knew this dream well, like he was reading from a script he'd seen before, though he'd forgotten it, always forgot it on waking. He'd come in the classroom for peace and quiet, to hide from the other children and read. But this twelve-year-old had gotten it in his head that they were friends, and would latch himself on like a barnacle to a skiff if he caught wind of Jack's passing by.

Jack's stomach cramped painfully, though he couldn't remember why it hurt so much anymore.

The boy held out his hand, and in it was a huge beetle. It lay with its legs spread out to the sides, perfectly still, and Jack wondered if it was dead. A flutter of its wings, and he knew it wasn't.

"Stay still!" the boy said to the insect, his face screwing up. Remarkably, it complied. Tony? Yes, the boy's name was Tony. "I'm glad you decided to stay here instead of run away. I think it's our destiny to be here." Tony's gaze was a little vacant. "Destiny's important. Gotta get your destiny, Jack."

The boy called Jack sighed, the pain fading. He really did not care about Tony or his beetle.

There was, however, a feeling of dread creeping up his spine again, cold and insistent. *Jackson,* Rosita's voice penetrated the fog over his mind, *tell me what happened in that classroom.*

"I don't know," he mumbled. "I didn't have anything to do with it." He began to sweat. *I don't want to be here.* He'd never liked this place. It wasn't safe, they said, not after they'd locked it down, boarded it up. His stomach began to writhe with pain again, and Jackson doubled over. *Make it stop. Please. I don't want to be here. Anywhere but here.*

"Are you okay, Jack?" It was the other boy's voice, but it was already growing distant. Jackson screwed his eyes up tight, and he willed himself to leave this dream world. He didn't want to linger on it anymore. He wanted the darkness back, the nothingness.

If I don't watch it, the dream stops, Jackson thought, hazy sleep-logic rolling through his mind. He heard the sound of footsteps approaching. *Don't think about the orphanage. That's what brought this on.*

"I found you," a man's voice whispered.

White-hot pain consumed him, and he felt himself falling forward. *Make it stop!*

Jackson doubled over, falling out of the kitchen chair, letting out a hoarse moan. His hands scrabbled on the tile of his home. His organs felt like they were being dragged through a compactor, getting smashed over and over again. He heaved, and a tiny glob of black bile hit the floor. Jackson panted and let the feverish heat wash over him, though his hands and feet were suddenly freezing. His head pounded in time with his heart, his breathing short and winded.

There was an uncomfortable peeling of paper from his forehead. It was the envelope, stuck to him with his fevered sweat, now wafting down to the floor. There, it stared up at him, uncaring of the bright pain now bursting across his skin. *FOR JACK.* Jackson stood, barely, and staggered forward. *Make it stop! I don't care anymore if this kills me. Just make it stop!*

He swayed out of the kitchen. The couch. He was going to lie down on the couch, close his eyes, and pray the pain, the dreams, the *horrible* buzzing in his skull would end. No more worrying about the orphanage, or Rosita, or the letter, none of it anymore.

Jackson's mind went dark. He didn't remember making it to the couch, but when he next opened his eyes, dizzy with fever, that was where he was. It was darktime still, and a heavy, aching fog was over his body. He looked up at the ceiling, ears ringing. His tongue felt so dry that he expected to find it shriveled, and something smelled *awful.*

"You're awake." Another voice pierced the darkness. Jackson jerked his head to look.

Sitting across from him in an old armchair was Agent Walker, one leg crossed over the other, sunglasses off.

Jackson meant to demand, "How'd you get in my house?", but his mouth had gone wrong, and all he managed was, "How... you... house?"

"Your door was open."

Jackson attempted lifting his head, but dizziness laid him back again, stunned. Perhaps the agent was a hallucination, or another dream. The line between those two things meant little to Jackson anymore.

The agent sighed and leaned forward. His voice had a tinny, faraway sound. "Who did this to you?" Jackson realized then that Walker was proffering a glass of water. He reached for it, but his hand shook too much to grab it.

Walker stood and closed the distance, lifting Jackson's head and tilting it for him, putting the water glass to his lips. Indignant, Jackson spluttered, but his body demanded the water, sucked it in. It felt as if his esophagus had painfully swollen, and his body wracked with coughs. Pain radiated out from his stomach, his headache flaring again, and he regretted drinking at all.

"Who. Did. This?" Walker's voice was getting foggier. A crystal-clear buzzing overrode him, and Jackson felt his datapad vibrating in his pocket. He fumbled with the device, and it fell to the floor, screen up. Walker's eyes narrowed.

Jackson knew in his gut the call was from was Rosita. "Have to tell her I don't know what happened." Why wouldn't she leave him alone, bother him about the classroom after all these years? All Jackson wanted was for the headmistress to be quiet and for the agent to leave. He wanted to sleep.

The datapad buzzed again. Jackson's fingers brushed the glass. "Have to tell her."

"Your datapad isn't ringing, Jackson."

"Yes it is." He felt it in his fingers.

"No, it's not." Walker grabbed the datapad and squinted at it. "You're delirious. You've been poisoned."

"Side effects," Jackson grumbled. "Tea. I'm going to be fine." He suddenly began to shudder as cold chills marched up his spine, and he coughed again, spasming.

And suddenly, Walker was gone.

Jackson didn't see him leave. It was simply as if time lapsed, and now, Jackson was staring at an empty space where the agent had once stood. His datapad was on the table. He felt the tide of exhaustion pulling him under again, his body spent. Darkness threatened to swallow him up.

A whisper seemed to drift from the datapad, though he hadn't answered the call. "Tell me about the classroom."

"I don't know," he mumbled.

"AWWW!" a screech shattered his waking dream. Jackson rolled his eyes to his right. A raven was perched on his datapad, beak open in a grating croak, wings unfurled.

"I'm delirious," he told it. "You're not real. I'm poisoned." And as he admitted it, he realized it was likely true. Perhaps he'd become inconvenient, his lapses in magical control a burden to the Order's cherished *secrecy*. Why not put the defective creature out of his misery?

"AWWW!" the raven cried out again. It spun, launching in a whirl of feathers and darkness, straight into the shadows on his wall. Then it was gone, as if it had never been.

"Witchbane?" A yell boomed through his head, and he gritted his teeth. The agent's shoes were earthquakes against his skull as Walker returned, and Jackson saw the packet of tea herbs in his hand, his wild stare. The agent's flashlight was a spear into his brain, and Jackson shrunk away. "Is this witchbane *tea?*"

"Mmmf?" *I don't know what you're talking about.*

"You did this to *yourself?*" Walker hissed through his teeth. "You stupid sonofabitch. Who the hell gave you this much witchbane, anyway?"

"Why... are you... here?" Jackson struggled to put the sentence together, but he succeeded. His muscles burning, he forced himself up, trying to stare down the agent. He still wasn't certain if Walker was even real.

Walker scowled. "Emergency developments dictated I see you immediately. And here I find you, door to your house hanging open, unconscious on the floor, talking to yourself and heaving up your guts. Now, why don't you tell me why the hell you're drinking this shit, and who gave it to you? And does it have anything to do with that letter that was in the kitchen?"

Jackson swallowed, the act causing him to spasm. Years of secret-keeping resisted the interrogation. He brushed back his hair, which was clinging to his forehead, then yanked his hand away. His skin felt like it was made of needles and fire.

"Your organs were shutting down, Dovetail, maybe still are, and there isn't a cure for this unless you fight it off. Frankly, I'm surprised you're bouncing back at all. If you'd like, I can put you on a suicide watch. You'd like that, right? A psychiatric evaluation?"

Jackson's lip curled. *Enough.* "Was told to increase dosage to three cups. Was supposed to help." He shook his head. "Haven't even read the letter yet. I… I stole it. From the Order." His body shook again, fear and nausea brewing together.

Walker's mouth hung open. "Three cups…? That's not… that's *insane…!* Why the hell would you drink it *at all?*"

Jackson was too weary to think of a lie, and it was almost a half minute before he could speak the truth past the nausea. "To sleep. I can't sleep."

"*To sleep?!*" The agent's eyes were flickering back and forth, as if he was piecing together a puzzle only he could see. "Did Huxley tell you to drink three cups?"

Jackson nodded in lieu of words.

"He's trying to *kill* you. He had the letter in his care?"

Jackson tried then to stand. The agent in his house, the sickness, the pain, it was all far, far too much, and he wasn't going to face it lying down. His knees buckled, and he pitched forward, barely catching himself before his face smashed into the coffee table. Walker was there in his personal space before he could stop him, one arm steadying him. Jackson resisted the urge to shove the Coalition agent away.

"Your fever is through the roof. There could be damage if you don't lower your body temperature."

"M'fine."

"Still need you alive, Dovetail, you unpleasant bastard." With a growl, Walker forced his shoulder into Jackson's side, a brace whether he wanted it or not. Now he had no choice but to move forward wherever the agent pushed. "I'll be damned if you die before I find out why the Order decided to assassinate you, and what they have to do with that letter-writing murderer."

The voice of Jackson's father resonated in his memory. *Huxley's an old friend. Do everything he says, Jackson. He'll help. I promise. We'll get you all better.* Jackson felt sweat and stench clinging to him acutely now like the pain, itching, chafing as he staggered forward. Walker pushed him up the stairs, almost lifting him with one arm. He saw the agent's shoe crunch a dark feather into the carpet. It looked as if Walker hadn't noticed it. "Where are we going?"

"Lowering your goddamn fever."

The snap reminded Jackson of Frank. Why hadn't he called Frank? This distracted him enough that he forgot himself in the haze, and when he came out of it, the two of them were standing in the master bathroom. Walker let him go, and Jackson managed to stay upright, holding on to the wall for dear life. "You need to get in cold water."

"I can do it myself," Jackson slurred, pressing his face to the wall, feeling its coolness, relishing in it.

"...Uh-huh."

Jackson glared, too tired for his mask. "Go away. I can do it."

Walker's arms crossed. "Fine. But you respond when I talk to you. You don't, or if I hear you fall, I'm coming in." Then, Walker left him there, shined shoes clacking in his wake.

Jackson tried not to think of the agent digging through his things. He had two stolen spellbooks in his desk drawer, and several *personal* notes he'd rather no one read but himself. *Get this over with, then.* His grip kept slipping, and it took two hands for him to spin the knob in the tub. The pipes creaked and gurgled, and then, they ran, water drizzling down from the shower like a cool rain against Jackson's forearm. The relief was instant on his skin. Perhaps the agent was... right.

What about calling Frank? He'd keep Walker in check. Cursing, Jackson realized his datapad was downstairs. He wished he'd called Frank earlier, or at least hadn't let the idea of getting lectured about "hoodoo" be an excuse not to. He should have done it, called the one person he trusted to guard over him. He was sick, he knew, and for all he wanted to disbelieve Walker about the poison, he felt like… like…

Like my organs are shutting down. Like he said.

Oh gods. I was dying.

And he'd almost done it alone.

Jackson stilled, sagging against the wall.

Given the nature of his career and his secrets, he'd never been able to keep anyone close unless they were already *informed*. He had no one to call, other than Frank. Now, he felt the loss, wondered if his chosen solitude might have cost him his life.

The boy from the orphanage floated up in his mind, gap in his teeth when he grinned. Tony. Tony wasn't just a bit of delirium; he had been a true memory, though one unremembered for years. Jackson knew they had both been at the bottom of the pecking order for being small and weird back when they were kids: Jackson with his nightmares and shadows, and Tony with his faraway stare and gapped teeth, the whistle in his words. Together, Jackson knew, they'd been less of a target than when they were apart. That was why Tony had kept nearby.

And Tony was the closest thing he'd ever had to a friend, besides Dad. Frank was paid, so he didn't count. Jackson didn't even know what had happened to Tony. He was fairly sure someone had taken the boy away, too. Maybe Tony had also been adopted? For the first time, he was troubled that he didn't know.

"You still awake, Dovetail?" Agent Walker's voice crashed through his thoughts, accompanying a pounding on the door. Jackson suddenly realized that he was in the shower now, shoes off, but all the rest of his clothes on. When had he even gotten in? How long had he been slouched there? His shaving mirror showed dark bile stains flecking his shirt, running off in the stream.

"I'm awake," he snapped, but his voice sounded small, afraid. He turned the mirror downwards.

Jackson sloshed out of the water, ruined suit dripping on the tile. He fought himself out of his jacket, and there was a small *thunk* as it hit the floor.

He stooped and rifled through the pockets, finding his keys, pocketknife, a flask, and the fresh, sopping pack of dream tea (witchbane?), and he glared at the bag, wishing that he'd never seen it, that he'd never drank a cup of tea in his life. A waft of spice drifted from the herbs, and a pain split his head, his vision doubling. Crumpling the packet in his fist, he flung it into the garbage. As if to compound this defiance, he unscrewed the top of his flask and chugged all the whiskey that remained. The scorching heat of alcohol lit up his mouth and the space behind his eyes.

Surprisingly, once the fireball settled in his stomach, his body gave no answering pain. A numbness spread where it touched. Jackson held the flask to his heart, dripping water as he stood. "Ha, still don't need anybody," he muttered. "Just booze. Ha."

Knock knock knock.

"I'm still here," he returned, hoarse.

And, so help him, the shower had cleared his head. His skin no longer glowed with angry heat.

When he opened the door, clad in drenched clothes and wielding a flask and pocketknife, the agent raised both eyebrows. Jackson ignored him and squished across his carpet, walking into his closet and shutting the door behind him. It was dark, but Jackson knew where everything was.

Poisoned.

Witchbane.

"Dovetail—"

"I'm here." Jackson stared at his rack of ties as if it held answers. He heard himself fall into his business voice, a practiced mask that he was finally alert enough to fuel. "What brought you here today, Walker?"

There was a long pause, one Jackson found he did not like. "This letter…"

Jackson's joints ached as he pulled on new clothes, then he opened the door, shuffling out. Walker had apparently decided to rip the letter open in his absence, and was staring at it now, an old yellow bit of paper that looked as if it had been pulled from a trash pile. On the back was an ancient subway schedule, stained and torn. Part of Jackson was glad that he himself had not been the one to open it. The idea of the greasy buzzing it set off in his fingers sent his stomach pains on fire again.

And yet, he was also offended that this agent would read his personal missive before he did.

Either way, Jackson sensed that he wouldn't have been happy about the contents. Walker's face was drawn and white. "That's where she died," was all the agent said.

"What?" Jackson walked around Walker, peering over his shoulder, unwilling to take the paper away. It was easy to read. The crayoned letters were large and bold, written with loops and flourishes.

294 Coffey St, the crayon said. *The Witching Hour, August 1st.*

That was all. Yet, the address sounded familiar. Jackson kept thinking of the smell of brine and rotten, genetically damaged fish. It was near the wharf around Red Hook, wasn't it?

"Rowan. Rowan MacGregor. She was from the Order. We found her body this morning at a warehouse at that address."

"*What?*"

"There was an illegal fighting tournament hosted there last night. August 1st. There was blood on the concrete, and not just hers. Teeth. *Other* things. And, her body, like some kind of message."

Jackson tried not to shudder as he realized that he'd staggered through near-death for two days, never realizing it. And, an old nightmare whispered in Jackson's ear as well: a man painted like a tiger tearing through flesh and bone, a ringleader in red laughing joyously at the harsh white lights, and the crowd calling for more. *It's not real. Don't let your imagination get the better of you.* "Fighting tournament?"

"Rings like that aren't uncommon. They make a lot of money. Militia has busted quite a few of them. But this one..." His eyes became sharp. "It was one *you* were invited to."

Jackson shuddered. "I know nothing of fighting rings, Walker. I don't know why he'd want me there, or who that woman was." He lifted his hands as if to defend himself, and saw they still shook. "I'm just trying not to pass out."

Walker's mouth became a thin line. "I know." He made a *hrmph* noise. "What about your associates? You ever hear about them attending things like this? Based on the warehouse, the blood, and the evidence of foot traffic, this fight was bigger than most. Almost Announcer level."

"I don't know what they do with their free time. I don't even... Announcer level? What does that even mean?"

"Figure of speech. Just urban legend. You know what... don't even worry about it for now. You're barely standing. Just... just go sleep, and try not to die. But before you do, I need you to arrange something for me."

"There has to be a cure—"

"There isn't. But, you're more stable than you were, at least. Drink water and bring your fever down if you start hearing things again. Don't go jumping out of the damn window or anything. Now, you need to tell one of your people to get a truck to the intersection at Willowbrook and Forest Hill at 8:45 tomorrow night. Under no circumstances can you be late."

Jackson struggled to piece together this request through his head fog. He was barely able to conduct business in his current state of mind. But, if he wasn't wrong... that intersection was right up on the compound where Anna was being held. His eyes narrowed. "What are we doing there?"

"You're going to pick up a package and deliver it. I will give your operative instructions on arrival. I don't think it would reflect well on your *fine* smuggling operation to ask any more questions than that, and I've spent enough time here."

Jackson's lip curled. Run number two, then? "Fine. There will be a truck there."

"Send your best. I'm leaving now. And *don't* contact anyone from the Order. Pretend you died. Wouldn't want them to try and finish the job, now would we? Get somewhere safe. I'll be in touch." With that, Walker's Coalition shoes were stomping down the stairs already, and Jackson knew the time for questions had passed. The door downstairs slammed shut.

Jackson began to hobble downstairs as well. Movement was still slow and painful, his joints creaking, the aches on the inside forcing him to hunch and wince. Pain rolled between his stomach and his kidneys. Yet, he was thinking in complete sentences. He was conscious. He heard no phone calls from the headmistress. *Did I really imagine all of that?* The ravens he had learned to ignore. Those other phantom things…

When he finally reached his datapad, he fashioned a message in the code-speak he and Frank preferred, giving coordinates and times in the guise of creating a haircut appointment. Walker had wanted his best, and Frank was his best, bar none. Fingers trembling, he also tapped out a code requesting a safe house. Frank had always said such negotiations could take a little time, and Jackson didn't know how much time he had. Huxley might send someone to check in on him, make sure the job was done. When had the grandfatherly old man decided he should die, just like that?

Had it been Huxley's choice? Was this one of those things the Order got together and voted on over their little potluck, who they should murder?

Jackson slumped back down on the couch.

Why is any of this happening to me?

He had been one of the few children that had never questioned his place in the world after being abandoned. Only his future had mattered, and he'd dedicated himself to wearing the Dovetail name with pride. But now, he began to wonder what The Order knew about what he was, what, perhaps, his biological parents had known before leaving him to die on the streets. *Did they know I'd see things, go crazy, do things I can't control? What is wrong with me? Why do they all want me dead?* For the first time in his memory, he yearned to know, to have at least one answer.

Exhaustion was creeping in around the edges of his mind again. He was too weak to fight it. The tide of sleep and the desperate need to heal was dragging him down, and Jackson shut his eyes.

He did not know if he would open them again, but he hoped he might.

CHAPTER TEN
Chainbreaker

Anna's eyes snapped open. Footsteps.

A new agent had come, this man wearing no environmental suit at all. She knew him. The man from the window. Those cold eyes stared at her not like she was a patient, but rather, she was a bit of interesting curios. "Matthews," he spoke with a frown. "Are you ready to be let out of those binds?"

My name's Dr. Matthews, Anna rebelled inwardly. "Yeah."

"No more outbursts?"

"No." She bit her tongue, but the words came out anyway. "Didn't have to be such asses, you know. Cutting me off from everyone, never telling me anything. I think I've been more than reasonable."

He ignored her, undoing the straps.

"And," Anna continued. "I want answers. What is Project Esper? Why are you still keeping me here? I'm not dangerous. Look! I'm all better! You're not even wearing a suit." She sat up, stretching her aching back, trying to keep the bedpan and her legs under the covers. She was back in an open hospital gown. Being pinned down for three days had taken most dignity from her.

"You cannot assault the workers, Miss Matthews. If you try again, you will be met with force."

I poked him with my finger! Anna wanted to scream. Instead, she only frowned, and stewed, sensing this man cared nothing for her situation. "Are you going to tell me why you're keeping me here?"

"I'm Special Agent Reeds. I've taken over from Agent Walker." The way he said Jaden's name left him with a subtle sneer on his face. "And you're a remarkable young woman. Tell me about your family. Are they like you, too?"

Anna blinked. "I don't understand."

"It's alright, you can tell me. I know Walker told you not to. I hate to tell you this, but he was using you for his own ends. He wanted to keep your discovery all to himself, to try and make up for his past mistakes. It's a good thing I was keeping an eye on him and his doings. I don't think you'd be getting the help you need otherwise."

Anna stared. "No, I really have no idea what you're talking about."

"Is that so?" Reeds took a seat, crossing his legs. Anna shivered. Reeds's voice altered in tone and cadence, like he was speaking with emotions, but not a single one of them reached his eyes. "You've been putting off radiation. And, I know you know that's not normal."

"I..." Anna bit her lip. "I'm reasonably certain his hypothesis was faulty. It's impossible for a human being to put off dangerous levels of radiation without getting sick."

"So true, so true. It is very strange that you seem completely resistant to it. I mean, you were sick for a while, but not from that. Did you know, Miss Matthews, that there are thousands of soldiers and agents who work out beyond the dome? They're good men and women. So many spend too much time in the badlands. They get sick. They die slow, and in pain. Even in the domes, we have a thirty percent birth defect rate, nowhere near what it was, but still... somehow being resistant to radiation, that old poison? Worth more than gold and silver."

Anna realized then that his fingers were clasped together on his stomach as he leaned back. And, on his left hand, only two fingers were present to do the clasping. The rest of the hand was melted and lumped. Birth... defects?

"I'm sorry," Anna said, apologizing for both his hand and his disturbing story. "But your tests have to be wrong."

Reeds sighed. "I don't think so. There's more to you, too, I'm certain. A skinny thing like you just threw three technicians ten feet. And then, there's this." He pulled out his datapad, tapping at the surface. "I'm pretty certain you can't wave this off."

The screen turned to face her. It was a camera feed of the room. She had been sleeping, before she was bound, and was winding around in her sleep, discomfited by dreams. Anna felt a sting of self-consciousness, wondering if they'd faithfully filmed everything she'd done. It looked like her dreams shifted for the better, though, and she curled up on herself, finally settling down.

Her skin began to emit what looked like a glow. Anna blinked, certain it was a fault of the recording. But then, her body lifted, and she felt a chill, making a whimpering noise. Her onscreen body hovered there, a foot over the bed, like she was in a demon possession film.

"I thought that was interesting," Reeds said. "You only did that for a minute, and no one actively watches these. I'm sure that if I hadn't been combing the past feeds for signs, no one would have noticed it at all." He shrugged.

Anna gaped, shaken. "That's *impossible*," she said. "It's impossible. I don't understand."

"Easy now. Don't want your radiation flaring, do we? Walker was insightful pulling in that Dovetail fellow to help get you under control, keep you from being flagged as an Esper without looking like he was too involved."

"But Jackson…"

"Jackson? He's a smuggler. Glorified drug mailman. He's no one's friend. I can help you for real, Anna. And your genetics can help the world. I'm just going to need you to do what I ask."

Anna realized she was shaking her head only when he gave her an annoyed look, and she kept shaking it regardless, the muscles in her neck on auto-pilot. "I just want to go home," she said, holding the words to herself like a charm. "You can't keep me here. I don't understand half of what's going on. Please. Let me go home."

Anna's eyes flickered to the window, the thick double-paned glass. She then glanced at the door. There was no movement or presence behind either.

She returned her gaze to Reeds. They were alone, perhaps. But, a gun bulged at his belt. "Come with me."

"Where are we going?"

"Medical. You're safe enough now to leave this room, and you'll need to be moved to a larger testing area. Medical will make sure you have all of the... accoutrements... you'll need." Anna brought her knees up to her chest defensively, wrapping her arms around them, feeling like a small, stupid girl. "You can go under your own power, which I'd like. Medical would like that too. Easier to get baseline readings if you're awake. But, I can tranquilize you again. What will it be?"

"I'll go," Anna whispered. "Can I have my uniform back?"

"No. We're running behind schedule. Don't worry, it's just a quick walk down the hall." Reeds jerked his head, and Anna rose, feeling the chill in her feet as she touched the floor. Flushed, embarrassed, terrified, she began to pad after him, drawing her gown as shut as she could behind her back with both hands.

Reeds pulled open the door and gestured she go first. The halls beyond were a sterile gray, so austere that no pattern or decoration broke the stretch of concrete as far as she could see. The agent fell in lockstep by her side, guiding her to the left. "I'm very much looking forward to seeing what you can do, Miss Matthews," he spoke with his crocodile smile.

Anna put her head down and kept walking, but her eyes darted to every side, taking in the extent of her prison. She heard no other footsteps beyond the echo of Reeds's sharply polished shoes, and saw no other people. The hush was suited to a mausoleum.

Cameras were situated in the corners where the hallways split into identical gray corridors. Anna entertained for a second the idea of suddenly tearing down one of these hallways, but the gun posted to Reeds's side crushed these fantasies.

Then, there were footsteps, an echoing click of heel. Anna kept her head down, and squeezed her gown shut tighter.

A woman rounded a bend, long, midnight hair pulled coyly over one side of her face. She was dressed in the white uniform of what Anna supposed might be one of the doctors. "*Reeds*," she smiled, her teeth flashing bright white. "You've brought her."

Reeds grabbed Anna's wrist and held her as he stopped. "We aren't at medical yet. That's where she transfers. Who are you?"

"Doctor Nyx," she breathed.

"There's no Doctor Nyx—"

And Reed suddenly crumpled as if an invisible man had cut his tendons, his head cracking against the concrete. Anna shrieked. He didn't move.

"Shh, shh!" The woman jogged to her. "You're safe now. You're alright. Well, almost safe. *Hola*. I'm a friend of Jaden's—you know, Agent Walker?" Anna nodded, dumbfounded. "Alright, we're getting you out of here."

Anna realized she was nodding automatically. "Okay." She looked down at Reeds, the cold floor, and her bare feet. "I'm ready to go."

A shrill sound filled the air, and Anna cried out in surprise, covering her ears. The woman hooked a hand around her wrist and pulled her. "The alarm! Come on!" She kicked her heeled shoes off into a corner, and they both began to run. Anna's gown flapped open, but she no longer cared. Thoughts of home, desperation, and fear pulled her now.

The hallways were a labyrinthine blur, the woman who called herself Nyx yanking her down them at a breakneck pace, dodging left and right like a rat who had memorized the maze. Anna heard angry shouts, the sound of stomping shoes, slamming doors. "Not long now!" Nyx called back, breathless.

They hit a dead end, a simple wooden door blocking them, and though Nyx yanked the handle, it was locked. "Really?!" she yelled. Then, "Stay back!" Anna teetered backwards just in time as the woman slammed both of her hands into the door at once, the sound of their pursuers, close, so close.

A hissing, crackling bang resounded, and the door splintered outwards into flaming bits under Nyx's hands. Anna stared up at the woman in disbelief, trying to articulate what had just happened. "No time, no time, go go go!" Nyx shouted. And then Anna was forced to her feet and was running again through the smoldering hole.

Her thighs and calves screaming, her chest gasping for air, she hit the stairs, endless stairs. Finally, when she felt like she would collapse, the hallway evened, the shouting behind them fading. Nyx still dragged her, but now the corridors were dark and nightmarish, only red lights pulsing above as the alarm sounded. "Down to emergency power here," Nyx gasped. "Should be able to—" The lights flickered on, searing Anna's eyes. "Shit! They got it back up! Move it!"

Anna stumbled after, and then, there was a hiss of air before them. With a neat *shink*, a thick plate of glass dropped in front of their path, blocking the hallway. "This area is now under emergency quarantine," a helpful voice said over the intercom. "Please, remain at your stations unless you are subduing the escaped patient. Again, this area is now under emergency quarantine."

The woman dragging her let out a howl of rage. Anna stared, wide-eyed, as sparks flew between Nyx's nails. Her palms glowed a deep red-orange, and she slammed them into the glass. The plate shifted color for a moment, taking on a reddish hue, then re-hardened. She did this twice more, to no effect. Then, she turned, and an apology was on her face, one sad and lost. "The power was supposed to... I'm sorry... it's our only way out."

Something in Anna snapped. The sound of marching feet was behind her, the shouts and orders, and so was imprisonment. Down that hallway came God-knew-what tests, and Reeds, horrible, condescending, ice-eyed Reeds. In that moment, the plate was the only thing between her and home, her mewling cat, her apartment, her soft bed, the lilacs on her nightstand. She yelled like Nyx had, tears coursing down her face now, and slammed her under-exercised, desk-job fist into the glass.

Anna heard the crunch, and was certain it was her hand breaking. A throbbing numbness exploded up her entire arm.

She pulled her hand back, and under it, a thick crack had split the plate.

"Nyx?" she whispered as she came back to herself, her heart pounding in her ears.

"Oh gods." Nyx moved behind her. "Keep punching. Just... just keep punching. I'm going to hold them off. If you take that thing down, you run, you hear me? You keep running, and you don't look back."

Anna, baffled, crying, wondering if she was dreaming, sniffled an agreement. Then, she hollered again, her throat hoarse, and planted her left fist where her right had been. A second crack grew across the first, spiderwebbing. *I can't do this. I shouldn't be able to do this,* her brain whimpered, and she wondered if it all might be a dream. Her third swing landed, then her fourth, and her fifth, her knuckles stinging now through the numbness, blood coming away and sticking to the cracked glass.

Anna gave one final swing, and a two-foot-wide hole in the barrier gave way, shards crackling as they fell. "Come on!" she choked. Then, she felt the heat of a furnace bloom behind her, and turned to see the woman called Nyx wreathed in fire. Anna gaped in awe. Flames licked out from Nyx's arms and hands, a pyretic halo, and she stood perfectly still, letting herself burn, somehow unhurt. Black-uniformed soldiers were rounding the corner, charging, jackboots thudding, and Nyx had her arms spread wide, blocking their way, flames boiling from her skin. "Come on!" Anna yelled, but Nyx did not turn, as if she couldn't hear.

Keep running, and don't look back.

Sobbing, Anna threw herself through the hole. The front of her gown ripped and tore, and as she pulled herself through, the ragged edges slashed at her legs and arms, no matter how careful her movements. "Hurry," she yelled, hoping Nyx would follow, hoping that whatever the fire covering her was, it would keep her safe. Then, Anna was on the other side, trying to keep her bare feet away from the shattered glass. Stinging pain shot up her heels and toes regardless, but she was running now, running, not looking back, praying her savior would be okay.

The lobby of the building was that of a plain, beige office, though the lights were off, and no one was there. Red lights pulsed above. The front door was smashed in, as if an explosion had blown it inwards. Anna stumbled through this, gasping for air, her gown damp with sweat, fear, and blood.

There was the gate, that barbed-wire fence. Where was security? It didn't matter. She had to keep moving. The open air, after so long, felt like a balm on her stinging cuts and scrapes, and she teetered onwards, the hard scrape of rough stone against her tender feet making her wince. Despite what Nyx said, she looked back. She wanted to see Nyx running out after her, telling her what to do.

She didn't.

Anna peered through the darkness, gripping the chain link in her aching hands. Belatedly, she saw the electrification warning. No shock had hit her, though. The fence was off. Now what? She could climb, but the spiked wire on top looked like more than she could handle without tearing herself open even more. It was also an fifteen-foot drop from up there. If she faltered... a broken leg might be the least of her worries.

A dull blue, glowing haze hung overhead against the stars. *The Barrier*, a memory whispered, Jackson's voice. Anna realized she couldn't process it then, not what it was, not what it meant.

She traveled along the fence, holding herself up with it, at a limping pace. It was so dark, she didn't see the hole in the mesh until she stepped on the broken wiring, stifling her gasp of pain with a hand over her mouth. Anna didn't question the blessing for even a second, wriggling herself down and through, noticing that it looked as if the edges of the chain link had been melted away.

The street beyond was cold and damp, and dark as if the power had gone out for blocks. If this was New York, and she wondered if it was, she had never seen a city so bereft of light or life, or even the noise of traffic. It seemed so wrong.

As if to oblige, a single car whizzed past her, almost silent, one headlight gone. It didn't even slow.

Anna limped onwards, and she wondered if her feet were growing numb from the abuse. They were hurting less and less. *Adrenaline. Have to get far away while it lasts.* The pain dimming, her limp corrected itself. She began to try a jog again, across the street this time.

A truck suddenly screeched to a halt before her, a ghost in the night with no headlights, a millimeter from running her down. Anna looked up, knees shuddering, raising her hands defensively. The truck was a plain white, a swooping dove painted on the side, and her heart fluttered in recognition. *Dovetail Parcel, Since 2042.* The passenger door clicked open. A thick, calloused hand beckoned her. "In!" a voice yelled. "Now!"

Anna looked at the dark, grim city beyond, and acted on the familiar dove, leaping up, grabbing a handle, and hefting herself into the cab. The driver, an aging man with dark, beady eyes and a pressed white uniform hit the gas, and the truck lurched forward.

"Where's the government man?" His voice sounded full of the road gravel that had been under her toes.

"I… I don't know…"

"Anyone following you?"

"I didn't see anyone…"

"Okay. Good. Put this on. Less conspicuous." He leaned to the side while steering with one hand, popping open a glove box and swerving almost ninety degrees down a different street. When her stomach settled, she saw that in the compartment sat a white uniform like the one he wore. Anna took it, clutching it to her chest, glancing back at him, uncertain. "*Put it on*, I ain't lookin'."

She did as she was told, scrunching down in her seat as the hospital gown came free, trying to cover herself with her elbows and a slouch, and being very poor at it. True to his word, however, the driver was keeping his eyes locked on the road, and down this deserted stretch, no one else was there to leer. Finally on, the uniform was a soothing, clean scratch against her skin.

"Now," the man said. "Take those scissors and cut your hair."

Anna blinked, and stared at the glove compartment. Blue-handled garden shears stared back at her. "Uh—"

"Do it if you don't wanna go back to prison, lady. Make it short, not like what you have now."

Anna stared up at the glowing blue haze on the night sky through the window, trembling. She seized the shears, sniffling, then began to hack. Blond hair fell around her thighs like dead leaves in the winter, some of it falling to the dark space where her feet rested, swallowed up in oblivion. When it was done, the rearview mirror reflected back a tattered pixie cut, the kind a child might inflict on themselves, and she realized that though she was shaking and whimpering, there were no tears coming at all.

"Alright, put the scissors back in the glove box. You did good. Just put the hat over it—there you go. We'll be stoppin' to dye it and change trucks, then takin' a ferry."

Anna blurted, "Is it 2147?"

"Yeah?" The driver gave her a sidelong grimace.

"Okay." That was all the words she had for it anymore, the dead emptiness the acceptance left, the realization that home didn't exist anymore. *Okay.*

A numbness inside was spreading, like the one in her toes and hands. Belatedly, she worried about getting blood all over the new white uniform, giving her away, and looked down at her shredded knuckles.

Though dried blood was caked along her hand, there were no slashes, no stinging loose skin that had been there before. There were only reddened scrapes.

Head foggy, she looked down, pulled up her pant leg, then whipped off the white tennis shoe from her foot. Her skin was bloodied, but... unhurt. A thousand glass cuts, gone. A shard fell out of the shoe. Anna sat back up, put the shoe back on, and leaned her head against the window.

Okay.

CHAPTER ELEVEN
The Starry-Eyed Man

Jackson slept a dead sleep, the darkness over his mind long and absolute.

And then, the air shifted, and his primal instincts knew something wasn't right.

His eyes snapped open. A starlit sky greeted him, and a shot of adrenaline coursed down his spine. He jerked upright. The comforting blue haze of the dome was missing. He was outside. *Outside.* He hurried to his feet and looked in every direction, heart racing. *Shit. Shit.* What the hell was this? Dark foliage obscured his view at every turn. Trees? *Trees?* He saw no roads, no derelict homes, nothing that would indicate nearby civilization. There were strange shuffling noises and rustling breezes on all sides. The air tasted earthy, bitter, and foreign. Jackson desperately tried to calm his breathing, feeling the beginnings of full-fledged panic.

He had never, never *ever*, been outside and away from the dome at night, and he'd never strayed from a human-made road.

Where was he? No clue.

How had he gotten here? He didn't know.

He had fallen asleep… the *poison*…

Am I dreaming? Jackson rolled up his sleeve and bit his arm as hard as he could. *Gah!* It *stung*. Was this real? Of course, he didn't think it ever occurred to him in dreams to question whether or not things were real. Did that mean…?

Oh gods. He had to get home. He'd been taken. A business rival, or perhaps someone wanting a payoff from the raiders for a body... or the *Order!* He'd been dumped out here. The poison tea had made him so sick; he'd been an easy mark.

Jackson fought the urge to tear off in a random direction until he found his way. Thankfully, he realized his stomach didn't hurt anymore, and his head felt squarely on his shoulders. The exhaustion had retreated. Against all odds, he'd gotten better.

He scuffled along the unpaved earth, his breathing getting faster. Then, a flicker of light caught his eye. It tugged at him like a lifeline in a sea of darkness.

A fire.

He found his feet drawn down the ill-trod path, weaving through sprouting shrubs. His business shoes scrabbled for purchase on smooth rocks. The light grew stronger, a dancing spot of orange.

Jackson neared the clearing where the fire sat, nervous, but hopeful.

Of course, the fire could have belonged to a slaver band.

His heart trembled, a betrayal to his stern facade that he had things under control. Slavers meant torture, shackles, living in pens, eternally bloodied and spit upon and *used* with no hope of escape. He had heard the stories, seen some pictures. Slavers were worse than death.

Who had he made enemies of recently? Pegasus Deliveries? Were slavers part of the Order's repertoire?

He drew his pocketknife, all he had for protection.

However, as he peered from behind one of the unfamiliar trees, he saw no scarred bandits nor armored soldiers around the fire. He saw just one man, a tall, hunched form, sitting on what appeared to be an old log. The man was dressed in a black suit, as dark as his skin, his face obscured by a waterfall of braids. Jackson watched him for a minute, sizing him up, realizing something was bothering him about this figure, but he could not put his finger on it.

Weighing his options made him realize he had little choice but to investigate. He finally stepped into the clearing.

"Ah, there you are. Welcome." The figure rose from where he sat, and spread his arms wide. His lips drew back, and a pearly, mischievous smile floated in the gloom.

Jackson's brain stalled for a second, finally realizing what was wrong. It was *him*. The eyes. His knife fell to the dirt. Those eyes bore down into his own, dark as the sky, and full of hundreds of glittering lights. Falling! He was falling into those eyes. Jackson sat abruptly, unable to turn away. Words seemed to dribble from his mouth, everything moving in slow motion. "Who... are... you?"

Finally, slowly, the stranger blinked, his face crinkling as if in silent laughter.

The dizziness in Jackson's head evaporated, and he shook his head several times. He could look again to the stranger, though this time, not directly into his gaze. Startled, afraid, he took in the rest of man's countenance. The braids running down the stranger's back were woven with strange trinkets and bones. His suit was well-stitched, custom made; Jackson's practiced eye could tell. It looked far better than the sweaty, sick-scented clothes Jackson realized he himself wore. They didn't seem fresh anymore.

A pair of wings suddenly unfurled on the stranger's shoulder, and Jackson realized a raven sat there, almost invisible against the layers of darkness that hung off the man like a shroud. *You again.* It made a soft frog-like noise, and then began smoothing down its feathers with its beak.

"She says hello." The man had a note of affection in his voice. He had an accent Jackson struggled to pin down, something that made his exacting syllables roll and dance. "She let me know you were *quite* unwell. I suspect you will remember our conversation this time."

Very few words managed to escape Jackson's confused stupor. "I... why... this time?"

"We have spoken, are speaking, will speak again. The fact that you have finally sought me out is good."

"I've seen you before..." This was an understatement. Dream after dream marched through his memory, always with this stranger in the shadows.

"Why were you in my head?" Jackson pulled up out of his dazed slouch on the ground and dragged himself up onto a log, anger rising. His head buzzed. Everything about this place was ever so subtly *wrong*. Even the dirt against his palms pulsed with a peculiar energy, and the air hung acrid on his tongue. He wanted to go home. Now. "Who are you? Where am I?"

The strange man simply cocked his head and sat back down across from him, silent. Jackson realized, as the seconds passed, that the man did not mean to answer these questions.

"How do you even know who I am?"

"Because you are mine!" The dark figure almost *vibrated* with giggles, rich and deep. "I like you. Ask another question."

Jackson scowled. "Yours? I don't belong to anybody."

"Of course not! But you are mine. Go on, go on. Ask another question!"

"No. I don't *belong* to *anybody*."

"Why are you repeating yourself?" The man put his chin in his hands, leaning forward like an eager child. "You are not being clever. Be more clever, Jackson. Now, ask!"

Jackson suddenly felt as if he was playing a game, and didn't know the rules. Demands rose and fell before they reached his lips. Fine. He would ask questions. "Well... I... why am I here?"

"Why *are* you here?" The man reached into his pocket, retrieved what appeared to be a half-crumbled cookie, and took a bite, chewing it thoughtfully.

"I don't *know* why I'm here, you—"

"You don't know why you're anywhere." The man shrugged. "You should work on that."

"Great. Thanks."

"You're welcome." Another bite of cookie.

Jackson tried again. "The raven... you can see them too."

The man shrugged. The raven made a chittering noise that sounded eerily like laughter, and nuzzled the side of the man's head.

They remained silent for a long minute, staring at each other, unblinking, Jackson growing irritated. Finally, the stranger sighed in exasperation. "Do you truly have *no good questions*? Why do you not ask the one you've always had?" Jackson blinked. "I see it in you, screaming to get out, deep, deep down there."

The man, unbothered by the heat, reached across the fire. His arm seemed to stretch and grow as the flames licked his sleeve, and he poked Jackson right in the chest. The touch set off a feeling like ice in Jackson's blood, and the old memories were finally sent bubbling up and out, after so many years, into the dreamlike night.

He remembered the whitewashed walls of Kind Hands Children's Home, the scents of sweat, urine, and children. He saw the suspicious eyes of the other orphans, sidelong glances, fear. Like a ghost's wail, he heard a young girl's piercing plea to the woman in charge. *"Jack brought monsters in with him! He's scary! Please, can't you throw him out?"*

He remembered the fat, golden tabby cat curled around Huxley's legs. The cat stared at him as if he were a tiny mouse, insignificant except to be eaten. Meanwhile, its master spoke. *"Jackson, I can't profess to know what accident of nature caused your arcane wiring to work the way it does. But it is not a gift. It is a disorder. I cannot teach you."*

He remembered trying to ignore a raven as it pranced upon his father's desk, as it looked up at the Dovetail patriarch and cawed plaintively, no one able to see it, no one but Jackson. His father was grinning and ruffling his hair like he wasn't nineteen. *"I'll be back around eight. Don't wait for me to come back before you eat something!"* Jackson had forgotten to eat, as per usual, but woke up the next morning wondering why his father hadn't returned... and then there was a knock at the door. It was a militia man. A week later, when Jackson came home from the funeral, a raven was perched atop the wall, eyes boring down into him accusingly. Had it tried to warn him of his father's impending heart attack? *Why didn't I understand?!*

"What am I?" The question tore out of his chest in the wake of the jarring memories, and it left a cold, fearful hole behind.

"Ah. There it is. Good job."

Jackson could hardly look now at the stranger's jaunty smile. His heart beat faster with terror.

"Do you really want to know?" the man said.

What if... gods, what if he wasn't human? What if he was crazy? What if he was dangerous?

"Tick tock, Jackson."

Would ignorance make him happy? He was *miserable*.

Jackson steeled himself and tried to forget the painful memories, and tried to stamp out the quaver in his voice. "Yes. Yes, I want to know."

"You... are my *Chosen*." The stranger let this sink in for a second. "Go on. Ask another question."

Wait.

What?

"Chosen?" Jackson stumbled over his words with all of the unsatisfied bewilderment he felt. The terror, the keen longing for answers—he wanted to *shake* this stranger until a proper answer fell out. "What the hells does that even *mean*?"

"Many things to many people." The man crossed his arms, considering the fire, as if he was monitoring something nestled deep at its core. "Many things." Jackson fought the urge to yell as the stars dimmed in the stranger's eyes. It was a long moment before the man continued. "Oh, Jackson. Your world, your stories are so full of sadness and horror. The earth dies. The sun weeps. Your songs circle around my ears with each passing moon. They are... not... pleasing." He heaved a sigh, and the dry leaves rustled in the trees. "You have the power to change this, however."

"Change *what*?"

"The stories, Jackson. The stories." The man gave another bright smile, seriousness melting away as quickly as it had come. "You are going to tell a new one. One I like. One the world likes. One you like. That is what you are." He spread his arms with a sense of finality, as if that answered everything. "That's enough questions for today, isn't it?" He stood and stretched, handing the last morsel of cookie to the raven on his shoulder. It gulped it down happily.

"Wait!" Jackson stood as well. "No, wait. You can't just-"

The night air fell still. "Oh? I. Can't. Just...?" The stranger raised his eyebrows in challenge, leaning forward again, grinning, leering. He suddenly seemed bigger somehow, as if he truly did not end where the shadow and night began. Something in Jackson's soul quailed. He licked his lips, mouth very dry.

"I mean…" Jackson's voice shrank. "What do you expect me to even do with that? Do I find others like me? What do you want? I don't even know your *name.*"

The dark man's face softened for a moment. He reached out and put his cold-tinged hand on Jackson's shoulder, and immediately, Jackson's entire left side felt like it had been put outside the Barrier in the middle of winter. But, he found himself unable to pull away. "I have been known by many names. Before. Now. Someday. The name I am most fond of, I have not heard for many moons. Perhaps you will find it?"

"Oh," was all Jackson could say to the non-answer, teeth chattering, wincing at the being's touch. The bone was starting to ache. "I'm Jackson." A beat. "But you knew that."

"Yes." The stranger seemed to think for a moment. "You have not heard the story, have you? The story that was kept from you. The book of stories."

"Story? *What book?*"

The man sighed. He looked like he was considering an answer, but then, something changed in his expression, his gaze shifting to the moon. Puzzled, Jackson followed his starred eyes upwards, and the raven took flight. Leaves were lifting from the trees and falling into the sky, splashes of green and gold as they crossed into the moonlight.

The hand left Jackson's shoulder. "The dream runs short. Keep well. The wolves circle ever closer."

"No! Wait. What do you *want* from me?"

"We will speak again by this fire when you have found the secrets which belong to you. They are yours, so take them." He flashed a conspiratorial grin. "Worry not. You *are* my favorite."

"But—"

Light suddenly flooded Jackson's eyes. He toppled to the ground.

The ground was, fortunately, soft, plush even.

He groaned quietly into the familiarity of his bedroom carpet. The light in his eyes was that of the sun shining through his window, illuminating his reading desk. An empty whisky glass lay toppled next to his head.

He had no recollection of coming up here, but he had fallen asleep in the chair, and fallen out of it, too. *It WAS a dream?* It was so vivid… why did he feel the need to even question what it was? This… this had felt so real. So important somehow. Every detail was burned into his mind.

Chosen.

The word seemed to whisper from one end of his brain to the other, and a headache followed in its wake, left worse by the memories the stranger had roused in him. He had wanted that answer, wanted so badly to know what he was, that it almost physically hurt to have only more questions. He curled up in on himself on the carpet, the sensation of the sickness and poison returning. The feeling of being unsettled by something larger than himself refused to leave, either. He didn't like it.

And yet, his stomach was calmer, his head was clearer. He felt as if he had slept for days.

Bang bang bang!

Jackson leapt up, heart racing.

Bang bang bang!

Oh gods. It was just the door.

He trudged downstairs towards the insistent knocking, rubbing his weary eyes, feeling the uncomfortable cling of days-old clothes. It felt as if something had died in his mouth, and he was certain that his hair was sticking up in unnatural ways. Still, he supposed he was alive, at least. Whoever was at his door and whatever they wanted had better be important.

Jackson opened the door, the insistent slew of knocks dropping off. Then, he blinked, long and slow. There was Frank, face stoic as it always was, come hell or high water.

And next to him, eyes glassy, hair dyed black, and hands smeared with dirt and blood, was Anna.

CHAPTER TWELVE
Sanctuary

Anna's butchered hair was knotty and greasy, her face caked in grime and a little blood. She knew her eyes were red and swollen from how they stung. She also knew Jackson was going to take one look at her and send her straight back to quarantine.

Her fingers reached to wheedle her hair in discomfort, but found only tiny shorn fluffs of indignity. Her hand fell back to her side.

She didn't run. She had run all night, and was too tired to go another step.

The man who answered could only be Jackson, though she knew he'd never seen his face before now. This man stared at her, mouth slightly agape—and to Anna's surprise, he wasn't the well-groomed, in-control businessman she had pictured. He was more gaunt and spindly than the bulky environmental suit had let on, all elbows and angles, as young as she was. His shirt was crumpled and smudged, his hair sticking straight up. Above all else, he looked pale and sick, with dark pools under his eyes. She cast her gaze to her feet again, wondering what to say.

Had he really arranged to get her freedom? The truck driver had told her in his angry way that she'd been a surprise, to say the least. Apparently he'd been expecting, at worst, a box too heavy for his aging back. Had Agent Jaden Walker kept everything from them? Would Jackson be angry, too? If this "Coalition" was the government, and had any true power…

Finally, Jackson seemed to come out of his daze. "Hi?"

"Boss," the big guy said, cracking his oversized neck. "You should let your lady friends know not to run half-naked around Staten Island at night." Then, he shoved past Jackson and into the hallway.

"Anna?" Jackson whispered as she followed with hesitating steps. "Are you alright?"

He might have been different than how she imagined, but his voice was the same: warm, concerned. Encouraged, Anna gave a small nod, then kicked herself, remembering that he was probably asking about her *condition,* not her health. "I'm not... um... unsafe. Are *you* okay?" It seemed like if the door shut too hard, he might fall over. He paused for a moment, like he was thinking about it, then nodded back.

The air was warm, and smelled a little like sandalwood. Her shoes brushed against a soft rug, none of the clicking and scraping from concrete and tile. No fluorescent lights. No whitewashed walls. No sterile aftertaste in the air. Peaceful.

She kept following her big-shouldered rescuer to a kitchen, wishing she could remember his name. Something about the stony set of his face had discouraged her from asking. Now he was rifling through Jackson's fridge and clanging through pots and pans like he lived there, grunting one-word instructions, and Jackson was making no move to stop him. There seemed to be a silent agreement in place that she did not have to talk yet, and she was glad.

The table was moved out to accommodate a third chair, silverware was set down, and water was set to boil. She didn't bother to ask why it looked like they were about to cook a meal. The prospect of something more than tasteless mush made her stomach ache in yearning.

Jackson kept glancing at her with curiosity. He cleared his throat and turned to her just as the big man (perhaps this was *Frank*, Anna finally remembered) began to grouse quietly about the lack of fresh ingredients in the pantry.

"You can use the shower if you want," Jackson spoke.

Anna seized on to the idea like a lifeline. A shower. A shower to wash away all of the madness. "Thank you."

"It's upstairs and to the right."

"You got ten minutes," Frank warned.

Anna tore past them, feeling somewhat sick. Jackson's guest bathroom was the most beautiful sight she had seen in weeks, and she intended to use it, wanted so badly to *stop* for a moment and rest. No more bouncing from one end of the streets to the next while Frank barked out orders as he had all night, no more Coalition doctors poking and prodding at her as they had all week. She shut the door behind her and felt the privacy in her bones. No one was watching her. For the first time since she'd woken up in this strange land, she was *alone*.

Don't cry. Don't cry.

She cried.

Her nausea passed, and so did the tears. Anna occupied herself by fiddling with the unfamiliar knobs in the bathtub. There was a groan in the pipes, and then, with a sputtering hiss, warm water tittered from the shower head—from heaven. The green block of soap in the corner smelled fresh and clean, like a young tree. The bottles were all unlabeled, but when she rubbed some of the cream between her fingers, she recognized the grain of baking soda paste. Homemade shampoo, like her roommate made! She almost hugged the bottle. It was so... so normal. So like what she knew.

When her skin was scrubbed pink, she felt the taint of the quarantine room slip away. For a while, she just stood in the water and breathed. Then, she pulled on the white uniform again, letting the sensation of *clean* sink in. Her brain asked her to pretend that she was in a nice hotel, taking some vacation, the twenty-first century waiting for her outside.

The illusion was shattered as she glanced down at her hands. The backs were now covered in tiny white scars. She rubbed her knuckles with the pad of her thumb, disquieted. The woman who stared back at her from the mirror looked haggard, desperate, a waxy-skinned stranger.

Voices drifted to her from the dining room as she padded down the stairs.

"I told you not to trust that hoodoo horseshit!"

"I'm fine. Or, I will be. Really. I feel better."

"You don't look it." A pause. "You been in that moonshine again?"

"Give me another day. Look... we have to talk about Anna. Where are you going to take her?"

Frank's voice rose, like the rumble of a volcano slowly waking up from its slumber. "Safe house, you dumb shit. The *hell* were you thinking, sending me off to smuggle an escaped Coalition prisoner? Don't get me wrong, I'm glad she's not in some damn petri dish, but *Christ*, boss! No warning? *Nothing?* You do know we don't have things set up for this?"

"*I* sent you to smuggle her? Frank, I had *no idea* what the shipment was Walker was talking about. He said nothing about the danger of this operation, or that it was Anna."

Anna wrung her hands. So, she was right. They'd been in the dark. Maybe they wouldn't have done it if they would have known. But could she blame them?

Frank was growing louder. "Oh? Why the hell'd you send a request for a safe house right after that then, huh?"

"No! Look, Frank... The Order might be trying to kill me."

Anna's eyes widened.

"THE *WHAT.*"

"The Order! You know... Huxley's, uh, crowd."

"MOTHERF—"

Anna hit a creaky step. The voices stopped. She kept her head held high as she paced into the dining room, pretending as if she hadn't heard a word as the two men looked up. Frank's hands were balled into white-knuckled fists, his jaw clenched with rage, but then, he blinked, and his face went flat, as if he'd been discussing the weather. Jackson gave her a weak smile.

There was a huge bowl of creamy white pasta in the center of the table, and a chair left open for her, and she sat, trying to pretend the tension wasn't so thick that it vibrated on her skin.

Jackson's expression softened. "Feeling any better, Anna?" She smiled back, though she knew it was no happier than his own expression.

"I'm... I'm sorry I got you involved in this... I didn't know Jaden was going to break me out, and I never wanted to hurt anyone—"

"Who the frick is Jaden?" Frank muttered at his plate.

"Um," she said, "Agent Walker. Sorry."

Jackson was shaking his head as if it didn't matter. "It's alright. We just need to get you somewhere safe, and soon."

"Thank you! I know... I know I'm just some girl, and helping me might be illegal or something..."

"Pssshhh." Jackson waved it off. "What's done is done, and this was the right thing to do, even if it was, er, a bit insane. So now, we make sure you'll be safe."

Anna nodded, and she felt her eyes swell and dampen, a hiccup in her throat. Frank glowered, and she kept the grateful sob inside. "Getting you out of the city will almost be impossible," Jackson continued. "The Coalition, for the last hour, has apparently begun seizing cargo trucks and inspecting every last crevice before letting them leave the dome."

Anna winced. "I'm sorry..."

"It's a hassle, but it's not hurting the business yet. And, fortunately, it's not just us. They haven't made the connection yet. You're going to need to lay low until this blows over. Do you know what you want to do afterwards, where you want to go?"

Anna sighed. "No," she whispered. "I don't have documents or anything. I... there's nothing for me to go back to, is there?" The hollow feeling pooled in her stomach again. She hadn't even tried thinking beyond the next day, let alone wrestle with the future. What could she tell the bank that had her savings, if they were even still around—that she'd decided to take a century-long nap? Every path she knew was blocked by people that would either demand identification she couldn't provide or think she was crazy.

2147. It's 2147.

Maybe she *was* crazy.

The table fell quiet. Then, Frank cleared his throat, glancing over at his employer. "Yeah, so, while she's thinking, get your shit together."

"Hm?" Jackson replied.

"Did you forget already? Safe house. Move it, people. This is a rest stop. You got five minutes boss, or I am leaving without you. Only reason I stayed this long was so you two could eat, 'cause I don't got that arranged yet where we're going." He turned to Anna. "Also, eat faster."

"We're leaving? Right now?" Jackson seemed startled.

"Well, the Coalition ain't watching the house, but that ain't gonna last. After all, how many people does she know in here?Besides, things might get dicey if any of those damn Huxley kooks turn up. *So haul ass.*"

Anna's hands shook as she spooned pasta onto her plate, not ready to ask questions, not yet. One bite of food, and the flavors burst in her mouth, almost exactly like cheap orange powdered mac-and-cheese mix, and oh God, it was beautiful. This minor miracle of "not porridge" distracted her so fully that she barely registered Jackson shuffling upstairs. This, this was the holiday dinner she'd dreamed about, and Frank's resentful stare was almost like Dad's anyway, so as far as Anna was concerned, the whole affair made her happy and warm.

God, if she could buy boxes of this cheese stuff, she would. And a pizza. She missed pizza, so, so much.

Eventually, some invisible alarm seemed to go off in Frank's head. He tugged at the bowl in her hands.

"Mmff," Anna rebutted, gripping it tighter, taking another bite.

"It's time, kid."

"*Mmmmf.*" *Just one more.*

He sighed, and took up all of the rest of the table settings before returning for hers, and she didn't fight him this time, though her mouth was still stuffed full. Then, he cleaned each dish with a meticulous hand that bordered on obsessive. She saw him spraying down the silverware with some kind of chemical wash, and she wondered if he intended to obliterate DNA evidence of her passing.

When Jackson came back down, he was wearing a white uniform like hers, and had only a small black bag in his arms, though the leather was stretched to near bursting point. Anna felt a strange pang at how malnourished he looked. Had he touched any of the food? She didn't think so. His eyes were wide and uncertain.

Leaving the house was unceremonious. Frank simply stuffed them into the back of a delivery truck while speaking into a wrist device under his sleeve. "We clear? *Five blocks out?* Shit… moving them. You alert me yesterday if you see something turning this way, and I don't care if it's a goddamn stray dog."

Frank had made several calls throughout the night along those lines. She supposed if she was the one smuggling people around, she wouldn't expect to do it alone.

Reeds's words about Jackson returned to her. *Glorified drug mailman.* Strange allies that she'd made. But, clearly, good ones.

The truck ambled down city blocks, bumping and skipping. Jackson stayed silent, bracing himself against a stack of crates. Anna, for the first time, became keenly aware of the quiet, realizing she couldn't even hear the motor. Perhaps it was electric. She wished she was better at conversation, but she didn't know what to say. *I'm sorry for upending your life, but thank you forever* didn't seem like enough.

She was surprised when they stopped a few times, and instead of ushering them into hiding, Frank just unloaded some crates. "Alibi for this truck," he grunted. "Gotta do this route." Jackson seemed to take it in stride, so she didn't ask. It was only when they reached a rundown navy blue high-rise that Frank whispered, "This is it. You both are couriers. Act like it. Get the cap down over your eyes—*there* you go."

She was handed a crate, heavy enough to feel like her feet were sinking farther into the earth, and then she was shuffled up through the building's entryway. The double glass doors were standing wide open, the panes cracked as if rocks had been thrown at them. Frank led them down a hall and past the boarded-up elevators, ducking into a stairwell. Anna heard Jackson's ragged breath behind her as he lugged a similar box up and up, one, two, three flights… but Anna realized she was breathing easy and evenly. Her arms weren't sore at all.

She tried not to think about how she had punched through reinforced glass. She never wanted to need to do it again. *Fear and adrenaline. That's what it was. Like the story where an old lady lifts a car off her grandson.*

That's why this was so easy, too, she imagined. She was almost shaking with fear. Every shadow could hold an agent.

But, six flights up and through the halls, and Anna saw not a single person. In some places, trash sat out in old bags, a sickly sweet stink, and she had to hold her breath. The walls were covered almost bottom to top in graffiti tags, and the few lights were sparsely placed, flickering or dead more often than not. It was a world that felt as abandoned as the dark roads she'd seen after crawling out from under the facility fence.

Finally, they stopped at apartment #614. The digits added up to a prime number. She had a friend at work that would take that as a sign of luck. Anna swallowed and figured she might as well start believing in luck, too.

Frank turned the key in the lock and pushed at the door. It did not open, instead squealing, the swelled wood grinding against the doorframe. He rolled his eyes and cursed softly, then thrust his massive shoulder into it, and the door wrenched open with a pop. Hesitant, Anna scuffled in after him. A whiff of mildew brushed her nose.

Unlike Jackson's home, this place did not put her at ease. Thick carpet swelled around her feet, stained and a little crunchy, the color of infertile dirt. Holes in the walls exposed pipes. She didn't have to go in the kitchen to know grime and old grease caked the appliances, or that in the bathroom, dark rings streaked the bathtub and toilet.

"Well," Frank lifted his arms as if to say, *Welcome!*, though his face still frowned like it knew no other way. "Bit lower end than what you're used to, boss, but it's got everything you need."

Anna turned to Jackson, who had padded in after her. His mouth was hanging open. By the look in his eyes, she could tell he was a little horrified as he let his crate topple onto the floor. "Er, these are the *accommodations...*?"

"Don't give me that. It's the best I could do in less than 24 hours. Lucky

I could find anything at all. And you know what? Ain't nobody knows you're here, 'cept me and her." Frank jabbed a thick thumb at Anna. "'Sides, you've lived on a lot less."

Jackson wrapped his arms around himself and fell silent.

Anna stepped further into the room, setting her own crate down. "It's not so bad," she spoke, fighting not to sound weak, forcing a smile on her face. A cockroach twice as long as her fingernail emerged from a hole in the wall and skittered underneath an ugly paisley couch. Anna swallowed back her disgust and tried again for optimism. "That, um, sofa looks pretty comfortable."

"It better be. I don't know how long you both gotta be here."

Jackson blinked. "Both of us?"

"Yeah. I got *one* safe house. I'm getting another one together. It's gonna take a couple days."

"Alright." Anna smiled at Frank. "Um, thank you so much. Really." No matter what stains and bugs there were, no matter the smells, it still was no prison.

He shrugged. "The boss is paying for it."

Anna moved to the window, feeling drawn there. The afternoon sunlight kissed her, and for a moment, the warmth made her feel like everything was going to be just fine, that at least the sun was consistent in a confusing and frightening world. She wasn't running around anymore. She had a bed for the night. She wondered if it would be strange to sit in this sunbeam and enjoy it for a while, like a child or cat would.

Frank came up behind her and slammed the blinds shut. "Now, look— you want this place to be safe, you have to keep it that way." He motioned to the window. "Keep this blocked. Don't answer the door for *nobody*. Anyone who ought to get in here has a key. Stay quiet. *Do not go outside.* Anything gets busted or stops working, you call me or report it to the delivery guy. He's gonna come once a week on Tuesday morning."

Jackson blinked through a dead stare, looking exhausted. "Is that... tomorrow?"

"Yeah. So there ain't any food here tonight. Tough it out until morning."

Anna sighed. She'd been freed, and she was still trapped. *No. This is better. This is only for now. Not forever, not like what those other people wanted.*

Frank jerked his head at Jackson, and together they disappeared into the kitchen. Anna heard them continuing to speak in hushed voices. She suspected it might have something to do with what she'd overheard earlier. *Jackson thinks some 'Order' is trying to kill him. Why? He... he seems so nice. Well. Even if he might be a smuggler. Is the Order with the Coalition?*

She worried her bottom lip, and knew she would ask him. Just, not until she knew how.

The cockroach crept out from under the sofa, lazily sensing the air and wandering along the floor. Perhaps it had made its home so long without humans that it had forgotten to fear them. Anna watched it go, repulsed, but too tired to chase it.

She, Anna Matthews, was on the run from the military, holing up with another fugitive. Her mother would have laughed so hard at the idea that she would have cried.

Mom.

Anna started to breath faster, and she squeezed her eyes shut, trying not to think about her family, feeling as sick as Jackson looked. Instead, she brushed her shorn hair back and padded around the living room, looking for books, a television set, anything. But, there was nothing at all, just a table near the sofa, the couch itself, and four walls.

She sat, the couch squeaking under her. A lamp was on the table, the bulb broken off. She centered the base, disturbing a ring of dust.

With that, she was on her feet again, going towards the bathroom. Underneath the sink, there was a shiny wire scrub pad and sponge, a bucket, a bottle of soap, and a tub of bleach that looked untouched. These walls, this dirt, it was her enemy now. She needed work. She needed *something*.

In the living room, she started scrubbing at the walls. Eventually, she heard a heavy stomping, and then the door slammed so hard that it rattled on its hinges. She stared at it. That... had to have been Frank. He wasn't one for goodbyes, it seemed. Jackson quietly padded out of the kitchen after. Anna resumed looking at the wall. The barest of the neutral cream paint was peeping out from under the layers of nastiness, the work of her scrub pad. After so long in bed, it felt amazing to work her arm muscles back and forth, pushing back the neglect, focusing only on it, on the improvement, on bringing *something* back to normalcy.

Jackson was silent. She heard the squeak of the couch, and knew he'd sat. She didn't need to look up from her work. She'd been shut up alone in that room for so long that his very presence was palpable in her mind, and oddly... reassuring.

Her hand kept looping its soothing circle on the wall. Now there was only the scrape of her cleaning pad on the plaster and the wait.

The tapping started about a minute later. She darted her eyes to Jackson, and saw his leg bouncing out a nervous rhythm as he stared at an empty spot in the air. At first, she didn't say anything, knowing he might need space to process his life turning upside down. She couldn't think of anything to say more than a stream of *I'm sorry.*

The tapping kept up for a good hour, as she worked at the walls as high as she could reach, finally completing two sides of the room. Anna decided to try, "Are you okay?"

The tapping paused. "Yes." His voice seemed oddly high. Anna glanced at the dark pall under his eyes, his face weary and his shoulders ramrod straight. *Hi*, she thought, *I'm the woman who thinks she's from another time, though I might just have schizophrenia. Can I make you more comfortable with this somehow?* But, she was going to make it, thanks to Jackson and Frank. She had to find some way to pay them back, help them not regret this. And... and Agent Walker. And the woman called Nyx. If they made it. They had to have made it. She wasn't worth them dying for.

"I don't suppose you brought any video games," she tried again.

Jackson ceased moving, processed this for a second, and then let out a bark of laughter. Anna smiled. It was a weak overture, she knew, but despite everything, a smile lit his face for a moment, and she saw a glimmer of the playful company she'd come to enjoy. "Frank confiscated my datapad. I just have a burner, and it doesn't even have wide data access."

The terms were a little unfamiliar, but she got the gist of the response. "Good for you then that I smuggled my Nintendo through time and space, and out of that government place. Had it under my hospital nightgown, you know."

He laughed again at her joke, though it took a second, and she wondered if he even knew what a Nintendo was. His stare returned to nothingness, and the conversation didn't continue, but his fidgeting didn't resume either. It was a companionable quiet. This continued until the sunlight around the edges of the blinds faded away. Anna reached for the light switch, flicking it on, but nothing happened.

"Um, I think we don't have power."

"Oh? Must be darktime." He checked his datapad. "Yeah. It is."

"…Darktime?"

Jackson stared at her. "Oh. Oh! No power to the residential grid. Right now it starts at seven. It'll be back on at six in the morning."

"Why on earth…? They just *turn off* New York City?" This hadn't happened in her cell, but Jackson's face seemed to convey that this was no new concept at all. "Do they… do they do that a lot?"

"Every night." He paused. "Did you really not have darktime before?"

"No! I guess a blackout happened now and again? But only for a few minutes!"

"You had power on *at night?*" The idea seemed so unbelievable he was gaping again. Anna felt adrift. Then, his eyes shut, and he nodded. "Right. Right, you wouldn't have had The Barrier in 2022."

This subject jabbed her like a hot needle. She was desperately curious about the glowing blue sky, and at the same time, she didn't want to know, because she sensed the implications of such a device being necessary. "What does The Barrier do?" Her question was only a whisper.

"It keeps out the worst of the radiation on the wind. And the raiders. It just… it needs a lot of power. We don't have the resources to keep it up, not and give everyone electricity all the time. It's not as bad as a few decades ago. But The Barrier is the most important thing we have. It can never fail. So, this isn't so bad, not as long as it stands."

Anna bit her lip, rubbing her arms, dropping the filthy scrub pad back into the bucket. *How was it built? What happened to the people that didn't have one? Why is there so much radiation?* Yet, with how her heart hurt, she was certain this was all the information she could handle for one day.

"Best thing to do at darktime is read. But, I don't think Frank loaded the datapad up. He's a bit overly practical like that. Might want to get some rest, Anna."

"Yeah."

Neither of them moved. Anna glanced down the hall. She'd only seen one bedroom, one bed.

"I'll take the sofa," Jackson offered.

"You don't have to."

"Oh no," He bounced up and down a bit where he sat. "It really does seem very comfortable."

Anna sighed, feeling bad, but knowing it might be fruitless to argue, wondering if she could talk him into a trade-off the next night. "Thanks. Um. Good night, Jackson."

"Good night," he returned, and she saw his eyes return to that same empty spot in the air as she walked to the bedroom and closed the door.

This room seemed to be free of holes in the walls and bugs. That was a good sign. It was hard to sleep with the idea of… skittering… things… getting on her. Yet, there were also no sheets, no blankets, no pillows. She fell back onto the bare mattress, trying not to think of its past occupants.

The world was quiet, far more so than she ever imagined New York could be. A New York with fewer people, she wondered. Fewer cars. Fewer animals. A quiet city under a glowing blue night.

How many of these apartments were empty or abandoned? The deserted hallways had weighed on her, as if the building would have to be very old to have accrued so much filth, as if the ghosts were still here from when it was shiny and bright. Was it possible that this place had stood when she'd been alive in 2022? If the world had been poisoned with radiation… how many were killed? Had it at least been quick?

A ceiling fan hung overhead, dead and still, and there was no way to relieve the sweat on her skin or the swollen ache in her eyes. Anna sighed and removed her shirt, balling it up under her head as a makeshift pillow.

There was a faint hum in her ears, foreign and constant in the silence. Was that... could that be the dome in the sky?

It was strange. It wasn't just a hum. As her mind slowed, she thought she heard a woman's voice, faint, just beyond her comprehension. The woman was singing.

She didn't know if she would be able to find sleep at all, but somehow, she did. Her dreams were disjointed, unsettling, visions of hallways filled with the dead. She heard thundercracks, saw monsters chasing her, and then, she fell on her knees in the wake of an overwhelming light, light so piercing she couldn't see at all anymore.

Anna awoke to a voice, muffled and strange. For a moment, as the sleep fell away, Anna thought of forests and campfires, though she didn't know why. After listening for a moment, she realized the voice was real, and was just beyond her door. Bleary-eyed, she saw it was still dark out, and she wondered how much time had passed since she'd lain down and, against all odds, slipped into dreams.

Who was talking? Jackson? Anna pulled her wrinkled shirt on and opened the door a crack, and his voice continued, quiet, erratic, and incomprehensible. Curious, she crept to the living room. Every instinct told her to reach for the light switch that her higher order of thought *knew* wouldn't work. The darkness was so absolute that she nearly walked right into the couch.

After a moment, she finally figured out what she was seeing and hearing as she squinted in the black. There was Jackson, fully dressed and curled up in a ball, twitching and sweating and dreaming, his mouth moving as if he was talking to someone. Now that she was close, a few of the words were understandable.

"...nothing to do with it," he said. "Not the classroom."

He rolled onto his other side and made a distressed noise, and Anna winced. She thought about going back to bed, feeling like an intruder on something private. Whatever was happening, though, it didn't seem pleasant. A friend would wake him up, right? Maybe she would say she couldn't sleep and wanted to insist he take the bed, let her try the couch. Yes, then he wouldn't be embarrassed.

"Jackson?" she whispered. He didn't respond, so she bit her lip and gave his arm a gentle shake.

He didn't open his eyes. *"No."* The response sounded almost like a plea. *"I'm not going with you."*

The lamp suddenly toppled off the table with a crash, and she jumped a half foot in the air. Jackson didn't notice, and his eyes kept fluttering in his sleep. Had he kicked the table? What had happened? Her heart hammered. She hadn't seen him do it, but...?

"Jackson," she tried again, heart tapping louder, shaking his arm. "Hey. Um. It's Anna. It's okay. I'm really sorry, but I need to wake you up."

Jackson made a noise, and seized her hand. Shocks burst through her palm. His eyes were shut and screwed up with what almost appeared to be pain, and his grip, though his fingers seemed thin, was iron. She struggled against it, but he just drew her in closer.

And then, Anna's hand, aching, began to glow.

She whimpered and tried to pull herself away, but Jackson's grasp wouldn't budge. A soft yellow pulse fluttered under her skin, and she recognized the same glow from the video Reeds had shown her, the *impossible* video. *Oh God oh God oh God. Stop!* Anna shook his other arm now, desperate to wake him up and get free, and still, he only locked her in tighter, mumbling, ignoring her frantic whispers. The soft light made the sweat on his forehead shine.

"Message," he said. "Message received."

He released her without warning. Anna almost smacked herself in the face as the tension went slack. Quietly, she stood, rubbing her aching fingers, panting, and the glow dimmed, like a faint heartbeat going back into hiding.

What... just happened?

The dark pressed down on her like a suffocating curtain. There were no answers. Jackson snored softly.

Anna huddled up on the other end of the sofa, heart dancing a frightened rhythm. She was both unwilling to retreat in the dark by herself, and unwilling to try waking Jackson again. Eventually, she curled up in a ball to match Jackson's, listening to his whispers, no longer words she could understand, but words that meant she wasn't alone. Long after the light under her skin subsided, Anna kept her wide eyes leveled at her hand, wondering if it would betray her again.

For the first time since she'd been a tiny girl, she thought about praying, and her plea was for morning to come.

CHAPTER THIRTEEN
Seeds

Jackson awoke with a start, uneasiness in his chest. For a moment he fumbled with the unpleasant mildew smells and the rough scratch of an unfamiliar couch, and he darted upright, heart pounding. Then, he remembered where he was, and he shut his eyes, shaking his head.

Without the tea, dreams had wound around his mind, and he'd shuffled through dark, dusty wastes in the night. A coffin-shaped box had sat in the middle of a clearing, a raven perched on the rim. But when Jackson peered inside, there was no woman. There was his dead father instead, staring up at him with glassy, accusing eyes.

The howling of wolves was sounding in the distance. There had been laughter riding through the wind, haunting and terrifying, and Jackson kneeled before the coffin, frightened, mourning, and unable to move. Yet, even stronger on the wind was the whisper of the starry-eyed man. *You are not being clever. Be more clever, Jackson.* The words refused to leave his thoughts, even after he woke up. And, woke up he had, seven times.

Still, as exhausted as he was, he kept returning to sleep.

He ran across the wastes, ran from the box, the panting of hot, animal breath on his ankles. For just a second, he turned to see what was chasing him. The tiger-man from the arena was there, bounding after him on all fours, tail bobbing behind, his face contorted into a demon's smile and wolves at his side.

The rusty spear was lashed to his back.

There was a flash of crimson in the trees, and the announcer in red stepped right into Jackson's path, blocking his escape. The masked man lifted his hands to the sky and crowed, "I don't think he's getting back up from this one, folks!"

Jackson's shoe caught on a rock. Claws sunk into his back...

...And he was falling, falling, and there was a boy with a beetle in his hands, a questioning whistle in his voice.

"Gotta get your destiny, Jack."

A door in a classroom was opening, and Jackson fell entirely into blackness, desperate not to know what was coming for him—

The final time Jackson awoke, it was the barest beginnings of dawn.

He caught the impression of another person in his peripheral vision, and flinched away. *Oh.* It was Anna. He eased, but only slightly, still shaking and alert. She lay on the other end of the couch, balled up as well, face slack, asleep.

What on earth was she doing there? Was there something wrong with the bed?

Maybe she just didn't want to be alone.

Jackson sighed, grounding himself. Despite the optimism and cheery talk, he knew she was frightened. He decided not to wake her. She deserved a little bit of peace and rest.

Her relaxed expression and easy breathing almost made him a little envious, really. Jackson sighed and smiled at her without thinking of it. The strange warmth and familiarity he felt with her tugged at him, that which he'd felt when he first saw her asleep, trapped in the box in the wastes. He reached out and brushed aside a bit of roughly shorn hair from her face. It had grown out a full inch overnight, a blond halo already over her head. *Is that normal for her...?*

He jerked his hand back. *You cannot get attached.* The voice in his mind was now Frank's. Jackson wrung his hands, embarrassed, angry with himself.

Last afternoon had not been pleasant, not with Frank. Apparently, all of the past week had bubbled and seethed inside of that balding, grimacing head, and the moment Frank had dragged him off to the kitchen without Anna, well... Jackson had known it was coming, like he had seen the shark in the water making a beeline for his boat. Still, he tried to dodge it, peppering his advisor with logistics. "What do you think we should arrange for business matters while I'm cut off from communication? Are you going to—"

"Boss," Frank started, as serenely gruff as he always was.

"...Yes?"

"Why don't you tell me what's going on?"

"What part?"

Frank's teeth had bared in a snarl. "*All of it*. I got almost *nothing* to go on, here, other than that frickin' Order is '*probably*' trying to kill you."

Jackson tried wiping the exhaustion from his face with his hands. It didn't help. And, when he spoke what he did know, Frank's look had turned darker.

"You didn't fucking *call me* when you mighta been *dying*."

"I didn't know I was dying! I thought I just needed to wait it out!"

Now, Frank's eyes were beady black fires. "And then that agent just took advantage of you, got you to arrange this *suicidal* run...!"

Jackson sighed, letting Frank's anger wash over him, too tired to argue. "You did well, though. Can't believe you managed to break out a government hostage. I'm glad she's okay." And, he was. For all of this madness, at least someone he liked was better off.

Frank's fists were balling up. And, suddenly, quick as a panther, he struck out, smacking Jackson under his left eye. It wasn't hard, it wasn't enough to do more than sting, and yet, the fact that Frank had done it at all made Jackson stagger back.

"You... you hit me!"

"And I'll do it again!" Frank rolled his thick neck, closing his eyes, as if forming words was difficult for him at that moment. "How long have we known each other, huh?"

Jackson glared, brushing his cheek.

"Right. Fifteen years. That's when your old man put me in charge of making sure you stayed alive, and I thought, great, I get to babysit this stupid teenager." His voice was still quiet, but it nearly simmered the air around them. "O' course, I figured you'd grow out of it. You snuck out of the house, I followed and kept an eye on you. You hit bottom when your dad died, I stayed on your couch for weeks to make sure you got out of it, poured all that damn whiskey down the drain. You kept getting into that freaky-ass hoodoo shit, and I let you sort it out, even though goddamn it, kid, I didn't sign up for that. But your dad was like family, and you are too. So, I was relieved when you grew out of most of the stupid, like I'd hoped." He leveled a finger at Jackson, as if trying to push the words through his head. "Now, finish growing up, *you dumb shit*."

Jackson fished for words, dumbfounded, largely at the fact that Frank had so *many* words at all.

"I get you *like* Anna," Frank continued in a low hiss, as if what Jackson liked was a nasty fungus. "But you cannot get attached to some freaky girl you found out in the wastes—*a mental patient*—that the government is hunting down. She seems nice and all. And, it ain't right, what the Coalition did. But you cannot get *attached*. The soonest chance we get, she's goin' in a different direction than you are, *for your own safety*."

Jackson stared. What the hell was he supposed to say? He could rail at Frank for insubordination, but it wasn't as if Frank would care. He could be furious that Frank still treated him like a child, but that, in itself, would sound childish. He could deny he was attached, but he... he couldn't. He couldn't even explain why. What were he and Anna? Friends? Fellow refugees? Why did he *care* so much that it almost hurt? "She's not a freak, and she's not a mental patient."

"Yes, she is. She's trouble, and way too much of it."

"I believe her." Jackson did not know why or when that had become true. Perhaps it was because he had begun to remember how impossible his own existence was, how many unanswered questions he had. "I'm not normal either."

"I *know*."

Jackson felt a little seed of anger sprout, one he'd nurtured for years. "Do you know *why* I'm like this, Frank?"

Frank growled, "No," as if to say he didn't really care.

"*I don't either.* And you cannot *possibly* understand what that's like. But you know what? Anna doesn't deserve to be treated like a freak, because I know how that is. I'm not going to let her go through that alone, like I had to."

"Boss, you're not gonna to tell her—"

"So what if I do?"

"That's *stupid!* What if someone gets to her, huh? What, you think she won't turn over your secrets in a second if they threaten her?"

"Frank, you work for me. Shut up. Anna gets moved to a different safe house on *my* orders."

Frank's face twisted into a scowl again, his fists tightening until his knuckles turned white. And, with that, the old man turned on his heel, leaving, and slamming the door to the rat hole of an apartment he'd brought them to. Jackson left the kitchen, sat on the couch, and a few minutes later, he could swear he heard the angry screech of a truck peeling out on the street far down below.

Jackson hoped Frank would not be so furious so as to prematurely retire. Still, Frank's churlishness and lack of respect *galled* him. The old man *never* would have spoken like that to his father. And neither of them would even be in this situation if not for Frank's insane proposition to get involved in the Coalition's messes…!

Anna stirred in her sleep.

Jackson sighed, mollified by her presence. *I guess… I did agree to that deal with Walker, too.* And, if he hadn't, Anna would have been found by the Coalition alone, and no one would have been the wiser. She'd be in that facility still. He was glad that, at least, they had changed that. Was it wrong that he should take pride that he and Frank's involvement should achieve her freedom?

Anna stretched and yawned lazily, her mouth upturning in a contented smile, her eyes still closed.

"Good morning," Jackson greeted, voice soft.

"Oh Jesus!" she cried out, sitting up with a jerk, looking around, panicked.

"Easy, easy! It's just me. I'm sorry."

"Jackson?" She blinked at him. Then, she rubbed her eyes. "Oh… I'm sorry. I thought… I thought you were a doctor for a second… from… um… that place." She frowned, yawned, and made a motion like she was trying to brush back her hair before realizing it wasn't there anymore.

Jackson shuffled his hands. "You didn't have an easy night either, I take it."

"No… sorry… I saw you were having nightmares, but you weren't waking up for anything." She rubbed the back of her head, looking awkward. "I guess I didn't make it back to bed."

"Oh!" Jackson's neck prickled with embarrassment, heat flushing his face. In his mind, he saw a tired Anna watching over him as he slept, mumbled, and drooled. He heard himself apologize again, felt his shoulders wrench tighter.

"Is it because… um… you're not feeling well? The nightmares?" Anna asked.

He winced, but he knew that perhaps anybody could have seen how sick he'd been. "Yes. I was taking some *medicine* to keep the dreams under control for years. I had to stop, recently."

"Why?"

"The medicine had some nasty side effects. Which is why I'm sick." There was an ache in his lower back, where his kidneys rested, still slowly working out the toxins. His blood felt sluggish, his eyes unfocused. But, Jackson knew, he was alive. He was getting better.

The witchbane packet was sitting in his suitcase. He didn't know fully why he'd taken it out of the bathroom trash. He didn't want to drink it… but he wanted to look at it, this thing that had been with him for so long. He wanted to understand it, the poison he'd always thought was medicine.

Anna was still giving him a concerned frown.

"I'm fine. They're… they're just dreams."

"What about? If you don't mind talking about it."

Jackson, startled she'd asked, wondered how much he could say. Would Anna understand…? No, it was too much, too soon. He might have threatened to Frank to tell her the secret about his background and abilities, but he didn't sense accepting magic's existence would be an easy conversation for her. Part of him didn't want to shatter something else in her world, not yet. "Thank you, but I'm alright." A weak smile.

She cast her eyes down. "Sorry, I'm prying. It's just... you've listened to my stories. You haven't called me crazy once. I promise there is nothing you can say that would make me judge you." She tilted her head, a soft smile drawing up her lips. "That's what friends are for."

Jackson settled back, somewhere between being perplexed and something he didn't quite understand. The unknown feeling left a warm tingle in his chest. Friends? He supposed that might be the word.

Either way, he didn't want to reject that tenuous trust in her eyes.

One secret, perhaps? One secret she could keep.

"Well," he said, his whisper filling the morning silence, feeling too loud. "I always see ravens. I don't know why. They've been in my dreams as far back as I can remember. Sometimes, there's an arena, with people fighting, trying to kill each other. And sometimes, there's this man in the shadows. He's usually laughing at me, or telling me to *be more clever*, or something equally useless. I don't know who he is."

Anna still appeared interested. "That's pretty Jungian."

"Er...?" Jackson didn't know what to make of this new word. "*Yoong?*"

"Jung. Um. I don't know if he's still taught."

Jackson shook his head. "I don't know. What did he say?"

"Well, I'm not an expert..." Her eyes apologized, but Jackson nodded her on. "Jung was a man who thought dreams contained universal symbols and archetypes." She paused, as if dusting off an old lesson in her head. "He thought that if you paid attention to what those dream symbols were telling you, you'd understand yourself and become a more complete person."

Jackson chuckled. "Ah. Dream interpretation?" Goodness knew he'd tried. His old therapist had dismissed the effort as stuff and nonsense. And, Huxley, well, was less than helpful with resources, seeing as Jackson wasn't One Of Them.

"I think there was one archetype that people could meet in their dreams who might taunt or challenge them. It was supposed to embody all the things in their unconscious mind that they didn't want to deal with. It was called..." she thought hard. "...The Shadow, I think."

Jackson's swallow caught in his throat in surprise and triggered a coughing fit.

"You okay?"

"I'm... I'm fine." No, he was not. "What else did Jung say about *The Shadow*...?"

Anna shrugged, her eyes again apologizing. "I, er, didn't put a lot of stock in dream interpretation either back then. I don't remember. Just kind of an interesting connection, I thought."

"Yes." A coincidence? The shadow man's pearly smile seemed to float in his mind's eye. *Chosen...* "I guess I see a lot of shadows in my dreams. Dark places. Sometimes, there are things I've only read about or seen in the old movies. Wolves. Forests."

Anna gave him a funny look.

Jackson wondered if she found him odd. No doubt she did. "I read a lot. It probably doesn't help my imagination."

"You've never seen a forest in person?"

"What? No! That's going beyond the *Barrier*. For fun? Gods, no. Central Park is enough."

"That's kind of sad."

"What? Was it common to leave the city in... your time?"

"Well, *yes*."

"Oh."

"One day, Jackson. One day, you should really go see. It's quiet. Peaceful. Nice."

Jackson sighed, not sure he believed that. Out there were the untamed wilds, unsafe water, bandits, and cancer. He rubbed his eyes again. But, for a moment—and perhaps it was just the way Anna said it—part of him suddenly craved sunshine and air that didn't smell like mildew.

"What does the shadow man look like?"

Jackson laughed. "It sounds ridiculous. He's wearing a fancy business suit, and his eyes are made of stars. And he has this grin like he knows a bunch of things he isn't going to share."

Anna was very quiet then, and he wondered if he had finally made her uncomfortable, or worse, bored her. But, after rolling around her thoughts, she spoke. "I think... that sounds really familiar somehow... stars... maybe he's from some old story you heard as a kid? Maybe one your dad read to you? I used to dream about fairy tales when I was younger."

"Oh, no, my dad didn't..." Jackson paused, eyes wandering. Perhaps she was onto, well, *something*. Had the stranger been in a book of his? This shadow man?

The story that was kept from you, the dream man had whispered. *The book of stories.*

"Your dad didn't what?"

Jackson sighed. "He didn't really read to me. I was already about thirteen or fourteen, they think, when I was adopted. Before that... I don't know much before that." Jackson fidgeted, reflecting back on the tattered old books stuffed into orphanage shelves. The headmistress had told him they had gotten him to read well before he'd begun speaking, when all he had to say were snarls and growls, habits from his extended time on the streets. All he could really recall of that time was a gnawing feeling in his gut, the baying of feral dogs, and the hard scrape of concrete under his soft, bleeding toes. And in all of this, he could remember nothing about a dark man with starred eyes.

And yet... there was *something* to this train of thought. He felt it.

Anna had been quiet for a while, letting him think. Jackson finally gave up on it. "I used to think about the past a lot," he said, "not knowing where I came from. It never comes back. There's just..." He waved a hand over his head. "...*nothing* there."

Anna regarded him for a long moment, worrying her lip. Her voice was suddenly very soft. "How do you become okay with that? Walking around with a huge blank spot in your life?"

Jackson leaned forward. He had the strange urge to pat her on the shoulder, do *something* comforting. Not wanting to do anything that might bother her, though, he kept his hands to his sides. "It doesn't matter near as much as you might think it does."

She blinked at this, looking as startled by this response as if she'd walked into a wall. "...Oh?"

"I never got my memories back. But, I'm fine. Can't be bothered by what I don't remember."

"It doesn't bother you *at all?*"

Jackson thought on this, then lied. "No," he said. "Not a bit."

"Not knowing anything about your childhood? What about your parents?"

"If my biological parents wanted to be important in my life, then I doubt I would have been found the way I was. I've had a while to think about it, and honestly, recovering the past like that... it's much more important to worry about the present and the future." He tried to give her a reassuring smile. And, though he saw her struggle with it, she responded in kind, eyes grateful.

"I still think it would be nice to know why I *traveled* through *time*. I know exactly how insane it sounds. And to not know..." Anna hugged herself. "But... maybe you're right."

Jackson kept smiling, although he knew it was a little hollow. It was true that he'd never wanted anything to do with the memories he lost... until he'd begun falling apart. Still, Anna looked like she needed comfort more than a complicated truth. "Are you going to be alright?"

Her mouth upturned a little stronger now. "Maybe."

"Are you at least sleeping well outside of a holding cell, when I'm not keeping you awake?" His insides shuddered with embarrassment again. He found he wanted her to think well of him, not get annoyed by his... oddities.

Anna chuckled. "I'm thinking too much to sleep well. I guess I'm trying to figure out what I'm supposed to do when I'm not being hunted by the government."

Jackson blinked, unable to help but feel a pang of alarm. He hadn't lingered on the thought... but how long would either of them have to be in hiding? "Um. You could try to get back into what you did before."

She whispered, "I'm not sure there's a place for it anymore."

Jackson waited for an elaboration, but her eyes seemed to beg him not to ask. "Well… I'm sure someone intelligent like you could brush up on today's basics quickly enough."

"…Really?" The sag in her shoulders lifted a little.

"Sure. I've seen you read a Geiger counter, right? Lots of rad tech work, if you have the head for it. There are classes, and not all require identification. Had one in high school." He turned on the datapad, ran a search for radiation technicians, and handed over the job listings.

Anna took it, looking at it skeptically. "You had a class all about radioactivity?"

"Of course."

"…Huh."

Jackson looked back up at her. "Wait. I get it. You didn't learn that back then, did you? Oh! Ha! Twenty-first century. I bet they didn't even give out Geiger counters!"

"Pffft, people didn't even know what they were, unless they were ambitious and nerdy." Anna readjusted herself. "I was both."

"Toddlers learn how to use them now."

"What? That's crazy!"

Jackson shrugged, then pulled something deep out of his memory, something the headmistress had chirped once. "It starts to click, don't get sick. Nothing to hear, all clear." Anna stared, and he felt the heat rise in his face again. "That's what they say! I know it's silly. It's for kids."

She laughed then, with genuine mirth, and he snorted, feeling strangely pleased that she thought it was funny.

Jackson saw the sun turn brighter through the slits in the blinds as their conversation threaded on. It was warm chitchat for the most part, like their first conversations, like how people got around town, or the difference between Queens and Manhattan—safe things that didn't involve bombings, death, or the government. He fished his Geiger counter out of his bag and set it on the table for her, just in case she'd want to take a look at it later.

Perhaps, Jackson thought, as he poured himself a glass of water, he would stop worrying about the dreams or magic. Perhaps once he relocated, he might put it all behind him again, just remaining vigilant about his meditation and self control. His night, as far as he knew, had been free of shadows.

Anna tinkered with the datapad's limited software, occasionally tossing him questions. It was companionable, pleasant, something Jackson had not felt for a long time. Her presence didn't even cause him to look over his shoulder.

Then, there was a light knock at the front door, and the lock began to click and turn. Tensing in the kitchen doorway, Jackson reached into his pocket for his knife on instinct, before remembering Frank's words that a delivery person would be along that morning with supplies. He realized with a start that the knife wasn't even in his pocket, anyway. Where had it...?

A chilling thought occurred to him. He had pulled it out in his dream of the starry-eyed man, and he'd dropped it in the forest clearing in shock, never reclaiming it before waking up...

Jackson shook his head. *That's stupid. You can't lose your things in a dream.*

A young man with dusty brown hair and a white parcel service uniform opened the door. He was a stranger to Jackson, an angry red swell of flesh gobbed taut over where his right eye should have been. Jackson had seen such defects before, and politely cleared his throat to let the man know he was standing in his blind spot. The deliveryman turned his head and nodded.

Anna stared up at the newcomer with wide eyes, then smiled. "Oh hi! Are you the guy that brings breakfast?"

"That I am, miss." The deliveryman tread to the kitchen counter, setting down a crate with a grunt. "Enough rations for the week here. Got a message for you also, sir."

"Oh?" Jackson leaned up against the counter.

"Ol' Frank's been coordinating with your department heads. Telling them you're on sabbatical, I guess. But there were some things he didn't know. I guess some new contract came through on the sunshine side." Jackson nodded, interested. So, a legal bid had been successful. "I think he said it was for some clothing company?"

Jackson stood straighter. "The Yi bid?"

The deliveryman shrugged. "I dunno. Bit above my pay grade, sir. But I think it was something like that."

"That's great news!"

"Well, apparently they can't find some files they need. You know the numbers, right, sir?"

Jackson nodded. He'd memorized them. He memorized most documents of import.

"Great. Frank wanted me to get you to a secure location to make a short call to your departments and get them the information they needed. Or, well, that deal won't go through so well."

Jackson blinked. "Can't I write the information down?"

Again, the dusty-haired man shrugged, scratching a scar under his ear. "I'd think so, but Frank kept saying you needed to actually talk to them. Sounded like they had some questions he didn't understand."

...*What?* "It just sounds like an unnecessary risk. What if I called them from here? There's a wiped datapad—"

"That..." the deliveryman hesitated. "Frank sometimes has a bit of a saying. I apologize; it's kind of... well, he says *you can't shit where you eat*, sir. This call might be traceable. So, I'd be giving you a secure ride, like on your way here. We go there, make the connection, talk them up, then clear out."

Jackson crossed his arms, staring at the warped and stained fake tile. Frank was a paranoid man, and shrewd, for all of his bitterness. He was never the type to advocate risks like this unless he was certain it was worth it. But, the Yi deal could be worth it, *especially* if the Coalition work dried up, as it might if Walker was connected to Anna's jailbreak. Jackson could only hope Dovetail Parcel would remain disconnected from the situation if Walker was found out, and plan for the future.

Yet, something about the whole matter didn't sit with him, an unsettling twinge between his shoulder blades. Frank didn't let just anybody in on the important details, especially not a no-name proxy. "Why didn't Frank come tell me?"

The deliveryman frowned. "I don't know, sir. I just do what I'm asked. Been working with Frank for ten years, though, and I guess he's got a lot going on. Been kind of... ah... gruff about it."

Jackson clenched his teeth. Most likely, Frank was still angry about their argument. *Old man can be a real asshole sometimes.* He supposed the information this man gave him would have to be enough. Something like the Yi deal wouldn't wait. "Alright. Let's go." He fished in the crate, grabbing a ration packet, looking forward to doing some work. Conveniently, he was still dressed in the courier disguise from yesterday—just a little wrinkled. That would do for the ride. He plucked up his bag from the living room, figuring he could change into a suit for the call. "Anna, you'll be alright?"

Anna nodded from the couch. Jackson saw she was wringing her hands. "Be safe?"

Jackson felt an inexplicable tugging in his chest that matched the twinge in his shoulders. "I'll be fine." If Frank trusted this man, then Jackson knew he could trust Frank's judgment. "See you soon."

"Okay. Good luck." Anna nodded again, her stare lingering a moment longer before the door shut between them, and Jackson followed the deliveryman down the corridor.

Outside, a raven was perched on a crumbling concrete wall. It hopped from one foot to the other, its feathers puffed in agitation. Its beak was open and its wings were flared, as if it was trying to get Jackson's attention. He paid the bird no mind. *No more of that nonsense.* Though its mouth moved, the raven was as silent as a ghost, and Jackson found it easy to put the mute hallucination out of his thoughts as the truck ambled him away.

CHAPTER FOURTEEN
Memento Mori

There was a tremble in Anna's fingers that belied her neutral expression. She tapped to the next page of the job site, trying to keep her thoughts mellow, even, in the now.

It had been a brave face she'd been putting up for Jackson. Maybe if she did it for long enough, maybe she would eventually believe it.

It was kind of Jackson to let her borrow the datapad, to stay up with her for hours, just talking. And, she considered... he might be right. Did her memory loss matter? From a scientific standpoint, if all of this was true, of course it did—time travel was incredible. It was groundbreaking. It was thought to be impossible.

But then, there was the fact that it had happened to *her*, had destroyed her life as she knew it. Whatever had torn her out of time, it was a hundred years gone, and agonizing over it would change *nothing*.

There was something screaming in the back of her mind, and she shied away from it.

Despite the sleep deprivation, Jackson's eyes had been brighter, and his skin had lost the waxy look it had when she'd arrived. After he'd made a run to the bathroom during their talk, washing up and shaving, he'd started transforming into the businessman she'd envisioned, a confidence entering his step. Anna was glad to think he might be out of the woods regarding whatever sickness had brutalized him so much.

She knew less about Jackson than any other person she'd called friend, but he was the only person here in this future that she even knew anything at all about, the only person who didn't seem to have an agenda. Everything about him put her at ease, for some reason, made her feel like she could laugh and be okay. She'd miss him, she realized, when she was moved to the other safe house.

Would that be today? Tomorrow, maybe? Where was she even going? She couldn't expect to be laying low forever. Thinking of the future, she'd poked at the handful of job sites Jackson had pulled up. *The Exciting World of Being A Rad Tech*, one blared. It involved endless soil and livestock analysis, nothing that was her first pick at a career... yet, in its favor, rad techs were most in need outside the dome, in the settlements under the real sky, none of the constant electric blue glow, that faint hum in the back of her ears.

The jobs were largely migrant labor. If that worked anything now like it did in her time, the Coalition might not be watching the migrants too closely. Perhaps the messy issue of citizenship papers would go away.

She sort of liked the idea of helping people make their lives and stay healthy. A part of her said *at least I would be doing some good*, then the rest of her felt terribly guilty for even trying to put a silver lining on things. Her mind began to quaver and reach back to her mentor, Dr. Appleby. That last day, he'd invited her to come on board to a new project. He'd respected her... Anna's stomach gave a terrible drop.

I'm sure someone intelligent like you could brush up on today's basics quickly enough. Jackson's words of encouragement echoed, dragging her back to the now, and she clung to them. She could do this. She had to believe she could do this, or she was going to curl up on the sofa and wail.

Anna stood up, flexing her tired hands and wrists, beginning to walk and think, trying to keep occupied. She knew that if she looked at the datapad any longer, she might be tempted to search for information about what had happened to the world in her absence, and she knew she wasn't ready for it. Glancing at the Geiger counter Jackson had left for her on the coffee table, she thought to tinker with it soon. It looked like it might operate in the same way in this time, but it was best to be sure.

A pair of dirty glasses caught her eye in the sink. Wanting a break from thinking about radiation, she washed them clean, and began to wander, looking for things to do, ways to be useful—*busy hands, busy mind*, a voice like her mother's informed her. If she could help with a little housework, then she was earning her keep.

The room Jackson had let her borrow had nothing out of place, no bed sheets to fix.

Anna frowned.

She wandered down the hall, looking for more. In the kitchen, it was much the same story. A home no one really lived in, and nothing to do.

Anna closed her eyes, breathing deep. An image of home sprung to mind. She saw her ancient appliances. She saw her bright-eyed calico cat. She saw the box full of old research papers from college, not ready to be thrown out, but not ready to be stored, either.

Then, Anna realized... she couldn't remember how it smelled, the place where her presence had been strongest, not over the scents here. Home's scent had been distinct, welcoming, comforting in a way she could not describe. But, the memory was gone. She was losing the details.

Shaking her head, uneasy, she began to leave the room.

Knock knock knock.

Her heart froze. The sound was coming from the living room.

Knock knock knock. Louder now. The door! But... who would knock? Frank had said his people would have a key. Anna's hands shook, her throat constricting. Coalition agents? *What do I do?* If someone was at the door, an agent, they might bust it down within seconds.

Anna inched to the living room. She didn't have anywhere to go, or hide, other than out a fire escape—but she knew that the Coalition probably wouldn't be so stupid as to leave a possibility like that unguarded. Then, a shifting of light caught her eye.

The silhouette of a bird was illuminated beyond the window blinds.

Knock knock knock.

"Really?" Anna said aloud, realizing where the sound was coming from. She parted the blinds a half inch and glared at the bird. It was surprisingly huge, taller than her forearm, and black as ink. The raven tilted its head up at her and ceased its tapping. "Awwww!" she heard it cry through the glass. It looked genuinely surprised someone had cared enough about its racket to come glare at it.

Anna sighed, swallowing her anxiety down. At least this might make a funny story later. That was, if she wanted to tell Jackson she'd been scared by a bird. *Good job, girl.* She lifted the window blinds just enough to pound back on the glass. The raven ruffled its wings and backed up, staring at her archly, beak open, as if laughing. Anna shook her head again, annoyed.

The kitchen lights flickered. Well, good. At least "darktime" was over. Maybe the hot water would be back, too.

And then, with no warning, Anna *remembered*, collapsing as if she had been hit with a truck.

Ravens.

The radio in her car was on, and she was nodding her head in tune with some pop dance remix—something about going to the club, where the singer rhymed "club" and "love" like they were remotely similar words. Still, the tune was keeping her awake as she hauled her old car through the Mojave Desert. Her dream job had not come with a dream commute.

The road was lined with an old wiry fence, which sagged and splintered in places, cordoning off barren, rocky land. Anna sipped her coffee and gazed absently at the fence and the road lines, watching them stretch forever into the horizon. The clouds had been flat wisps, the landscape a painting frozen in time. And then, she had seen them.

Ravens.

Nearly twenty of the massive birds were clustered on a segment of wire. She normally would have thought nothing of the flock. But, as she passed, in the span of half a second, they lifted their heads and turned with her, as if they weren't twenty birds at all, but one mind in many bodies.

Her stomach made an apprehensive leap. Some old story in her memory surfaced. *Omens of death. Ravens.* She laughed it off, trying not to think about how their beady black gazes had unsettled her, and took another sip of coffee.

Anna arrived at work, slid her badge, and sat patiently through the twenty minutes of security screening, even though everyone here knew exactly who she was. She'd wished the old guard well and gone to her office... but something, something pulled her out into the hallway again...

It was a scream.

Anna's breath came in short spurts, her sense of time and place fogging.

Oh God. The world was a blur.

Screaming. Her friends, her colleagues, panicking, running. So much screaming.

Oh God. Oh God. A man with fire in his eyes and death in his hands. Screaming. Terror. Gun shots, so, so many gun shots. *Screaming.*

Anna came to her senses, and realized hot tears were streaming down her face. The tile under her cheek was damp and cold. Her throat was raw. Had she been yelling? Weakly pushing herself up, she rested her back to a cabinet, drawing herself into a ball, letting herself cry. Her ribs ached and her lungs hurt like she had been running straight from the memory and into the present.

Oh God.

She only had flashes of what came after the memory, pain and grief and confusion. It was still mostly a blur. Her chest hurt, a pellet of fire blazing under her skin. Anna massaged the tiny spot between her ribs.

I was shot.

This was something she couldn't quite remember. It was something she just... she just *knew*. Her body remembered.

I was shot! Who shot me?

Vertigo gripped her. Anna grabbed the edge of the sink and dragged herself up, leaning over it, trying not to heave.

Why did they shoot me?

The pain in her chest began dissipating as she made the sink her life raft, but it was slow.

Click. Click.

The Geiger counter looked up at her damningly from the table. It was taking a reading.

Not again. Anna forced herself over to a chair, stomach still turning, shutting her eyes, her chest throbbing. *Breathe in. Breathe out.* She tried to bring back her mental image of a beach, but it kept dissolving. She knew they were all dead. Knew it. Had known it from the moment she'd seen the dome instead of sky. But as long as she hadn't thought about it, it wasn't real. It had happened to someone else.

She couldn't hold it at arm's length anymore.

Everyone was dead.

Her co-workers were dead. Her roommate was dead. Her family was dead. Her mentor Dr. Appleby was dead. They were shot, or they were disintegrated in nuclear hellfire. They were murdered a hundred years ago. Everyone was dead.

Everyone except... me.

Click. Click click.

Anna's breathing hitched and cracked, tears streaming. She tried again for the beach, but it wouldn't hold. The only thing she could draw out of herself was a long wail, a mournful cry for her mother, the woman who, despite everything, she'd loved. She cried for the dead. She cried for herself, not knowing why she was alive.

It was many minutes before the wailing stopped coming out of her chest. Anna came to herself again, still trying to focus, to find some shred of peace left in her soul.

It's starts to click, don't get sick. That silly child's rhyme. In her mind's eye, there was Jackson, awkwardly reciting the Geiger counter jingle. He'd asked her what she intended to do that day, never questioning her story or memories. She put herself back on that couch, sharing a conversation with her friend.

The clicking slowed, and she ran through that memory over and over again, slamming her grief back into a box, shoving it down into her mental basement. No one was dead, not if she didn't think about it. There was only a childish rhyme, awkward laughter, two smiles, and the flickering of thoughts of her future.

Nothing to hear. All clear.

The clicking stopped.

Anna let out one last breath, head dizzy and achy from crying. She closed her eyes again for a few moments more, putting her horrible memories as far from her mind as she could, thinking about rad tech jobs and sunshiny beaches, the mildewy smell and the memory of serenely scrubbing a wall, over and over, circling a hand forward, then circling it back. Detached, she analyzed the numbers on the Geiger counter. The meter's reading had not crawled so high as to be dangerous. Everything was okay. Everything was okay.

I'm going to be okay.

No. No, I'm not.

Don't think about it.

She scooted her chair back out, wringing her hands, turning around.

An old man was standing in the kitchen.

Anna shrieked and backed up into the table. *Click. Click click.*

The stranger blinked at her owlishly, and stayed put. Though he'd badly startled her, he was making no aggressive moves, and Anna frantically tried to slow her racing heart again. Somehow—and perhaps it was because she was surprised enough to forget her pain—the counter stopped.

The stranger had the look about him of a lost grandfather, glancing around as if getting his bearings, even giving her a pleasant smile. He was short and unassuming, the top of his curly-haired head only coming up to her chin, and he wore a waistcoat with gold buttons covering his portly belly. His eyes shone bright over a white, sweeping mustache. "Oh my," the man said with a polite look of befuddlement.

"*Who are you?!*" Anna demanded. The words came out angry. Chastised, not meaning them to, she bit her lip.

He merely blinked. "Who are *you?*"

Anna's mouth opened and closed, her nerves shot. Her logical mind presented her with several options. One, the man was from the government.

This was unlikely, as he did not seem to recognize her. Two, the man was some friend of Jackson's or Frank's who had a key. Still, he didn't seem to be there to deliver anything, just seemed confused to see her, so this didn't sound believable either. Three, the old man was in her head, and she really *was* crazy.

Anna struggled to think of a fourth option, not liking any of the above.

"Oh, I'm sorry, my dear," the old man withdrew a handkerchief and wiped his forehead. "You must be *Anna*. Jackson's told me about you." Anna didn't know how to respond. Jackson hadn't warned her about any visitors she should expect, nor did Jackson strike her as someone who would go around telling just anybody about the government refugee holed up in his safe haven. The old man only continued giving a beatific smile, like he was speaking to a favorite grandchild, and fiddled with the tip of his fluffed mustache with two fingers. "Is Jackson here?"

Anna heard herself politely squeak, "I'm afraid he's at work right now."

"Oh?"

"...Who are you again?"

"I'm Huxley. Theodore Huxley. A pleasure." He extended a hand, several thick rings glittering on his fingers, and Anna shook it, not knowing what else to do. Huxley's eyes twinkled.

Well... he feels solid. He doesn't feel like a crazy hallucination. Anna ruled out that explanation. "Ah... so... how can I help you?"

"I'm just a little concerned about Jackson's health, lately. I was checking in on him. How is he?" Anna bit her lip again, not feeling it was her place to say. "My dear, you can be honest with me. We Huxleys and Dovetails... we go back for generations. I've known Jackson since he was just a boy, and, to be truthful, I'm concerned he's not taking care of himself. He's been having a lot of bad dreams lately, hasn't he?"

"Um. Yeah. I guess so." Anna reached behind herself, unobtrusively hefting the heavy Geiger counter and letting it rest in her spacious back pocket. Whether or not this stranger was all grandfatherly smiles and twinkling eyes, she'd rather be paranoid than sorry.

Huxley continued, "Jackson seemed so glad to have met you. He's spoken highly of you. He's also spoken of your difficult situation—and the very, very confusing things happening to you—and he truly wants to help. As do I."

Anna, startled again, relaxed her grip on the Geiger counter. She still didn't know what to make of this man's appearance, but... well... suppose he was just there to help? And Jackson sent him? He was acting nothing like the other government agents. Perhaps Jackson had just forgotten to tell her Huxley was coming by, with everything else on his mind?

"Thanks," she finally said. "Jackson hasn't been feeling well. Did he know you were coming?"

"Of course."

"Sorry he's not here, then..."

"Quite alright. Has he been taking his tea?"

"What tea?" Anna blinked. "Sorry. I don't know."

Huxley gave a deep frown, smacking his lips. "Stubborn boy. Well, nothing to be done about it now. Anna, Jackson told me you're having issues with radiation. I may be able to aid you in getting this under control, but only if you accompany me right away. The head of the organization I represent has requested evaluating you personally. We don't want the Coalition getting wind of you being here, so I've arranged a safe transit."

Anna gaped. "I... what? Organization?"

"Yes. We help people like you. You're experiencing a flare. We deal with this all the time."

"*All the time?*"

"Well, it's not always the same. But Anna, there isn't a lot of time to waste. Your condition could be dangerous unless you have help. Will you come with me?"

"I..." Anna, though uncertain, stepped forward, feeling the Geiger counter in her pocket. It's chirpy click weighed heavy in her memories. "Yes. I need help. Thank you. *Thank you.*" Silently, she sent a warm thanks to Jackson, too.

Huxley nodded, and clapped his hands together. "Excellent! Let's get started, then." And, he began to mutter, a whispering chant. Anna raised an eyebrow. The chant had an odd quality to it, as if it was beginning to resonate through the air, through the floor, through her body. She stepped back, suddenly afraid. The strangeness of what the old man was doing struck her, and fear—did she know who this Huxley was, really? What was he doing? Why was the room tingling and thrumming?

A crushing pressure exploded in Anna's head.

No! She backed up into the table, and her legs seized with paralysis. She felt herself fall. Her eyes went blind. Panicked, she tried to thrash, a thick air plugging up her lungs.

Without warning, the pressure vanished. The feeling in her muscles returned, and she could breathe, though she felt like she was made of jelly. Carpet pressed into her face. Groaning, she staggered up, vision still dark, a panic beginning to boil.

The scents of incense and spice told her that somehow, some way, she was no longer in the safe house.

CHAPTER FIFTEEN
For Jack

The sky above roiled with thick slate-gray clouds beyond the electric blue Barrier sheen. Thunder rattled the air, rain popping in firecracker shots against the energy field, never to make it to the city below. From where Jackson sat in the truck, it looked like the heavens were simmering.

The driver had been quiet for the last twenty minutes. Jackson pulled his hat down, unsettled by the tension in the air and the feeling of being out in the open. The breakfast ration bar was mealy and flavorless in his mouth. It seemed his stomach wasn't entirely ready for food yet. "Where is this location?"

"Not far, sir."

"Good. But, that doesn't answer my question."

The driver sighed. "Old subway station. Closed since the Bombings, up on 175ᵗʰ St."

Jackson narrowed his eyes. Some rat-infested, shuttered train stop? "And we'll have a connection in there?" The city's coverage was sometimes iffy inside of his own home, much less underground.

"Frank's got it set up. Been using it for years. Don't worry about it."

Jackson sighed and figured it would have to do. At least, it didn't sound like the kind of place where he would find the Coalition, either.

The electricity of the thunderstorm felt like it had settled in the tense spot between his shoulder blades. His knee bounced. He didn't like this, abandoning the cover of his safe house not twelve hours after stepping inside. *But, we do what we have to do.* He only hoped Frank wasn't using this opportunity to go against his directive about moving Anna.

You know he's right about it being safer.

Jackson huffed at no one.

He did have to hand one thing to Frank, though: the neighborhood the truck pulled into was nigh deserted. A rise of rusted fence with chips of teal paint marked the abandoned station, the stairway down blockaded by rubble and plywood. The driver ignored the fencing and drove past, parking in a discreet garage almost a block away. Then, he took a deep breath as he shut off the engine, as if he too was wary. "Alright. Now, I'm going get some packages and drop them off at the apartments across the street. You're going walk to the back of the garage and go into the maintenance closet."

"The closet."

"Yessir." The driver rubbed the taut red welt where his eye might have been, as if it itched. "You'll find another door that's unlocked for the next five minutes, and a tunnel going down. It's going to take you to the station."

"*Frank* had a *tunnel* dug."

The driver snorted. "No, it's been there who knows how long. Useful, though. My colleague will meet you at the bottom, tell you what you need to do. I'll be up here until you get back."

With that, the driver scampered out of the cab. Jackson eased himself out as well and began walking to the back of the garage, leaving his half-eaten breakfast on the seat and taking up his bag. A green door labeled *Maintenance* caught his eye, the same teal the station fencing once was. He glanced over his shoulder to confirm with the driver, but the dusty-haired man was in the back of the truck now, the clanging sounds of a dolly accompanying his work.

Jackson turned the doorknob.

As promised, a supply room lay beyond. Canisters were toppled haphazardly on shelves, grime and rust so thick on them that the labels were long since illegible. Someone had thrown cardboard boxes against the wall in a wet-smelling pile. On the ground, swinging out from behind the boxes, was a door's path traced in the filth.

The boxes were empty, and easily moved out of the way. There was the door, and as promised, it opened. A crude dirt tunnel wound down into the dark.

Jackson was glad for his good night vision. His hand traced the wall as he strode without hesitation into the gloom, his shoes scuffing against the dirt, well-packed and well-trod. It seemed it was true that the tunnel had been in use for a while. Perhaps it had been dug even before his father's time and used by other smugglers. After a short walk, it opened up to reveal a hole in a cinderblock wall, a haphazard entrance smashed into the station. No one had bothered to conceal the tunnel on this end. Jackson supposed no one was going to find it anyway, not unless they dug out the main entrance first. The shuffling of his shoes on dirt changed into the clack of tile and the crinkle of archaic paper and garbage, the chitters of rats flying before him.

The station smelled of old rot and damp filth. This level of darkness, even for Jackson's practiced eyes, was almost suffocating. Where was this person that was supposed to meet him?

As Jackson listened, his ears picked up the almost hidden hum of a generator now. He kept walking, hand to the cool wall, following the sound. A little light met his eyes further down the station corridor, where the train stop itself sat. Was that... the catch of a voice? Jackson pressed on. He hoped this call was quick. Every last one of his nerves was painfully on edge. He didn't like this place. The air felt... greasy somehow. Like it buzzed.

His shoe caught the edge of a shattered bit of tile, and he stumbled, catching himself. Grunting, knee stinging, Jackson stared at his feet and the old litter.

The low whine of an alarm began in his mind.

He saw an old flyer, disturbed from the fine layer of dust that had settled over it. The ink was barely visible anymore, especially in the dark, but Jackson caught a smear of a familiar timetable. It was a subway schedule, circa 2022.

He scrambled up, the paper brittle in his hands, tearing and slipping. No, it wasn't a mistake. It was the same sort of flyer he'd been given that crayon letter on, that invitation to the underground fighting arena. *FOR JACK.*

Shit!

Jackson backed up.

Coincidence. It could be coincidence.

No. No, he wasn't going a step further. An unfamiliar driver, a surprise deal, the *exact* same bit of trash…!

Click.

The cold weight of steel rested against the back of his head.

"Huh," a gruff voice intoned. "And 'ere I thought ya were just gonna walk right in without any coaxin'. Well, least I earn my keep. Raise yer hands."

Jackson did so, knowing they shook. *Gods. Damn. It.* He willed his face and his breathing to slow.

"Ya gonna walk or not?" The steel nudged his skull less gently. Jackson began to move forward. He stumbled over the refuse, and the presumed gun fell into a relaxed press in the middle of his back.

"Who are you?"

"Who cares?"

"Who do you work for? The Coalition?"

The voice scoffed. "The *Coalition?* Ha. Hahaha."

Not government, then. "The Order?"

"Order of what?"

Not a mage. "Pegasus?"

"Who the hell are they? Tell ya what, why don't ya shut up. Make this whole thing go quicker."

Jackson pursed his lips and did so. A yellow, dim bulb burned his eyes as they rounded the bend, illuminating the platform and two yawning black tunnels in either direction.

"Watch yer step. Now, just stand here."

Jackson didn't try to run. He stood, breathed, and let his eyes flicker across the room. Trying to run down a tunnel was a bad idea, despite the fact that no train had used this line to go this far north in over a century, and he doubted they would start now. He turned his head though, just a little, to give his captor a sidelong look—a thickly built thug, nothing interesting or familiar, only a shaved head and a scar across his nose.

"Don't get uppity." The man waved his gun at Jackson, gesturing for him to turn back away. "Geez, yer a scrawny one. Weird choice. What the hell are ya, some kind of accountant?"

Jackson's mind spun. *They haven't killed me. They need me for something. We're waiting for someone else.* "You have no idea who I am."

"No, why should I?"

"I'm the president of a wealthy company. We've been in business for over a century."

"Good for you."

"Jackson Dovetail. Dovetail Parcel. Now, I can tell no one else is watching us. If you escort me back to the surface, I will pay you three times what your boss is paying you."

The thug was silent for a moment. Jackson felt a trickle of sweat run down his neck as the gun tapped the back of his head again. "...Oh. Yer *Jack.*" The name was spoken with a hush, like a whisper reserved for the dead.

Jackson's heart rattled, fear in his throat. "I'm a businessman and a man of my word. Ask my clients."

"*Oh* no. Nope. Keep yer money, Jack. I'm not touchin' a chit of it."

Jackson felt his jaw muscles grind trying to keep in frustration and panic. "Why?"

"Even if ya *weren't* who ya *are,* my boss is a lot scarier than any amount of credits in the world can pay to keep away."

Jackson swallowed. "And what does your boss want with me?"

The thug didn't answer, and Jackson knew he probably didn't know, nor did he likely care.

They stood in silence for long minutes, listening to the hollow drip of water. Jackson found himself wondering what would happen to the welt-faced man who had led him down here in the first place. *How much money does it take to betray me?* To get access to the safe house, that courier would had to have been one of Frank's most trusted.

A tiny part of Jackson wondered if Frank himself already knew. Business wasn't good. Extra money, a new boss...

No. Frank's practically family, no matter what. Frank wouldn't do it.

...Would he?

A sound began to echo in Jackson's ears. It was a steady swish and grind, swaying in from down the tunnel. Surprised, he whipped his head to listen. *That can't be...*

A light pierced the gloom, and a train car ground to a halt, lining up neatly with the ancient demarcations on the platform. Jackson gaped. There were no trains here. Everyone knew that. Yet, this ghost car hadn't gotten the memo. It was rusty, scratched, and worn, clearly a car time had forgotten, nothing like the ones that ran on the still-maintained lines. Draped across it, spilling over the side and covering the windows, was a rich red banner, sparkling with sequins. Calligraphic gold letters shouted: *Welcome to the greatest show in New York!*

The door neatly swished open. "Please watch your step," a crackled, yet soothing female voice spoke over an intercom.

"In ya go," the thug intoned, poking Jackson's head with the gun again.

Jackson, hesitating, stepped inside. Twenty pairs of eyes turned to meet him, curious looks glancing up from flutes of champagne. A crowd of people in their finest black tuxedos and shimmering gowns regarded him from velvet-lined seats as they lifted tiny hors d'oeuvres to their lips. All of their faces were obscured behind what looked like party masks. As quickly as he'd interrupted their enjoyment, they turned away, smiling, resuming conversations with each other.

"Have a seat," the thug said into Jackson's ear, holstering his weapon. "I will draw my gun again and blow yer head off if ya bother the other passengers."

Jackson sat and put his bag by his feet, unnerved by how clean, well-lit, and plush the train was. He looked to his left. Someone had set down a platter of crackers and what looked like—and this startled him—*real* sliced ham. The odor curled under his nose, and, for once, his stomach didn't turn. While watching his escort, he nicked one and popped it in his mouth, chewing slowly as the thug regarded him with a look of disbelief.

"The hell are ya doing?"

"Hungry." Jackson snagged an unassigned champagne flute from beside the platter and took a swig. "And I need a drink. Do you want one?"

The thug raised his eyebrows and shook his head, but sat back and let Jackson continue.

"I couldn't believe the match last month," a gentleman two seats away from them spoke, talking with his hands, the sapphire in his cufflinks flashing in the subway light. His mask was of blue velvet. "That boy with the club was fantastic! I hope we see him back again. The way he moved in his fight! What was his name… ah, it doesn't matter, you know the one—he smashed in that other one's head…?" There was a chorus of assent around him.

"I hope he's *not* here tonight," a woman next to him sighed. Her sculpted white mask slanted around her eyes as if to give the expression of laughter. "I like it when they end it, quick and painless. Just because it's a fight doesn't mean they need to stretch it out. It's not necessary."

"They know what they're signing up for," the man replied.

"I meant for the audience. It gets boring when they want to parade around every head they've cut off."

"Keeps them happy and off the streets."

Jackson found he wasn't really hungry anymore, not even for expensive pork.

"I'd like to do a paid match," the man in blue continued, squaring his shoulders. "I bet I could give some of them a run for their money."

The train car began to ease its roll. The crackled, pre-recorded voice came back. "Next stop, 168th St. Please watch your step." The doors opened again. And, this time, as the crowd looked up to see who was getting on board, their eyes widened. They did not turn away, nor did they resume conversing.

A slim, angular man dressed in cherry red strutted inside, smoothing back gold trim and fastening the shining buttons of his jacket. He was a good head taller than anyone else on the train, and wore the hat of a circus ringmaster, a glittering silver mask, and a smile wide and white. Jackson felt the champagne flute fall from his hands and clink onto his shoes, a trickle of alcohol splashing his ankles. His heart pounded.

The man in red from his dream. The announcer himself.

"WELCOME!" the man spoke, and his voice echoed and boomed, as if he had a microphone, though there was none. "Welcome to the greatest show in all of New York! Welcome to a night unlike any other! I promise, there are things tonight the likes of which you've never seen!" He spread his arms as if embracing them all.

The car erupted in applause. Even the thug to Jackson's right was politely clapping and smiling.

And then, the man rose up on his toes and floated down the center of the car, arms still spread wide, beaming smile unfading. The hushed crowd scrambled back into their seats to give him as much room as they could, like he carried some sort of infection. Jackson felt the blood drain from his face as he felt the sensation of sick buzzing washing again over his skin. The nightmare man drew closer, and he finally knew the magical signature in the air for what it was. "Jack!" the man declared, parting his audience like the sea, drifting. "You came!" Jackson saw now that the man's eyes flashed gold in the light, slitted and reptilian under his shining mask. A merry laugh boomed out of his chest. "You came!"

"Hello. Yes. Yes, I did." Jackson had no idea what more to say, trying to clear his head. "How are you?"

The announcer stopped floating, his feet resting on the floor of the car again. He threw back his head and cackled. The rest of the car was still silently watching. The man with the blue mask was clutching the woman's hand by his side, hunching and making himself smaller. The announcer dropped into the seat between this man and Jackson, then chummily threw his arms around their shoulders. "Tonight is a grand night!" he boomed again. "My dear friend Jack has joined us! Have a round in his honor! To... Jack!"

"To Jack!" the train rumbled, filled with false smiles and cheer, glasses tipping in salute.

The man in blue made a whimpering noise.

Jackson smiled at the room and waved. *Who the hell are you? Why do you know me? Why are you even real?!* "Thank you for the invitation. It's good to, ah, finally be here."

The announcer giggled. "It's so hard to get ahold of you, Jack! I had to be more *direct* this time." He lifted his hand and snapped his fingers, and the train doors shuttered, the wheels grinding to life again, pulling the car along. It was hard to tell if he'd commanded it, or if it was going to do it anyway.

"I don't think The Order meant to pass along my invitation," Jackson said in a low voice. "I only found out about the, well, *thing* on August 1ˢᵗ after it already passed. My apologies."

The man in red frowned deeply. "The Order! Makes a lot of promises they don't keep, don't they? Liars. Rule breakers. Will have to deal with them eventually."

Jackson nodded. "Yes. They've certainly done me no favors."

"Did you get my *gift?*" The announcer's knees jiggled in excitement.

Jackson blinked. "I... don't know?"

"Jaaaack! Of course you got it! She's why you're here!"

Jack, they told me to leave this here for you. "You mean... you mean *Anna?*"

"Who's that?" The announcer popped a cracker in his mouth.

"In the box. The woman in the box. In the wastes."

"Ohhhhh." He rolled his eyes up, as if in thought. "Maybe she was named Anna. I didn't ask. Figured she'd be dead before you got there. Not that it matters. Dead. Alive. They'll talk at you all the same."

Jackson, baffled, felt his mouth moving but no words coming out.

"So, here you are!" The announcer lifted his arms and wiggled his hands in a jazzy way.

The intercom chimed, "Now arriving at 157ᵗʰ St. Please, watch your step." The door swished open, and a party of three entered, a man and two women. They were chatting, unaware of the uneasy silence that had commandeered the car. Then, they looked around, sensing it, troubled looks dawning. The man's eyes fixated on the announcer, and he stumbled in surprise, barely catching himself on the edge of a seat.

Suddenly, though the smile never left the announcer's face, his eyes shifted to the meet the newcomers, and quick as a cat, his head snapped to follow. "What...? What do you think you're doing?" His voice, though it had been smooth before, had a jagged note.

"I'm so sorry..." the man who had tripped stuttered. "Just a bit clumsy... ah, I can catch the next car if you—"

"She *says* to please *watch your step*. It's the *rule*."

There was a whine beginning in Jackson's ears, as if the diseased buzzing in the air was vibrating, faster and faster. He gritted his teeth.

"Sorry again. I'll just—" The man moved to back out of the car. The doors swished shut in his face. "Ah. Hm."

"You can't just... can't just *break* the rules." The announcer's eyes were wide now, a mad light dawning in the snakelike orbs.

"Very sorry," the man whispered again, moving to a corner. The two he had arrived with drifted away from him to stand on the opposite side of the car.

The whine in Jackson's skull rose in pitch, and he tried covering his ears, head starting to hurt. It did no good.

The announcer's voice was airy and high. "No rule breakers. Not in *my* city, not on *my* train."

Jackson sagged, holding back a moan as the mad whine filled his brain.

The newcomer suddenly stumbled forward, clutching his chest. "No, no, I—!" There was a popping noise, and the group nearest him screamed. The man's eyes rolled up in his head, his body collapsing on the floor, and blood began to seep from his eyes and ears, spreading out in a pool under him from his heart.

The announcer rolled his head on his neck, grinding his teeth as the car quieted. "No," he said. "Not on my train."

The train in question began to peaceably carry them onwards again. The whine in Jackson's head was gone. He sat up, dizzy, feeling sick. The announcer was smiling brightly at him, as if nothing at all had happened.

For the first time, though, through the haze in his mind, Jackson saw the announcer's smile wasn't straight and perfect, not really. Between the two front teeth, a gap persisted.

It was then Jackson realized his life had no luck, no coincidences. It was all destiny.

Gotta get your destiny, Jack.

"Tony," he whispered.

Two snake eyes smiled. "Jack. It's *so* good to see you again."

CHAPTER SIXTEEN
The Order

"There, there, take a breather. First trip is the hardest."

Anna whirled as her vision began to clear. Slowly, Huxley began to take shape. "What did you do? *Where am I?*"

"Teleportation, my dear. I know it's a lot to take in. But, it will come with time. Welcome to our library." His smile continued to be beatific and disarming. Anna staggered back as her eyes flew side to side—true to what Huxley said, she saw towers of books sprawled in shelves, reaching the ceiling, and cluttering the floors. A sound was on her left. A man in torn jeans was blowing off an old tome's cover, sending a shower of sparkling dust motes into the air. She watched him for a long moment, but he seemed to be ignoring them both.

"Teleportation isn't real," she finally spoke, voice wavering. Of course, neither was time travel. The more these impossible things happened, the more the foundation of her world cracked a little, threatened to give way.

"Well, it's certainly not something we advise doing just for *fun*," Huxley said, as if that excused the matter entirely. "But, our Archmage was unwilling to risk you on another method."

"*Archmage?*" Anna shook her head. "Mr. Huxley, I appreciate your, um, hospitality, but I really just want to go back. I'd like to learn about all this later. A lot later. There's just too much—"

"Nonsense. I'll explain everything as we go. Come along!" Huxley beckoned she follow. "You'll be fine. It's always overwhelming for a new initiate." Then, he strutted away, twirling his mustache, not paying attention to further hesitation. Anna hugged her arms around herself, wary eyes on her surroundings. After a long moment, not knowing what else to do, she followed.

Outside of the library, the halls remained hushed. Trophies and decorations passed them by: weapons, dusty vases, glittering jewelry in cases. Plaques graced some of the displays, but they were scribed in a squiggly tongue Anna didn't understand. Dust and the smell of furniture polish filled her nose.

"Now," Huxley began. "What's happening to you is perfectly normal."

Anna quietly disagreed.

"Those that are able to touch the magic of the world might feel some of it coming back into them. Left untended, that magic can make your body experience *flares*. It's usually when you're younger—bursts of elemental power, like heat, light, or energy. According to Jackson, in your case, it seems to be radiation."

Anna swallowed, her mouth dry. "So… you're saying I become radioactive because of *magic?*"

"Quite possibly."

Oh, no. New Agers. I give up. "It doesn't make sense."

"How so?"

"Radiation doesn't come out of nothing. It's a by-product of certain types of decaying matter. There are *reasons* for it."

"Think of it this way. The mage is a channel, converting a force that most never see or sense into an energy or form we can, bending it to his or her will. There *isn't* anything in your body giving off radiation. You are converting an unseen force into another form. It's only bad luck that it's harmful. Fortunately, most magic users are immune to their own flares, hence your resistance. And worry not about your powers causing harm here. These walls are quite warded."

For a moment, Anna stared at her hands. Then, she glanced back at the old man out of the corner of her eye. She wouldn't lie; any explanation, no matter how implausible, was desperately appealing. But, what she felt was trepidation. Calling something *magic* smacked of laziness and hand waving.

"Do you have questions?" Huxley prompted.

"I… I don't really believe in magic, sir. How do you know Jackson, again?" *It would be my luck if the only normal and friendly person I've met in weeks turns out to be in a cult.*

"Oh! He was a potential initiate, once. But he didn't have The Gift, upon closer examination." Huxley straightened his waistcoat.

"…Oh. And you're saying I have a gift. To, um, convert magical energy." Anna resisted the urge to use her fingers as quotation marks.

"*The* Gift. Possibly. The difference is whether you only brush against magic, or if you can control it. The latter requires a great strength of character, and a lot of training. There's also the challenge of keeping those magic-touched a secret so they are not abused. The Coalition… well, we would rather our system of power not be known to those who continue to lord nuclear firepower over a burned world."

Anna sighed. She didn't doubt Huxley seemed to mean well. Still, she was beginning to wonder if this "training" in a "system of power" would be available to her for twenty easy payments of $99.99. It bothered her more that she didn't know how Huxley had gotten her here, had no rational explanations, and no warning before it happened. "Does… does Jackson actually know where I am?"

His face fell. "…No." Anna tensed. "But not bringing you could have endangered you and those around you. I cannot stress this enough. He will be contacted. I'm sorry I lied."

"Why didn't you just say so?"

Huxley faced her, bushy eyebrows furrowed into a pleading look. "I was worried you might refuse to come along, and I hardly would force you. Anna, I know this is difficult and scary, and should have been handled better. But, please, meet with our Archmage. Let him give you an assessment. Then, I promise you, you are free to go, no strings attached."

Anna frowned. She saw no doors or exits. What was she going to do? Huxley had every look of sincerity about him. A weight tugged in her back pocket. Reaching behind, she put a ready hand on the Geiger counter, wondering if it qualified as a weapon if, for whatever reason, she would need it. "If I talk to him, you'll take me back?"

"Yes, absolutely. I swear it."

"…Okay." Anna's hand fell by her side as she followed Huxley again.

After another minute, they came into view of the only door Anna had seen yet, tall, imposing, carved of dark-stained wood. The strange writing from the plaques was burned into the surface, an artistic arch. "Here we are." Huxley rapped three times, clearing his throat. Anna heard no response, but, after waiting a few moments, Huxley turned the handle and pressed forward into the room beyond.

Beyond the door, a fire burned low in a hearth, leaving most of the room in deep shadow. A man with slicked black hair and a dark beard sat behind a desk, a glass of amber liquid in his hand. Anna squinted as her eyes adjusted. He was dressed in a strange sort of finery, a black suit with red accents that she would have thought to call antique even in her time. Victorian, maybe? On his desk was a datapad, jars filled with withered herbs, and a thick, leather-bound book.

"Anna," this new man spoke, his voice smooth, a faint British accent coloring his tone. There was a twitch to his mouth that might have been an attempt at a smile, but it was hard to tell in the dark. "It's so *good* to finally meet you."

Anna took a deep breath. "You're the 'Archmage'?"

"Yes. I am." He stood, and as he moved, his eyes caught the firelight like gems. Anna now saw his beard had strange symbols shaved into it, like the kind on the door and on the displays. She couldn't help but wonder how long that took him to eke out in the bathroom every week.

"OK," she said. "So. I'm told you're supposed to tell me something about 'magic'. And then, I'd like to go back to where I came from."

He peered at her in response, holding his chin in a gloved hand. "Administer the tests," he finally said. Then, he leaned back on his desk, wearing a dispassionate stare.

Huxley came up alongside her, proffering a smile. He was holding two stones in his hands, one clear quartz and one deep obsidian. "Hold these. Ah, the black one in your left. There you go."

Anna grasped the rocks, feeling very silly. "Er, what am I supposed to do with…?" Her left hand grew frigid. "Ack!" A frosty, pulsing light took hold around the edges of the darker stone. A painful freeze stole up her arm, and she dropped the rocks like they'd bitten her.

"Hm! Interesting," Huxley said. The Archmage said nothing. His pupils continued to burn.

"What *happened?*" Anna demanded.

Huxley traded the stones for a book, ignoring her question. He fluttered through several pages, squinting as if he too was struggling in the low light. Finally, however, he arrived at his destination with a smack of his lips. "Take a look at this." He spun the open page to face her. Anna stared, flabbergasted. The page was an old, brittle yellow with ink spiraled into nonsense diagrams. Huxley's chubby finger was pointing to an ornate block of text. "Can you read that?"

Anna blinked. The style of the words matched the writing scribbled on everything else around here, and was definitely not English. She couldn't even sound it out. "I don't know that language. Sorry."

"Keep looking at it for a minute. See if it comes to you."

"Uh." Anna wrung her hands. "I'm not going to understand a new language by staring at it, sir. Can you tell me what this is about?"

Huxley's eyebrows furrowed into a surprised and bushy caterpillar. "Huh!" he said, clapping the book cover shut.

"That's enough," the Archmage's voice broke the silence.

"But there's still—" Huxley began.

The Archmage waved a dismissive hand, and Huxley fell silent. Then, the portly old man quickly left the room. Anna's stomach dropped. *Where are you…?* A soft *click* told her the door was now locked. "Anna. Tell me. When did you first see signs of your powers?"

"I don't have—"

"Your *radiation*." There was a dangerous edge in his tone, his lip curling.

Tell him what he wants and get out of here. "I... a couple weeks ago. I woke up, and it was happening. That's all I know."

"What's the last thing you remember before that?"

The menacing chasm in Anna's mind yawned open when she tried touching her memories. She tried not to think about it. "I... It's blurry. I don't remember. I'm sorry. I was at work. Then I was suddenly in a box, and... and I saw Jackson looking down at me..."

"*Jackson.*"

Anna stared. She didn't like the way the Archmage hissed. She didn't want to answer any more questions. She didn't even want to give lies for answers; she'd never been talented at lying anyway.

He watched her as she squirmed, then gave another not-smile. "You look simply terrified."

"I just want to go home."

"Well, I have news that may be to your relief."

"What?"

"You are most *certainly* not a mage."

"...Oh?" Anna blinked as the Archmage sipped at his glass. This actually *was* a relief. She didn't want to come back. "Huxley said... well... I'm not sure I understand."

"Of course you don't. But, here is our problem. You've certainly been *touched* by something magical. Tell me." His words coiled. "Do you see *ravens* sometimes?"

"Like, the birds?"

"Did I stutter?" A hand wave beseeched her to hurry.

"Sure. Yes. Why?"

"Mmm. I *thought* so. But you're not his. No, no... your face is too open for that. You're not a woman of secrets and *lies*, now, are you? Oh my. Those flares... the stones... you're *hers*, aren't you?" It was then that the dead smile on the man's face contorted wider and the sheen of life finally entered it. "What a treat! *Do* tell me about yourself."

Anna's mouth was dry. Her gaze settled on a closed window to her left, blinds drawn shut. This man hadn't done anything but talk, but everything in Anna's mind screamed *Don't trust him!* How high up were they? Would she be able to jump and run for it? She stalled, thinking. "I'm a scientist. I monitor radiation levels at my site. That's it. Nothing special."

"And how did you meet Jackson?"

"He found me outside the city and brought me back to get help. I don't know how long I was out there."

"Hm. Yes. I wonder why he kept visiting you, though? Are you *friends?*"

"Well, yes! Maybe." A keen wobble kept vibrating along her spine every time he spoke, as if there were traps in his words. The window would be too risky. If he got closer, then maybe she could knock him in the head with her Geiger counter, find a way to call for help.

"It's curious, how you would wind up in Jackson's proximity so quickly after escaping."

Anna swallowed. Then, she thought of Reeds's unsettling stare. Could this man be...? What if she was getting Jackson into trouble? "Are you with the Coalition?" she finally asked. "Jackson may be my friend, but he didn't break me out. He didn't do anything illegal."

The Archmage's laugh filled the room like the wispy wheeze of dying things. "Oh, no. No, dear Anna, and the Coalition is far from what you should be worried about at present." He smirked, letting his finger lazily trace a pattern on the black book on his desk. Then, Anna saw a red light in his eyes wholly apart from the fire in the hearth. She stood in alarm, clutching at the Geiger counter, but her limbs froze, her body taut. "Eghh!" she protested, cement in her bones, jaw unwilling to move. The counter fell from her hands, thudding into the soft carpet.

Click. Click click, it intoned.

A cold sweat bled down her neck. She could only breathe now, and cry out in her head. *Oh God. I can't... I can't... What's happening?*

The Archmage ambled from behind his desk, as if he had all the time in the world. "You'll be a suitable peace offering to one of my most useful. Ah!

Two birds with one stone, of course, as that tired old phrase goes. You're one of the birds, I'm afraid."

He leaned down near Anna's face, observing her eyes, pulling her lips apart as if checking her teeth, then pacing around her in a circle, his eyes alight. Every muscle in her body screamed to recoil, flee, but she was locked in place. He was close enough for her to smell him, a cold, yet sweet odor, something that made her gag.

"Just a quick peek then, before you're off to your fate." He placed two icy fingers in the center of Anna's forehead. "Relax, my dear. This will probably hurt quite a lot."

Anna sucked in a breath, vision whirling, trapped in her head and screaming. And then—

—then she was at her desk at work, head on her arms, staring at a wall.

What?

The world was fogged. Drowsy, she sat up, pulling her long hair from her lips. "Ptoo," she said, her hair falling from her mouth. *Did I fall asleep?* Something at the back of her mind was humming, a simmering anxiety, but she couldn't remember what had caused it.

Anna, still fuzzy, looked around. There was a folder on her desk, a bit of Dr. Appleby's handwriting peeking out of the edges. She seized it, hoping it hadn't been delivered while she'd been slumped over, sleeping.

A jolt hit her. *What if I'm late? What if I slept through the meeting?*

She whipped her head around to find the wall clock, then heaved a sigh of relief. Three hours until it was time. *C'mon. You've got this.* She'd gone over the subcritical test presentation so many times that she could have recited it in her sleep. The data would be used for improving the bomb simulations, and, Anna knew, cement her reputation a little further. If only public speaking didn't scare the bejeezus out of her. But, if today went well… maybe, eventually, she'd get to work with the decommissioning team. She looked forward to a day when constant safety simulations weren't necessary for the missile stockpile, and the world didn't need these weapons anymore.

The note in the folder stared up at her now.

Dr. Matthews,

Take some time to go over this proposition for your career. Falcon wants minds like yours in the development sector, not just running subcriticals!

Also, breathe, your meeting today is going to go fine. Routine, really.

Anna breathed, but the unease still oozed under her skin. Sighing, she decided that after today, she was going to get a good night's rest for a change.

The lights went off.

Anna's eyes flickered up. *Darktime already?* Then, she blinked and wrinkled her nose. *That* was a nonsense thought. *The power's just out. Maybe someone else knows what happened.*

Her hands were shaking for some reason. But, she stood and opened the door.

The hall was gloomy, windowless, and whitewashed. Today, Anna found it suffocating, though it had never bothered her before. She walked with a brisk step, glancing over her shoulder.

BANG!

The noise was shattering, a ringing left in its wake. She froze, the hair on her neck prickling.

Was that a…?

BANG BANG!

A shriek pierced the air, and then, the pounding of shoes. A crowd of almost twenty personnel began stampeding around the corner, one dressed in the deep green and browns of the Army. The soldier flew off his feet as another ear-splitting *BANG* resounded, his head cracking into the wall. He didn't move as Anna's screaming coworkers raced over him.

Anna's legs were paralyzed. Her mind froze.

A bobbing brown mustache caught her eye. Appleby! His eyes were wide with fear, and for just a second, they met hers. He surged ahead of the crowd, grabbed her shoulder, and almost tore her off her feet, throwing her into her office. Then, he followed, shutting the door, and slumping against it. The rest of the group didn't even seem to notice as they mobbed past.

"What's happening?" Anna cried.

"Shhhhh!" Sweat was popping on his forehead. A bright red stain was seeping down his arm.

"You're hurt!"

"I'm... I'm f-fine..."

Muffled stomping sounded. Jackboots.

"Get behind the door," he whispered, dragging himself to his feet. His face was ashen as he adjusted his glasses. "So it'll cover you."

"What?"

"We have to warn the Pentagon. We've been overrun."

"*What?* By who? What do they want? Why *here?* Aren't the soldiers—"

"I don't know." He swallowed like it hurt. "I was taking a break. Some of the Army started shooting at us. It was too quick to see, to understand why. T-two soldiers pulled me inside, then, and started returning fire. I don't even know who is who right now. Power's out. Communications are down. I was with that group trying to get into a safe room, but the soldiers turned on us..." He swallowed, throat bobbing. "Nowhere's safe. I think... I think they're trying to get at intelligence, or our fissionable material. Only thing that..."

BANG!

Anna heard a scream in the hall, and then, terrible silence. She shook, feeling hot tears. Appleby put a hand on her shoulder and smiled at her. "It's going to be okay." He guided her behind the door as far as she could go, then motioned her to stay there as he took a place at her desk.

Before Anna realized what he intended to do, the door drifted open with a soft creak. She held her breath, trying not to cry. The black steel barrel of a gun was hovering through the door now.

"Can't a man bleed to death in peace from the comfort of his own office?" Appleby snapped.

"You going to help, or not?" A man's voice.

"No."

BANG!

Appleby flew out of the chair, a flash of red in Anna's vision. A high-pitched whine rang in her ears. The door swung open further now, her small frame barely shielded behind it. The assassin was checking the corners of the room. Anna saw he was in an Army uniform, saw the buzz cut fresh on his head, but she'd never seen this soldier before today, had no idea who this man, this murderer, was.

She stopped herself from breathing so she wouldn't scream.

And then, with a swish, he was gone, his boots thudding down the hall.

Anna sagged, letting out her breath, sick. *Oh God. Wake up.* Her breathing was ragged now. Her mentor was dead behind her desk. *Wake up.*

She wasn't waking up.

Then get up. There was a voice in her head now, one she barely recognized as her own. It pushed her to her feet, even though she shook.

The safe rooms were under guard, if Appleby was right. Any of the soldiers she could have called on for help could be the enemy. Could she afford to hunker behind her door until help came? What would happen to the others? What about the people these maniacs could hurt if Dr. Appleby was right? She couldn't imagine them getting far with anything stolen. This wasn't a launch site. There had to be backup on the way.

But what if they *did* override the security measures, managed to steal even one thing? What if backup didn't get here? Anna knew the exact payloads of every missile on site, and knew the destructive capabilities of even the intelligence they guarded.

You have to do SOMETHING. You can't let this happen.

She staggered out from behind the door, peeking around the edges to see the hall beyond. Her head was still ringing, her hearing clouded. There were bright spots at the edges of her vision, as if the world wasn't entirely real.

No one was guarding the hall. She scurried out, as quietly as she could, trying not to look back at her mentor, or the crumpled body of the soldier.

What... what now?

With the power cut, sensitive areas would be locked down. *"You gonna help or not?"* the assassin's voice echoed in her brain. Her chest ached. If these people were forcing the personnel to aid them and did restore power, they could open a lot of doors.

180

She couldn't fight armed soldiers. She couldn't hide or disable the dangerous things they kept here, not quickly, even if she could get at them. *I need help.* Appleby was right. The Pentagon had to be contacted. But if the usual channels were down or guarded...

Do skip ahead, my dear. A man's imperious voice, tinged with a British accent, shuddered through her bones, almost making her heave. *I don't have all day.* The edges of her world felt like they were warping.

And, she was surrounded by junk, dust and electronic decay in her nose. Anna jerked her head around, something pausing her thoughts, making her wonder why she was there. She shook her head, clearing it. No time. The soldiers could find her at any moment.

The supply closet was claustrophobic, and she could barely see. She struggled to keep her shaking hands in check, to sort through the dusty, unused bins of government hoarding. The United States nuclear complex hadn't been a favored funding destination since the Cold War had ended. For soldiers, it was stressful and dead-end. For personnel, it was a time warp. Anna had been baffled on her first day, when she'd seen floppy disks sitting on a desk. She'd been told they were getting phased out. Eventually.

The supply closets were treasure troves of technology the rest of the world had left behind. Why would anyone bother guarding them? Anna suspected most of the intruders' efforts were in herding, murdering, and getting what they came for. They thought her wing of the world had been cleared. Thanks to Appleby.

There was the barest of keening noises coming out of her throat. She forced her muscles to contract and stop it.

There it was, what she'd been looking for. An old HAM radio, circa 1980s. Anna, hopeful, scooted it from its resting place, leaving a layer of grime behind. She wheezed, hefting it and the accompanying microphone, wondering if she had any hope of a signal reaching far enough that someone would hear. There wasn't power, so she'd need to either get to a generator... or... or... was *that* a box of old flares?

Ahhh... I see... and what then? A sinister male voice in her head prodded her, the ground twisting and the walls shuddering, the world reforming itself once more.

Now, the trash can barely hid her body. She could see her car. And, she could see five armed soldiers. Anna had no way of telling which side they were on, but she could assume.

The black flare gun was lead in her hand. She didn't know if it would actually fire, old and ill-maintained as it was. Would it explode in her hand if it didn't? She held her breath, pointed to her right, and squeezed the trigger, her entire hand screaming with the pain of tension.

The flare ignited. It whizzed spectacularly into the side of the building, bursting and ricocheting, then exploding with a deafening crack. The soldiers turned for just a moment to see the bright red light scorching their eyes. And, Anna ran the twenty feet to her car, head down, ducking behind the tire. Someone was yelling.

BANG!

It felt as if someone had punched her thigh with a rock, and she screamed, diving, yanking her door handle as she fell. Boots thudded. Anna crawled up through the passenger seat, locked the doors, started the car, and threw it in reverse without any thought on where it would go. She couldn't see. Her leg howled. The sound of shattering glass blistered the air as the tires squealed and guns boomed, and she shifted to drive, barely looking up, her hearing destroyed.

The road peeled on before her. Anna lifted her head as she tore through the open gate, free by sheer luck, bleeding, crying, terrified. She couldn't hear their shouts anymore, but she could see them running in her rearview mirror. She knew they would chase her. The cord to the old radio was thick in her hand; her laptop charging adapter only accepted the plug after three tries. Anna struggled to remember any of her experiments with radios as a kid, flicking a switch, one eye on the road, hoping the default wavelength would work. "This is Dr. Matthews, at the NNSS. We have intruders, wearing Army uniforms. People are dead. You have to contact the police, the military, *anybody*. Tell the Pentagon."

Silence. No, no, she was doing it all wrong! Her hands felt awkward and fumbling, and she couldn't stop to look. There was a drag in the tires, and she suspected they'd been shot. *You don't have time. Make it count!* Anna had never known her inner voice could ever be quite so clear when the world was falling apart.

No. I don't care about how you lived. The intruding male voice split her head one last time, an impatient edge curling it with disdain. *Tell me how you died.*

Her eyesight burbled and twisted again, going black as she felt her world leap. It wasn't far ahead this time.

The sun baked down on her face through broken glass. She looked at the sky, exhausted. *Was I...?* Anna collapsed against the seat, head heavy and mind thickening. Her hand on her thigh came back sticky, seething with bright red blood. The engine idled, but the hood was acquainting itself with a gnarled Joshua tree.

A dust cloud spilled over the horizon line. Military jeeps, closing in.

Anna fiddled with the radio dial. Only now as she stopped and breathed, burning her precious last minutes, did she finally think that she got the tuning right. The signal *might* go through.

If anyone was listening. If.

"This is Dr. Anna Matthews of Falcon, at the NNSS." Blood from her hands smeared the microphone. "We need help! I repeat," she sucked in a breath, feeling her head getting fuzzier. "This is Dr. Anna Matthews, from Falcon, at the NNSS. Please... anybody... intruders in Army uniforms... you have to warn the Pentagon..."

She heard a door slam.

"Look at this crazy bitch," a voice said, muffled by the ringing in her ears. "I bet she thinks that's going to work."

"Just shut her up. I just had to drive two miles through this desert to catch a goddamn Honda. Can't believe she got through." Anna could swear she recognized the voice of the man who had murdered her mentor. She looked up, then, to finally see his face, but instead saw a dark hole in the sky, a gun barrel.

BANG!

Her chest split open with lancing, burning pain.

BANG BANG!

"One would have done it." The voice was a distant echo. Her vision blurred. There was only the sun burning down on her, a white light washing out all else.

"Dr. Matthews?" she heard as the light took her sight. The faint, static-littered sound was almost lost to the whine in her head. "This -bzzt- Casey Rogers. -bzzzzt- Message received. Over."

The light burned, embracing her. And, Anna was gone, floating away on the desert breeze.

INTERLUDE

Frank opened the door to the safe house, a scowl on his face and a coffee in one hand. Only an empty apartment lay beyond.

"*Goddamn it.*"

He was reaching for his datapad now, war in his eyes.

CHAPTER SEVENTEEN
Snake Eyes

"We've all been waiting for you, Jack." Tony, the man in red, pulled back his fingers, a dozen cracks popping through the dead air.

Jackson swallowed. "We?"

The announcer did not elaborate, grin pulling even wider. Mad lights twinkled in his reptilian eyes.

Jackson tried to recall anything he could of his past. Tony tagging along in his shadow. Tony standing on a desk, declaring one day, he'd be on stage. *"Everyone will know me!"* he'd crowed. But the rest was faded, far gone.

This man was no wide-eyed boy. In his presence, Jackson felt as he had in the dream of the starry-eyed being, as if he was before something too vast to be real, something that would crush him by accident if its mind shifted in the wrong way.

He wasn't certain when he'd picked up his bag, but he now hugged it close, as if it could shield him. It held just his change of clothes and a tube of toothpaste: a poor defense. "So," he said, trying to keep his voice light. "It's been such a long time. How did you get into this business? You really look to be in your element. I'm happy for you."

Tony was silent for a long minute, boring his alien eyes into Jackson's soul. When he finally answered, it was a whisper only they two could hear. "Do you remember what happened in the *classroom?*"

Jackson stilled. "No."

There was an indefinable sadness in Tony's face, dimming the mad brightness. A shiver went through Jackson's mind, horror, shame, regret, and a million pinpricks he didn't have words for. He didn't want to know why. All he knew was that in his head, there was an empty room, and a boy with a beetle in his slender hand. Jackson's breath was coming in shallow spurts. "I don't want... I can't..." He couldn't think about it. Everything in his body told him he would regret it.

"The bad man came for you, Jack."

It was something in Jackson's peripheral vision, ignored for the last fifteen years, and all he needed to do was turn his head just a little to see.

No. Don't look.

Tony leaned forward. "He found us. He's been watching us ever since."

Ice shattered across Jackson's skin, as if the starry-eyed being was touching his mind again. And, the dam in his mind finally burst, sweeping him away.

"I *found* you." The words were a hiss, and the boy called Jack looked up from his book. The boy named Tony made a startled squeak as the stranger entered.

The intruder was dressed in a suit, black and rigidly pressed, a red tie at his throat. He had a strange beard, one cut with foreign letters. But, it was the eyes that made Jack stand, made him clutch his book to his chest protectively. They were the kind of blue that made him think of the ice that crept through the graveyard during the winter. "Finally." The man's face was engraved with hate, and he blocked the exit, looming. The door closed, though he didn't touch it. The lock twisted shut by itself. And, he began creeping closer, gait like a prowling wolf.

Jack's instincts fired, sending him running for a window, despite the fact that they were three stories up. He was certain he could monkey himself down the side of the building if he had to.

Then, Jack's body seized. He cried out in fear and surprise. A red light was glimmering in the man's eyes beyond the ice, and Jack was all gurgling breaths and pain, fighting to flee in a body turned to stone. He heard Tony make a similar cry behind him.

The man's voice chilled the air. "Easy, boys. Now. *Jack.* You certainly have been a difficult Chosen to find." A silver knife bloomed in the man's hand, drawn from some hidden place. Jack screamed without sound. "Clearly without talent, though. Perhaps these days, he's just sending out the leftovers." The knife flourished under Jack's nose, the intruder's movements robotic and precise. "Don't worry. It will only take one cut. I've become *very* good at this."

He lunged.

A hand seized Jack's collar, yanking him back. A thin slice of wind kissed his throat. The man gave a startled snarl, the red lights shining brighter. "How did you...?"

Jack stumbled, his limbs still numb and dead, as ten-year-old Tony threw him back under a desk. There was a whine in his ears, a horrible buzzing, like the world was about to vibrate apart at the seams.

The air around Tony coiled and breathed. And then, it *exploded.*

An electric force crackled in Jack's lungs, something searing outwards from Tony's body, tearing up anything in its path. The plywood and particle board shattered and groaned; the air filled with splinters and pain. The man with the knife screamed in agony, a howl that echoed in Jack's ears over and over again, and Jack squeezed his eyes shut tight as he could, the debris tearing at his skin.

He opened his eyes again, and he was covered in red. A great beast had reached inside the room with its teeth, gnawed and broken the bloodstained wood like bones. The wall was blown out, dust and rubble. The man was gone, and so was the buzzing, the air flat, dead. Someone was screaming, far away.

Tony was in an unmoving ball in front of him, soaked in blood.

Jack sat under the desk until the headmistress came, and she'd cleaned him, covered his eyes, and taken him away to a solitary room. A glaze of unreality had taken root in Jack's mind, as if, should he try hard enough, he would be able to peel back the world and find only blood and vertigo beneath. And, when the headmistress asked what had happened, pleading, wondering if he and Tony had built a bomb somehow, he could only sit on his bed and stare at her in silence.

The man with the dark sunglasses came the next day. He sat on the far edge of the bed, smiling at Jack, who scrunched himself into the wall. A woman with long, dark hair was there too, crouching before Jack, searching his wary gaze. The headmistress stood in the doorway, wringing her old wedding ring.

"Hey. I'm Nyx," the dark-haired woman said. She reached out to touch his shoulder, but he shied away, and she gently drew her hand back. "No one's gonna hurt you. We promise. This is my friend, Agent Walker. He's with the Coalition. You know, the people that try and keep everyone safe?"

Jack kept his silence. The man took off his sunglasses, his face furrowed in sympathy. The lack of stern eyes or tired wrinkle lines—things all adults had—made Jack unsure.

The woman continued. "What you saw Jack—we need to know about it. No matter what."

Jack shifted uncomfortably. No one ever believed him. "He exploded."

"*Jack*—" The headmistress began to interrupt, but the agent raised a hand, cutting her off. Nyx nodded at Jack, as if encouraging him to continue.

"A man came in the room with a knife. I couldn't move. He... he was trying to kill me."

"Do you know what this man looked like?" Agent Walker asked.

"He had eyes with lights in them. His beard had weird letters in it." Jack struggled with the words, trying to say them forcefully enough that they would seem true. "Tony pulled me away. And, he exploded." A quaking had entered Jack's voice, and he didn't know how to convey the ear-splitting screeching or the screaming or how much blood there was. "Where *is* Tony?"

"He's going to be fine," the agent said.

"I'm very sorry," Rosita interjected, words rising over the agent's shushing motions towards her. "Jack might not be a... reliable witness. He has some *conditions*, behavioral issues. He likes to tell stories. We have him talk to a therapist."

No one seemed to acknowledge her, but Jack hung his head, well-used to Rosita's apologies on his behalf. He was broken, and everyone knew it. "I saw it," he mumbled. "It happened. Where is he?"

The agent sighed. "Tony's going to come stay with my people for a while."

"He's going to be going to a special school," Nyx chirped. "With a lot of kids like him. Don't worry. We're going to make sure he's safe and happy."

"Oh," was all Jack could say, alone in his corner on the bed. "You don't believe me, do you?"

"You saw what you saw." Nyx reached up, putting her hands on each side of Jack's face. He tried to twitch away again, but her fingers were soft, cool, and seemed to stick. He felt his eyes getting heavy, his muscles sagging. She smiled. "Don't worry about it, kiddo. Get some rest. This will all be a faraway dream when you wake up. Just a bad dream."

Jack mumbled in assent, too tired to do much else. He laid back on the bed, curling up, exhausted and worn.

"What did you do?" he heard the headmistress ask.

Walker's voice was growing hazy, drifting into the distance. "He just needs some sleep. He shouldn't remember this. It's for the best... let him have some innocence." A sigh. "We'll keep an eye on him, just in case."

The boy called Jack closed his eyes.

And, the man named Jackson opened them.

The lights in the train car were lancing his sight, halos in the air, and when he turned away, he saw his shadow flickering and sputtering, though no one else's was. He realized he'd had his face in his hands, shivering, cold, lost in the flood in his mind. Blood was still seeping out onto the floor of the car from the dead man's body. It was less blood than when Tony had torn apart the world. Still, it was quite a lot. One woman had pulled her heeled feet up onto the seat with her so as not to step in it, and was staring resolutely ahead, as if nothing at all was the matter.

"You remember, don't you, Jack?" There was a keen edge in Tony's voice, like he was still a lost little boy.

"I... remember." Jackson breathed, shaking, in his mind sitting under that desk, covered in red stain. A cold finger traced his spine as he thought of the man outside of Huxley's manor, runes in his beard, a stare full of hate. *He tried to kill me when I was thirteen.* He didn't know what to do with that revelation. And Agent Walker. The bastard! The lying government bastard! Walker had kept his eye on him since he was a teenager, made him *forget.* He took Tony to some special "school"—a government facility, most likely. Was that the only memory he and his companion had stolen?

Walker was using me to get to Tony. Of course he was. Tony had slipped the leash, hadn't he? He was out of control. And the agent hadn't just *happened* to need the insight of some random smuggler to track him down, magical background or not. "The Coalition took you away."

Tony's face seemed to spasm. "Number Thirty-One. That's me. I asked to write you, Jack, so many times, and they didn't let me. I tried anyway." He reached in his vest pocket, pulling out a tiny purple crayon, so old it was only a nub. This he rolled slowly between two fingers. The air simmered, a rot under the surface.

"What did they do to you…?" Jackson let his words dance around the matter of dead man on the floor. This madman had saved his life once, had been his friend, and clearly still thought he was just that. *Perhaps*, Jackson thought, *he won't hurt me.*

Tony made a creaky squeal of excitement as he refocused on Jackson's face, insanity in his burning eyes. Jackson reconsidered. "They taught me the rules. I found my destiny." He popped another cracker in his mouth, carelessly crunching, some of the crumbs dusting his well-stitched suit. "Now I just make sure the world runs… smoothly. But they were always trying to get in my *head*. I didn't like it. No. Not. At. All."

"I'm sorry." *They wanted to control you, use you, study you, didn't they?*

"It's okay. I'm all better now."

All better. Jackson shuddered. "Do you know what they wanted?"

"They said I had to be the best I could be." Tony grimaced. "We all have to be. That's a rule. We must do what we're told. That's another, *very important* rule. If they want us to fight, we must. Give blood? Yes. Kill? I always did what I was told, Jack." His voice took a cheerful swing. "They made it hurt *so* much when I didn't!" The smile stretched until it looked like his face might break.

"But, I had a secret, Jack. Like you. I *saw* them. The *ravens*. They listened to me sometimes, and told me stories. Like when they said if I left *her* there, outside the dome, you would finally get my letters, and you would come. I didn't tell anyone about it. Even though I was supposed to." His face spasmed again, as if fighting off any expression that would interrupt his painful-looking happiness. "Never tell. A secret. Between friends." He reached out, hesitated, then gave Jackson's shoulder a ginger pat.

Jackson's thoughts skittered around the ravens. The idea that they were real, in some way, was far easier for him to accept than he wanted it to be. In a way, he'd always known they were. Just like his nightmares. Like his shadows.

"Who were you supposed to tell about Anna?"

Tony twitched and fidgeted, the whine of strain in his voice. "Can't say. The sky opened up, Jack. It opened up, and out she came, and I heard the singing, so I came to see. But they were going to take her away, like they took me. Get in her head. *Her head.* For their Project, Jack. The Project. I... stopped them."

The disquieting whine in the air ebbed and flowed. Jackson's mind stalled. The sheer destruction and death in the valley's ghost town stared back at him, the awful, cloying, copper stench and the sick, yellowing sky.

"One of them had a peanut butter sandwich in his pocket," Tony continued, his eyes going vacant. "It was good."

"I..." What could Jackson even say to that? *Thanks?* He worked the dry lump in his throat, struggling for something polite. "Anna is very nice. I'm glad you stopped them from taking her to the Project."

"Sure! Who's Anna, again?"

"...The woman in the box."

"What woman in the box...? OH! That one. Yes. I'm sorry. I see a lot of them. They have trouble with that, you know. Boxes. I figured it was okay, letting her get her destiny later. I knew I'd see her again." Tony continued munching on snacks. Then, he uttered with a sacred hush: "I know why you're *really* here, too."

Jackson tried to still himself, tried not to think of blood and death. "...

You do?"

The train car was rolling to a halt. The crackling pre-recorded voice began to play again. "Next stop—" It cut out. All the doors slid open, and the crowd came alive, swarming for the exits, hopping and shimmying around the dead man on the floor. Expensive shoes click-clacked away down an echoey platform. Jackson sat right where he was.

Tony, however, rose. He beckoned with one hand, no whistle in his words at all anymore. "Yes. Follow me and see."

He turned and strode out the exit, not even bothering with dancing around the blood. It splashed on his shoes, leaving a trail of red prints behind him. A throat cleared to Jackson's right: the thug, entirely forgotten. The man raised his eyebrows as if to say, *Go on, then. Do I really gotta pull my gun to make ya go?*

Jackson stood, legs shaking, and crept after the bloody footprints, *tip-tap, tip-tap*, headlong into the dark. He had no choice.

The station was ill-lit, but it was enough to see by. Sounds of clicking shoes and echoing voices drifted from far ahead like old ghosts. Laughter. Jackson had forgotten how happy everyone in that train car had been before Tony had graced the crowd with his presence. *They fear him. But they pay money to come back and see his show. Night after night. How long has this been going on?* His stomach clenched. He had rubbed shoulders with the wealthy before, especially before the business had taken a downturn, and he wondered if some of his clients were down here. Perhaps they were eating hors d'oeuvres, cheering for the blood sport to begin so they could make some money on their wagers.

Tony himself was strutting as if he owned the tunnels, a bobbing red ringmaster's hat in the darkness. He swayed his arms at no one, conducting an invisible symphony, muttering something under his breath. Then, without warning, he turned down a separate corridor. "Backstage! VIP!" he sang. Jackson heard only the dripping of water and the whistle of a breeze down this new path, one that had been blasted into the station wall. Swallowing his fear, he followed.

They continued for some minutes, the thug silent, and Tony humming in bursts, like he was filling in for parts of his imaginary orchestra. Finally, however, the music in his head seemed to stop, and he affixed Jackson with his disconcerting grin. *Having the time of my life*, it said.

"So... uh... what do you do down this way?"

"I make the magic, of course!"

"...I see. Then. Thank you for the tour. Bit of an honor to see the behind-the-scenes."

Tony tittered. "Well, you've seen the show, anyway, Jack, from out in the audience. This is a *special* night."

"Special?"

Tony waggled his fingers and did not elaborate.

"...How did you know I've seen the fights? It was only in dreams...?"

"Doesn't matter! I have a *special* surprise for you." Tony's golden eyes glistened as his head turned, and he darted his neck this way and that, finding his way forward as if he were scenting the air.

Jackson did not think he would like the surprise. But, he resolved himself to smile and nod as he was presented with it.

"You want your destiny, right?"

The question very nearly made Jackson trip. What would be a good answer? "Who doesn't?"

"You want to know what the man by the fire wants? You want to know the secrets?"

Secrets that were kept from you. Jackson's heart pounded. "Yes."

"Good." Tony gave a satisfied nod. "It's settled." And, he walked on, saying nothing more.

The door hadn't led to the surface. Another tunnel greeted them now, and it dipped down, winding, carved out of stone and dirt. It felt like an endless walk, and Tony himself was distressingly silent. Jackson's nerves failed when he tried to think of anything more to say. Eventually, the dirt gave way to a brickwork tunnel, a canal running alongside them. Was this... an old sewer?

Strange drips echoed off of the bricks and stone as they marched on into deeper dark, no lights guiding their way anymore. Tony didn't seem to mind, and Jackson's eyes adjusted readily. The tunnel was crumbled, molded, the arches and passageways often blocked by rubble. How far were they from the station? Could he even find his way back if he had to? He knew the answer was no.

Then, a sensory wave washed over Jackson: the smells of sweat, fear, and excrement, the unsettling undercurrents of groans of pain. Hard, metal edges greeted his straining eyes as they rounded the corner. There were cages stacked upon cages, the shuffling of prisoners and the clink of chains. *How many...?* He recoiled.

"Come on." Tony beckoned again, unfazed. Jackson swallowed, and continued walking.

Eyes met him from behind the bars, suspicious, angry gazes. Jackson knew what this place had to be. Most fighters, he imagined, did not arrive voluntarily. Jackson hoped no one could see his face in the gloom, blame him for not being able to act against their slavery. "These are my stables!" Tony was smiling again as he gestured across the room with one arm, as if to say, *ta da!*

The prisoners held their tongues, but a seething tension hung in the air. They were caked in dirt and things Jackson did not want to think about. Some cast their despondent eyes at their feet, but many stared right back at him, teeth bared in snarls, as if sizing him up.

Jackson looked away, unable to meet their challenge. He was not like these angry ones, these defiant ones, ready to fight, looking as if they knew how. These prisoners had scars, a lot of them. Some were painted in lurid tattoos, animals and birds, and some had sharpened teeth, points overlapping their lips. These... were not normal citizens. *Wait. Those aren't tattoos.* They were too crude, too alike. *Brands.*

"Most of these people are raiders," he thought aloud.

"Ding ding ding! Very good." Tony examined his gloves.

"Where did you get them all?"

"Here." Tony's matter-of-fact statement made Jackson shiver. It was an answer no New Yorker wanted to hear—that the Barrier, their cherished protector, had any flaws. "They always sneak around, steal people away, try to get in under us in the tunnels. I find them burrowing sometimes, or bribing their way in, stealing from my city. My arena. But I won't let them. Always protect New York. Always kill raiders. Those are rules." He kept moving forward.

The Coalition tried to use your powers to protect their interests. They had you kill our enemies for them. Jackson was almost certain of this. It was what the Coalition did: protect the cities, by any means necessary. The sanity of a small, fragile boy, he wagered, would mean little to them against the safety of millions. Still, that left one question. *Why the death matches?*

"It's how you live," Tony said.

Jackson wrung his hands, thinking he'd only asked the question in his mind. "I don't understand."

"It's *how* you *live*," Tony re-emphasized, narrowing his eyes, as if annoyed. "It's the rule, Jack. You must be your best to get your destiny."

Jackson found he did not want to press at anything Tony found... irritating. "Of course."

"You don't understand?" Tony came to a full stop, his eyes going wide, as if in shock. "How can *you* not understand?"

"Of course I—"

"No, *no*, NO. Don't lie! Don't break the rules! You'll make me... You DON'T understand, Jack!" Tony was wincing again, the agitated sizzle in the air sending bits of steam rising from the puddles near their feet. There was a smell as if something was burning, acrid. Jackson's eyes watered. "How? You're like me!" Tony slammed his hand down on a cage they passed. "Here! Look! LOOK. *Do you understand?*"

A horrified wail floated up from the cage. Jackson could tell right away that this cell's occupant, unlike the others, was no bandit. She wept freely, and looked up at them both in terror.

"Please let me go," she whimpered.

"You don't want *that*," Tony soothed. The water at his feet stopped boiling. "No. Don't worry. Your time is after the headliners tonight."

Jackson swallowed. "She's not a raider," he ventured.

Unwarranted hope flashed in the woman's eyes. She turned to him, desperation on her face. "Please! You're right. They kidnapped me. My name is—"

"This is Barbara!" Tony patted the top of her prison fondly. The woman cringed into silence. "I call her Barb." He then made a gesture to Jackson. "Say hi, silly. Don't be rude!"

Jackson's voice was small and awkward in the dark. "…Hello Barb." He tried to apologize to this woman with nothing but his eyes.

"She was kidnapped and sold off to the raiding party over there." Tony waved at a cluster of cells on the far end of the room. "I got her for free when my people ambushed them! *Filthy trespassers.*"

"Please," the woman said. "I just want to go home! Please…"

Tony rolled his eyes. "No, you don't. You need this. You just don't understand it yet." There was a desperate conviction in his smile. "You see it now, right? Right?" Jackson shuddered and nodded, unwilling to disagree or rile Tony any more. "They need their destinies, Jack. They *need* them. Everyone does. Barb's life is ruined. Her family is destroyed. Her sister is dead! The raiders killed her." The woman burst out into tears. Jackson could do nothing to comfort her. "She's lost. She's a shell. Why would I rob her of the chance to look her enemies in the eye, try to kill them for what they have done? Why would I rob her of the chance to seize her life, her death? Her destiny? She *must* face them. She *must* fight. Or she will never be her best."

Oh. Suddenly, Jackson understood exactly what Tony wanted of him. "I," he said, backing up.

A metal barrel tapped into in his back again. "No breaking contract," the thug behind him intoned.

"Absolutely right," the ringmaster of the arena crooned through his rictus smile. "You're here for destiny, Jack. You've agreed to it. So, don't try to run. You won't get far."

CHAPTER EIGHTEEN
The Light Within

Drip. Drip. Drip.

Water echoed, a maddening constant in the dark hole. The world smelled of grease, stagnant liquid, and fear.

Anna lifted her head. Her eyes were red and puffy, but she'd run out of tears. Joints aching, she pulled herself up, manacles clinking, wrists and ankles chafing with a sweaty sting.

She didn't think of the pain, though. *I'm dead.* Anna stared out into the darkness beyond her cage. *I died.*

And yet, here she was, a hundred and twenty-five years past a man murdering her in the desert, her blood trickling into the car seat. She'd given her life for just a chance that no one else would have to. She didn't even know if it had helped.

Message received.

Maybe it had.

The dark was no longer so deep. A soft light was glowing under her skin, pushing it back, if only a little. She hoped she wasn't giving off radiation again. In the blackness, she could hear an occasional sob, or a rattle of metal from chains. She knew she wasn't the only prisoner.

The weight of her memories had left her fading away, and she'd awoken here. The Archmage was gone. *Off to your fate*, he'd said. He likely wanted to dispose of her. Apparently, whatever she was didn't interest him for long.

Where am I? The ceiling was too low to allow her to sit up all the way. All she had was the vague outline of thick steel bars, her light feebly reflecting off of them, highlighting old rust.

"Hello?" Anna called out in a wavering voice, her head throbbing in time with her heart. No one answered. She tried to move closer to the bars, her ankles yanking at the cuffs on her feet. There was a dog bowl in the corner filled with water, and another with a few grainy-looking biscuits. Anger filled her then, pushing down her fear and grief.

"LET ME OUT OF HERE!" she shouted, but her words died in the gloomy quiet. "HEY!"

Not even the faraway sobbing paused to acknowledge her.

Anna wasn't sure how much time passed, but eventually, there was the creak of a door opening, the click of shoes on concrete. She peered into the dark, eyes straining. As if in answer, the light under her skin burned stronger. She could see now that she was surrounded by crates. Whoever her crying neighbor was remained a mystery.

The tapping of shoes came closer. And, a sallow man in a bright red suit rounded the bend, nimble fingers fiddling with buttons that gleamed gold as he neared. His waxed mustache made an expressive twitch. For all the world, he looked like a circus ringmaster. The yellow light from Anna flared up over his face, making him blink, recasting his cheery smile into a sinister skull-grin. Two snake eyes sat in the sockets. Anna tensed. His was a dead stare, unsmiling, no matter what his mouth was doing.

He kneeled, peering at her. "Hello. I'm so glad you came back to me. Both in one day."

Anna shook her head. His eyes were strangely hypnotic, almost making her dizzy. *Contacts*, the desperate part of her mind said. "Who... who are you?" She steeled her voice, trying to make it forceful. "Where am I? What am I doing here?"

"Oh, good. You have some fight. That's always good." He took out a tiny notepad, making a few scribbles with what appeared to be a purple crayon.

"You are here with me again, Anna, to meet your destiny. Isn't that *wonderful?*"

Anna found nothing wonderful about it. "What are you talking about?"

"Don't worry. Even if you die, it's a very good time." He patted the top of her cage, a gentle rap. "You're for tonight. Lucky! Some people wait weeks!"

"Did the Archmage bring me here?" Anna's hands grasped at the manacles, looking for weak spots, for hope.

"Well, yes." The man giggled, a trill that left behind an unsettling echo in the room. "Knew Jack wouldn't be long after you, somehow, someway, whether he knows it or not. Connected."

"...Jack..?"

"Wants him to see you die. It's a *test*. But, the Archmage doesn't appreciate the art of what I do. He lied to me. Many times. *He broke the rules.*" The man's voice bled a harsh and discordant edge. "Will have to deal with him. But not first. Wanted to deal with you first."

"What are you *talking* about?"

A spasm wracked the man's face.

And, suddenly, the crate to Anna's left exploded. She shrieked and flinched back, holding up her arm to protect her eyes from flying splinters. Stinging needles embedded themselves in her flesh. *Ah!* When she lowered her arm to look where the crate had been, nothing remained, as if the box as large as her cage had disintegrated entirely. Blood was trickling down her wrist, and she sucked in a breath, pulling out the largest of the splinters, fingers shaking.

The man's face kept its skull-smile, as if nothing had happened. "Oh, we haven't been formally introduced! How *rude* of me. I'm The Announcer." He spread his arms wide and bowed his head. His words were spoken with such clarity and confidence that it might truly have been what his parents had named him.

Anna reached back to her pocket before remembering she had lost the Geiger counter.

"Oooo, you look about ready to *snap!* Careful! Once you go, there's not a lot of putting yourself back together. Haha. *Trust me.*" He made an elegant swish at the air with his hand. "Jack's getting prepared. I'm thinking... a club.

Always a spectacle! For you, I'm thinking—"

"You're *crazy*." Anna didn't know why she had to say it out loud. There was just so much insanity peering down at her that she couldn't help it.

"A stabby thing for you. A big one. Yes. A sword. Lady with a sword. Crowd pleaser. And tonight, you will choose your destiny. You're going to fight, and you're going to kill, and it will be *beautiful!* And, if you live, I'll let you go. That's the rule, Anna, above all others. You *must* kill to live. The Archmage doesn't get to change the rules whenever he *wants*."

Anna wasn't sure what broke inside of her then. Perhaps it was the sting of the manacles, or the madness, the memories of her death, or the dog bowls. Everything within her suddenly lunged forward, furious at yet another cage, at yet one more dose of horror and confusion. The chains on her ankles went painfully taut, wrenching her joints, but still, she struggled, she fought, and she yelled to high heaven.

The Announcer smiled, made several excited clapping gestures, and then spun on his heel and left as she ground her voice down screaming after him. She screamed for herself, and for everyone who'd risked their lives only so she could wind up here. She screamed for her friends and family, for everyone she'd left behind, and the death of the only reality she'd ever known. And, when all of the shouting was done, she saw the one thing that might save her life.

One of bolts holding her chains down, after her lunging and thrashing, was jiggling.

Anna began to struggle anew, wrapping her ankle chains around her bare hands until her knuckles felt about to break from the pressure, tugging, getting the bolt just a little... bit... looser. As she worked, her hands began to glow a little stronger, the fluttering light a butterfly under her skin.

Anna yanked. It gave a little. She tugged again, twisting and grinding the chain, then pulling as sudden and as hard as she could. It rattled a little more. *Do it! You can do it!*

With a cry, she pulled with everything she had, desperation singing in her blood, the light now pulsing so brightly she nearly had to close her eyes.

It sprung free! She tumbled, the bolt clattering, her back slamming into the steel bars. There were spots in her eyes, and she was just as surprised as she was happy. *Yes!*

Anna righted herself and scuffled to the door, her feet still bound to each other. The steel was old, scratched, and half rotted with rust from the damp. It might have held against most prisoners. But her? *What have I got to lose?* She'd died once already, anyway. Was this reincarnation? Had she been such a terrible person? Was this really where cheating on a 9th grade English test had gotten her?

Her fist connected with the lock, sending the cage vibrating and clanging. Hot certainty was in her chest. She wanted her life back. She wanted her cat, her friends, and an entire pizza with pineapple and onions, but if she couldn't have that, then by God, she was going to have the sun on her face again, and she was going to *exist*. She was going to *live*. No more madness, fear, and blood. She swung again. *CLANG!* And again. *CLANG!*

"Agh!" Her knuckles throbbed in agony. Painful trills were spiraling up her arm. The metal hadn't rotted through so thoroughly, after all. Of all the times she wanted to be some super-girl, *wanted* these powers to do something, and she was falling flat. The light wavered.

"Shhhhh!" A frightened whisper drifted to her. "Stop doing that!"

She looked up. One of the crates now gone, she could now see a woman across the room was staring at her, hunched over in her own cage. Her fists balled up nervous bundles of stained flower-print dress. "I'm getting out of here," Anna told her.

"No! Just… be quiet! It's against the *r-r-rules* to try to leave." The woman was blinking rapidly, covering her eyes, as if she had been in the dark so long that it hurt to look directly at Anna's light.

Anna blinked in disbelief. "I'm. Getting. Out. Of. Here." Biting her lip, tensing her entire arm, she cocked back her fist.

"What the *hell's* going on in there?" There was a sound of someone stomping their way through the cages. A grim-faced man stormed into view. Anna hesitated. The light flickered and faded, until it was almost gone. Something about the way he moved reminder her of Frank, but the coiled tension was ready to be unloaded on *her*. There was a gun belt wrapped around his hip, and goggles on his face, black and green. *Night vision…?* "The hell happened? How did you get that bolt loose? You making trouble?" He sneered at her, grabbing the door with his meaty fists and shaking it, just, it seemed, to make sure it was secure. "You're new, bitch, so I'm going to explain—"

Anna reached down inside of herself, squeezing her eyes shut, trying to grab hold of her courage, that indefinable feeling of warmth when the light surged through her. And, it was if a bright fire burst ablaze under her skin, right in this man's eyes.

"Gah…!" He tore at his goggles, startled and blind. Anna snapped her hand through the bars, grabbing his gun out of his belt, praying the explosive force of the bullet would succeed where she failed. *Over 800 pounds of force*, an old bit of physics homework reminded her. She had one shot, and she could only hope it didn't ricochet.

Anna aimed at the lock, the weakest, rustiest point she could see, and squeezed the trigger.

Nothing happened.

"Crap!" She flicked off the safety, and squeezed the trigger again.

BANG!

The sound shuddered through her soul, almost sending her to her knees, but she fought to stay up, to not lose herself in fear and memories. The bullet exploded against the lock, punching a massive dent in it, and Anna followed with her fist.

CLANG!

The cell door gave, flying open with a squeal and a crash. But, the thug had wrestled off his damaged goggles, and she was a beacon in the dark. He lunged for the gun. Anna swung wildly at him. Her fist crunched into his chest, and he made a surprised "*Urk!*", eyes bulging. He dropped. His breath was a gasping wheeze.

Anna stared down at the crumpled man in surprise. She nearly panicked that she'd collapsed his lung. "Sorry!" Then, she wondered why she was apologizing.

On his belt was a ring of keys. Anna tore it away, then skipped back as he recovered, glaring up at her in disbelief. She leveled the gun at him.

"Great. Another freak." The thug stiffly sat to his knees, blood trickling down his lip.

"Uh! Get in a cage! And don't call for help!"

He stared at her, scowling. And then, resentfully, he stood, turned away, and began a slow shuffle, one hand nursing where she'd hit him. An empty pen was only a few feet away. He crawled inside, as if it hurt to crouch, and shut the door behind him. The lock clicked. "Stupid," he wheezed. "You're not gonna get far. You should know better."

"Thanks for your advice," Anna breathed, lowering the gun.

"Hey! Glow-witch!"

Anna turned. A scrawny, darkly tanned prisoner was waving at her. He was covered in tattoos, a scraggly beard scraping his chest. "Those keys. You'll get me outta this, right? I'll follow you to hell and back if you do!"

The light around her had receded from her assault against the thug, but it still burned bright, and Anna suddenly realized how many shines of eyes there were in the darkness. Thirty, maybe more.

"Me too!" Someone called.

"HEY! Don't forget me!"

"N-n-no!" The first woman in the cage called again. "Get back inside! Before it's too late!"

"Don't listen to her," the tattooed man muttered. "Broken, is what she is..." And yet, she wasn't the only one making distressed noises, as if the idea of leaving was too much to bear.

Anna swallowed, coming to terms with what she was about to do. "I'm not leaving anyone behind." Her hands shook as she rifled through the keys. "And... and you stay quiet," she told the thug in the cage.

"Couldn't yell if I wanted to," he wheezed. "Christ. Your right hook..." He coughed, spitting a dark glob onto the cage floor.

There were only five keys, but it took Anna a minute to figure out which went to cages, and which to manacles. Her chains fell away with a click and a clatter. A subtle thudding had begun as she worked, stomping, chanting. "Glow-witch! Glow-witch!" She wasn't sure how she felt about this name, but she supposed it wasn't as bad as it could have been. Jogging, she reached the tattooed man's cage, trying the keys in the lock. He smiled, and Anna tried not to wince at the fact that all of his teeth were filed down. "I'm Rat. You single, lady?"

"Uh. Yes. But, not for you."

He laughed, but there was too much white showing in his eyes, as if the laugh was part hysterical. His lock accepted the third key Anna tried, and opened with a grinding swish. "We have to get outta here." He scampered out, favoring his right leg. "Now."

Anna snapped two of the keys off of the ring, passing them to him. "Go around opening the cages. We're not leaving without everyone."

He shook his head. "That asshole's not the only guard. There are patrols."

"Then hurry!" Anna dashed to the crying woman's cage, setting down the gun so she could use both hands. One of her keys worked. The woman shook her head over and over, shying from the door. "Hey," Anna whispered. "Come on. Let me open your chains. We're all gonna get out of here. What's your name?"

The woman's eyes were wide with terror, and she stared over Anna's shoulder at the other cages getting opened. "B-barbara." Anna followed her stare. More prisoners were free now. Many were tattooed like the first man. "I c-c-can't g-go."

Anna considered the effort it would take to heft this woman over a shoulder, but she knew it wouldn't work. She made a pleading gesture, her palms up. "I don't understand. Why don't you want to run?"

The woman only shook her head. "It's… it's okay. I'll be okay. Will you send help? P-please?"

Guilt tore at Anna's heart. "Alright. Okay. I promise." She backed away. "Are you sure?"

"Y-yes." The woman reached out and closed the cage door with a final *click*.

She wasn't the only one. As her and Rat moved through the room, Anna counted six of the thirty-odd prisoners who would refuse to leave. They sometimes stared straight ahead, gazes vacant. They sometimes shook their heads, like Barbara had, quietly shutting their doors. One muttered. "Rules," and turned away. But, the rest were a rowdy bunch, stretching out disused limbs, rolling necks, leaping from foot to foot. Almost all of them shared Rat's sense of fashion: scarification, ink, and muscled anger. *A gang?* Well, if she was going to get out of this, she realized, it might pay to have dangerous friends.

"Um." Anna weaved through the growing mob and tapped Rat on the shoulder, right in the middle of a faded image of a viper eating a pigeon. He jumped. "Okay. We can go now." She cast one last look behind her. *I'll send help,* she promised.

"About time," he muttered. "Shark here knows the way out, he says."

He jabbed a rough thumb over his shoulder at a mountain of a man, red ink tattooed in a splash over his face as if it were a mask. This man's eyes were steel and fury, and a rumble began in his throat. "Dragged up there. Fought three times. Won." His fists clenched into steel boulders. "Yeah. I know the way."

"Okay, then, Mr. Shark." The hairs on Anna's neck refused to lay flat when she looked at him. "You lead."

He smiled, filed teeth rotted, some missing. "Glow-witch. You stay with me. Walking flashlight. Rat takes the gun. He's a good shot."

The initial burn of courage was straining to hold. Anna remembered the terrified jelly in her limbs when she'd left her office for the last time over a hundred years ago. Now, she had no Pentagon to reach, no radio. She had no friends down here. Just Rat, Shark, and a horde of disquieted, angry gang members. She swallowed, bracing herself. "Okay."

It bothered her, surrendering the pistol to a stranger's outstretched hand, but she couldn't deny she had no idea how to really use a gun. *Perhaps he can do better.* Despite her wariness, it was as if a burden lifted when the firearm passed from her fingers to Rat's, the object like the one that had ended her once before. She hated the thing, and never wanted to see another one again.

They moved as a sea out of the door, no hesitation in their steps, no arguments on their lips. Anna took the lead next to Shark, a small beacon lighting their way. Her shoes were dirty and wet, making mousy squeaks against the stonework, the shuffle of the hoard behind her. The tunnel bent both left and right, stretching on endlessly in either direction. Shark chose the right-hand path, moving quick and low to the ground for his size. The group followed, Anna keeping her eyes and ears open, knowing that if anything happened to her, they would all be dead in the dark.

Then, a guard turned the corner. "What the-!" he called, reaching for something on his belt.

"GO!" Shark roared. Five people split away, as if trained. They threw themselves as a mob at the guard, who drew his pistol, sending bright flashes and explosive cracks into the blackness. Two painted bodies went down, unmoving, no one even crying out. The remaining three, silent, overwhelmed the thug, pinning him. Anna winced as she heard him shriek in pain, and then, a gunshot silenced the struggle. Her head rang, her eyes stung. The three survivors rejoined the group, a woman clutching the gun, a cut over her eyebrow bleeding profusely. Her stare was grim. None of them moved to retrieve the fallen.

"What about—"

Shark put a meaty palm in her back, shoving her forward. "Leave them. Did their job. All of us dead if *he* comes back."

Anna hesitated. But, she let herself be pushed on, not knowing why it hurt her chest so much to leave those two strangers' bodies behind in the dark.

It was an endless rush through decaying stone tunnels, the smell of stagnant water and mold filling their noses. More than once, Shark stopped, grumbling, swaying his head back and forth as if unsure. He'd gesture Anna come closer to illuminate something he was squinting at, make an exasperated grunt as if coming to a conclusion he didn't like, and would guide them down a new path. Sometimes, he would pause, kneel, and examine the stonework for minutes on end, running his hand over the slime on the surface.

"Man, what are you hoping to find down there? A damn sandwich?" Rat griped. "I thought you said you knew!"

"*Shut up*. I do." Shark growled, contemplated, and moved on.

Anna wasn't sure how long they stumbled about in the tunnels, but then, the terrain subtly changed. Rotted stone and concrete shifted into tile. She heard echoing—voices? Unsure, she glanced at her guide. The man had an ugly smile pasted on his face, his teeth causing his bottom lip to bleed.

"Is this the way out?" she whispered.

"Oh yeah, Glow-witch. Only way out."

Something about the way he said it made her spine wobble. Trash and debris crunched under their feet, and then, she saw for the first time down here a light beyond her own. The sunshine in her skin dimmed in greeting it. There was a grinding hum in the air, the artificial bulb flickering gaudy fluorescence on the dirty white walls, revealing the hallway beyond. At the end, there was a teal elevator, bright red and gold banner framing it, velvety and tasseled. "Welcome to the greatest show in New York!" it cheered.

"*Only* way," Shark intoned again, still smiling, pressing his meaty thumb into the UP button.

The elevator made a polite ding, and opened. Anna was shoved inside, Shark lumbering in after. The crowd poured in, filling every space, elbows and chins digging and squishing as their bodies panted and lurched. The air was sucked out of the tiny space. Anna could no longer see anything but inked, scarred skin.

"Up," Shark grunted.

The doors swished shut with another mellow ding, like he'd commanded it.

And, when they opened, a roar filled the air, screaming, cheering, applause. Anna froze.

"Show tonight," Shark rumbled, flexing his enormous fists. "Home game. Better run, if you don't want him to catch you again."

The crowd of prisoners seemed to understand what he meant. They gasped and pried themselves from each other, bare feet and worn shoes tearing out down the new hallway. Anna, in the back, took a long breath as the stench in the elevator began to lift. *You heard him. Go!*

Shark fell into a lumbering gait, taking up the rear, and Rat scurried in his wake, still limping. Anna slowed, staying in the back with them, letting the first of the prisoners spill ahead. At first, she didn't understand why she felt she needed bring up the rear. Then, Rat tripped on his bad leg, and she grabbed his arm, righting him, tugging him forward, and understood. *No one else dies,* she thought. She had survived, somehow, when her entire world had burned. No one else had to get killed. Not even creepy Shark and Rat. Not if she could help it.

The harsh artificial lights gave way to darkness again, but this one hushed and soft. The hairs on Anna's neck rose again. On instinct, she knew this dark was engineered for atmosphere. Startled yells and shouts greeted them. They'd crashed into a crowd, it seemed, hundreds of people in finery, business suits, and masquerade masks, glasses in hand. More than one face seemed upset that the jostling had spilled their alcohol. Bright stage lights beamed down on their far right. A stage stood under the lights, a fighting arena, no lines or ropes, but unmistakable all the same, old blood stains seeped over the edges. Anna understood then where she'd been slated to go that evening. *Lady with a sword. Crowd pleaser.* She shuddered.

A splash of red mobbed her peripheral vision. She stumbled, her mouth dropping, nearly tripping Rat a second time. The man in ringmaster red. He was *floating.* He descended down from the ceiling over the stage, arms outstretched and silver mask glittering in the spotlight. Though he gave no sign of having seen them, Anna felt his eyes washing over the room, the cold snake orbs almost freezing her like a startled deer. Even with the rush of prisoners just breaking into the crowd, no one had torn away from his spectacle long enough to sound an alarm.

"Ladies and gentleman," he called, his voice sharpened silk. "This is a special night."

The crowd roared. And, Shark suddenly let out a bloodthirsty cry, peeling off from Anna's left, teeth bared in a frightening, malicious snarl. He dove into a nearby cluster of richly-dressed men, eyes filled with rage and satisfaction.

The onlookers screamed, but were drowned out in the cheering for what was happening on stage. And, Rat was the one grabbing Anna's arm now, tugging her onward when she moved to stop Shark.

"LEAVE HIM!" Rat yelled. "He's got what he wanted!"

Chaos had hit the immediate crowd, some backing up to watch Shark attack the audience, some yelling and fleeing, some still oblivious to the scene and applauding. The Announcer had not stopped his opening ceremony, and Anna prayed the bright lights had blinded him to them. He was keeping most of the gathering under his spell. "Our headliner tonight is my personal favorite. This is the fight I've waited *years* for." He took a deep, satisfied breath, letting his congregation marinate in anticipation. "Good people of New York, Give a great welcoming scream for... *JACK!*"

Anna turned for just a moment to see, the announcer's voice curling around her ears, as if he'd walked up and spun her, demanded she look. And, what she saw made her heart drop. That couldn't be...? He wouldn't have... No. *No.* The crowd jeered, and Anna pulled against Rat's grip, grinding them both to a halt.

"*What are you doing?*" he yelled.

There under the spotlights was Jackson, trembling, bloodied, and staring out at the crowd. The white illumination washed out his pale skin even further, making him look sick and weak. In one hand, he dragged what looked to be a club twice as long as his arm and three times as thick.

"Fodder!" Feet stomped and voices roared. "Fodder!"

He came for me.

Anna cried out his name, but it was lost in the fervor. His opponent entered the arena now, disdain and triumph on his face, thunderous approval exploding from the audience.

He's going to die.

CHAPTER NINETEEN
Raven Song

The primal roar of the crowd vibrated up through the cold cement floor into Jackson's bare feet, so much worse than in the dream. Spots danced in his vision as he staggered under the hot, white lights. The arena was a long, rectangle slab, faded blood flecked in the cracks, open air along one end, the crowd reveling there beneath him. There was no fence to prevent him from trying to flee into their ranks—but running would be against the rules, wouldn't it? A powerful voice carried over the audience, joyous and reverent, yet with an edge to it like a serrated knife. Tony's voice.

"Ladies and gentleman, give a great welcoming scream for *JACK!*"

The hoots and cheers pounded against his ears, but a terrible undercurrent of laughter and chanting was swelling beneath it.

"Fodder! Fodder! Fodder!"

The arena lights allowed him no secrets. Jackson looked down at his body, now stripped of all but a pair of shorts, as if seeing himself for the first time. He was smooth and soft, flesh pale from lack of sunlight. His wiry, underdeveloped muscles gave him away for what he was. A businessman. A man who handled money, not labor. There was no fighter here. And when they'd taken everything from him, slapped this club in his hand, and shoved him out the door at gunpoint, there had been nothing he could do to stop it.

The pain-stricken faces of the arena's victims from his dreams floated into his mind. Their snapped and skewered bodies were shuffled away like trash, the blood still pooling on the ground.

Jackson's hand ached already from the heavy club. Sheer terror almost made him drop it. A weakness and lightheadedness had clouded over him in those dark tunnels, and it was everything within him not to vomit in front of the bloodthirsty masses, right now.

"Fodder!"

No. He could not show them how afraid he was of all of them, of whoever walked through that other door. Jackson instead raised the club as high as he could and let out a dogged cry. The club only went up about halfway, and he had to use both hands to even manage that. The laughter of the crowd vibrated through him. He imagined he looked like a puppy trying to act bigger than it was.

"Fodder!"

NO! He was not going to lay down and let himself get his throat cut on their sick little entertainment alter. He would fight. He had to. Jackson bore his teeth, holding the club fast, wanting to scream back at the crowd. *This is what you want? You want me? Come get me, then!*

"I know he doesn't look like much, dear audience, but look at that spirit! It's too bad his opponent today is our five time champion…"

Jackson felt a coldness in his bones. He knew exactly what the announcer was about to say, knew in that moment, there was no other path.

Destiny.

"…THE TIGER!"

Jackson let the club rest with a heavy thud as the opposite doors opened. As if out of hell, The Tiger paced forth, the same animalistic lightness in his step, the same cold nothingness in his eyes. The peculiar lifelike tail lashed behind him, and he bared sharpened teeth in a snarl, fiery warpaint blazed over his body. The cruel, rusted spear was bound to his back with a strip of leather, still caked with someone's blood.

The final piece of his nightmare was complete.

Jackson stared. Then, he felt a shuddering in his core. It twisted his insides, hurting, until he couldn't hold it in anymore. Something broke.

He began to laugh.

His executioner halted his restive pacing for a step, cocking his bestial head in something akin to confusion. Apparently, this was not the reaction he was used to inspiring. But, Jackson found he couldn't stop. Chuckles were bubbling up through his throat and spilling out like some sort of wellspring of hysteria had uncorked in his brain. He shook, tears starting to roll down his face.

There was a restless muttering in the crowd. Jackson looked out at them, laughing harder now, knowing they would never get the joke. He was crazy, saw things that weren't there, had dreams about things that weren't supposed to be real. Except, here they *all* were, in the flesh, and they were about to end his life.

Oh gods, he was going to die.

The laughter pouring out of his chest trickled to a stop.

Then, an eerie giggling began anew, and Jackson realized it was no longer coming from him. The laughter washed over the silent and uneasy crowd, amplified by a microphone. Even The Tiger was glancing back over his shoulder, nervous.

It was *him*. Tony. His chuckling became a high-pitched, insane trill. "HAHAHAHAHA! Ahhhh. Like I said! Such spirit!" The man reached under his mask, as if to wipe away a tear of joy. "I'm not counting Jack out just yet, and *you shouldn't either*. Now, my Jack, my Tiger, ARE YOU READY?"

The audience hadn't yet recovered from the air of disquiet. A few yelled and cheered, but an apprehensive muttering had taken root.

No time to think about it. The announcer howled, "BEGIN!"

Distracted Jackson was hit with a blow to his side like he had been smashed with a bag of bricks. He toppled and rolled, gasping with pain, club falling out of his hands. The Tiger had somehow covered the distance between them, far too fast for any human Jackson had seen, and was stalking back and forth, as if challenging him to get back up. Jackson scrambled to his feet and pedaled backwards, trying to get out of reach. His ribs ached with each breath. He was disarmed. The club was too far away now. *Shit! Shit!*

But The Tiger did not reach for his spear just yet. Instead, he let out a growling shout, spreading his arms wide, as if in a dare.

Realization dawned. The Tiger could kill him in less than a minute. But this wasn't just an execution. This was a show. A spectacle. He had to toy with Jackson, draw it out, excite the crowd.

Jackson tried to stop hunching over like his side wasn't killing him. His eyes flickered to the discarded club.

The authorities would not save him. Not Frank, not anyone else. He was alone.

The Tiger pounced.

Jackson was too soaked in adrenaline to know how he evaded the grab. Perhaps it was because he had seen it before, in his dream, when a young man let his guard down and met his end. Somehow, though, Jackson dove through The Tiger's deft grasp, heard the grunt of surprise. His hands made a frantic grab and curled around rusted iron and wood: the spear on the man's back. The Tiger swung around wildly, and his meaty fist connected with Jackson's face. Pain and starry lights bloomed. Jackson's jaw crunched in an unnatural way to the side.

There was a snapping sensation in his hands. He was flung back several feet, teetering backwards and landing hard on the floor. Lights were still dancing in his vision. The crowd was cheering again. One eye was blurred. The other made out The Tiger's snarling countenance as the man grabbed for the spear on his back in a fury.

The spear did not draw—only a broken haft of wood.

Dizzily, Jackson looked down to his own hands. He clutched the other end of the haft, knocked back so hard that the rotten thing had finally snapped. Jackson tried to stand, to hold the cruel, rusted iron edge before him, but the world was veering on its side. So, he backpedaled as fast as he could with his feet, still half-lying on the ground, as The Tiger let out another raging shout, storming towards him.

Gaining the weapon was a hollow victory. The Tiger wore a cold look of satisfaction that said he knew he had won, and Jackson's silly, untrained spear-waving would get him nowhere. He began to dance around the feeble slashes and smile, the crowd whooping and cheering. His shadow cast long and dark over Jackson now, all the more monstrous with the stark lighting at his back, eyes alight with bloodlust as he advanced.

Be more clever, a haunting voice resonated somewhere in the back of Jackson's mind.

And then, with sudden clarity through the dizziness and pain, Jackson knew exactly what to do.

The Tiger's shadow was cool under his empty hand. It felt like an autumn night, like an old friend. An odd sensation of peace was stealing over Jackson now, of wordless understanding. And, the shadow *rippled*. It flowed up and over The Tiger's ankles like it was made of water, almost looking like a trick of the light.

The Tiger's eyes went wide. His foot caught on something unseen. With a surprised grunt, he toppled and fell, arms waving to catch himself. And, he landed on his opponent, all thick muscle and bone, brutally forcing the air out of Jackson's lungs. Jackson struggled, unable to move, flailing to breathe. His opponent let out a gurgling roar, and rolled off of him, delivering a crushing kick to his knee in the process. Jackson almost went blind the fresh pain, feeling as if a knife was under his knee cap. He was dragging himself away from his opponent with just his arms now.

Yet, The Tiger was not advancing. He was regarding Jackson with a baleful glare, clutching his side, doubled over on the ground. Blood spattered. The spear head had found its way deep between The Tiger's ribs. If Jackson didn't collapse from pain and weariness first, he might fall over from relief. *No one gets up from that.* The bright red was seeping too fast through the man's fingers.

Then, The Tiger struggled to his feet, shaky, but furious. "Oh, come on," Jackson wheezed. The Tiger's stance was flagging, the bloody spear hanging from him like a hideous ornamentation… but impossibly, he stood.

"Not die." The Tiger's words were rasps, yet Jackson had been wondering if he could speak at all. "Will not die. Not to *you*." He staggered forward, eyes fixated on the club that had fallen between them not long ago. Even though he looked half in the grave, he kneeled and hefted it up in one hand. Jackson let out a cry of anger and fear, reaching through the shadows one last time. But now, though The Tiger lurched and stumbled, he didn't fall, as if he was moving under the power of some unstoppable engine.

The Tiger came to a stop just over Jackson's prone body. They had dragged themselves to the edge of the arena. There was nowhere else to go.

"Done now. Finally done," the bestial man wheezed. He raised the club up high, blocking out the light.

Jackson heaved himself up with a strength he didn't know he had. The shadows felt as if they pooled around his body, a tingling surge of reassurance, of power. With every last ounce of will he had left, he grabbed for the spear in The Tiger's side and pulled, feeling the shadows pull with him. The club crushed against his back, missing his head, causing his arms to go explosively numb. Yet, he held.

They both howled in pain as the spear came out in Jackson's grasp. Blood began streaming down The Tiger's side, faster, unstoppable.

Then, The Tiger grabbed the spear from Jackson's shaking, useless hands. With no further contemplation, he thrust the spear into Jackson's chest, pinning him like a stuck insect to the floor.

Jackson's limbs went limp. He stared in disbelief at the object sticking out of his body. A whimper. A gasp for air. The spear throbbed in his vision like a hallucination. It burned and ached, eating him alive. He couldn't breathe. His arms twitched weakly. Warmth, life was trickling out of the wound, down his chest and sides. Above was the beast-man, eyes hungry and triumphant.

There was shouting then, and a rapid series of loud bangs. The Tiger flew off his feet as if he had been punched by an invisible fist. He landed somewhere off to the side, but Jackson was unable to look away from the shaft sprouting from his lung and protruding towards the ceiling.

He kicked his legs futilely. He was desperate not to die.

He was certain he wouldn't live.

A fist was clenching his weakening heart, squeezing, tighter, tighter, spots swimming before him.

Someone was screaming. A lot of someones.

The harsh arena lights were like the sun, drying Jackson's blood to his skin. Flickers of black wheeled in his vision against the light. Then, they weren't flickers anymore. They were dark-feathered birds croaking their song overhead, circling, watching.

His companions until the end. Always.

The edges of his sight were blurred and distorted, and he was spiraling downwards, down a shadowy hole. In the pinprick of light there was left, he saw a glittering silver mask move overhead, the patient reptilian eyes behind it watching him fall.

Tony's voice was gentle and quiet now.

"The ravens are coming for you, Jack. Don't worry, though. I'm here."

And all was darkness.

CHAPTER TWENTY
Deal Made

Anna watched, horror-struck, as a war-painted man stalked around Jackson, the spectators laughing cruelly. His arms were as thick as Jackson's head. Anyone could see her friend had no chance. He looked terrified, like he was paralyzed, too stricken to move in the face of the bloodthirsty crowd.

There was a yank at Anna's wrist again. "Glow-witch! HEY!" Anna snapped back to see Rat, one of his knees twisted in, like he couldn't put any pressure at all on his right foot anymore. Bright fear was in his eyes. "We gotta go! NOW!"

"I can't!" She swung a hand at the stage. "I have to stop them!"

"Are you crazy? He kills all of us then! Come ON! I need you to get me out!"

"Shoot that guy!" She pointed at The Tiger's meaty backside.

"*No!*"

The crowd burst into a hearty cheer. Anna snapped her eyes to see Jackson flying back, stumbling into a dizzy pile, looking as if he couldn't see straight. Blood ran down his face. He had somehow gotten the spear from The Tiger's back, and was waving it like a drunk man.

"Shoot him!" she yelled again. Anna then noticed a sharp-eyed man splitting the crowd, a cold brutality in his clenching fists. *A guard.* He was drawing a weapon. Someone had finally noticed them. They were running out of time. Not knowing what else to do, she raised her fists, putting herself between Rat and the advancing threat twice her size. Her knees shook, her mouth going dry with adrenaline.

And then, only a few yards from reaching her, the guard stiffened and trembled as if struck by lightning. His eyes rolled back in his head, and his tongue lolled out between his teeth. He dropped in front of her, a heavy thud.

Behind him stood a man in a dark suit with dark glasses, holding what Anna could only assume was a stun gun. The tip crackled and arced. "Anna! Are you alright?" He outstretched a hand, eyes wide.

"…Agent Walker?" Anna didn't lower her fists, but relief and confusion blossomed in her chest. She was even more surprised when she looked to Walker's right. There stood a balding, broad-shouldered man, salt-and-pepper eyebrows knitted in what might have been annoyance. *"Frank?"*

The crowd was shrieking now. The frenzy had finally begun to spread, and people were whipping their costumed faces around, catching sight of Agent Walker and, further back, Shark. They were dropping their drinks and fleeing. Anna ran to him and Frank, grateful they were there, and pointed wildly at the stage. The Announcer was cocking his head at his audience now, a befuddled statue.

"Is that…?" Walker holstered the stun gun, drawing another pistol. On stage, The Tiger was towering above Jackson. He'd gotten the spear, was raising it in an arc.

"STOP HIM!" Anna yelled.

The Tiger plummeted the spear into Jackson's chest. Jackson's limbs seized up, and then settled, twitching.

Time seemed to slow.

BANG BANG BANG!

Bullets exploded from Walker's pistol, and The Tiger's head snapped back as he flew off his feet. He landed in a heap, blood, froth, and muscle.

"Violators! Violators in my arena!" It was a hushed call, yet it carried over the crowd like an unsettling specter. The Announcer was descending from his perch on high. "Who would dare break the rules *here?*"

Anna broke and ran for the stage, filling with hot pangs of grief and desperation. The startled masses had made for the exits, but they still swirled and trampled, a confused tangle of finery and masks. Arms smacked her and legs threatened to trip her. She shoved them out of her way. *Please be alive, please be alive, please be okay enough for someone to help.*

A shrill voice barked. "Is it *you?*" The Announcer's reptile eyes fell on her, the skull-smile still paralyzed on his face. A spotlight swayed of its own accord, beaming down on where she stood, blinding her. "You left your *cage?* Don't you know what that *means?*" He thrust a palm out, fingers curling, like he was attempting to close them around a delicate egg.

A deep pain pulsed under her left breast. She staggered in her run, dizzy, head snapping forward. "Agh!" Hot sweat burst on her back, her eyes blurring, and she fell to her knees. *What...!* Her skin itched and thundered with her pulse. Blue veins were popping in spiderwebs against the surface of her arms, her vision blurring in time with her heartbeat. It hammered faster now, faster. Her breath came in constricted pops. Her heart felt like it was about to tear in two-!

A dozen cracks rang out in the air, and The Announcer ripped his head away from her. The horrifying sensations subsided, her heart slowing down, and she collapsed, almost sick. There was warm blood under her nose, dripping down her lip. As her vision cleared, she saw what could only be soldiers now, camouflaged men and women storming through the crowd with rifles, pistols, and bulky bulletproof vests. They were throwing the straggling arena patrons to the floor, blinding them with bright flashlight beams, training their weapons on The Announcer. Anna tried staggering to her feet, thinking of Jackson, but her vision swayed and shifted, and she could barely put one step in front of the next.

The Announcer was backing up on the stage floor now, teeth bared. Anna saw him kneel over Jackson, saying something. A dozen rifles lit up red dots on his brow.

"We have you surrounded!" a voice shouted.

The Announcer raised his eyes, his face contorting. Under the brilliant lights, his expression trembling, he looked like a mournful actor in a tragedy, one about to pierce the air with a soul-rending song. Anna dragged herself onwards, trying to see her friend.

"Put your hands over your head!" More men and women in uniforms were storming through the dark, these in dark blue, a golden badge glittering on their chests. Their pistols were raised. At the fore was a woman, her body ramrod straight, her furious commands splitting the air without any aid. "Do it, now!"

The Announcer's reply shuddered through the room, a reverberating roar to dwarf her. "*Rule breakers!*" His spittle flew before him. "I will be back to deal with *all* of you!" And, he put his palms on the concrete stage, and screamed.

Anna would remember that the only sign of what was to happen was the rumble in the floor, just for a moment. An earthquake teased her feet.

And then, the stage *burst.*

Concrete dust swelled in a wave. Shards of rocks and rubble rocketed outwards, dropping several agents where they stood. Splashes of blood danced in the air before the billows of dust plumed over them, choking them, wiping out their vision.

The world was a muffled haze. Anna was floating in a dark cloud. Her lungs burned. She managed to get to her feet and pressed forward, unable to see, the light under her skin flaring, trying to guide her way. It was useless. She stumbled, feeling an arm or a leg under her feet, a warm body, but she couldn't tell if it was Jackson or a Coalition agent, couldn't check if they were alive or dead. She kneeled, putting a hand on this person's side, as if to comfort them.

She didn't know how many minutes passed, the world a tide of concrete sand. Finally, however, the dust began to settle. Anna coughed, expelling it. Her nose was plugged, her tongue smearing grit on the roof of her mouth. She could see now her hand was holding the sleeve of someone who used to be wearing camouflage, now ashy gray. His pained face seemed to plead with her, coffee-colored lips drawn back across white teeth in a grimace. He wasn't an agent—the colored bars on his shoulders seemed to indicate he was a soldier. There was a bright red spot spreading down his torso, pierced by what looked to be rebar. It had gone right through his armored vest. Anna saw his front moving up and down, weakly clutching at breath. She still couldn't see far ahead, but, hesitating, she looked down at the soldier's frightened eyes.

There was a tag on his jacket that read *Waters*.

"You're gonna be okay, Waters," she choked out. He nodded, dazed.

Heart sagging, knowing how bad this soldier's injury looked, she scanned the room. The spotlight was still shining down, setting the dust aglow. Both The Announcer and Jackson's body were gone.

Anna sniffled. *He might still be alive.*

There was a shouting now. It sounded like the agents and soldiers were recouping, searching.

I don't really have anywhere to run, do I?

Anna put her palm into the soldier's gaping wound, trying to staunch the flow with the cloth of her sleeve. Waters winced.

The glow under her hand grew stronger then, brightening around her fingers. Waters made a strangled gasp. Unsure of what she was doing, but certain now that it wasn't anything bad, she let her fingers stay. Then, she reached down inside of herself and encouraged the glow. It heated her palm, a friendly light. The metal stuck in his chest trembled. It seemed to push itself out, rolling down his side and clattering to the floor.

Waters's blood ran slower now. He stared up at her in wonder.

Click. Something cold and heavy came to rest in the back of Anna's head. "Stand up with your hands over your head, Dr. Matthews." The emotionless voice was the one she'd dreaded hearing.

"Reeds." She didn't stand. "I think I'm helping this soldier. Wait, okay?"

"Haven't you gotten uppity. I said, stand, hands on your head."

"Let... her... help..." the soldier gasped, glaring up over Anna's shoulder. She stayed kneeling, focusing on the warmth in her hands. On the edge of her awareness, she felt her toes getting cold, then her feet, like the light was leaking from her body. It left a shaking weakness behind. Anna, afraid, bit her lip, letting the coldness creep up her legs until she was numb at the knees.

Waters's bleeding stopped. He let out a deep sigh, closing his eyes. "...

Thank you. Whatever you did." Anna nodded and moved to stand, stumbling on her freezing and numb ankles. The light flickered out. She collapsed again.

"Having trouble?" Reeds intoned. "You've certainly given me enough of that."

Waters began standing too, grimacing, slow. He gave Anna's shoulder a tug, helping her to her feet, offering a shoulder.

"What are you doing, Sergeant?" Anna could hear the narrowed eyes in Reeds's voice.

"Helping her. With all due respect, sir, she doesn't look like she's going anywhere fast."

Anna trembled, staggering, leaning on the soldier's good shoulder. She felt jelly in her muscles, like she had when she thought she had radiation sickness. Still, she walked. Together, they found the door outside, an exit from the dust and darkness. Everyone was shouting, running, and Anna saw more than one angry, searching face.

"He got away," Anna whispered.

"Looks that way," Waters agreed. "Never seen anything like that in all my life." He helped her to the tailgate of a truck, the Coalition handshake emblazoned on the side. Medics in white were scattered around it, seeing to injuries. Anna could do nothing but sit, an ashen ghost staring at the sky. Waters leaned against the vehicle too, closing his eyes, looking almost ready to fall over again. The arena looked to have been in an old brick building, no defining signs, and Anna didn't know New York well enough to know this neighborhood. The block was lined with shuttered gates and garbage. If there had been any other people here, they'd fled when the government had shown up.

"If you try anything…" Reeds warned, joining them. He holstered his gun and posted himself nearby, tapping his ear with his one good arm. His eyes fixed into a middle distance, and he started whispering. Anna guessed he was using some kind of communication link.

A row of thirty well-dressed patrons were corralled in a corner. Their masks were torn away, their wrists pinioned behind their backs in cuffs. None of them looked up from their feet. They acted as if letting the setting sun reveal their faces was an embarrassment beyond compare. Anna found she wasn't sorry for them, not even a little.

And, hogtied on the ground nearby was Shark. His tattoos were almost entirely covered in dust, but there was no mistaking his sharp-toothed smile. He was making sure to affix it on the arrested arena guests, his eyes wild and happy, even though he was stuck on his stomach. Anna thought she saw red stains on his hands. She looked away.

A familiar, wheedling voice rang. "You don't understand! I was kidnapped, too! I can help you find him!" Anna jerked her head up. Walker was hustling Rat out of the door, who was in cuffs and limping badly.

"Keep moving, raider," Walker snapped.

Frank followed these two, brushing dust from his balding head and looking thunderous.

"Hey! Glow-witch!" Rat's eyes flickered to Anna's. "Tell them! Tell them I was a prisoner! I'm okay! I'm a good guy!"

"Glow-witch?" Reeds mumbled with disdain.

Anna had no idea how to respond. She waved at Walker, as if asking without words for him to come closer, and to bring Rat if he wanted. Walker shoved Rat onward until they approached the truck. "Anna. Do you know this one?"

Rat's eye pupils were surrounded by frightened white. His tattoos were fierce, his beard a scraggly, angry mess. But, he looked like a man on his way to the executioner, one knee twisted in, scrawny frame trembling. Anna wondered why he was a *raider*, what he'd done that had earned him New York's distrust. "Rat," she began.

"Yes'm!" He nodded. "See? I'm her friend."

"Do you know where The Announcer would take someone really hurt?" Anna worried her lip. "Someone so hurt that they couldn't move on their own?"

Rat clicked his teeth. His eyes darted. "Uh. Maybe. Yes."

"He doesn't know," Walker sighed, moving as if he was about to yank his prisoner away again.

And, then Frank walked forward, grabbed a hold of Rat's elbow, and twisted it, pressing his palm into his shoulder. Rat crumpled, shrieking. "Do you know or not?" Frank bellowed.

"Agghh! Shark! SHARK DOES!"

"And who's Shark?" Frank demanded.

Anna rose one shaking hand and pointed at the giant ball of smiling muscle thirty feet away. "He said he fought in that arena three times. He probably did have to get healed up a lot." Frank eased off Rat, but stared him down as the man stood and shuffled out of arm's reach. "Also... there still people down in the tunnels. Prisoners. Shark knows the way back to them, too."

Walker glared at Shark, then yanked Rat over in that direction, thrusting him on the ground into a sitting position. They shared words. After a moment, Shark turned, and smiled at Anna, sending the creeping chills down her spine again. Walker rose, re-handcuffed Rat to a nearby pole, and then stormed back.

"And what's your report, Walker?" Reeds sighed, sounding bored. "That, as we've noticed, we've lost this so-called 'Announcer' of yours for good?"

Walker bristled. "No." He lifted his hand to his ear. "Director."

Reeds straightened. "I demand to be in on this call."

Walker glared. "We found Antonio Bertinelli, sir." There was a long silence. "Yes, sir. He's The Announcer. The rumored fighting rings. They've been operating out of the unused subway and sewer tunnels. I'm going to send you my report. Level 10 Esper activity." A pause. "No sir, he got away. But, we might have a lead. He's a raider—former prisoner of Bertinelli's. I advise we do anything and everything to follow this one, sir, or he's going to vanish again."

"I demand to be in on—" Reeds stopped, astounded, as Walker held up a finger of silence.

"Reeds is requesting to be on the line," Walker continued, tone flat.

Reeds straightened, tapping his ear. "Director! I've apprehended #46, Matthews. She was involved in this fighting ring. Permission to bring her back to the base."

"Our raider lead claims he will *only* talk to Dr. Matthews, sir," Walker interrupted. "Anna led an escape among the prisoners in the fighting ring after being captured, securing his safety. If she's taken away from this operation, this man might shut down, and Bertinelli is lost to us. Raiders are well conditioned against interrogation, as you know. And, I repeat, Bertinelli is a *Level 10.*"

Anna blinked, staring at Walker and Reeds, who were busy sizing each other up, and, finally Frank, who only scowled at the sky. A little of her strength was coming back to her now that she was in the fresh air, the feeling returning to her feet and ankles. She shoved off from the tailgate, shaky, but ready to move.

Reeds was grimacing deeper now. He suddenly tore off his sunglasses, crushing them in his fist. "Yes sir," he spoke. "Understood." The destroyed glasses fell from his hand, and he tapped his ear one last time, sneering.

Walker smiled. "Anna, can you walk?"

"I don't know." She was quaking. "I want to help find Ja—" she cut herself off, eyes darting at Reeds, who was seething besides her. "The other prisoners."

"We need to hurry." Walker turned to Reeds once more. "I need ten soldiers and a medical team. Our best."

"I volunteer, sir," the soldier named Waters stepped forward, silent though he'd been by Anna's side. Walker nodded at him.

"You *will* bring her back to the facility intact," Reeds growled, pointing at Anna. "Or I will make sure that so-called *former* associate of yours, Nyx, names you in her interrogation."

Walker frowned. "Director's orders, Reeds."

Reeds spun and stormed away, muttering. Walker heaved a long sigh.

"Um," Anna whispered. She limped away from the truck, close enough to Walker so he would be within whispering earshot. "Hi. Thank you." She looked down at the ground.

"Good to see you're okay." He seemed very tired, and much older than when Anna had seen him last. "You've had a rough week."

"Shut it," Frank snapped. He was reloading his gun. "Don't care. Get your team. We're going, now."

Walker grimaced, then made his way back to Shark. Waters posted himself just behind him. And, Anna teetered after the two in Frank's shadow, weighing her words. "So…" she began. Frank gave her a sidelong stare. "How'd you find us?"

"You know the guy that brought you breakfast at the safe house?" Frank snarled.

"Um. Yes."

"He didn't run quick enough."

Anna swallowed.

Walker calmly added, "Mr. McSheffrey here called me in when he found out his former employee had made a move to cross the border today, and wasn't able to be reached. I, of course, have access to the border records. So, chasing him down was relatively simple. And, he talked."

"Like a weasel." Frank scowled. "Can't believe I had a weasel under me for ten years!" He squeezed the grip on his gun tighter, fury baring his teeth.

"We all make mistakes," Walker whispered. It didn't sound as if he was talking about only Frank, but he did not say more. Instead, he stopped before Shark, then nodded to Frank and Anna, and nudged the big raider with his toe. "You."

"Coalition scum," Shark greeted, nodding. "And Glow-witch! Nice. Much better to look at." Anna crossed her arms.

"You'll talk with her. You'll take us to 'The Announcer', and to the other prisoners. If you do, I might just be convinced you're a reformed and productive member of society, and let you go outside the border with a car and some supplies. You don't, and I might have to shoot you."

Walker's voice was flat and cold, but Shark gave a cheerful nod. "Yeah, and my tiny brother too."

"Your what?"

Shark jerked his head at Rat, who was despondently slumped by his pole. "Tiny brother Rat."

Walker scowled. "*Fine.* But he's not coming with us. He's injured, and he'll slow us down."

"That is okay. But if I don't see Rat when you let me go, I rip your throat out."

Walker closed his eyes, like he had a headache. "Deal made." He tapped three fingers to his chest.

Shark nodded. "Deal made, Coalition scum!" His fingers waggled from their bonds behind his back. "I would salute you back, but...?"

The agent rose and extracted what looked to be a tiny chip from his pocket. He waved it over Shark's back, and the metal ties retracted, letting his arms and legs fall flat. The giant rose, rubbing his wrists. "Haha. And don't forget to kill all of those people for me." He made a careless wave at the group of once-masked spectators, then tapped three fingers to his chest, as if in belated response to Walker's gesture.

"They'll be going to trial, and it is out of your concern."

"Trial? You do not just kill them for forcing your people to murder each other?" Shark grunted. "*Savages.* It is okay. I killed a few for you. Nothing makes good killing like a nice bunch of *citizens.*"

Walker drew his pistol, aiming it at Shark's head. "If anyone dies because you need to keep standing here posturing, our deal is off."

"Coalition scum have no sense of humor." And, Shark turned, waving them on, back into the rubble and dust. "C'mon, Glow-witch. I speak with you now." A team had formed at their back alongside Waters, as Walker had requested. Anna guessed that Reeds was loyal to this Director figure, and accepted his orders. Still, if the opportunity to run presented itself, she was going to take it—she didn't know if Walker could or would stick his neck out for her again.

At least... she would run after she knew if Jackson was okay. She took a place again by Shark's side. He winked. "Good thing we brought a light, eh?"

"Yeah," she mumbled, marching through the ruins of the empty building, right back to where she'd been running from only fifteen minutes before. Her shaky legs had stabilized. "So... Rat's your little brother?"

"*Tiny* brother," Shark corrected. "He's so small! I could break him in half!" Anna nodded like she understood. Shark's voice dropped to a low growl. "They want to catch rulesmaster man. That one... he's like *you.*"

Anna shook her head.

"Yes, yes. The way I think, that means *you* make sure he doesn't kill us all."

Her heart thumped, remembering The Announcer's cold stare, the way it felt as if her chest was about to implode. Disquieted, she wiped at some of the blood that had gushed from her nose after The Announcer's attack. It had already dried. "I don't know if I know how to stop him from doing anything. My special talent is calculating large numbers in my head, Shark. I'm not like him at all."

But, she knew exactly who he *was* like: the Archmage. The man that had frozen her in place with only a look, had somehow broken into her mind. Had he been watching? The Announcer had said he'd dumped her off here as some kind of test to lure "Jack". Jackson. Connected, he said they were. She shuddered, not sure why. *Jackson might have died here today because of me. We both could have died. What do they even want with us?*

She wasn't sure if she could share her worries with Agent Walker yet. Even if he was trustworthy, there were too many strangers that would be paying close attention to the human light bulb in their midst. So, she kept her silence, and thought, and tried to give herself hope.

Heading in an arc towards the tunnels, Shark took them past the broken body of Jackson's opponent. The lights were still shining down overhead, as if their last purpose was to highlight the death of this gladiator. His striped war paint was dull with dust now. Some kind of tail was secured to his pants, torn, limp. Shark stopped and kneeled. Then, he took two fingers, and shut the eyelids over the dead man's glassy stare. "Hunt in peace, Father Tiger," he whispered.

He rose and kept walking, not looking back again.

"You knew him?" Anna ventured.

"Aye yeah. Of course I did. He led us once. Until his team never came home. And here he's been, killing and hunting inside the great blue wall!" Shark gave a rasping laugh, one that made his eyes squint in good humor. "Killed by a citizen! Haha! Such a *little* man, too! Ha!"

Anna wrung her hands. "When we find the man he was fighting, you can't hurt him."

"*Hurt* him?" Shark's eyes bulged in their sockets. "I *congratulate* him! No one thought anyone could ever kill Father Tiger. Even if the little man had some help. Or died for it. Ha! Good to see Father's final fight!"

Anna sunk her teeth into her lower lip and said nothing. The spear in Jackson's chest loomed in her mind. Her rational mind knew that was fatal. But, her wishful heart told her that she was in a new century. Maybe it could be fixed. *Something* about this world had to be better than what came before it. "How far until we reach this place where they're keeping him?" she asked.

Shark shrugged. "Better question is, how long it will take the Coalition scum to surround it, take it, and lure the rulesmaster out? How long it take them to *die?* You punch through steel. You are the only one that *can* fight him. That should be what you think about. Yes?"

Anna fell into thought, and said nothing more as Shark guided the team to the prisoners deep in the labyrinth. His sense of direction seemed unerring. And, as they walked, the team whispered behind her about the light under her skin, mouths hanging open. Walker silenced them all with a look.

The medics saw to the chained ones, coaxing even the most reluctant from their binds, guiding them back to the surface. Then, they trudged back to what appeared to be a train station—train absent—and Shark led them down an abandoned track. It was an hours-long walk. Rats and giant cockroaches skittered before them as the team pressed against a wall, careful to not touch the charged rails. Her skin crawled.

Walker didn't say anything either, but Anna caught the worried looks he was giving her out of the corner of her eye, as if he was on the cusp of reassuring her, and then not. She knew that every minute that passed meant it was less than likely they would find Jackson in a state they that could treat.

Worry about it when we get there. Not if. When.

At one point, Shark paused, offering to carry her on his back, let her be a "portable flashlight", as he put it. He wiggled his fingers in an unsettling way. She declined, not that tired, not yet. But, they sat for just a moment, a medic passing out ration bars so they didn't drop. These tasted like carrots and nutmeg, if it was slathered over sawdust. And, as Anna nibbled, she busied her mind with self-analysis, asking herself what she was going to do if that man in red turned his gaze on her again.

In the end, she didn't have a plan.

But, she did have the inner voice that had urged her on when the NNSS was attacked. It was the same voice that saw her lead the breakout. *You're going to do it*, the voice said. *You don't know how yet, but you will. You have to. Why else would you be alive, after all this? To die here?*

Anna decided to call this voice *courage*, and she hoped it was right.

CHAPTER TWENTY-ONE
Champion

Jackson opened his eyes.

Blackness. Endless blackness.

"Up you go, Jackson," a faint voice whispered.

He struggled to see. His attempt to move sent bile and agony up in his throat. His tongue was dry and swollen, and he ran it over his cracked lips like it might help the pain. It did not.

"Go on, sit up, boy." It was a stern tone, but it held no real anger. Jackson found, however, that he could not sit up, no matter how much he tried. Perhaps he would go to sleep again. Perhaps he could forget the pain for a little while.

In the darkness before Jackson's eyes, a man began to appear, as if the shadows were pulling back to let him through. His expression was soft, if troubled, and his shoulders were set as a man's would be if he were trying to hold the world on them. He stroked his fingers across the hint of silver that had snuck into his brown mustache. Jackson knew him instantly, wanting to cry out.

Dad!

But sound refused to come. His jaws were cemented together, and all he managed was to breathe louder, air scraping his windpipe on its way out.

Peter Dovetail kneeled at his side. He was wearing the same business suit he had worn when Jackson had seen him last, before he left for the office, before the heart attack had taken him forever. "Jackson," he said, "You've slept in long enough. Get up. Business waits for no one."

Jackson blinked, the sting of tears in his eyes. The darkness pulled back further, revealing a room. Every available space on the walls seemed to be packed with books, glorious and wasteful in the way pre-Bombings objects were. Dust and musty scents hung in the air. He was in a bed with tight, clean-smelling sheets, and his father was in a folding chair next to him.

"What? You're going to sit there and let the company fail because you're sleepy?" The Dovetail patriarch rapped his walking cane on the floor in challenge.

No. No, of course not. I just hurt. All over.

His father didn't seem to mind that Jackson could only think the words. "Good, because I'm supposed to make you President some day, and what will everyone say if you burn the business down? You've got three generations to live up to, son."

Of course, of course... I... Jackson tried to sit up again, but he was paralyzed. He could only turn his neck. *I want to sleep. Let me sleep.* His hazy thoughts stumbled, as if they were stones thrown into a pond, sending up ripples, messes of noise. *Dad... you're dead.*

His father smiled gently and raised a glass of water under Jackson's nose. The liquid was cold, precious. It ran down his throat until he coughed and sputtered.

"Never let a silly thing like death stop you from doing what's important," Peter advised. Jackson found enough strength to lift a shuddering arm and reach out, though his father was too far away to touch. "And what's important to you, boy?"

Jackson blinked in confusion. *They're depending on me.* And, for just a moment, his mind was filled with thoughts of blond hair and a nervous smile. *So is she. I met someone like me, Dad.*

"That's all well and good, son, but hoodoo, yours or anyone else's, won't pay for a cup of coffee." Peter lifted an old datapad, as if checking the daily messages from work. "You want to get out of this? You just need to be more clever."

What...?

Peter got up, smiling, ruffling Jackson's hair. "I have to go." He snapped the datapad under his arm. "I'll be back around eight. Don't wait for me to come back before you eat something."

No, wait! That's what you said... come back. Please... stay here.

But, his father faded, and Jackson's mind grew fuzzy again. He lost track of time. Perhaps an hour went by. Perhaps twenty years.

Jackson found himself blinking again, rapidly this time, and wasn't certain if he'd just woken up, or if he'd been awake all along. The room was as he remembered it, piled high with books and dusty smells. He was alone, sprawled back on white sheets. He coughed. A knife lanced through his lungs. Jackson, able to move for the first time, peered down at his chest, neck grinding as he did so.

The spear was gone. Its passing wasn't.

Linens and bandages were wound across his torso, blood drying at the edges. He labored to sit up, and a fresh red smear began to spread, the spot hot and wrenching. He stopped trying to move. There were far more dark stains on the wrappings than not. Bruises spilled over his legs and arms. Something smelled of harsh disinfectant, lemons and ammonia.

A polite creak at the door let him know he wasn't going to be alone for much longer. He again made an effort to right himself, barely managing to budge his legs. It felt as if ghost of The Tiger was quite simply sitting on him, far from done with making him suffer.

A slight woman entered the room, a stranger, her brunette hair pulled back in a tight bun. Her scrubs and bag gave her away as a medic. Jackson relaxed.

"You're awake!" She trotted to his bedside. Jackson tried to form words, but realized that there was a reason he hadn't been able to speak. Something was secured to his face, metal and padding. He settled for a questioning grunt. "Don't try to talk yet. That's holding your jaw in place so it heals right. In fact, don't move at all. You're tearing yourself open already."

She held a disc of some sort aloft. Golden whorls were engraved on the surface, and Jackson had never seen anything like it. Suddenly, it began to glow with a sunny light, making the woman's hazel eyes shine. Jackson's heart began to pound. *Magic!*

Strange words were pouring from her lips as she traced symbols with her finger over the disc's surface, then, holding it to Jackson's jaw, began to trace again along his skin. His heart calmed. Warmth was suffusing his face. His headache vanished. His thirst dimmed. When the light faded, she gently reached behind his head and unhooked the strap, removing the braces. "There we go," she said finally. "Your jaw was broken in two places when you came in, and you almost lost a few teeth. That's actually not too bad, considering The Tiger's right hook."

Jackson's tongue told him that all of his teeth were still there. He cleared his throat a few times, trying speech again. "Thank you…" His voice was strained and harsh. She unhooked a canteen from her belt and handed it to him. The liquid was cool and sustaining like the water his father had given him. This thought left a sad hole behind. *Just another dream.*

The medic began examining his bandages, unwrapping some, tightening others. She was silent. He found this uncomfortable, and itched to talk, no matter how much the words hurt to speak. "You used magic."

"Yes, well, so do you."

Her shrug of apathy almost derailed him completely. "How…?"

"How what?"

"I never got to learn…"

"It looks like you figured it out on your own, then. Shadow manipulation… tricky application." She was going over his remaining injuries with a deft, all-business hand.

Jackson reeled. It was as if she couldn't care less. What had he even done back in that fight? He'd thought all magic required incantations to be used properly, as Huxley had said. But, this…! For once, the shadows had been *his*, not an outside, tormenting force.

"Might have some serious scars," she muttered. "You've been out for a few hours, and it *should* have been a week." She made a disapproving grimace. "But, he wants you fixed ASAP." Her hands were jittery now. "Healing like this is *dangerous*, I say. No. Doesn't care. He's probably going to die anyway, I say. Better off to let him die quickly. No. Doesn't care. Says it's *destiny*." She snarled like she wanted to tell a particular someone just where to put *destiny*. "You were broken. You had a jaw break, a concussion, a cracked kneecap, and, well…" She gestured towards his torso. "I should hope you remember *that* one. Blood was filling your lungs. Needed to resuscitate. He'd have gotten you to me a second later, and it wouldn't have worked. Still not sure of the side effects."

Jackson tried to focus, fuzzy. The healing had left him even more tired than before. "Who *are*…?"

"Just the person keeping the champion breathing as if her life depends on it, because it does. Which is a painful irony for me." She placed the disc on Jackson's chest now, centered, where the spear had impaled him. It began to emit a pulsating glow once more. The dull ache cleared further. Breathing felt easier.

"Champion?" The word held little meaning.

"Concussion. Great." She drew a tiny flashlight, blinding his eyes as she shone it into his pupils. "Yes, champion. On a technicality. The Tiger died first." Her sleeve drew back, just for a moment. Jackson saw the tattoo of an eye. "Everyone could tell he was dead on his feet anyway when the government stormed… hey! Stop that!"

Jackson struggled back, no longer trusting her healing. His bones ground and his muscles shook. "You're from the Order!"

She glared. "Yes. I am. And, I'm here to help. Now, *stop moving*."

"The Order…"

The nurse clenched her jaw, her face reddening. "It doesn't matter, *Jackson Dovetail*. I have a vested interest in your health. Now, let me do my job." She reached forward, but again, he shied back, barely able to do more than quake. "I *cannot* have you struggling when the difficult part starts."

"Why are you helping me? Why are you here?"

Her lips pursed. "Will an answer stop you from undoing all of my work?"

Jackson stared. The pain burned bright. He knew he was trapped. "...Yes."

"Fine." She nodded and gestured that he come forward, that he lie back down, but he did not. She scowled. "The Announcer was useful. He keeps the borders safer and can help someone get rid of problems, if you understand. A beneficial arrangement was easier than eliminating him."

She beckoned again, but he ignored the request. "Arrangement?"

"*Yes.* He takes care of our requests, and we make sure he stays hidden, that he gets a healer so he can continue with his *hobbies*." She made a little mocking bow. "Although that won't do him any good now. Protection has been withdrawn. The Coalition's coming, and we're probably all going to die. Now, lie down."

Jackson stared. "He murdered for you. And now he's turned on you, too. But you can't kill him. You're scared of him. The Order is *scared* of him."

Her lip curled. "You know nothing. Something happened that broke whatever was left of his sanity. Took some gods-blasted wander into the wastes and came back raving about a Jack—surprise, that's *you*—then killed every mage here when we protested his ignoring our other requests. But, he still needed me. Mind you, I've been warning the Archmage that this was an eventuality, and he was going to be more trouble than he was worth someday..."

"You know who I am. Tell me why the Order wants me dead."

The woman's eyes narrowed. "This was not part of your original question. And it matters not now, you stupid—" And, she fell silent. Her eyes shifted subtly to her right, over her shoulder. As the flashlight-induced spots in his eyes began to fade, Jackson realized that another figure had entered the room behind her now, and was leaning against a bookshelf, arms crossed. His distinctive suit and gold buttons were a beacon, even in the dark. Tony. The monster and the boy. The medic, as if on silent command, gave Jackson one last resentful look and removed the disc from his chest. Then she spun on one heel, exiting. She was careful not to look directly at Tony or touch him as she passed.

He approached Jackson's bedside, hands behind his back. His silver mask was gone, and Jackson could see the swarthy complexion from his boyhood had long since turned anemic and pale. And yet, he seemed to have taken great care with his appearance, his thin, dark mustache perfectly waxed, his black hair slicked down, not a strand out of place. Dark brown patches splotched his clothes from his head to his toes, visible even on the red fabric, stinking of death. Jackson recoiled again, every muscle shrieking.

"Shhh, shhh, Jack. Don't worry." He was whispering, but his voice was high, sing-song. "You're doing fine. Lucky, lucky!" He lifted off the ground, then drifted back to sit in a nearby chair, propping his feet up on the bed. There were dried brown flakes scraping onto the sheets where his heels now rested. "I made sure you'd have lots of books while you're here! Your kind *likes* books." The grin never dimmed.

Jackson summoned his most polite smile, which hurt as if he might have been driving nails into his face. "Thank you." He swallowed. "What time is it?"

"It doesn't matter." Tony crinkled as he shifted. His pockets were overflowing with bits of scrap paper, crayon messages littering the margins. "I wish you had come sooner. I needed to tell you things, Jack. *Important things.* Things I've had to write down so I don't forget them." The eerie smile vanished. An edge wavered into his tone. "It took you so long to get here. I wondered why. Maybe you didn't want to be *friends* anymore."

Jackson choked out his words. "Of *course* I wanted to be friends." Tony's lip stopped curling, and his mouth upturned ever-so-slightly instead, his eyes shining with purpose. Jackson continued. "We should... catch up. Yes. I... those papers in your pockets... what did you want to tell me?"

Tony glanced down at his coat, then poked at the bulging mess of notes, making them whisper. "Oh! *Yes.* I've seen the *secrets*, Jack! Sometimes, I see them, just for a second. The destinies. I have to write them down right away, or I forget. Mustn't forget. *Mustn't forget.*" His face screwed up, a mournful note creeping into his voice. "I can't keep it all straight in my head sometimes. It gets *lost.* It's always changing."

"That's okay. It's fine. You're fine."

"No," Tony said, face twitching, mouth a stern line. A low growl rumbled in his chest. "It's not fine! *I'm* not fine!" He snarled, slamming his fist down into the arm rest over and over, like a nervous tic. Then, he stopped, his eyes clouded, and a beaming grin split his face, as if his brain had spun a dial. He leapt to his feet. "What was that? Oh. You need to heal. Secrets when you're done. They're coming, Jack, so *hurry it up.*"

Jackson licked his lips. His body was collapsing with exhaustion, his eyes almost shut. "What are…"

Tony drew in further, only a foot from Jackson's nose, as if he was going to confide something. Then, he lunged forward, seizing Jackson in a bear hug, making his entire body shriek in pain. Jackson barely stopped himself from screaming. Tony was shaking with what might have been sobs or giggles.

"Happy!" Tony announced.

Jackson felt howling warmth seeping into his bandages, his chest wound reopening. Tears, involuntary, leaked down his cheeks.

Tony drew back, hands in the air. "And you'll only get better! Think of your next match!"

Jackson lay back and wheezed, seeing spots, his stomach twisting. "…Next."

"Yes! A champion must defend his title, after all! And that's what you are, Jack. You're a champion. You're *Chosen.*"

"What—"

"And Jack, we have so many rule breakers to sort through! You can help me deal with them. Finally! Nothing else in the way. No more *Archmage.* No more *Coalition.* Nothing they can do, not anymore! You'll make everything all better. And the Coalition, they're almost *heeeere.*" The buzzing in the air around Tony rose in pitch, stiffening the hairs on Jackson's neck, crawling under his skin. And then, Tony turned and barked over his shoulder. "Claire! Fix Jack. *Now!*"

And, he spun and left without another word, the bloody footprints and tingling, sick air all that remained in his wake.

The medic returned. She stared down at Jackson and frowned. "Perhaps I'm not going to help kill you," she muttered. "But even with your luck, there is little chance you are going to live until nightfall."

She tapped a finger in the center of his head. This gentle push was all Jackson needed to reel back into oblivion.

He didn't know how much time passed after that. Occasionally, he would wake for a moment and see the medic again. She would not speak. The glowing disc in her hands would pulsate, and she would start her work, not bracing him for the creaks and twists her healing magic wrought on his body. Jackson would pray to pass out in these moments. It seemed they had reached the "difficult part". His bones stitched far faster than they should have and his organs cried out as they ran out of fuel. It was no longer pleasant warmth. Everything in his core was burning, burning to heal the damage. And when she stopped, she would force food and water down his throat, and they would begin again.

The blackness was his only reprieve. The treatments were endless.

And then, one moment, his eyes snapped open, and he knew with every fiber in his body that he could walk, even if the world was veering.

The medic was not there. With a lurch, he sat up, moaning, feeling his head throb. *Go. Have to get out. Now.* He cast off the covers, a chill striking his exposed legs. How long had he been there? Anna must have been worried by now. Had she called Frank? Had Frank started a manhunt?

Moving his muscles still made him see white, though he felt no trickle of warm blood on his skin. His bandages were gone.

Tony had said the Coalition was coming. They would either rescue him or kill everyone in the area. Jackson guessed what their decision might be. He swung his legs off the bed. They felt more spindly than he remembered, like too much weight on them might snap them in half.

A glint of sunlight on metal caught his eye. A wheelchair was parked in the corner. His knees buckled as he made to stand, and he grasped the bed, holding himself up. The center of his chest, for just a moment, burst with fire. Determined, he squared his feet into the carpet, reaching out to a bookshelf with one hand. He tottered. But, he stood.

Dare he just stagger out the door, naked and weak? Were they waiting for him?

The wheelchair caught his eye again, and a tingle of dread pulled at his mind. On the seat was a neatly folded bundle of clothes—his. It was the suit he'd had stuffed into his bag, though it had been confiscated before the fight. When he staggered to it, grasping the cotton with one hand, he realized it had been dry cleaned and pressed to perfection. He was expected.

His hopes dimmed, small as they were. But, he pulled the shirt over his head, his shoulders grinding. He couldn't hook all of the buttons—not without his chest feeling like it was splitting open—even though all that remained of the spear was an inflamed red scar. Still, Jackson persevered, and finished dressing. For a moment, it made him feel less vulnerable. He swayed, however, dizzy from exertion. Spots danced in his eyes again.

A bulge in his jacket pocket made him pause. It was soft, and crinkled when pressed. Part of him expected to find notes stuffed in there, the "secrets" Tony had for him. But, on reaching inside, a repulsive smell hit him so hard that he almost dry heaved.

Tea! Gods-damned tea! The one Huxley had given him, the fresh packet he'd stuffed in the bag to study. He'd forgotten to take it out of his luggage when he left the safe house. Now, someone had gone to the trouble of making sure he'd get all of his belongings back, tucking the tea away in his pocket. Right next to the packet was a tube of toothpaste. *How helpful.* Jackson would have thrown it away right then if he didn't have more pressing concerns.

Pulling his jacket tight so the smell disguised itself, Jackson tottered to the door again, leaving the wheelchair behind. As bad as he felt, his arms and chest were far more useless right now, and he didn't think he could move the wheels under his own power at all.

The door wasn't locked. Jackson blinked, startled, in the sputtering lights beyond his room, a corridor illuminated in two directions. It was scrubbed tile and grout. He was still underground, likely still connected to the train system. What, had they burrowed a library and hospital room out of a maintenance closet? Shaking his head, unable to care, he tottered on.

"Hullo, Jack."

Jackson froze. The affectation left him knowing exactly who spoke, even before he turned. Sure enough, it was the thug from before, the one who had kidnapped him in the subway station. The man had one hand on his gun, the other scratching the scar on his nose.

"You," Jackson spoke.

The corners of the thug's mouth tugged upwards, but it couldn't be called a smile. "You're still walking. And ya won against the goddamn Tiger because he *tripped*. Wouldn't have believed it if I hadn't seen it."

Jackson's mouth went dry. Tripped? Well. He supposed most people wouldn't know the difference. "I was... very lucky." Jackson had to pull in another breath to speak any further. His lungs felt shallow, weak. "Where are you dragging me off to now?" He had no doubt the man had been waiting for him, had popped out of some room nearby.

"Got some troublemakers on the way."

Jackson wondered how long he'd been a prisoner. Hours? Days? Weeks? Hope and despair warred in his chest. "I see," was all he said. Deep in his lungs, he felt an alarming rattle.

"Boss wants to see you 'bout those troublemakers."

Jackson wheezed softly in reply.

The thug didn't take him far. It was only a five minute pained shuffle by Jackson's estimate, and they emerged into a huge open platform. The rusting old train was parked on the tracks, velvety welcome banner still flying. A set of stairs caught Jackson's eye to his left, sang to him of the surface world.

He turned away. He would not be able to run. The thug still had his gun.

A huge chunk of the platform was cordoned off in velvet rope. In the middle of this long section, surrounded by cups, books, dishes, and other oddments, was Tony, a brilliant spot of red, pacing back and forth, muttering to himself. His pockets were still stuffed with notes. A fresh bit of paper was in his hand, crayon poised over the surface as if it was waiting for inspiration.

"Boss," the thug intoned in a manner so like Frank that it made Jackson wince.

"Hrmmm?" Tony ceased pacing at once and glanced up. His teeth flashed. "Awake! Awake! Very good. Good job, Claire. Won't kill you after all." The medic in question was nowhere to be seen, but Jackson imagined she might find the release from her death sentence pleasing. Tony unhooked one of the velvet ropes blocking off his rectangle of space, and made a gesture indicating his guest should enter. Jackson did so, then collapsed into a chair, trying not to make it look as if the act was torture. Tony re-hooked the rope. "You always have perfect timing," he spoke, taking a seat across from Jackson. "*Perfect.*"

Jackson said nothing. There was a box full of credit chits right next to his elbow. The numbers on just the visible sides soared into the thousands. Tony must have been a millionaire. What did he even do with that kind of money? Were there more boxes down here with the rats and leaking pipes?

"Now," Tony said, his eyes darting around the train platform like a spooked school of fish. "Claire says you need more time, but she doesn't understand *your* kind of time. No. You're the champion. You have responsibilities, now." He pointed both fingers at Jackson, like little guns. "We will settle the rule breakers. You and I! Couldn't do it without you. It was your championship fight they *ruined.*" Tony frowned and shook his head in a woozy way then, his eyes drifting. There was what looked like an unnatural breeze stirring around his feet, carving circles in the dust around where he sat. "No one escapes destiny, Jack. No one escapes the rules."

Jackson nodded, tearing his eyes away. "Okay." His core shook. He was more terrified than he'd ever been in his life, sitting in front of his former friend, the diseased aura sliding across his skin, the weight of it making it even harder to breathe. Was he now Tony's pet prisoner? Was he expected to kill on command? His brain whirred over his surroundings, desperate to find some talking point, some way he could barter freedom, something that would make sense to Tony's broken mind. There was so much clutter. Kitchen supplies. Changes of clothes. Electronic rubbish. Why all here, in this space, divvied off with rope? Just another sliver of madness?

"Interrupted your victory celebration," Tony was muttering. "I don't have any cake. Can't believe there isn't any *cake.*"

The statement was so quiet and nonsensical that Jackson almost ignored it. And then, his spine tingled and stiffened.

An idea.

An insane one.

A clever one.

"It's alright." His throat swelled painfully with the words. "I don't really like cake." There was a shuddering in Jackson's body now, like there was a hysterical laugh hiding in there, but he kept it inside, as much as it made his eyes tear up with anguish. "But, you know what I find always helps me celebrate?" he rasped. "What always makes me feel *better?*"

Tony clucked his tongue, looking wary. "What?"

Jackson smiled. It was perfect, agonized calmness. "Tea. A nice cup of tea."

CHAPTER TWENTY-TWO
Tea Time

The stale air hung tense and coiled around Anna's shoulders. She rubbed her arms against the underground chill and tried to listen for any sound in the tunnel beyond the government team's whispered reports. There was nothing. Not even the skittering of rats.

"Anna," a mutter came to her left. She jumped, her hands coming up before she could think about it. It was Agent Walker, adjusting a pair of goggles above his eyes. "Sorry," he said.

"It's okay. Um. I'm just jumpy."

"You hear it too, then."

"Hear what?" Their whispers seemed to dispel like mist in the endless dark.

"The nothing," he said. "The vermin, the bugs. They've run."

Anna squeezed her arms tighter around herself. "Yeah. I noticed that."

Walker's lips became a thin line. "You'll need to put the light out in a few minutes, if you can. We have night-vision. I don't want them to see us coming—I suspect we're getting close, now."

"We are," Shark growled. "I remember the last station. Saw it on the way to get my arm reattached." He rolled his right shoulder. For the first time, Anna noticed a messy scar ringing his bicep there, splitting down an image of a snarling dragon.

Anna turned away, not wanting to stare. A little bit of hope burned brighter, though. If The Announcer could heal injuries like severed limbs...

"How will Shark and I see?" she asked. She doubted either of them were about to get their own pair of Coalition-issue night-vision goggles.

"You're both going to hang back once we're ready to move in. His job is getting us there, and yours is getting him to cooperate. You've done that. Good work."

Anna frowned. "I haven't really *done* anything."

Walker shook his head. "Raiders don't cooperate with anyone, usually."

"For good reason," Shark grumbled.

Walker ignored this, dropping his voice. "Even if there isn't anything else you can do, Anna, we wouldn't have gotten down here without you. It was lucky you were here."

Anna bit her lip, then decided to be upfront. "Yeah... about how I got here. That guy you caught that worked for Frank... I don't think he had anything to do with it."

Walker raised an eyebrow. "He did only confess to taking Jackson."

She nodded. "After they left, an old man came to the safe house. He told me he wanted me to be evaluated by his organization, by a man called the Archmage."

Walker looked like he nearly stopped walking. "What? The Order *found* you?"

Anna's mind spun, connecting the dots. "That was the Order? The Order that's been trying to kill Jackson?"

Walker cursed under his breath. "I can't believe it... God damn it! I thought that idiot would have placed wards on your safe house, at the very least...!"

Anna flickered her eyes down the tunnel, then back to the agent. *Wards?* "The people I saw, the Archmage..." She shuddered, the memory carrying a sense of violation. "They dumped me here. The Announcer told me they wanted to get rid of me, but also to draw in 'Jack', which I'm certain is..."

"Jackson. That doesn't make sense... did he say why?"

Anna shook her head. "No one really told me a lot. But, they were going to make me fight in the arena. I managed to get out."

"Hell yeah we did." Shark rumbled. "No chains. Never again."

Anna wrung her hands, nodding, feeling as if she understood the weight that was put into that sentiment. "Yeah. Never again." She leveled her stare on Walker, who seemed somewhat taken aback. She wondered if there was more steel in her eyes than when they'd first met. "If there's any other way I can help... I pack a pretty good punch, you know. It seems to be part of what I do now since you found me." This was a strange irony to her. She was a scientist, and growing up, she'd never even liked sports, athletics, exercise—none of it. Now, here she was, offering to beat up a supervillain in a desolate train tunnel.

Walker paused, as if sizing her up. "You're not combat trained. You'd get hurt. Mr. Bertinelli is... well... you'd be lucky to get close enough to even *think* about hitting him."

Anna bit back her frustration. "What *is* he? You said he was an Esper. Reeds said he wanted to put me in 'Project Esper' back at your facility. Sounds related, you know?" She scanned the dark, continuing to find nothing. The stale air hung dead around them. Yet, she couldn't shake the sensation that something was watching them, something that made her hairs rise and her breathing tighten.

Walker sighed. "It's a bad time for—"

"It might never be a good time."

There was a small upturn of his lips, but the smile didn't reach his eyes. "It's best if you don't know details. And don't let anyone hear that I had anything to do with you being out."

"But you did, didn't you?"

Walker's face became utterly blank. "If I did, the Coalition would make me *disappear.* That's what it will do to everyone that it caught breaking into the facility, after it finishes interrogating them. Treason isn't something you do lightly."

Anna stared, stricken.

"But Nyx, I know, would have done it again in a heartbeat even if you weren't Dr. Anna Matthews."

"She knew who I…? But I'm nobody—"

"You *were* the woman who made the call when the NNSS was attacked in 2022, weren't you?"

Anna almost froze. She stumbled, but kept walking, pretending nothing was wrong. The phantom pain flared from the bullets once in her chest and leg. It made her breath shallow. "You… you know about that? How? You really do believe me?"

"There's a lot of questions about why and how you're here, and I've made sure those questions stay to myself. But, I had a friend dig through some archives. I verified your prints and DNA." Walker was checking his gun as they walked, opening the chamber, peering inside, as if to make sure all was ready and well. "I don't have answers, but I believe you."

Anna didn't know what to say. Her denial of her reality had only recently fallen away. And then, as the memories came back, as every new, impossible thing kept piling up, she'd even started to wonder if she'd gone crazy. Heck, she'd considered *reincarnation*. But… she was real. She still had her DNA and fingerprints. She was fundamentally *Anna*. And, this thought almost made her cry with the comfort it provided.

"There still aren't a lot of accurate records of what led up to The Bombings," Walker was continuing. "But, I did find that that your alert was picked up by a radio hobbyist. Then, the police, and then, the federal government. They took back the NNSS before the terrorists got away. Most everyone was dead, but the site was secured."

Anna's breath hitched, her eyes welling with tears.

He made an awkward throat clearing, as if he'd remembered he was speaking about events that, to her, were no century away. "And, after being tipped off, they stopped attacks on five other important locations that were triggered at the same time. Some people believe the terrorists intended to use what they found to obliterate what was left after the bombs dropped. Could have meant thousands, or millions, of lives saved when you sent out a warning. We don't really have any way of knowing. Either way, what Dr. Anna Matthews supposedly died doing that day was heroic."

The tears leaked from the corners of her eyes now. Anna lifted a shaking hand to wipe them quickly away. *Message received.* "They heard me."

"Yes. They did."

A sob escaped her throat, and she covered her mouth with her hands. Walker put a hand on her back. Her entire frame was jerking with such relief that she couldn't speak for a long time. Then, her eyes still blurred, the voices of her friends and colleagues in her ears, she finally asked: "Who were they? Why did they do that to us?"

Walker gave her shoulder a squeeze. "I'm sorry. I don't know. But maybe someday, when we get out of here, I can give you the history lesson, and maybe what you saw can solve the mystery once and for all. And… maybe we'll know why I found you outside of New York, the only woman alive once Mr. Bertinelli was done with everyone."

Anna's mind didn't want to come back to their present problem. The past was big enough. The faces of the dead and the soothing sound of *Message received* was playing over and over in the halls of her soul. *They heard me. I saved people.* Still, she knew she had to focus, and she wrenched herself away from it, promising herself she would give it the remembering it deserved later. "So… so what's an Esper, Jaden?"

She felt his hand stiffen and pull away. "You should not repeat this. Understand? It's just… you probably deserve to know. Project Esper found people with extraordinary abilities, things humans typically aren't born with. Like what you currently have. Like what Mr. Bertinelli can do."

"Like what Nyx can do."

Walker frowned even deeper. "Yes. Like that."

"Reeds said he wanted to look at my genetics, my radiation resistance. He said he wanted to use me to help people."

"That is *part* of what the Coalition wants."

"I don't mind helping people. But, they kept me prisoner. They didn't explain anything, Jaden." *You didn't either.*

He looked like he was grinding his jaw. "I know. I'm sorry. Some people want benign things out of the Project, Anna. They did back then, too, on the first Project. But, some people want other things, and they don't care if they have to lose a little of their humanity to get it."

Anna regarded the agent, feeling a wariness towards him she hadn't known before. He had helped her, had put much on the line for her. But the way he spoke implied that he'd worked alongside monstrosities, and not all of them were madmen in red suits. "Was the Announcer... Mr. Bertinelli... involved in the first Project?"

"Yes." It was a clipped response. A fine sweat was visible on his brow in the low light, and under her questioning stare, his jaw kept working, like he wanted to elaborate, but was deciding against it. "It is strange," he finally said, "That I finally found him, after all these years of hiding, the week I find you. I wish I hadn't brought you in, that I'd had enough talent to see the signs that you were a far stronger, more varied Esper than I'd thought. I wouldn't have tried to hide you under their noses, downplay you to them. I would have found another way, ignored my orders. I wish... well, I wish a lot of things."

"Bertinelli was a Coalition prisoner too?"

Walker's eyes widened, as if he'd been slapped. "No," he said hoarsely. "No. Never. Not... not at first. He was just a kid." His face wrenched in an odd way, as if it was trying to hide its own expression from her, but wasn't quite strong enough to do it.

Anna hugged herself tighter. "Not at first?"

Walker was silent. He gripped his gun tighter, craning his neck like he wanted to peer down the tunnel further. Perhaps he was only trying not to look at her anymore. "I called in a lot of favors for you, so you wouldn't end up a repeat of the past. There wasn't just Nyx. It's not a stunt I can repeat. If you get a chance to make a break for it in the confusion, you need to take it. Will you do that?"

Anna bit her lip. "Yes," she said, honest.

"Good. Get out of here, and put the Coalition and those damn mages far behind you." He unhooked something from his belt, pressing it in her hand. Anna took it, confused... until she heard the tiniest, whining clicking as it touched her skin. "You'll need that more than I will. Now, put that light out.

You and Shark need to move to the back of the unit."

His expression said that he was turning his attention away, and the conversation was done. And so, clutching Walker's Geiger counter to her chest, she let the light go back inside. The cold, underground darkness swallowed them all whole.

And that was when she heard the growling.

Everything stopped.

There had been nothing in the dark. And now, there was a hiss of air, as if it was escaping between wet, sharp teeth. Twin, pale orbs flickered for just a moment down the path, hovering in the darkness like tiny moons. They swayed, reflecting the weak light, observing.

And then, there was another pair.

And another.

And six more.

"We've got mutants!" Walker screamed. "Guard dogs!"

And with that, a braying howling cracked through the tunnel, and the orbs shot towards them, scrabbling claws and hissing breath. Anna felt a strong arm throw her to the ground, knocking the air from her lungs. And then, the world lit up with gunshots and thunder.

Jackson heard the flat, dull words come out of his throat, and he had no idea how they didn't waver and chuckle with panic. "I brought some tea of my own, of course."

"Of course you did! Good, reliable Jack! We *can* celebrate!" Tony was one bright smile again, and he took the witchbane packet without question. Two cups lifted themselves from a box and drifted through the air. They hovered before Tony, as if uncertain, then settled down between the two men on a little table.

Tony began an eerie whistling tune as he pulled an old water jug from behind his feet, pouring an equal amount into each cup. Jackson wondered if the water had even been purified. He could hope.

Almost as soon as the water sloshed inside the little cups, steam began to rise over the brims. Jackson, alarmed, peered inside. The water was boiling of its own accord. Tony seemed untroubled. He was pinching out a particularly strong dose from the bag. "How much?"

Jackson stared. *That much would have killed me.* He felt a twinge that might have been guilt, but he knew it would not bother him if he lived. "That's just right."

Tony nodded, rubbing the dried plants between his gloved fingers, obliterating the leaves to a pulverized dust. This settled into the steaming water, transforming it to a bright yellow-green. The warm, spicy scent puffed up under Jackson's nose.

Lavender. Coriander. And, something else.

He looked back up. Tony was silent and completely still, save for a wincing spasm under his left eye, as if an insect was biting him over and over. The notes in his pockets began to rustle as he shifted his legs in an impatient cadence. "When does it work?" he barked, shrill.

"It needs a moment to steep."

"It has *had* a moment."

"Okay." Jackson smiled, bringing up his hands in a soothing gesture. "Then it's ready."

Steam was still rising from the cups. Tony picked up his tea and knocked the whole thing back. He coughed and sputtered in pain as he finished, slamming his cup back down as if it were whiskey rather boiled leaves. "I don't like tea! I don't *like* it."

"It's an acquired taste." Jackson stared at his cup now, and then lifted it to his mouth, pretending to take an appreciative sip. The liquid stung and burned. He smacked his lips.

Tony's eye was twitching quicker now, his waxed mustache wrenching back and forth. "*Why?* It's awful!" His hands flexed open and closed. The queasy buzzing of his magic was rising. Jackson wondered if Tony was more perceptive than he'd been in matters of poison. "You're not even drinking yours!"

Jackson prepared himself to, quite possibly, never rise from his seated posture again. "Of course I am." He steeled himself and took a real swig now, letting it scorch his tongue, praying to whatever gods there were that he had built up some kind of tolerance. "You should try another one," he offered, trying not to choke. "You might like it better the second time."

Tony frowned. With that, he poured another cupful of water, making an impatient rub of herbs between his fingers. "Fine. It's your celebration." Jackson almost couldn't believe it. *Is he really doing this because he thinks it will make me happy?*

The tea was already souring in his belly. He could feel it.

It was then a metallic *BANG! BANG!* slammed into his ears, echoing off the platform walls. And, for a moment, perfect silence shattered the air in its wake. Tony cocked his head like a curious puppy. Jackson held his cup to his lips, listening, waiting.

"They're here," the thug announced. He said it as one would mention a change in the weather. A scream pierced the air, far off, a wailing ghost. Jackson shuddered, his stomach turning again, but this time with real fear.

"Wonderful!" Tony rose, his eyes bright, setting the second cup of tea down untouched. He clapped his hands as if he was welcoming the moment. "Come, Jack!"

Jackson stalled. "Perhaps… we should…"

Tony was already skipping to the rope entrance. "Come!" This was an irritated bark, a command for a disobedient dog. Jackson swallowed. And, he hoisted himself out of his chair, feeling his sweat beading already, sticking his clothes to his aching back. He shook as he walked.

Tony could have easily hopped over the line with his long legs, but he unhooked the rope with a delicate hand anyway, as if the thought never occurred to him. The rictus grin was in place, and the man was already striding ahead as if he were the commander of an army.

All Jackson saw was the scarred thug and himself, an injured businessman. But the screams kept echoing up the tunnel, and report after report of gunfire.

Jackson realized he'd stopped breathing when they entered the tunnel, the darkness engulfing them as they rounded a turn. He blinked a few times, his eyes adjusting, and exhaled, his chest pounding with the painful memory of the spear. Tony was humming again, motioning with his hands, his invisible orchestra returned. The screams punctuated the beats in his song.

Jackson thought desperately of the stairs behind them, the hope of the surface. He prepared himself to run for it the first chance he had.

BANG BANG BANG BANG!

Rapid gunfire peppered the air again, and an inhuman howl resounded, chilling Jackson's blood. There was no warning, no transition between the echoing noises and the chaos of battle. All of a sudden, it was simply upon them.

The tunnel rounded a bend, and the world lit up with flashes and thundercracks. A slavering, snarling hellbeast charged out of the dark, tearing past Jackson, its fangs glimmering with blood and foam, its eyes pure white. It bounded into the tunnels beyond. He threw himself behind a thin strip of concrete edge in the wall, using it as cover as bullets clanged from the stone, and clutched his ears. The tunnel was an echo chamber of deafening clamor, and he crumpled in on himself, trying to stay small, praying not to get hit from a ricocheting shot.

Yips, howls, and all too human screams of pain punctuated the gun blasts. Jackson couldn't even see the fight, only blurs of furred creatures on the other side of cover, the brief flare of gunfire.

And Tony kept walking, undeterred.

He was still smiling.

A clatter sounded next to them, and Jackson heard a hiss. Choking gas started to pour out of a canister. His barely-healed lungs started to seize and burn, and he toppled, cheek into the concrete. He scrabbled back from the billowing cloud of tear gas.

And, the flash of red that was Tony jogged to his side, kicking the can straight away into the far tunnel from where they'd come. "Wheee!" he announced. The canister soared away, leaving a trail of choking mist behind it.

Jackson's eyes burned and watered, his air passages fighting not to slam shut. Tony stood there, smiling down at him, as if he'd forgotten what he was doing, making no effort to protect himself. Jackson wondered at first what kind of devil's luck saw him not getting mowed down… and then, he saw a shined, pointed slug hanging in the air. It simply drifted there, a foot from Tony's unfocused eyes, as if stoppered in invisible molasses.

There were other bullets, circling around Tony in an off-kilter halo, as if caught in the sludgy current of his aura. Jackson pressed further against the wall, as far away as he could get.

There was a scream nearby. Jackson saw Tony's thug reel back and drop to the ground. Tony then spun, a look on his face that said, *Oh, right.* He outstretched his fists, clenching them.

And, the gunfire stopped altogether. A terrifying ringing was left in Jackson's ears. There were no more howls. There was no more thunder. Groans began to float up the tunnel, as if Tony, with one gesture, had turned his opponents into tortured spirits.

"C'mon!" he crowed. "It's easy once you've done it the first couple of times! Just like they taught me!" He resumed his strut down the tunnel, no resistance meeting him at all anymore. Jackson struggled after, despairing, lungs burning and spitting with pain.

So much for the Coalition.

Dog-creatures were littered on the tracks, mutated, scrawny creatures. Their mangy fur was patched with blood, their bared flesh lumpy and tumorous, their overlarge teeth bared in an eternal snarl. Blind, bony tunnel creatures, large enough to tear off a man's arm. Tony hopped over the bodies. Jackson shuffled after, keeping his distance from the dead dogs, catching for a moment that the thug on the ground was still moving. The man hissed in pain, rolling onto his side, and shot Jackson a hate-filled glare. It said that the why's and how's of his injury didn't matter. The blame was solely on Jackson's presence.

Jackson ducked his head down and pressed on, terrified of what he might find.

Tony finally stopped. He lingered in front of a man dressed all in camouflage and armor, standing and holding up his rifle like a posable child's toy. Blood caked his leg from what looked like a bite from one of the dog beasts. As Jackson got closer, he saw the sweat pouring from the man's brow, saw the frightened eyes as Tony's reptilian stare bore into him. "Mrrmmm," the soldier said. His gun trembled, aimed point-blank at Tony's chest. It did not fire.

Waters, read the soldier's name tag.

Jackson wheezed, wishing he might be invisible.

Tony was clenching his fists once, then twice. "Why isn't it...?" He squared his stance, outstretched an arm, and made a squeezing gesture.

The soldier turned darker, his eyes bulging as if he was choking under Tony's pantomimes. But suddenly, his voice seemed to break free of the spell. "He's here!" he screamed. "He's got us!" And then, his throat seized a final time, and he toppled with a wet scream. There, he twitched on the ground, his fingers weakly clawing at his neck.

"Aggh! It's not working right!" Tony tore at his hair, clenching his fingers over and over, teeth bared. Jackson felt his aura stronger now. If it was a river, it was now blocked by a dam, and Tony wasn't controlling the ebb and flow as he once did—it splashed and warped in sickly, burbling waves, sloshing uncontrollably one way, then the next.

The poison. It's starting.

"I'm free!" someone cried out from down the tunnel. Jackson heard a dusty, shuffling step, heard the scrape of shoes once held in place.

And then, something changed, far down the tunnel, in the dark.

It was a pinprick of light, barreling down the tracks.

Jackson threw himself against the wall again, for a moment convinced it was a train. But, it seemed to bounce, was bobbing and twisting as it charged towards them. Tony looked up from his brutal work with the soldier as well, startled.

The light had blond hair. It was a woman.

Jackson wondered if he was hallucinating. *Anna?*

"*You!*" Tony made a throaty scream, and Jackson felt the diseased magic aura lurch and claw at the dam in its path, pressure building and roaring and fizzing over the top.

Tony extended his hand to her.

No! Jackson didn't think on it for another moment. He slammed into Tony, forcing the extended arm up over their heads.

The sickened and trapped aura collided with him and exploded, a bomb going off. A wave of air pressure crushed into Jackson, sending him into the air. Concrete and stone screeched and cracked. And then, it burst. The world was dust and rubble and fiery pain. Jackson choked and flailed in the black.

There was nothing but air above and below. Stones bashed into him as he rocketed up in the force from the blast, a yank on his collar where Tony's hand had hooked into him.

THUD.

His skin burned and scraped as he hit concrete again, tumbling, legs over arms, a pained heap. He blinked and tried to breathe, but his eyes blurred and his lungs heaved.

It was impossible, but for just a moment, he thought he saw the sun.

CHAPTER TWENTY-THREE
Rule Breakers

The ceiling was gone.

Anna gaped upwards at the ruinous hole, oblivion ripped straight out of concrete, dirt, and steel. Her ears were ringing from the explosion.

She'd caught only a glimpse of a red blur in the blast, shooting up, as if propelled by the force.

The glittering blue of the dome could be seen now, and beyond that, a white-hot flare of sunlight. The government team cried out in surprise, tearing off their goggles, blinking, trying to adjust in the shower of dust. Someone was wailing with pain.

"GO! GO!" Walker hollered over the noise, muffled by the oppressive ringing in Anna's ears.

But the soldiers stumbled, confused, hurt from the hail of rubble and the pressure of the blast. Anna had been spared that, at least. The debris had bounced from her, bruising her, but causing no serious harm—and the hurts it did cause felt as if they were healing already. She bounded ahead of the soldiers, snagging a handhold in the maimed dirt. Her arms screamed as she pulled herself up, forcing her hands into new nooks, finding purchase for her feet. She never would have been able to do this in her past life. And yet, now, it seemed like she should, and she was hardly surprised when it worked.

She knew the light was flickering under her skin again, even though she couldn't see it in the bright afternoon light. It was a warm pulse, urging her on as she climbed.

She inched up, further, further, out of the torn earth. She heard someone else scrabbling beneath her, and above, there was the sound of wailing and shrieking. Feet pounded. A siren started to blare.

Just above her, Anna knew, was a mess of people that had no idea how to deal with what had clawed its way out of hell.

Jackson rolled over, spots and stinging dust in his eyes. The sunlight above almost overwhelmed him from so much time in the dark. He retched, feeling the remnants of the witchbane poison dribble off his tongue. His body shook with chills, his stomach clenching, as if it had gone into overdrive to repel another round of toxin.

His head was clearing. He hoped it would be enough.

"Get up, Jack," a wavering hiss spoke above him.

Noise clattered in Jackson's ringing ears, shouting, the stampede of feet. He saw the tapered angle of the Flatiron Building. Tony had torn his way up into the middle of Midtown Manhattan. How had he gotten above ground...? Had the blast...?

"Get. Up."

Jackson's neck wrenched with painful whiplash as something seized his collar and jerked him to his feet. He was spun, his knees threatening to give way at the tilt, and found two golden snake eyes burning furiously into his own. His breath stuck in his chest, as if something wet was blocking it, punching his lungs at the point where The Tiger's spear had been.

He wasn't standing anymore. He was hovering off of the ground, the burning grip in his chest and on his neck not from hands at all. Tony had those curled into angry balls at his sides. The man was bleeding profusely from a gash in his forehead, his black hair askew and smeared with gray dust. He was holding Jackson in the air by pure force of *thought*.

It felt much as if someone was wrenching hooks into all of his blood vessels and suspending him like an old suit on a rack. Jackson made a creaky noise of pain and fear, eyes swinging. There were people running, citizens probably on their way home or to work, wide-eyed and peering at the blood-stained man who had torn his way into the street, hauling a sagging victim with him. But, they turned away, and they ran, and Jackson couldn't even form the words to scream *Help me!*

It looked like the wayward explosion of Tony's power had caught bystanders as it surged up out of the street. There were twisted limbs under the chunks of concrete. There was blood on the ground. There were screams. The windows had been blown out for three stories in the building to their left. And now, cracks were spiderwebbing out into the asphalt under Tony's feet, as if he was about to short-circuit a second time.

Jackson heard sirens, but they were far away, too far.

Tony jerked his head to the left for a moment, facing the bystanders. Some had foolishly paused, taking out their datapads. Tony spasmed. "Filming! *Against the rules!*" A car screeching around the fleeing crowd suddenly lifted, spun, and went careening into the mob. A deafening crunch of glass and steel assaulted Jackson's ears, but there was nothing he could do. Tony turned his attention back, his mustache twitching. "That... wasn't what I wanted to happen." His eyes darted like a frantic lizard's. "Nothing is. Nothing is! What did you *do* to me, Jack?" He snarled, and Jackson felt the invisible hooks digging tighter, his breath coming only in burning, painful bursts. "*Why did you stop me?*" Tears were leaking from the snake eyes, his face blurring as Jackson's vision began to waver. Tony screamed, his face contorting with betrayal. "It's against the rules! You're not *supposed* to be a *rule breaker!* Why did you have to be a rule breaker?"

"We... can... talk... this... out..." Jackson stalled. Bits and pieces of debris were orbiting around Tony, as if he were small star. Confetti-sized bits of metal whistled as they sang past Jackson's shoulder, banging and embedding into the wall behind him like scattershot. Stinging pain blossomed across neck and arm where three pieces did not miss, raking his flesh.

Desperate, he flickered his eyes to Tony's shadow, long in the setting sun.

He tried to touch that patch of darkness, his synapses fizzling and misfiring. There was a concrete chunk the size of a fist sitting on the cracking earth. Jackson had no words for quite what it felt like to reach through the shadows this time, but the area felt more solid, somehow, around that bit of rubble.

Jackson tried flinging the shadow-gripped concrete chunk. The darkness punted the debris about a foot, where it settled pathetically, tapping Tony's shoe. Tony's eyes flickered down to it, then back up to Jackson.

"Sorry Jack," he said. "Very sorry. Very sorry. Tell Inoki I'm sorry. The rules. Must follow the rules."

Jackson felt hope leave him. The hooks dug in even more, a burning under his skin, hotter and hotter. His head rolled, his neck cracking with pain as his lungs began to constrict, his breathing becoming impossible. He saw his hands. The veins looked as if they were fighting to get out, a network of blood and life trying to burst out of his body.

And then, his vision shut down, a merciful blackness as he felt his body readying to tear itself apart.

⁕

Anna launched out of the hole shredded in the earth and asphalt. Shrieks met her.

It was late afternoon, sunlight sinking behind the high rises, making them glitter. The streets had been alive, the intersection bustling with business people, students, and workers. Anna swung her head around, trying to see what was happening. A car's horn blared, its tires screeching, as it swerved past her and ended its journey with a ear-rending crash. She whirled to look. Screaming filled her ears, the chaos of a hundred pounding feet.

For just a second, Anna was back in her workplace hallway, a gunman driving her colleagues in a stampede towards her.

In the present, hundreds of people were mobbing her way. The crowds were wailing, parting like the sea around her and the hole in the earth.

She heard a howl. It was him, not ten feet away. The man in red was staggering back and forth beyond the fleeing crowds, clutching his head and screaming at the sky. Anna dove into the swarm of people, not letting them drive her back even as they smacked and tripped her.

The road was making a grinding rumbling under her feet, cracking and seething, faults splitting out from under the man in red's feet. He spun back and forth, spittle flying free from his sagging mouth. "Jaaaaack?" He howled.

'Jack'...? Is Jackson... here?

Anna ran towards The Announcer. There were bits of rubble and debris spinning around his body on an axis. "I'll find you! *Rule breaker!*" he was slurring.

She ducked around a cluster of dented, stopped cars, avoiding his wild search, and there she stayed for a few minutes, paralyzed by indecision. The cars' drivers were getting out and getting clear on foot, the hole blocking the road. At least, most of them were. Some were just honking their horns, as if they might convince the madman and the chasm to get out of the way.

Then, she heard yelling and chattering to her left. Some people in the fleeing crowd were stopping. They had taken out their datapads, and were pointing them at the scene in a posture she'd known even back in the 21st century.

The Announcer whipped his lolling head towards them. "Filming! *Against the rules!*"

Anna heard a squeal. A car was rising off the earth. Its driver was panicking, slamming his shoulder against the door as if trying to get out. He managed it, toppling to the street, but the car rose higher... and, it turned, its headlights pointing to the crowd.

Oh my God.

"Get out of the way! Run!" she yelled out at the stragglers, but her shouts died in the cries and chatter around her, the sounds of the earth cracking open. The car was swinging down at the crowd like a wrecking ball. *No!*

Anna wasn't sure what she did next—it was almost as if she tripped one moment, and then, the next, her mind was reaching out for the people about to be flattened. Suddenly, her feet were both off the ground, and she was hurtling through the air. Anna got an armful of frightened faces as she tackle-scooped two women out of the way. The car drove so hard into the earth that its windows shattered out.

Anna breathed. The two women in her arms thrashed, trying to stand. Slowly, she got up, the world feeling as if it was moving slower than usual, her ears ringing.

"Did you see *that?*" someone was shouting.

"Holy shit!"

"The car fucking flew…!"

"*She* flew! She's glowing!"

Anna, alarmed, looked down. The pulse under her skin was still alight, a soft aura around her. She was hovering almost a foot over the earth. Both women she had saved were staring at her, wide-eyed.

Then, one leaned forward, hand outstretched. "Are… are you an angel?" she whispered.

A deranged howl sounded behind Anna again. "You have to run!" she yelled at the crowd. "Go! It's too dangerous here! You could get hurt!"

She breathed a sigh of relief as they listened, and they fled.

Where is Jackson?!

She turned away, feet touching the earth again, hiding behind the totaled car The Announcer had driven into the ground. Broken glass crunched under her tennis shoes. As she tried to take in the scene, her eyes finally found him.

So had The Announcer.

Jackson was *floating*. His legs were kicking weakly, purple outlines tracing up his neck. Anna heard a strangled, gargling noise coming from him. Blood was leaking out of his nose, down his upper lip.

Something about her world slowed down further, became sharper, clearer. She forced herself to stand, despite the hurts, despite the shortness of breath. And, she charged. With a jarring thud, she threw her whole body into The Announcer's. It didn't even look like he'd seen her coming.

The Announcer's head cracked against the concrete as they went down together, and he let out an angry screech. Papers flew from his pockets into the wind. Anna was flailing and punching, and sometimes even connecting. Her head whirled with adrenaline as she pounded at his face and chest, every last indignity and desperate hope in those blows. She heard the sound of Jackson's body collapsing behind her, but she was too scared to turn, to take her eyes off her target for even a second.

A block of concrete slammed into her side, knocking her off The Announcer, sending her rolling. She curled up into a ball, crying out as she settled, nursing what she was certain was a side full of cracked ribs. Her mind went black for a second, but then she was back, blinking, trying to clear her head.

There was an insane giggling in the air.

"Oooo, the girl can fight! I knew you were *special*. You're like *us*."

She heard him scraping his shoes across the asphalt, and she tried to shove the pain and exhaustion into the back of her mind. She staggered to her feet. There he stood, smiling, as if her all-out assault with fists that could shatter walls was nothing. Purple and red bruises bloomed unnoticed on his face.

"You shouldn't interrupt people when they're talking. It's not against the rules, but it is a *little* rude."

Jackson was a crumpled heap behind him, mouth open to the sky. He wasn't moving.

The Announcer saw her eyes flicker. "You seem upset! Really, this is a matter between me and Jack."

"I'm not going to let you kill him," Anna said. She had never felt more certain of anything.

The Announcer's voice was like a little boy's. "Why? Did he tell you that you're friends or something?" He snorted. "They always lie." His too-wide eyes narrowed, his face contorting. He shouted over his shoulder, keeping his eyes on Anna. "You hear that, Jack?! You're a liar!"

Anna stared into the face of insanity. Then, she saw something that gave her hope. Jackson stirred, lifting his arm. She gave no sign of recognizing this. Instead, she kicked a crumbled bit of asphalt as hard as she could at The Announcer's face, before he might turn and see it too.

It stopped within an inch of grazing his head, spinning in the air as if uncertain. Then, it disintegrated to dust. "You'll have to do better!" the man crowed.

And, with a mighty shrieking groan, another car rose from the ground of its own accord. It flew towards her, a moment away from grinding her into the street.

Jackson was dazed, floating, drifting in and out of unconsciousness. He tasted an unpleasant, coppery tang in his mouth. Blood. So much blood.

His face hurt where it was scraping into the road. His muscles stung as if all the little imaginary hooks were still embedded in them. But, Tony had dropped him, had spared him. Why...?

It was too late. So much damage had been done. And, he'd already cheated death once. He didn't think he was going to get a second shot. There was so much blood in his mouth. Everything hurt.

It was easy to close his eyes and sink away, to try not to feel anymore.

"*Jackson...*" A voice was in his ears. It was merry, bright, and far too pleased with itself.

Jackson no longer saw the world around him. In his flickering sight, he saw a campfire. He saw trees. He saw the light in Anna's eyes, the dust of the wastes, and smelled the old leather of his favorite chair, tasted the pungent coffee from the spot in Red Hook. He saw his father smiling down at him before his growth spurt, before he'd gotten tall enough to meet Dad's eyes. He saw Mrs. Rosita handing him a rag to clean the counters at the orphanage, and Frank handing him a fistful of napkins, telling him to set the goddamn table like a civilized boy. He saw ravens, and he saw dreams, and he saw all of his life in between.

And there was a press of something cool and hard in his hand, something he knew, something familiar.

"You forgot something," the merry voice spoke, a breath touching his ear.

Jackson's eyes snapped open. His veins burned. His lungs struggled, the wet rattle in them worsening, his breath a gasping wheeze.

I'm still alive. He didn't know how, but he was still hanging on, if only by a thread.

A woman screamed.

Jackson lolled his head to the left, vision blurry. A flash of dirty, stained white tumbled through the air, blond hair flying. Anna rolled and stood, despite her body making an unpleasant thudding on the ground. She was clutching at her ribs. Jackson saw Tony now, heard the trill of his laughter, his suit of ringmaster red a beacon, even to blurred eyes. She kicked something at Tony, but it didn't look like it connected.

No... Anna... get out of here...

Tony's back was turned. He was shouting at her, and Jackson saw Tony's fingers twitch. The rubble was drawing up off the ground as he passed, whizzing and clattering in every direction in his aura's field.

A car shuddered and groaned, creaking off the ground, one wheel dropping off and rolling away. It swung through the air.

But, Anna dove for cover, ducking behind another car. The looming vehicle crushed itself into a torn pile of machinery on her right.

Tony didn't have precise control right then it seemed, and was swaying from the poison. But, eventually, he'd cause enough destruction to kill.

Jackson staggered up, stumbling, not sure how he managed. And, he felt something in his hand. It was cold, familiar, hard. Eyes wide in disbelief, he stared down at his grip.

His pocketknife. He was clutching his lost pocketknife.

Jackson didn't let himself think on it. He ran, almost tripping over his own confused feet, stumbling toward his once-friend. And, with a shout, he swung the knife down in an arc.

Tony turned, his eyes widening.

The knife sunk all the way between his ribs, his chest smacking the side of Jackson's fist. Red wetness bloomed, sticky and warm.

Tony stared, his mouth dropping open. Jackson stared back, unable to move, unable to do anything at all but hang onto the knife, keep it where it was lodged. Tony's clothes were torn and rumpled as if he'd been battered. Bruises were swelling his face. How he was still standing as if nothing was wrong was baffling.

But now, he seemed to notice.

"Jack...?" Tony sagged. His voice cracked. His eyes shone with surprise and hurt. It was as if he'd forgotten they'd been fighting at all. "But... why would you...?"

"I'm sorry," Jackson said, but he wasn't apologizing for the knife. He was sorry for all the years and the fates that had brought them there.

BANG! BANG! BANG!

Shots rang out. Tony staggered forward, falling into Jackson, his mouth a surprised "O!" Immediately, he snarled, shoving Jackson away, then reeling back, grasping for the little blade in his ribs.

Jackson let him go. He couldn't move anymore. His lungs burned. In the distance, he saw a man in black, sunglasses torn away. Agent Walker. His pistol was getting reloaded now.

Tony fell down onto one knee. His slicked hair was stringing apart with sweat, plastered to his forehead. His fingers kept failing to grasp the knife. The snake eyes seemed to focus on something far away, something only they could see.

"I don't understand..." he sobbed.

And, he crumpled, his hand making to catch himself. He did not. His body made an unpleasant crunch and scuffle on the asphalt. Jackson heard a whimper of pain.

Then, there was nothing. Tony was still.

Jackson dropped to his knees. A sharp pain was building in his lungs. He was hyperventilating. His vision flashed black. He fell back much as Tony had, barely managing to catch himself before his head smashed into the concrete.

The sky whirled above him. A bird whistled by overhead, large and black. A raven.

Jackson stared at the clouds, sucking in pain. The flock had returned, the *unkindness*. They skittered across the rubble, perched on the rocks and broken cars. They croaked and cawed, calling something out only they could understand, as if delivering speeches as the sun set. What was it? Were they trying to tell him something again?

But Jackson realized, as they passed him by, that they weren't here for him at all, not this time. Their beady black eyes were all on Tony, the red of his suit a brilliant, bloody splash on the street. They mingled around the spot where the madman had fallen, their heads bobbing, their talons shuffling. The unkindness of ravens closed into a circle. And then, their heads bowed as one, and they became solemn avian statues.

Tony was dead. Jackson knew it now. The ravens had come to see him off, the one who had listened to them, who had interpreted their cries. It didn't matter that he was a monster, a lunatic. They were here for him anyway.

Jackson, stunned, lay back on the hard, dusty road, trying to breathe. It was all he could do to watch the setting sun shimmer across the glowing blue of the sky.

⬥

Anna staggered to her feet. The Announcer was in a heap thirty yards away. She drifted over the shattered road, over the chunky potholes that could sink her car. Her opponent wasn't moving. She didn't know why, but she sensed that this kind of unmoving meant he was gone.

And, there, not far away from him, was Jackson. His face was covered in blood, bright red, pointing up at the sky. She stumbled to his side, her body singing with soreness and bruises.

Jackson looked up at her as she moved in front of the sun. His hair was askew, his eyes dull and hazy, his skin sallow and sweating. The blood was leaking from the corners of his lips and his nose. She kneeled, taking stock, hoping she knew what to do. "I'm here," she reassured.

"They're mourning," he answered, then coughed, a violent, watery sound. "Why?" His eyes refocused on her. He managed another whisper. "You're okay. I'm glad."

She swallowed. "Shhh." How he'd managed to fight through his injuries this long was beyond her. She put her hand to his chest. He winced. His breathing was shallow. A wet, jerking rattle caught inside of him as he inhaled.

The noise made her cringe.

"Let me help," she whispered. *Please, let this work.*

His eyes questioned her, but she narrowed her focus to the wound, the horrible shredded lesion where the spear had punctured him.

Anna felt something new under her touch, something she hadn't perceived when she'd healed the wounded soldier. Thoughts were coming to her that she had no business knowing. She felt, in the tingle in her fingers, that this wound had broken what could not be fixed. Even if Jackson recovered now, the rattle would get worse until it was fluid, then blood, then choking pain, and death. She felt that something had forced him back together again, had tried stitching shut all the damage, but it was an unnatural bandage applied out of desperation. It had destroyed him. She could *feel* his life force leaking out through the cracks, like steam hissing out of a pipe, slowly, slowly.

It was a miracle he was alive at all.

And yet, through all this, she felt that this grievous wound wasn't beyond her capabilities. She didn't know how or why she thought that was true.

Anna closed her eyes and pressed her palms to his bare chest, nudging aside his shirt. His skin was smooth and cool, though a haggard, angry red scar lay there.

He wheezed. "Anna, I—"

"Don't move." Something opened in her mind then, in the heat and electricity in her fingers, that she hadn't felt before. It was almost like a tether between her and Jackson, a tugging between her life force and his. Jackson gave a startled suck of air, and she knew he felt it too.

"What's—"

"Shhh," was all she could say. And, the warmth began spilling out of her fingers again, down the tether, down into the gaping pool of wrongness in his chest. His breathing seized, and she felt his heart start to pound, his lungs taking in sharp, panicked, shallow mouthfuls of air. It was as if his body went into shock and was trying to tear away, but she had a firm hold on that tether now, and their bodies were glued together at her fingers. No matter how much he wrenched, she could hold him down.

And, she had to. His chest jerked, erratic. His legs kicked. A coldness had started in her toes again, and it was spreading, sucking up the feeling in her ankles and shins in only seconds. Anna gasped with surprise. *No! Focus!* Her instincts told her that if she somehow let go, she might botch the job, and he'd be worse than when she'd started. Her knees were gone in the cold, her thighs, then her hips-

Jackson breathed in once, long, full, and clear—no rattles at all in the way. He stopped thrashing.

She released him before the freeze reached her chest. The tether snapped, leaving a hum behind, all the way up her arm and into her heart. Then, Anna leaned over, her head drowsy and dizzy, her legs feeling useless. Unable to stop herself, she slumped her head into her arms on top of him.

They lay like that for a long minute. Jackson was breathing, a free, clear sound, and Anna was trying not to faint. She lifted herself when the dizziness began to pass, the rough asphalt digging into her palms. "Are you okay now?" The world tilted.

There was a long silence. Then, he rose, slowly. There was a healthy glimmer in his eyes that said more than words could. He took in another gulp of air, like he was savoring oxygen for the first time. "I feel... I feel amazing. It doesn't even *hurt*. What *was* that?"

Anna smiled, tired. "I'm some kind of super-mutant. And I don't know."

They stared at each other, and then, Jackson snorted, his eyebrows raised, and he barked out a laugh. Anna started giggling in response, a happy *we're still alive* chuckle tearing itself out of her soul too. She was groggy, hurting, and starting to hear the shrill whine of panic in her brain as sirens approached. But, for now, she was alive, and so was he. And, everything in the world felt like it might eventually be alright.

CHAPTER TWENTY-FOUR
Exile

Anna was sitting there, smiling softly, and Jackson's mind was reeling. He felt whole, healthy. No poison. No bruises. No crushed lungs. It was the best he'd felt in so, so long.

And, for just a moment, he'd been wired directly into Anna's being. What she'd done had taken that strange sense of familiarity he'd felt with her since they'd met and amplified it a hundred times over. The connection had been electrifying. And, so help him, he wanted to feel it again. He wanted to lean in close to her giggling, bright face dusted with ash and dirt, and he wanted to kiss her, wanted to run his hands through her hair, wanted to hold her to him until the militia got there and dragged them both away.

His skin hummed, and he found himself chuckling, though he wasn't sure at what. *Am I… drunk?* His eyes widened. *On magic?* He almost didn't care.

Except…

A nasty, coppery taste was on his tongue. His mouth was… *ugh*. Blood. So much *blood*. Disgusted, he wiped it away with the back of his hand as best he could. And, somewhat cooled, he saw now that Anna's eyes were almost squinting from exhaustion, her body sagging. "Anna… are you…?"

"Jackson. Anna."

Jackson looked up, and so did she. Agent Walker had closed the distance.

He looked haggard, his Coalition suit ripped and sullied underneath a bulletproof vest. He nursed a long slash under his eye, and it looked to be bleeding far more than it ought to have been. "Are you alright?" The question was hushed, but the sound carried.

For a long moment, the three just stared at each other, as if asking what they should do now. The giddy fog in Jackson's mind was parting. Twenty feet away, one of the battered cars gave up the ghost, its crumpled passenger door tearing off with a crunch and a shatter as it met the concrete. Other quiet voices were on the breeze now, people leaning out of windows, peeking out of alleyways, seeing if the danger had passed. Even those who had fled were inching back.

Jackson appreciated that his fellow New Yorkers were incapable of fearing for their lives appropriately, but he wished they weren't peering at him right then.

Walker was holding his gun up. Jackson followed the line where it pointed to Tony's body, a dusty red spot on the black asphalt. The agent had a pinched expression on his face that said that if Tony gave so much as a twitch in the wrong direction, he was unloading the magazine.

"He's dead," Jackson said. Another raven fluttered from above, perching on the lamppost above the body. It spread its wings and made a great croak, as if delivering a proclamation. Then, like the others, it bowed its head.

"That remains to be seen." Walker did not lower his gun.

Anna made to stand. Her limbs wobbled as she brought herself up. Jackson sprung to his feet and offered her an arm, amazed at how easy it was to do so, at how far the pain had been banished. She nodded, giving a tired sigh, leaning most of her weight on him. *She's not okay. We need to go.*

"For a fight with someone like Bertinelli," Walker spoke, staring, "you both look to be in good shape. In fact, you're looking... well, alive, Jackson."

Jackson gave no answer, uncertain how much Walker knew.

The agent snorted, looking like he was swallowing back words. "Look," he finally said, "Backup's coming from the west. If you go now, they might forget to chase you for a while. I can stall them." He waved at the destruction around them. "We have a lot to handle."

There were other men and women in uniform now, climbing up through the hole. They looked tired and hurt. It seemed as if they wanted to do damage control and go home.

Anna made a throat-clearing noise. "Thank you for letting me go," she whispered.

"You're letting us *both* go," Jackson observed. "Why?"

Walker swallowed. "Just go."

Jackson knew he should. It was wisest. And yet, he couldn't. "No. No, I want answers. After all this, I want *answers*."

Walker's eyes went wide in disbelief. He swallowed. "Fine," he snapped, not lowering his gun. "Fine. *Project Esper* has been revived, and I'm not getting consulted. Ask Anna if you want to know more. Neither of you are safe from the Coalition right now; not you, Anna, with your powers, and not you, Jackson, if you're even *half* of what I think you are."

A spark of anger fired in Jackson's chest. "What the hell is Project Esper? Is that where you took Tony? Is that why you wiped my memories?" At Walker's startled expression, he added, "Oh, yes. I *remembered* that. Is that why you were using me to get to him?"

"...Tony?" Anna asked. Jackson pointed at the dead body. "You *knew* him?"

Walker's gun wavered. "*Tony?* Really?" He looked at Jackson as if he'd gone mad, his words an agitated hiss. "Alright. Yes. I brought him to Project Esper. I asked Nyx to make you forget all of that so you wouldn't get nightmares every night for the rest of your life. Seemed a mercy at the time."

"You didn't do a very good job," Jackson snapped.

"Well, you're not the only kid I failed. I failed Tony and everyone else like him when the Project got pulled out from under me. He's here, he did all of this, because of me, because I couldn't stop the others from getting in his head and trying to brainwash and weaponize him. He got out. He killed every Esper and supervisor we had. Where he went after that, I don't know—but I've been tracking him down for years so I could end this. And I got called in to that mess outside of the city, something we only saw when Tony got out the first time, and I find a note to a *Jack* on that box... yes, I decided to leverage you, to see what you would see out there, and it all just fell into place." Walker grimaced, then wiped his cheek with his hand, trying to clear away the blood that was leaking down his face. It didn't help. "Now, there isn't time, Jackson. I thought maybe I'd get a second chance. I thought I could help you, Anna. But, apparently, the people around me didn't learn from the past. So, go. Get away from the Coalition. Get away from the Mage Order, whatever they have to do with all of this. Ward yourselves. I won't say a word about your involvement. I won't tell them where you are. I won't say what you are. Go." He turned back to Tony's body. "And I'll make sure they'll have no hope of getting any more secrets out of Antonio's brain."

Jackson scowled, furious and frustrated, though he knew the agent was right, and there was no time. Walker was already stepping away towards the red-suited corpse. The ravens raised their dark heads as he approached.

Then, Walker stopped.

Jackson, torn, saw what the agent was looking at. The papers Tony had stuffed in his pockets seemed to be long gone. The flailing and fighting had sent them into the wind. But, there was one left. It was sticking out of Tony's sleeve. It was as if Tony might have moved to grab for it before he fell back for the last time.

Walker kneeled, tugged the paper out of its resting place, and, without looking at it, passed it Jackson's way. "I suspect that's for you."

Jackson stared, feeling an itching break out on his skin, even though Tony's aura had vanished from the world. Then, he reached out a hesitant hand, snatching the note away. As he unfolded and read it, his eyes widened. His fingers trembled harder.

"What is it?" Anna asked.

"Nothing. There's nothing on it. Just trash." Jackson crumpled it back up and stuffed it in his pocket.

Anna's soft hand slipped into his, and he almost jumped. He realized it suffused him with warmth, a small wisp of the healing magic he'd felt before. "What are you going to do, Jaden?" she asked. "Are you going to go back to them?"

"I can't leave. I won't leave Nyx to them. Maybe I can still help her." Walker gave a smile, a sorrowful one. "Maybe, if luck is good, I'll be in touch with you someday. Maybe I can get this project shut down, and the Order, and all of the ghosts I keep seeing. And maybe then we can trade our stories." He turned his back to them.

"Come on," Anna said. "He's right. We gotta go."

Jackson nodded. She was putting less weight on him, more weight on her own two feet. Perhaps she was starting to feel better.

There was nothing more to be said. Together, they began to walk.

And, suddenly, a black militia van swerved around the rubble, going up on the sidewalk to avoid the hole in the earth. It screeched its brakes to a halt in front of them. *NYM*, the side blared in gold. Jackson stared, wondering if he was about to be arrested.

Frank popped his head out of the driver's side window. "Get the fuck inside," he snapped.

Jackson, in that moment, had no idea why Frank was in a militia van. But, it was as if a guardian angel had descended from on high.

The back door opened. A grinning, tattooed mountain of a man, not Frank at all, leered down at them. "Hurry hurry!" the man crowed. He seized Jackson by the collar, throwing him back into the seats before Jackson could even think of protesting. Anna followed, landing next to him with an *Ooof!* The door was slammed shut, locking them away from the destruction and the peering crowds, and Frank floored the gas, sending them all flailing into their seats by sheer force of acceleration.

There were three gunshots behind them, and Jackson knew what Walker had done. In his mind's eye, he saw the ravens disturbed from their vigil, taking flight. *Goodbye, Tony.* "Frank?" he asked aloud, voice weary. He wondered if he should say hello, or if the *get the fuck inside* covered all of that. "Is this a stolen militia truck?"

Frank sneered. "*No*, they let me *borrow* it." The sound of sirens blared around them. Jackson hoped it was their own. Frank then chuckled to himself, the noise like a gasoline engine that was failing to turn over. "Never should have shown me how to hotwire these things," he whispered to himself. Jackson decided that was a story that could wait.

"Hello, Shark," Anna said, her voice so quiet as to be almost unheard.

"Hello, Glow-witch!" the hulking tattooed man replied, a yell.

"My name's Anna..." she whispered, lying back into the seat, shutting her eyes, as if it took her quite a bit of energy to talk at all.

Jackson leaned in front of her, protective. "And who are you...?" he finally asked of this "Shark", alarmed both that he was here, and that Anna seemed to know him. This man's teeth were filed down to points. This was a raider. In a militia van. With them. *Unchained.*

Said raider ignored his question. "Hello, small man! Slayer of *Tigers!*" He thumped his fist with his chest. Frank swerved the van violently around a corner, and Shark gave a roaring shout as he nearly careened off his seat.

"We're past the police line," Frank said. "They thought we were one of them long enough not to check us out. They won't be thinking that for long once they realize this van's off of their grid now."

Jackson saw then that the militia radio had been torn out of its socket in the dash. Its lights were dark and dead. "Where are we going?"

"*Out.*" Frank silenced the siren on the van, merging into traffic. Jackson saw through the windshield that they were headed due north. "This city's bad for your health, kid."

Jackson stared. *Out.* "You can't *possibly* mean—"

"I *mean* you better hope you brought your toothpaste, because I ain't dropping you off at your house after everything that just went down. That guy you just killed, he's probably got friends, and I'm not letting his organization gun you down, or the Coalition, or the goddamn freaky Order that's gonna come lookin' for you. You're done here. You're getting out."

"What? Outside the *Barrier?*" Jackson was shouting now too. "I can't just leave!"

"Whaaat? Slayer of Tigers is worried about a little fresh air?" The giant raider made a *tsk*ing noise.

Jackson felt the blood leaving his face. "Frank. You cannot be serious. The business. My life. It's *here*. And Anna might need medical help."

She was still sagging, eyes tired, distracted. Her head flopped a little on her neck when Frank made an abrupt lane change. "I'm okay," she insisted, voice faint.

"It's not like you're getting banished," Frank said. "It's just an *extra-safe* safe house."

"We can have one of those within the dome!"

"No. No, we can't." Frank's voice took an unsettling descent into a growl. "We've got rats, kid." Jackson swallowed, thinking of the one-eyed courier that had delivered him to the train station. "And where there's one, there's more. I can't guarantee your safety right now. I can't trust any of our people. Not until I flush them out." He shook his head. "Shark and I here, we've worked out an *understanding*. And he's going to show you where to squat this out until it's over."

"Yes. Understanding!" Shark said. "You will be welcome in my camp. We have good space for people like you."

Jackson gaped. *"You're dropping me off at a raider camp."*

Frank shrugged. "I'm keeping you alive. I'll be back for you once this blows over. The company will take care of itself."

"No, you can't…!"

The traffic slowed for a moment. Frank braked to a crawl, then turned away from the road and reached behind the seat, grasping Jackson's arm. He locked his stare onto Jackson's, pinning him under his gaze. "You *will* be okay. I *will* be back for you. And the company *will* be fine."

For just a moment, Jackson felt again like he was nineteen, the day after his father's death. And Frank had been there, hovering and patting his shoulder with giant, calloused hands. *"You'll make it through this, kid,"* the older man had said. *"It hurts, but you'll make it. Trust me."*

It was that stare Frank was giving him now. Jackson stared back, and then, he settled back into his seat, quieted. He had no alternative path or solution that would stop their enemies. A raider camp was madness. But… if Frank *actually* thought this "Shark" was going to listen to him… who would look for them in one of the worst places on Earth?

Frank was right. Frank was *usually* right. Even when the plan was desperate and horrible.

The suggestion still repulsed him.

They stopped once, only to ditch the militia van and clamber into an unmarked black version, no militia gear at all in this one. Jackson helped Anna to her feet, helped settle her in to their new transport and secure her safety belt. She still seemed a little hazy, but she smiled and assured him, again, that she was fine. "Moving again, huh? Is it going to be safe? Out there?"

Jackson sighed. "I doubt it."

"It's a damn sight safer than in here right now," Frank growled.

Jackson swallowed his arguments.

Anna sighed, resting her head against his shoulder. Jackson's muscles tensed. Even given his attraction, one he didn't even know if he wanted to pursue, he was unused to such a familiar touch. "At least we're not alone," she said. "We're in this together." His heart skipped, and he nodded. "Besides, anyone tries to hurt us, and I'll pop 'em in the jaw." Jackson snorted, unable to stop a laugh, especially when such a small, tired woman looked so very serious about this. But given how she'd handled Tony… he supposed there was something to her words.

Perhaps there was no one better to go to hell with.

The edge of the dome was coming into view. Frank braked for the border inspection line, then reached under the seat and extracted a credit chit. Jackson could only see several zeroes on the end. *Some lucky guard is about to get an inordinate amount of money.*

His thoughts drifted back to the millions of credits buried in the tunnels in unmarked, dirty boxes. Tony's fortune. Likely the Coalition's, now, alongside all of those trinkets and oddments, teacups and books.

"What did Jaden mean?" Anna asked.

"What did who mean?" Jackson tried not to think of all the things he was leaving. His bed. His book collection. That little coffee shop. Any semblance of sanity or normalcy. The guard was getting closer, would wave them on and lock his world behind him.

"Jaden. Agent Walker," Anna replied. Jackson decided it was best not to look too interested in the border patrol. He turned to meet Anna's eyes, though they were closed. She seemed half asleep. "He said he suspected you were something that the Coalition would want for Project Esper."

Jackson froze, his shoulders clenching tighter. "Oh. *That*. I... I don't know."

Anna frowned, her eyes opening long enough to lock onto his with a long stare of certainty. And, Jackson knew that she knew he was lying. It was the way her look glimmered with a touch of hurt.

He bowed his head. "I'm sorry. I shouldn't have said that." Lying had become reflexive.

"Jackson." She sat up straighter. "What is it? Why did we just go through all of that?"

He saw Frank's hands tightening on the wheel, the knuckles whitening. Yet, the old man said nothing. He only shuffled his papers and rolled down the window as a guard approached. The raider seemed to have the common sense to be hiding behind the seat, somehow cramming his bulk back there. Jackson dropped his voice. "It might not be the best time to—"

"You can tell me." Her tone seemed to add that he could tell her right now, if he knew what was good for him.

Jackson shuddered away from her prying, confused gaze. "I don't know what they want with me."

Her face crumpled with frustration.

"I mean, I don't know *exactly*. But..." Jackson's heart thudded, his mouth running dry. *No more outs. Nowhere to run with this.*

She deserved the truth by now, didn't she?

"Look." Jackson grabbed a credit chit from his pocket and cupped his hands, bringing them low behind the seat. The guard was chatting with Frank, exchanging a knowing look. Frank was saying something pleasantly gruff about the weather. The bribe had been accepted.

A small bit of shadow pooled in Jackson's grasp. He wondered, for a moment, that he'd ever forgotten how to do this. It was beginning to feel like the most natural act in the world. He wasn't even sure if he was afraid of it anymore. It had saved his life.

The shadow wriggled and flickered, then rose as he held his concentration. The chit lifted along with it.

Anna made a small choking noise.

He waited for her to say something, anything, the chit spiraling in the impossible pool of darkness in his palm.

"I don't know why it works," he said, breaking the silence. "It just does. It always has. Although I couldn't control it for most of my life." He could now. Why? Did it have something to do with losing his fear, or no longer taking the poison? Was it both?

"That's…" Anna spoke.

Jackson stared, unsure, a slight shake in his hands. He waited for her to tell him to stop. He waited for the flash of fear in her face, like he had seen in so many others, before they turned away, before they made him someone else's problem or refused to speak to him about it again. He waited.

Her eyes turned to him, then back to the shadows. She opened her mouth, shut it, then opened it again. "That's *really* cool."

Jackson started, his concentration shattering. The shadows dissipated. The chit dropped back into his hand. "I… I guess?" A chuckle of relief built up inside of him. She smiled, just for a moment, nudging his shoulder. And, in that moment, Jackson felt even worse for keeping his silence. "I'm sorry. I just wanted to help you. And I'm sorry I dragged you into this mess—"

Anna breathed in and out, and reached for his hand, squeezing it again, closing her eyes. "It's not your fault."

Something about her face still made him anxious. "You're angry, though."

"Yeah." She bit her lip. "Yeah, I'm little mad. I can't believe you didn't say anything. Do you know how much it would have helped if I'd have known I wasn't really… *alone?*" The way she said the final word tore at him, as if it described terror itself. He knew exactly what it was like to be *alone*. He did.

Jackson felt an unhappy anxiety building into a hard little ball in his chest.

"I should have told you," he muttered. "Everything was just happening so fast... and there were so many other things you were dealing with..."

She squeezed his hand again, and he wasn't certain if he was forgiven, but he hoped he was. He didn't want to be *alone* either. Not again. The guard was waving them on. Jackson let out a breath he hadn't realized he'd been holding.

"I guess it makes sense that you knew how to calm down my, um, *powers*," she said. "Are a lot of people like this? Is it just something in the air now? The radiation?"

"Thankfully, no," Frank growled. "Can't you people wait until the checkpoint's passed to vent your damn secrets?" He was pulling away now. The glimmer of barrier blue overwhelmed the windshield for just a moment, the familiar crackle raising the hairs on Jackson's arm and neck. There was a faint humming noise, comforting, almost primal. And then, it passed over them all, and it was gone. Jackson had been past the walls many times, but he'd never felt the loss so keenly.

"All that *humming!*" Shark grumbled.

Jackson frowned, trying to ignore him. Instead, he tried to whisper just to Anna, trying to be helpful, to soothe her questions. "I'm the only person I ever knew like this until I met you, outside of the one man I knew from The Order."

Anna's eyes sharpened.

Jackson looked away. "I don't think we're quite like them, though." But, he had no way to find out the full story. He suspected he wouldn't learn it from a camp in the wastes.

"And you've always been able to do that, with the shadow things?"

"As far back as I can remember."

She yawned. "Okay," she said. And, she leaned back, put her head on his shoulder again, and her eyes fluttered shut. "You're gonna tell me about everything when I wake up. And I'll tell you everything, too. We're in this together, Jackson." She looked to be fading fast.

"Anna, are you really okay?" he asked, growing more concerned.

"Do you hear that singing?" she mumbled.

Jackson shook his head. There was no music beyond the rumble of the road, decaying under the wheels the further they got from the Barrier. "What singing?"

"She's singing again… I keep hearing her…" Anna's eyes unfocused, and then, they drifted shut. "I feel like… she's saying it's going to be okay…"

Then, without warning, her breathing evened. She gave a little snort and a snore. Jackson blinked at her. His heart was pounding with uncertainty. The abruptness of her sleep left him unsteady, and he could feel her warmth now blooming in the crook of his arm, growing. It felt as if she was fevered.

"Frank," he whispered.

"We're not going back now, so she better just be tired." Frank sounded exhausted then too, sounded as old as he was. The towers of the city, of home, were shrinking in the rearview mirror. Flustered, Jackson glared and shook his head at no one. He knew there was nothing he could do. But, he resolved himself to watch over her, help her somehow, this one woman like him in all the world.

If he was honest, it felt as if the tether hadn't fully severed between them. It was a feeling that defied words for any relationship he'd known.

The raider climbed from his hiding place now into the passenger chair. He began talking to Frank about where they were going, his enthusiastic broken accent grating Jackson's ears. *Frank is really going to trust us to this "Shark". To a bandit.* It boggled his mind.

We're alive. At least we have that.

Alone with a sleeping Anna and his anxiety, Jackson let his knee bounce. The wastes passed them by, dilapidated houses, weeds, and dust. Potholes and cracks rumbled underneath the tires. It was just as when they'd left the city with the agent in tow, only a few weeks ago, though it felt like a lifetime. And, for just a moment, Jackson caught a flicker of black perched on an old trash can, and he knew what it was, even if the van was moving too fast for him to get a long look.

The ravens were coming with him.

His knee bounced harder.

A crinkling noise. He let his gaze fall to his pocket, where his leg's anxiousness had disturbed the contents. It was the paper Tony had written on, the one Walker had pulled off his body. Jackson had said it was just trash.

He'd lied then, too.

Jackson didn't want to look at it again. He wanted to roll down a window, let it flutter off into the breeze and into oblivion, like all the rest. After all, his brain argued, why should he let himself get worked up over the ramblings of a madman?

Tony's voice was still in his head, whispering his incomprehensible mutterings. None of them made sense to him, even now, but they tempted him, as if they were riddles demanding to be unteased.

You want to know what the man by the fire wants?

That's what you are, Jack. You're a champion. You're a Chosen.

Sorry Jack. Very sorry. Very sorry. Tell Inoki I'm sorry.

Why should he put any faith in Tony's so-called "secrets"? And yet, he couldn't part with the paper. Something deep inside told him that would be a mistake.

The message was burned in his mind now either way. Two lines of cryptic crayon: Tony's final words.

He's under the floors, Jack. He's in the walls. He's waiting for you.

HE'S LISTENING.

TO BE CONTINUED

HELLO, DEAR READER,

Thank you so much for spending this time with me and this tale. I hope you enjoyed *Raven Song*, the first in a series I hope will surprise and delight you. Feel free to write me at i.a.ashcroft@ravenchosen.com to let me know what you thought! You can also find out what's coming for Anna, Jackson, and everyone else by visiting ia-ashcroft.com and signing up for notifications about this series. There are some free short stories that will be coming to e-mail subscribers, too.

Now, let's get personal.

Readers like you make or break a new book. I would be deeply grateful if you would consider leaving a review on Amazon: the parts you loved, hated, are looking forward to—anything! It would only take a moment, and it would mean the world to me as a writer.

May you have pleasant wanderings as you return to the waking world. And, see you next time in *Eclipse of the Sun: Book Two of Inoki's Game.*

- I. A. Ashcroft

CPSIA information can be obtained at www.ICGtesting.com
Printed in the USA
BVOW08s1409300616

454106BV00002B/21/P